THE GREAT DARKNESS

By Jim Kelly

The Great Darkness
The Mathematical Bridge

THE GREAT DARKNESS

JIM KELLY

Allison & Busby Limited
12 Fitzroy Mews
London W1T 6DW
allisonandbusby.com

First published in Great Britain by Allison & Busby in 2018.
This paperback edition published by Allison & Busby in 2018.

Copyright © 2018 by JIM KELLY
Map © 2018 by PETER LORIMER / PIGHILL

A CIP catalogue record for this book is available from
the British Library.

10 9 8 7 6 5 4 3 2 1

ISBN 978-0-7490-2292-1

Typeset in 10.5/15.5 pt Adobe Garamond Pro by
Allison & Busby Ltd

The paper used for this Allison & Busby publication
has been produced from trees that have been legally sourced
from well-managed and credibly certified forests.

Printed and bound by
CPI Group (UK) Ltd, Croydon, CR0 4YY

To Rowan Haysom,
for his insight into the City of Cambridge
and sharing a generous sense of place

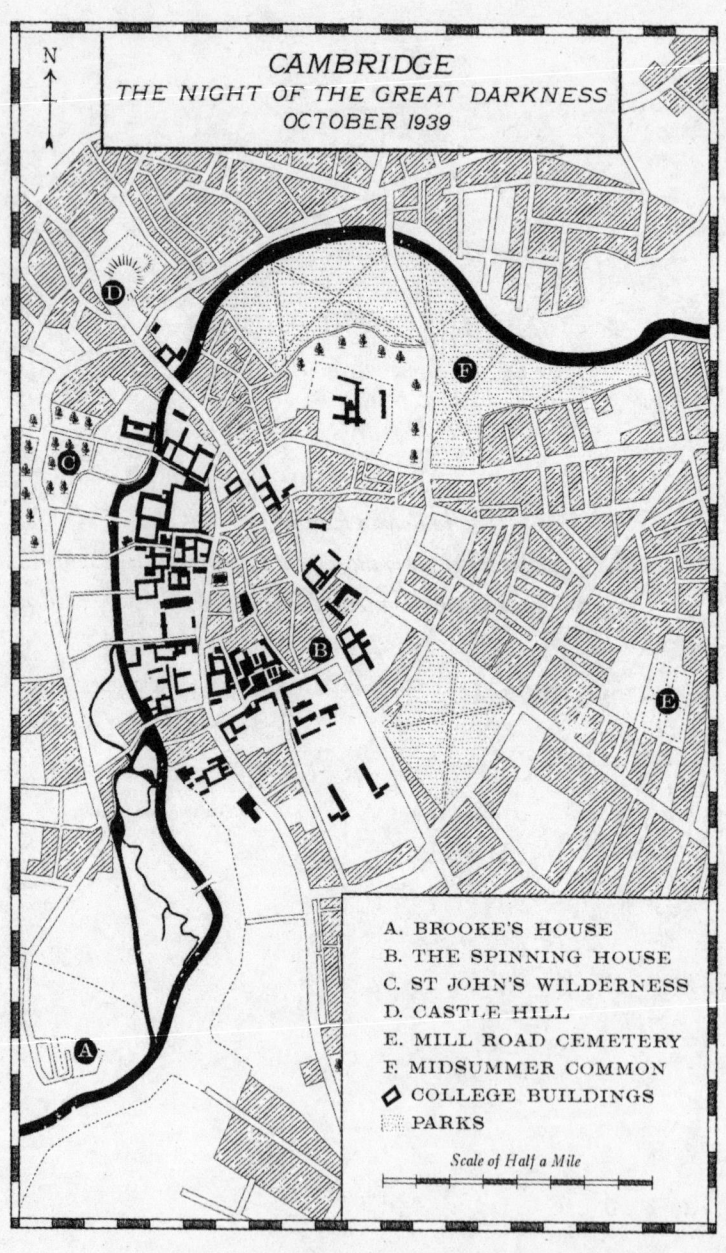

CAMBRIDGE
THE NIGHT OF THE GREAT DARKNESS
OCTOBER 1939

N

A. BROOKE'S HOUSE
B. THE SPINNING HOUSE
C. ST JOHN'S WILDERNESS
D. CASTLE HILL
E. MILL ROAD CEMETERY
F. MIDSUMMER COMMON
◇ COLLEGE BUILDINGS
PARKS

Scale of Half a Mile

AUTHOR'S NOTE

The City of Cambridge is one of the principal characters in *The Great Darkness*. Like all fictional characters it is in part a combination of reality and imagination, both in terms of its geography, and history. The City of Sheffield is a minor character, but the same applies.

CHAPTER ONE

October 1939
Cambridge, England

The secret place lay at the end of one of Cambridge's many blind alleys, through a small oak door. Brooke had the key which turned the well-oiled antique lock. Slipping down the narrow, mossy steps, he reached the river. Here he sat in the darkness on a stone ledge, setting his ochre-tinted glasses on a shelf in the brickwork. A wooden box, with a slate lid, hid a canvas bag containing bathing shorts and a towel.

For a moment he sat listening to the old city, unseen beyond the high walls. Water trickled in drains, pans clattered in a college kitchen, and close by a bicycle rumbled over cobbles. And something new, the sounds of war: soldiers marching, synchronised boots fading away towards the station, and the *silence* of war, the empty streets, the buses and trams confined to depots, the cinemas and theatres boarded shut.

To the south, a pair of searchlights crossed and uncrossed in the sky like knitting needles, on the watch for the parachutes of spies.

Brooke filled his lungs with the night air, laced with the scent of the river, that unmistakable concoction of river weed, sodden roots and banks. Coal fires brought a smoky softness to the night. The great Fen fields to the north, harvested of beet and potatoes and cabbages, added an earthy edge, the signature of the deep black peat below. And, tonight, a trace of air fuel from the fighter base on the outskirts of the city.

Setting his hat on a nail in the frame of the door, Brooke took a minute to change, folding his clothes neatly in the box. For a moment he hesitated: swimming after dark had been banned, and the army ran a motorboat on regular patrols, armed with a searchlight. But such rules, for Brooke, had always amounted to a challenge.

He used his palms to raise himself the inch needed to allow a forward slide from the step into the cool, forgiving stream.

He lay on his back, floating, looking up into the mercy of the night. Closing his damaged eyes, he drifted with the current, which ran in its ancient canyon of stone; dark tonight, not overseen by the jewelled windows of college rooms. Especially dark tonight, for all of Cambridge was cast in shadow, the streets patrolled by air raid wardens, every window blind. The Great Darkness had fallen by Whitehall decree across half of England, an official blackout in preparation for the bombs that would fall.

For now the war itself, a month old, had been branded 'phoney' – the German offensive in the west, following the surprise attack on Poland, was not expected until the new year. The Poles fought on, but were clearly losing. The Russians had invaded from the east. The French had managed a token sortie in the Saar, while the British Expeditionary Force camped along the Belgian border.

But there were casualties, even as the world waited. In the Atlantic, a U-boat had sunk HMS *Courageous*, with the loss of more than five hundred men. One of the dead had been a former scholar at Brooke's old college. They'd posted his name on a board by the porters' lodge, a little ceremony which brought the loss closer to home. For Brooke, just forty years old but a veteran of the Great War, it felt like an augury.

He swam north, where open meadows lay on the west bank, a fen marked on one of Brooke's beloved city maps as St John's Wilderness. The river ahead retained the ghost of its reflection: a sinuous bend of faint luminescence, slightly blurred by a rising mist. Somewhere, he heard the dull thud of a poacher's gun, repeated, matched by echoes. Submerging his face, his eyes, then his ears, he listened to the river turning over the tiny pebbles of its gravel bed, a treble, set against the bass note of the water, the deep rumble of the main stream, as it ran between its banks.

As he surfaced he caught, or rather finally identified, a noise that had been present for some time, and which he'd confused with the under-song of the river itself.

A trundle, a murmur, as of cart wheels.

But he could see nothing: the darkness seemed to rest against his eyes.

The cart wheels came closer, with the trudge of boots matching the pace of the turning wheels.

Finally, he glimpsed shadows on the bank.

And heard a voice: 'Grim work.'

A half-bar of a song in three voices followed, the melody tangled.

'Quiet there! Right, we're under the trees, boys. Those who want to smoke, can.'

A match flared, then another, the light passing from face to face. Brooke saw it all in a moment: a line of three empty carts, the traces horseless. A dozen soldiers, each with a spade, stood in a circle as the cigarette smoke rose. Recalling the scene later for Claire, his wife, he noted that the men appeared cowed, shoulders down, heads bowed, one leaning on the next.

Soldiers had become as common as students on the streets. In the weeks since Chamberlain's broadcast had marked the advent of war, Cambridge was an armed camp. Tents in rows filled Parker's Piece, one of the city's great parks, as if re-enacting the night before Crecy, or Agincourt. Anti-aircraft guns, dug into pits, formed a necklace of encampments along the borough boundary. Even the sky was defended, dotted with barrage balloons, held by cables over the railway lines and factories, braced to deter dive-bombers when they came, flying low.

But given the strictures of the Great Darkness, what had brought this platoon of men out to the meadows at midnight?

A voice from the riverbank: 'So no pocket money this time, eh, Sarg?'

'You've done alright. I told the lot of you, stick with me and you'll not go short. Next time they'll pay double.' This accent came from the North, a strange guttural sound Brooke couldn't place, but the questioner was a Londoner.

Brooke caught a sweet smell on the breeze.

It was as if the next speaker had heard his thoughts. 'That's you, Spider – the stink: you haven't had a wash this year.'

London again, the East End, reeking of the market stall and bargain calls.

'Christ. The stench is on the spades,' said another.

'Use the river.' The sergeant's voice this time, losing patience with his men.

Brooke saw the white splashes where they plunged the tools in the water.

'Right. Let's get some grub,' said the sergeant. 'Put your backs into it . . .'

Cigarette butts sizzled in the stream, and the soldiers were gone, tramping south, man-hauling the empty carts away to the north.

The sticky sweet smell went with them.

Treading water, Brooke pushed thick wet hair out of his eyes. He thought that anything undertaken by night came freighted with connotations: shame, secrecy, guilt. What had the soldiers buried? Where was the pit?

Detective Inspector Eden Brooke swam back to the mossy steps.

CHAPTER TWO

Brooke was a nighthawk, but he was not alone. Over the years since he'd been invalided home from the last war, his insomnia had deepened, and the wounds to his eyes had failed to heal, so he'd taken to strolling the streets at night. He found them inhabited by fellow travellers: those who couldn't sleep, those who didn't wish to sleep, those whose work began when the sun went down. They offered a warm fire, a friendly chat and sometimes inspiration when a case proved intractable. Each night he did, finally, find rest: at home if Claire was not on night shifts at the hospital, or in a cell at the station. Sleep, when it did come, was always brief and sudden. In the dark watches of the night his life often felt like a clock winding down.

Rose King, at her tea stall on Market Hill, had been his first nighthawk. Returning from the Great War, Brooke had joined the Borough – the city's own police force, one of the oldest, and smallest, in the country. After training, he'd secured a night beat, a preordained path which led him across Market Hill, the city's central square, each midnight. Rose had provided a hot drink and, beneath a wide awning, an oasis of golden light.

But even the resilient Rose had to abide by the rules and regulations of the Great Darkness, and he found her hut boarded up in the corner of the square, amongst the empty traders' stalls, and partly obscured by a wall of sandbags. A chalk sign read simply: CLOSED BY GOVERNMENT ORDER.

Brooke stood in the silent square, considering his next move, lighting one of his precious Black Russian cigarettes. He watched the flame consume the paper, edging down towards the golden filter. The mist was thickening, seeping up through drain covers and out of culverts, a milk-white flood which threatened to engulf the city. The night was getting chilly, and his damp hair made him shiver. The strains of a piano came and went from a nearby pub, but there was no light, just a half-line of a song.

Something of the scene he had witnessed on the riverbank refused to succumb to a rational explanation. Many people are curious and ask questions, but Brooke was driven by an innate conviction that he had a right to know the answers. The result was a restless life. Why order soldiers to dig at night? Why promise to *pay* soldiers to dig at night? He needed a fresh perspective, to rise above the moment, and he knew precisely which nighthawk to visit.

Leaving the shadows of the old market he made his way down Petty Cury, the narrow street a procession of shop windows taped up in criss-cross patterns against bomb blast. His footsteps echoed, thanks to the Blakeys on his brogues: metal studs to protect the leather, an army trick he'd adopted for civvy street. He circled St Andrew the Great, playing his torch over the stained glass, noting the familiar image he'd been shocked by as a boy: the severed head of John the Baptist, neatly set on its silver platter, awash with the saint's blood.

An echo of this grisly martyrdom waited a hundred yards along the street, where Brooke paused outside Sidney Sussex College. His father, a professor of medicine, had been a distant figure, but had once returned home from dinner at the college with a sensational story, which he'd told his son while sitting on his bed, an unheard-of degree of intimacy that had cemented the moment in Brooke's memory more than the gruesome tale itself.

'I've seen a man's skull tonight,' his father had said, his eyes bright in the candlelight.

The story was richly Gothic. The body of Oliver Cromwell, the great republican and a former student of the college, had been dug up from his quiet grave by supporters of the restored King Charles II. The head, hacked from the body, had been hung from London Bridge, beside that of common criminals, where it was pecked at by birds.

'The eyes were first to go,' his father had explained.

Blown down in a storm, the top of the skull had fractured and had been spirited away by supporters, taken north to Cambridge to be hidden within the great man's old college. Only two trusted fellows ever knew its hiding place at any time. On special nights, the lights over dinner were doused and the custodians despatched to find the treasure, which was set on the polished mahogany table, supporting a candle.

'He was with us until the port and cheese,' his father had said, tucking Brooke in. 'Then he was whisked away.'

As Brooke surveyed the college facade, he saw a flickering light, briefly, in one of the lancet windows: the selected fellows, perhaps, returning Cromwell's head to its hiding place.

Pressing on, he cut down an alley full of metal bins to a fire escape, which took him up six flights before decanting him onto the roof of one of the shops. A metal ladder led a few feet further aloft to a lookout post, one of several set up across the city by the Observer Corps, with a sweeping panoramic view across the rooftops, ideal for spotting enemy aircraft and the fires their bombs and incendiaries might ignite.

Jo Ashmore emerged from a conical hut at the rear of the platform, straightening her uniform, unable to stop herself retouching her short, expensively cut brown hair. Tall, willowy, fashionably boyish, she smiled broadly when she recognised her visitor.

Brooke swept his hand across the scene below. 'The Great Darkness! A success, and no doubts. But what have you seen, Jo? Tell me all.'

'Always questions, Brooke, never answers.'

'I'm a scientist. Sorry, I *was* a scientist, of sorts,' he said, taking off his hat and running a hand back through the thick black hair. 'If you want answers, you must ask questions. Ask the right one, at the right time, and the world makes sense.'

She peered at Brooke's shadowy face and laughed, retrieving a powder compact from her uniform and holding the mirror up. The detective took off his glasses and stared at his own image: the high forehead, the pale blue eyes, the hair flopping forward. A long strand of green river weed was stuck to his cheek.

'You'll be growing webbed feet next,' she said.

Ashmore was Brooke's newest nighthawk recruit, tonight marking her first full month as a member of the Observer Corps. She'd grown up next door to the Brookes, played with their children, free to come and go with her brother, Marcus. The houses, a mirror-pair of detached villas, were set in meadows down by the river. The families were close in that entirely natural way which means that nobody can recall how the threads had become entangled.

A racy reputation had marked her coming of age: there were parties in London, boyfriends with fast cars, smart clothes. She'd abandoned it all at the outbreak of war for her post, a mystery Brooke suspected she felt cast her in a Romantic light. He noted that she'd expertly applied lipstick to create a delicate bow of her lips, and that her tin hat had been hand-painted with the elegant motif: *OC*.

From her post she watched for EA: enemy aircraft, especially bombers, of which, so far in this war, there had been none. But the whole country had its eyes on the sky, when it wasn't trying to ferret out spies and German parachutists hidden in garden sheds. This was the intolerable burden of the phoney war: a time of watching and waiting.

Not a single light betrayed the city below. Rooftops stretched north towards the Fens, south to the Gogs, a range of low chalk hills, dimly seen against the stars. Mist lay in the streets, as if college sheets had been laid out on the cobbles.

'I saw you earlier,' she said, a smile widening under the tin hat. 'It's a good job these glasses aren't really powerful otherwise I might have seen more than I should.'

She enjoyed teasing Brooke about his looks. When she was a child she'd been told the tall, pale man with the odd glasses had fought with T. E. Lawrence in the wildernesses of Egypt and Palestine. The great hero's dark good looks found an echo in Brooke, a wounded knight, brooding, soldiering on. And there'd been a medal from the king, for some always unspoken act of heroism, which added lustre to the legend. As a ten-year-old she'd once spent an evening with Brooke's daughter searching the upper floors of the house for his missing desert robes.

'You didn't see anything else when I was swimming?' asked Brooke. 'On the far bank, just there . . .' He pointed to a spot in the gloom beyond the rooftops.

She went back to her hut, reappeared with a box file and handed Brooke a typed order sheet:

CAM 005/OC ADVISORY
20–21 October 1939

Duration of scheduled blackout 21.30 hrs to 6.30 hrs. All troop movements cancelled. All vehicles confined to depots by midnight.

NO FLIGHTS LOCAL – DUXFORD.

Air Ministry advises two overflies by RAF reconnaissance, Stanmore.

Night exercise St John's Wilderness. Ignore all sound. No plot required.

EASTERN COUNTIES COMMAND.
MADINGLEY HALL.
Office of CO Eastern: COL. SWIFT-LANE.

'It's odd, isn't it?' said Brooke. 'Why hold a night exercise when we're all supposed to be tucked up in bed behind our blackout blinds? I doubt our lads need that much practice digging holes in the ground. Did you follow orders and ignore all sounds from St John's Wilderness?'

'That would have been a challenge,' said Ashmore. 'They made a racket, actually. Civilians first, dragging spades down before dusk. They disappeared into town later, promptly replaced by soldiers, and carts . . . Looks like the civilians dug a hole, and the soldiers filled it up.'

Brooke studied the order paper. 'I saw the soldiers. A sergeant and a squad. They'd been working, alright. No other orders like this?'

She handed him five more notes, all referring to the same location and at similar times, stretching back over the previous month.

'You can keep the bumf,' she said. 'If we could produce Spitfires and bullets as fast as red tape we'd win the war hands down.'

They stood in companionable silence, during which Ashmore checked her watch at least three times.

'I'm waiting for the moon to come up,' she explained. 'Which it is due to do – according to my chart – any moment now. Madingley Hall has been on the line to say they've lost three barrage balloons.'

Madingley Hall, a Tudor mansion on the outskirts of the city, was military headquarters for much of Eastern England.

'They broke free from their cable moorings an hour ago a mile south of the station. So they're headed this way. Three runaway airships out of control – what fun, eh? No one has any idea where they are until we get some moonlight. If I see them I have to phone in a position.'

Brooke peered into the darkness, disturbed that three sixty-foot-long cigar-shaped balloons could remain invisible right before their eyes.

'Someone will cop it for letting them slip,' said Ashmore. 'A week ago, according to the grapevine, they lost six in a storm on the East Coast. Drifted across the North Sea and took down power lines in Norway. Havoc, apparently – it's the cables underneath and the netting that do the damage. They snare stuff. The sooner we can spot the blighters the better. Once I've radioed their position it's someone else's headache. Anything for a quiet life.'

Brooke had never before associated Josephine Ashmore with the quiet life. He wondered what really lay behind her decision to volunteer for lonely work, at night, on a cold rooftop.

'There's the moon, at least . . .' she said.

A bright light had appeared on a college roof, lodged between tapering medieval chimneys. Within seconds it had revealed an arc of its circle, moving quickly against the silhouette of the buildings. Silver light washed over the Cambridge skyline, revealing the four great pinnacles of King's College Chapel, the distant, brutal tower of the University Library, the colleges running down to the river, which lay in a great meander opposite open meadows, along a stretch every student learnt to call the Backs.

Brooke watched the moon rise, imagining the gentle hum of celestial mechanics until it was free, gliding into the sky, the light spilling out and seeming now to ignite the river, which gleamed like steel sliding from a furnace.

'There!' said Ashmore.

A balloon, the size of one of the city's buses, hung in the air a few hundred yards downwind of the cube-like tower of St John's College Chapel, a network of cables ensnaring the building. As they watched it rippled, waves moving over its surface, as it strained at its moorings.

'And there,' said Brooke, pointing away from the river towards the open fenland to the north.

This balloon, several hundred feet up in the air, had got much further and, glimpsed beam-on, was heading swiftly towards the distant coast, impeded only by what appeared to be the remains of a tree held within the net beneath its 'belly'.

There was no sign of the third balloon.

Ashmore plotted the two within sight and phoned in the data, sitting down to make out a report on paper by torchlight.

'Bumf,' she complained. 'Bloody bumf.'

Finished, she lit a cigarette.

Then they saw the third stray balloon.

A sudden flare of yellow-blue flame flashed and lit up the sky over the distant railway station. A few seconds later came the strangely elongated pulse of sound, like a hot, jagged hiss. A burning balloon, caught up in power lines, crumpled over the large grain mill beside the station. As the 'skin' burnt away it revealed the structure within, crashing towards the ground. The distinctive *crump* of the collapse shook the rooftops.

A fireball of escaping gas lit up the night, a pulsing vision in yellow, dripping with flame.

The pain in Brooke's eyes was needle-sharp despite the yellow-tinted glasses, and he had to grip the plotting table for support.

An air raid siren began to wail.

Brooke pulled the rim of his hat down over his eyes. 'So much for the Great Darkness.'

CHAPTER THREE

Brooke, climbing down the ladder from Jo Ashmore's OP, felt momentarily giddy – a delayed effect, perhaps, of several hours without a meal, combined with his nightly swim. He'd left Ashmore on the landline to the Fire Brigade and Civil Defence, trying to direct them to the smouldering wreck of the barrage balloon, which after its brief explosive flare had subsided below the roofline, although a sickly orange sheen persisted in the southern sky.

By the time he was back on firm ground the sound of fire engine bells echoed in the streets, competition for the wailing siren. His immediate need was food. He set off along Trinity Street, past the Old Divinity School, its pale carved heroes of theology standing in their niches against the red-brick facade. As a lonely schoolboy, he'd cultivated an interest in the city above eye level. He was an only child, whose mother had died when he was young, while his father's work restricted him to the laboratory. After school, and at weekends, he'd explore the city, finding in its maze-like alleys a puzzle he could gradually master. Wandering the streets, he'd examine the stonework, the statues, the gargoyles and saints. In his mind, he set them upon a mental map of every court, every archway, every cobbled lane. By the age of ten he held the city in his head.

One favourite was right here at the Old Divinity School; the third figure along the facade was Bishop Joseph Lightfoot. On tiptoe, Brooke could just touch his shoe, a feat beyond him as a child. He'd always admired the way the sculptor had set a heavy book in the old man's left hand, which seemed to weigh him down. Curious, he'd read a brief biographical note on Bishop Lightfoot's life in one of his father's reference books, and memorised one of the cleric's pithy dictums which he admired: *I will not be discouraged by failure, I will not be elated by success.*

The siren died, fading away, to leave a ringing silence.

Opposite the gatehouse of Trinity College, Brooke saw a car approaching, its headlamps masked with tape but for two narrow strips which gave it the appearance of a hunting cat, down low, dragging itself forward, ready to pounce. As it passed, a match flared, illuminating the driver and his passengers, and Brooke glimpsed a silk scarf, a bow tie, a silver cigarette case. Despite the war, and the blackout, the joys of a night life still survived for some.

Brooke turned into All Saints Passage, the entrance to that part of the city which had once been the Jewish ghetto: a warren of narrow paths between high walls, incapable of holding a true compass point for more than twenty yards. This labyrinth had been committed to Brooke's internal map, but it had taken several years of patient study to survey its full extent. One of his maps revealed the view from above, as it were, like a cross-section of the human brain: an organic, convoluted puzzle.

In the darkness, he had to find his way by touch, as the alleys led him away from the moonlight. The darkness here was of a new order, making him briefly stop to examine his own hand, just visible, a few inches from his nose. Trailing his fingers along the wall, he made his way to the first corner, turned right, then left at the next. The stonework was damp, slightly wet from the mist which had even found its way into this echoing labyrinth. The bricks were icy too, with that faint glaze which heralded a freezing dawn. At one corner, where a water fountain stood against a wall, he stopped; raising his hand, he was able to touch an iron gutter clamp, cast in the shape of a dog's head. He patted it once, as he had many times, and walked on, until he reached a small trapdoor, set within a greater door of studded oak.

His knock, evolved over years of use, consisted of one sharp tap, then two, delivered with his signet ring on the metal hinge.

A lock turned, then another, before the door opened.

Stepping over the wooden ledge, he entered the porters' lodge of Michaelhouse. The light inside made Brooke stop, pinching the bridge of his nose, the pain behind his eyes penetrating his brain. Quickly, he substituted the ochre-tinted glasses for the darker green. He carried four pairs: ochre, green, blue and black, each one affording a higher degree of protection against the light.

'Fire in the sky, Mr Brooke. What's afoot?' asked Doric, the porter.

'Barrage balloon alight. What's the news here?'

Doric was Brooke's most reliable nighthawk. But for an enforced two weeks in January when he travelled to his sister's in Margate, Doric was as much a part of the night as the Pole Star. For a detective like Brooke he also offered the untold wealth that was college gossip, communicated through the brotherhood that was the college porters of Cambridge.

'All quiet,' said Doric as he switched off the light, leaving the lodge lit only by a glowing coke fire and a small desk lamp over the ledger on the counter. As a student before the Great War, Brooke had often admired this room for its weathered snugness, the wooden panels as polished as a ship's cabin.

Doric stood by the kettle on its gas ring, waiting for it to boil.

'Everyone tucked up in their beds?' asked Brooke, pushing his black hair out of his eyes.

A sturdy, solid figure, Doric walked stiffly to the counter and studied the open book, whistling tunelessly.

'Phipps, Torrington and Jordan – our three natural scientists – left at eight with Lux, the visiting Yank,' he said finally. 'I asked if they were dining out and they said they couldn't tell me as it was *classified*. Careless talk, all that. Pompous little arse-wipes. Anyway, I knew where they were headed, which tore the smiles off their smug faces. Porter at Emmanuel put the news round about a hush-hush meeting in the new anatomy building. The Galen?'

'That's it,' said Brooke. 'One of my father's heroes, Doric. Galen of Pergamon, the father of medical science.'

The mention of Brooke's father, Professor Sir John Brooke, always stilled the porter, who glanced at a board by the desk, decorated with the gold-painted names of the college masters. Sir John's mastership, from 1910–1921, embraced the Great War which had almost killed his son.

'Wouldn't get me in the place for love nor money, not this side of death,' said Doric, executing an exaggerated shiver. 'Cutting stuff up. It didn't suit Phipps, Torrington and Jordan either. When they got back – minus Lux – they didn't want the cold mutton the cook had set aside, although Jordan ordered three bottles of the Saint-Émilion. Looked like they needed it.'

Brooke's hunger resurfaced. 'Any leftovers about, Doric?'

The porter lifted a cloth from a tray to reveal cold mutton, potatoes and a chicken leg. The tea was strong and black, although the porter produced a tin of condensed milk, two holes neatly punched in the lid, and set it down beside the mug. Brooke let the steam play on his face before adding the oily cream. The resulting colour, an almost fluorescent orange, was unique in Brooke's experience to the British Army.

He placed his glasses on the window ledge and massaged his eyes.

'I saw a platoon of soldiers on the riverbank. East End accents, 'cept for the sergeant. Who would they be, Doric?'

The porter's eyes flitted to the shadowy wall by the post room where a military flag hung, pinned out flat, the regimental colours gossamer thin and darkened by fire and shot.

'Can't be the London Regiment. They're gone, disbanded like my lot. A scandal that. So, I'd say the Buffs. The East Kent. But that's odd because I'd not heard they were with us too. Mind you, every other bugger is. There must be two thousand troops on Parker's Piece, you seen 'em? And more on the Backs. But you say this lot was down by the river, tonight?'

Brooke nodded. 'See if you can find out more?'

Doric sat at his desk, his fat fingers thrumming on the arms of the chair. Retirement, when it finally came for the porter, would spell a kind of death. There were rumours the college night staff were to be laid off for what they were all now calling 'the Duration'. Doric faced the prospect of enforced retirement, or worse, working days.

Stillness was not a quality the porter had ever achieved for even a fleeting second. By an effort of will he set his hands down flat, but then the tuneless whistle returned.

'There was a smell, too, on the riverbank. Chemicals, maybe?' offered Brooke.

Doric rearranged his feet under the table. 'It's gossip.'

'Is it now? Care to share it?' said Brooke, leaning back, the chicken bone in his hand.

'Story is there's been an air raid. A bad one, but the papers can't print it.'

'Scotland?'

'Right, you've heard it too, then. Firth of Forth, the docks. But I heard Glasgow too, maybe Liverpool. Streets of rubble, hundreds lost, but not found. London too, the docks. Bodies out in the open they can take away quickly. But there's no time to search the ruins in a city, and they want it all hushed up. Morale is the thing; you don't want civilians taking to the roads. So they send in trucks and load up the lot: bricks, window frames, staircases, furniture – and the bodies, or what's left. All in one. Army's got to find places to bury it all. There's pits round the country. They cover 'em up with lime, that's the chemical. Maybe your cockneys are burying the stuff.'

Brooke tore a shred of meat from the chicken bone. It was a good explanation, but it didn't explain why they'd be paid for the work.

'Sounds like a tall tale. What have we had? One raid on the west coast, three aircraft, nobody hurt. It's not exactly the dreaded Blitzkrieg, is it?'

Doric threw up his hands. 'You heard it as I heard it,' he said. 'I'm just a college porter. You're the detective inspector.'

CHAPTER FOUR

Brooke's nightly swim had let the frosty air get into his bones. Walking along King Street, with its infamous run of seedy pubs, he stopped outside the Champion of the Cam. Putting his ear to the door, he heard the gentle murmur of bar chat. A sharp knock brought the landlord and, recognising Brooke, he let him slip inside. Lock-ins such as this, after time, were one aspect of everyday life which had not been snuffed out by the war, even for the Great Darkness. He sat in a corner with a whisky, watching a group of students arguing the toss on Hitler's offer of a peace conference with the Allies.

Half an hour later, out on the doorstep, he still felt chilled, as if a globe of ice was slowly forming in his guts, coalescing, despite the Champion's glowing coal fire and the onrush of blood from his skin to the pit of his stomach. He needed company and warmth. He needed Claire.

Walking along Fitzwilliam Street, past the blinded traffic lights opposite Little St Mary's, he reached the open iron gates of the hospital. Even in the blackout he could still see the steam rising from the ducts and pipes of the great building, as if the interior was boiling over. A single down-light marked the main entrance, where an ambulance stood abandoned, its doors open.

Claire was the sister on Rosewood, on the third floor. Taking the steps two at a time, he arrived invigorated, gently pushing open the double doors to reveal the full length of the ward, his own silhouette stretching out in an elongated shadow.

A thin voice chattered in dreamlike conversation, and a set of bed springs grated. In the shadows to the left he could see a pale hand searching for a glass of water on a bedside table.

At the far end, Claire sat at a desk, a green-shaded lamp illuminating paperwork. On his nightly walks when he wondered how she was, this was the image that came to mind.

He tried to walk softly down the tiled floor but the Blakey's marked every step. She watched him approach, checking the time on her pendant watch.

'What's wrong?' she asked, standing. She was slim and neat, with white-blonde hair cut in a bob which always seemed to fall into place. 'You're shivering,' she said. 'And you're as pale as a ghost.'

'I'm cold. The river was chillier than expected. I'm frozen. What do you prescribe, Nurse?'

'Wait a moment,' she said, walking over to a bed where a side-light revealed a young man lying unconscious, most of his body under a white sheet, his bandaged hands on top, both of them bloody. Claire took his pulse and laid a hand on his forehead.

'What happened?' asked Brooke, examining the soldier's pale face.

'According to the pal who brought him in, the lad's a

"winchman". I didn't entirely follow the details but he runs a machine which raises and lowers barrage balloons. The cable snapped and he tried to haul it back. His hands are dreadful, Eden, cut to shreds, down to the bone. Each cable is made of thousands of wires, and when it breaks they splay out, like frayed hair. Every one is as sharp as a razor blade. They should give him a medal, but they won't, will they? He's just a private. I think he's a hero.'

She tucked the soldier in. 'Odd thing is, a sergeant turned up and got very officious, said the work the lad had been on was classified. He told his pal to get back to barracks. He had the nerve to tell *me* not to repeat anything I'd heard, or might hear, overnight. I said he could relax because I'd given the patient a decent dose of morphine, so he'll be out cold until dawn at the earliest. I think it's the least he deserves.'

Satisfied the patient was comfortable, Claire fetched a junior nurse from the ward kitchen where she was washing bedpans and installed her at the nurses' station, explaining that she was ready to take her half-hour break.

Brooke followed her to a side door which led out onto the fire escape. A corkscrew iron staircase led down to the ground, then two more flights descended into a basement.

An iron door was marked STRICTLY NO ENTRY.

Claire unlocked the door.

The boiler room was dense with a dry pulsing heat. Claire had brought with her a fresh towel. Brooke pressed his back against the metal boiler and felt the burning metal, the gentle rumble of the hot pipes, the subtle flexing of water close to boiling point.

'It might be time to leave the river to itself for another year,' said Claire, pushing away his hands to dry his hair, and unbuttoning his shirt.

She'd brought him here before.

'Did you bolt the door?' he asked, kissing her on the lips. 'We wouldn't want to traumatise the night watchman.'

'I've locked the door, Eden. I am a practical and meticulous nurse. It says so on my latest record card, and that's a doctor's opinion, so it must be true.'

Later, holding each other in the half-light, Brooke broke a long silence. 'Tonight, from the river, I saw a platoon of soldiers on St John's Wilderness. They'd been digging pits. Doric, who is omnipotent as you know, says the rumour is the army's burying rubble from bomb sites.'

'Bomb sites?' asked Claire, standing up and letting her uniform fall past her shoulders, her arms held high. 'There've been no raids. There've been sirens, and alarms, and quite a bit of hysteria, but no planes.'

'Doric says the government's hushing it all up. That there's casualties, and the mangled dead are mixed up with the rubble, and there's no time to sort it all out and besides they want to keep it a secret, to maintain morale. It sounds like hogwash to me, but could you ask around? Doric heard the raid was in Scotland, Glasgow maybe, but he'd also heard it might be the East End. If it's true, the doctors will know. The survivors must have been treated somewhere.'

'I'll ask,' she said. 'But you know as well as I that curiosity is going out of fashion.'

CHAPTER FIVE

Romsey Town, a working-class district of narrow streets set in a ladder pattern, lay just beyond the railway line, reached only by a Victorian bridge of rusted iron. Once crossed, the medieval city was left behind, while ahead lay an industrial suburb, grimy terraced houses set in cheerless rows, smoke seeping from chimney pots. A Methodist chapel stood sentinel by the bridge, opposite a pub, the Earl of Beaconsfield, its windows etched with enticements to drink: *Windsor Ales* embellished with a scene of the great castle, *Lamb's Navy Rum* adorned with a Union Flag. A slit between two blackout screens revealed the convivial light within.

Built for railway workers, the 'town', as it was known, was impregnated with coal dust from its own humble fires and the steam trains which thundered past on the mainline to London, or shunted trucks in the marshalling yards. Every stone and every brick was black, slightly sticky to the touch, and sooty. The drifting smell of cheap coke, mixed with fumes belching from the sugar beet factory, gave the district a raw, burnt stench.

At ten-thirty a disparate chorus of bells marked closing time in a string of corner pubs. A light flashed on the pavement outside the Earl as three men spilt out into the night, fastening up coats and putting up collars, the door hastily locked behind them from the inside.

'Right, let's do it,' said Henderson, the largest of the three, and in charge. With Lauder, the Scot, and Popper, the doctor, Henderson represented the committee of the East Cambridge & District Branch of the communist party. In the Earl, they'd talked about the football, carefully avoiding politics or any mention of their plans for the rest of the evening. The Soviet invasion of Poland, in cahoots with Hitler, had placed the Party in a precarious position. Whose side, the newspapers asked, was the Party on? Arrests had been made in London, national leaders interrogated, and there was talk in parliament of banning the Party altogether. If proscribed they'd have to go to ground, so no point now in getting noticed.

The three of them stood waiting for their eyes to get used to the dark, then Henderson led the way down a side street to a dead end, where an alleyway cut along the backs of the houses to a school and then to the top of a railway embankment which looked over the yards.

A man stood waiting on the girder footbridge which spanned the main line.

'Chris?' called Henderson.

'It's me,' said the young man. 'Can you see it? There's a fire up at the station. Do you think it's a bombing raid?'

'I doubt it,' said Henderson. But they all stopped on the bridge, examining the sky, which pulsed gently with a yellow glow.

'We need to get on . . .' said Henderson, leading them down the steps on the far side and over a series of rails, past a looming water tower, to a large shed built of corrugated iron. For a minute he wrestled with the lock, before ushering them inside, where his torch revealed a tank engine on rails set in the centre of a concrete floor. Producing candles from his pocket, he asked Popper to set them out, while Lauder was instructed to get chairs.

Finally, Henderson produced a wooden box from a store, set it down on the floor, then climbed aboard the tank engine and perched on the running board above the wheels, his legs dangling.

'Right, let's use our imagination, boys,' he said. 'We are now sitting in the splendour of court number one at the assize on Market Hill, Cambridge. I'm on the bench, Judge Henderson presiding. Christopher Childe, you're in the dock. So stand on the box. Tomorrow, this will all be for real.'

Childe nodded. Popper and Lauder took front row seats.

'At the moment, Chris, you're registered as a conscientious objector. A conchie. A coward, like the rest of us. *Conditionally* registered. We all know what that means. You have to do what they bloody tell you to do. Hard labour. Tomorrow the military tribunal will sit in the court and decide if you are worthy of *unconditional* registration as a conscientious objector. That would mean you'd be free to work for the Party full-time . . . A rehearsal like this increases your chances of success in front of the tribunal fourfold, Popper's got figures from Party head office to prove it. This . . .' He spread his arms. 'This is your rehearsal. You're a lucky man.'

'Can I sit down?' said Childe. In his early twenties, he had a pale round face with a small button nose, below which was a thin moustache. A receding chin thrust his lips forwards, so that they caught the candlelight.

'Pull yourself together,' said Henderson. 'You'll have to stand tomorrow. And stop snivelling. I know we're all conchie bastards, but it's a cliché.'

They all nodded, and watched as Henderson took a copy of *Peace News* from his pocket and threw it down on the floor as if it were evidence. The paper was produced nationally to rally support for pacifism.

'It might be a rag, boys, but it reaches out to the proletariat,' said Henderson. 'Most of all, it's read, unlike most of the tedious screeds churned out by the Party. That's why we help distribute it. If Chris is successful tomorrow we can use *Peace News*, comrades, to reach the masses. We can print our own page, a news-sheet, and slip it inside. We need you, Chris – full-time – as editor and printer.'

Childe tugged at the collar of his overalls. The paleness of his face was in stark contrast to what looked like dirt on his forehead. His hair, short and tufted, looked dusty too, and his fingers were grimy, the nails black.

'First things first,' said Henderson. 'For the real thing – and it is *tomorrow* – have a bloody bath.'

'I've been digging trenches,' said Childe.

'Exactly. That's why we need you to go in front of the tribunal.' Henderson cracked his knuckles. 'So, first off, they'll ask you to read your personal statement. Frankly, they won't take in a word. What's important is the answers you give to their questions, and your *demeanour*. You have to convince them you have genuine issues of conscience.' Henderson coughed. 'Let's get started. Do you object to taking life?'

'Yes.'

'Are you a vegetarian?'

Childe relaxed slightly, shifting his weight onto his left leg. 'That's a puerile question. I object to—'

'Never question the questioner,' shouted Henderson.

'They hate it,' said Popper. 'It's not a debating society. It's not like the last show, Chris. They'd have shot you in 1914. There's a real chance they'll let you get on with your life. So calm down.'

'You have a sister?' asked Henderson, his voice taking on a hostile edge. 'If a German soldier was raping her in front of you, would you use violence to help her?'

Childe's eyes filled with tears. 'I need to learn answers, to prepare a crib . . .' he said.

'That's the last thing you need to do, laddie,' said Lauder, slumped back in his seat. 'They hate that. They're not military types. There'll be two from civvy street. Bound to be a lassie as well . . .'

'And try to stop shaking, Chris,' said Popper.

'I *can't* stop shaking,' said Childe.

He stood down from the box. 'I've had a real shock tonight. They marched us out to St John's Wilderness to dig pits on the riverside. They said soldiers would come later and that they needed the pits. But they didn't say what for. We dug for three hours . . .'

Lauder scoffed at Childe's aversion to hard labour. 'What did you expect, lad? A cushy number?'

Childe shook his head. 'My answer to all this, to all of you, is that it doesn't bloody matter what the tribunal says because I've seen something tonight that makes it clear it's too late. The war that's coming, comrades, they won't need soldiers. I saw it with my own eyes. I know what they're burying in the pits . . .'

CHAPTER SIX

The mist, thickening, was now flowing like a river in the empty streets: skeins of it, like shrouds in sinuous procession, nosing round corners, licking damp archways of stone, insinuating itself under doors. Brooke turned up the collar on his greatcoat and headed back towards police headquarters. Claire always said she could spot him in a crowd from a hundred yards: his hands thrust deep in overcoat pockets, steps marking a relentless line, so that his silhouette appeared to narrow to a single point of contact with the earth, his hat brim folded down.

Moonlight revealed King's Parade, a line of grand shops and cafes which faced a series of wide lawns, beyond which rose the splendour of the colleges. To Brooke, the street was always uplifting because it reminded him of a seafront: stately Eastbourne, perhaps, or Regency Brighton. The parade looked out to sea, but found instead the clipped lawns, the honeyed stonework and tracery of the medieval facades beyond. The wide-open space, the starry sky above, stood in contrast to the narrow alleys and passages of the rest of the old city.

A great horse chestnut, set against King's College Chapel, had gathered the mist around its roots so that the soaring stonework appeared to float free of the earth, the four great pinnacles hooked, perhaps, on the stars. The silver grey of the great tree's boughs was a match for the stone of the college, as if it too had been carved by the medieval masons. A century old, it was one of the city's treasures, the highest branches stretching up a hundred feet, supporting the autumn leaves. But even here the war had left its mark: grey felt and tape obscured the chapel's towering East Window, the precious medieval glass whisked away to safety in the city's cellars.

Brooke walked to the Bull Hotel, its windows shuttered, and turned towards Silver Street bridge, college walls pressing in on either side, so that he was able to stretch out his arms and touch both sides at once. Ahead he could just see a police radio car at its appointed time and place on the bridge, the half-masked tail lights shining feebly through the mist.

A uniformed driver sat at the wheel, an elbow on the open window ledge, filing in his logbook, watching Brooke's approach in the rear-view mirror.

'Take a break, Constable,' said Brooke. 'I need the radio.'

The young officer jumped out.

Slipping into the seat, Brooke lifted the receiver off its cradle and put his glasses on the dashboard. The windscreen was fogged with fallen ash from the incinerated balloon, so he swished the flakes aside with the wiper. For the first time that night he saw his breath, misting the glass.

'Brooke on four,' he said, against a backdrop of static, repeating the call-in three times, finishing each time with an obligatory 'over'. Impatient, he fished out the pewter hip flask Claire had given him that Christmas and took a sip of water.

Still no answer: the duty sergeant was no doubt cradling a mug of tea, trying to judge the right moment to pick up. Or was he below in the cells?

In the slit-beams of the car's headlights, Brooke could see the constable at the rail of the bridge, the mist waist high, flowing gently from south to north, enveloping the unseen bridge, leaving him in mid-air, and mid-stream.

'Desk here, sir. Over.' Brooke recognised the voice: an elderly sergeant they'd enticed out of retirement to swell the ranks of the Borough, depleted by conscription.

'Anything on the station fire, Sergeant?'

'Auxiliary Fire Brigade has two engines at Kew's, sir, the flour mill by the station. County brigade in support. I've sent the night shift pair from here on foot. We're told it's barrage balloons from down the London line, apparently the cables broke. One's drifting north, so I've rung Ely, Downham, even Lynn. If it keeps going it'll be at sea by dawn. One balloon at St John's College, tangled up with the chapel roof. The porter's got the master out and he says they can deal with it once there's some light.'

'Any customers downstairs in the cells?' asked Brooke.

'Three drunks, but we'll let them go in an hour. Wardens report the streets are empty. But who knows. Broad daylight may tell a different story. One thing . . .'

The rest was lost in a burst of static.

Brooke got him to repeat.

'Foot patrol – PC17 – called in from the police box outside Shire Hall, up near the Castle. He found three lorries stopped on the up-slope a couple of hours ago. Drivers having a kip. He says their papers look dodgy, so he's taking down particulars. I said I'd check out the haulage firm in the directory, but there's nothing in Kelly's. The address on the side of the lorries is York. I'd ring the nick there but the lines are down. I'll keep trying. Over.'

PC17, Brooke recalled, was just out of training and heading for military call-up by Christmas. The name eluded him, but he recalled the file: previous occupation register office clerk, at home with documentation, forms, signatures, permits, regulations.

So what was 'dodgy' with the lorry drivers' papers?

'I'll wander over,' said Brooke, cutting the line. He'd had in mind taking one of the cells for an hour, but the thought of those three lorries, parked in the shadowy night, changed his plans.

The radio car's constable was still on the bridge. When he saw Brooke, he ditched the cigarette in the water with a dart-like action.

'Sir,' he said, standing straight.

Brooke's reputation went ahead of him: brisk, impatient, he had no time for fools, or the slipshod. The detective's ability to spot bullshit was also a local legend. Keeping out of Inspector Brooke's way was widely seen as a valuable career strategy.

'It's PC Woods, isn't it?' he asked.

'Sir.'

'Later, after the sun's up, stretch your legs along the riverbank, north of Trinity Bridge.'

'I'm supposed to stay this side of the river, sir. Car three's . . .'

'I know that,' interrupted Brooke. 'But we're police officers, Constable. Not bank clerks. Do you think all the crooks stay on this side of the river too?'

'Sir.'

'Right. So, take a walk along the west bank. Keep your eyes open. I saw a platoon of soldiers out there digging at midnight. See if you can spot the pit, anything else that catches your eye. Leave me a note, my desk, before you knock off. Got it?'

CHAPTER SEVEN

The three lorries had pulled over on the left-hand side of Castle Hill, a wide street which rose up from the misty river towards a rough circular grass mound upon which stood the medieval remains of the city's once imposing fortress, now co-opted as the county jail. The lorries faced uphill, as if heading out of town. The street, of several pubs, a brewery and a sawmill, lay still in the moonlight. A red gas lamp had been lit and posted at a junction halfway up, casting a warmer patina over the scene.

Ascending the hill on the pavement, Brooke found the driver asleep in the first lorry, slumped forward, the moonlight catching false teeth thrust slightly forward of the lips. Fifty, fifty-five, with a heavy head, his face was fleshy, the folds of skin falling to a double chin pressing down on his chest.

The next cab was empty, the passenger door wide open. A cigarette smouldered in an ashtray set by the gearstick. Moving on to the last lorry, Brooke heard voices and, coming level, found a police constable standing in front of the cab, taking notes, talking quietly to a man in worker's overalls.

The constable saluted. 'PC Cable, sir. This is Mr Turl, charge hand for . . .' He checked the paperwork. 'Turl Haulage, of York.'

'What's the problem, Cable?' said Brooke, taking a step back, giving Turl a half-smile.

The driver was five foot eight or nine, with a very light build, small head, black hair with a widow's peak, maybe twenty-five years of age. An open face, deferential, almost submissive. Brooke thought he was very young to be a charge hand, and might be the owner's son, given the company name. His limbs hung loose in baggy overalls, large hands working a rag, giving the impression of restrained energy.

He should be in a uniform in France, thought Brooke, but then recalled that road haulage was a reserved occupation. If the fighting started in earnest such dispensations would not last.

'It's the paperwork, really,' said Cable. 'It's just a bit of a mess. I've rung in some details to the desk to see if they can cross-check the basics.'

He nodded over the road. A police box stood in the shadows of a tree, offering a landline to constables on the beat, a first-aid kit and a fire extinguisher. Rumours at the Borough suggested several were fitted with a paraffin stove for brewing tea on cold nights, and even the occasional bottle of beer. A faint light showed from the half-open door.

'Sergeant said he'd ring the box if he gets anything,' added Cable, handing Brooke the vehicle log book. 'ID card's fine. I've not checked the other two. Goods were picked up from a depot in north London, medical supplies and clothing, en route to a store at Goole docks, on the Humber. Hunter's Shipping. Ouse Wharf. The full address says *South* Riding.'

Cable looked up, incredulous at the error. 'It's West Riding. East would have been an understandable error. But there isn't a South Riding. Never has been.'

Turl shook his head. 'It'll be Meg in't office,' he said. 'Lass is getting married this weekend. Bit ditsy, mind. It's her big day.' He smiled at Brooke and there was a genuine warmth in the eyes. 'Bit of a stunner, our Meg.'

'Yorkshire lass, is she?' asked Brooke.

'Born and bred,' said Turl.

'So you think she'd know,' said Brooke.

Turl kept smiling.

Cable ploughed on, 'Two of the vehicle registration numbers don't match the actual plates – one's a number out, 3 for a 5, the other's GJ, not SJ. The travel permits are fine, but the issuing stamps are smudged . . .'

Brooke held the piece of paper as Cable played torchlight on the circular blue stamp across which had been scrawled an indecipherable signature.

'Odd travelling at night. Especially *tonight*,' said Brooke, studying the young driver's cheerful face.

'We'd pulled up. Bit of a kip until dawn. Then we're off. Your man here woke me up. I was well gone. We got this far by eight. Driving on the curfew lights is dodgy, 'specially long distance. So we laid up. Bit of shut-eye.'

'Your mate's missing from the next lorry down,' said Brooke.

Turl looked blank. 'Ginger? Weak bladder, that lad. He'll be off down an alley. Nature's call.' He nodded his head as if agreeing with his own explanation.

'What do you think, Constable?' asked Brooke. 'By rights we should keep them here until we've checked everything. But we can always get York to run the paperwork tomorrow. I'm sure it's just a slip of the pen. You happy with that, Mr Turl? You'll need to go to the station, present the documents.'

'Not a problem, Inspector,' said Turl.

'We'll just take a quick look at the loads,' added Brooke. 'Let's start with Sleeping Beauty at the bottom of the hill.'

Turl had started sweating, so that his clear skin shone, and the whites of his eyes were wide. 'Nev having a kip, is he? It's been a long day. Good luck waking him up.'

Later, recalling the moment for Claire, Brooke was uncertain which happened first: either the light on the top of the police box flashed, or the phone began to ring.

Whatever the trigger, the result was instantaneous: Turl ran. The word 'greyhound' didn't do him justice.

PC Cable set off in pursuit.

Brooke walked quickly down the hill to the lorry at the bottom. The cab was empty; the sleeping driver had fled, the passenger door on the far side wide open.

Three lorries, all padlocked. Three drivers, all gone.

CHAPTER EIGHT

The Borough police force was based at the Spinning House, a one-time workhouse and prison, set on seventeenth-century foundations. It had been the university's jail, where the proctors and their fearsome constables – the 'bulldogs' – had imprisoned prostitutes in a bid to protect the morals of students and scholars. The women were set to work on spinning wheels in a large room on the top floor, beneath a great oak roof. The Victorians had subsequently used the building to house the deserving poor and the destitute. The workhouse was just that: a place of toil, offered in exchange for thin soup and shelter at night. The original cells below were still in use and, according to several recent occupants, haunted by the ghosts of past prisoners.

The facade of the building was of fine stone, elegantly simple, with small lancet windows on the ground floor below grander bays above. The door, set in an imposing archway, opened into a hallway of panelled wood, the station night desk barring the way forward to offices beyond.

As Brooke arrived, the sergeant covered the mouthpiece of a phone pressed to his ear. 'York's adamant, sir. No such firm as Turl Haulage, certainly not on their patch. Which makes you wonder about the ID cards. Cable just rang in, by the way. Lost the driver, good and proper, out towards Bait's Lock.'

Brooke was impressed by PC Cable's stamina. The lock lay out on the edge of the city, where the inter-war suburbs bled into the open fen.

The sergeant finished with the station in York and dropped the phone on its cradle. 'I've got everybody out looking, sir. But you know – needle, haystack, same old story.'

'Any progress on bolt-cutters?' Brooke asked. 'We do need to get inside those lorries, Sergeant.'

'First thing tomorrow, sir. Garage is locked up till day shift comes on,' the sergeant said, nodding in the direction of the station yard. 'Before the war we had twenty-four-hour cover. But needs must. Radio car will keep an eye on the lorries on Castle Hill until the mechanics can jump-start the lot, bring 'em back here.'

Brooke nodded. 'That'll have to be good enough. When you can spare someone, post them on the spot, will you? We've got three men on the run, I don't want one back-tracking and driving off.'

The sergeant looked at Brooke. 'You alright, sir?'

'I may borrow one of your cells, Sergeant. And a candle. I'm tired. It's been a long night. Number six free?'

The cell, at the end of a short corridor, consisted of a bare stone box with no windows, no ventilation, just a bunk and a clean bucket. It had been Brooke's refuge many times.

Lying down, he made a pillow of his coat, slipping a book out of his coat pocket, holding it up at an angle to catch the wavering candlelight.

He read the title: *Vagrants and Thieves Wanted*.

Each page carried a short note, a description and a mug shot, the book reissued every six months by the Home Office. He carried it always, filling spare minutes with a quick revision of the faces he'd memorised. The skill was not to study eyes, or lips, or broken noses, but to somehow register, and store, an image of the whole face. Brooke found that when he had to search a crowd for a robber, or a street for a thief, he could animate that image, turning it like a sculpted head, a three-dimensional creation of his own mind.

He flicked through twenty pages, looking for the ghost of Turl's whippet-like features, before he felt himself sliding away. He checked his watch, closed his eyes, and actually heard the book hit the floor before darkness descended. It was more like oblivion than sleep, and as he slipped away his limbs jolted, as if his body was in free fall.

The last time Brooke had slept, in what his doctor liked to call the common or garden fashion, was in late October 1917. It was the night before his capture by the Turks in the desert, at an oasis fifteen miles east of Gaza. The Egyptian Expeditionary Force had been on the road for three months, fighting its way east into Palestine, shadowing the construction of the new rail line from Alexandria. When a halt was finally called, some care had been taken in the setting up of a proper camp.

Brooke's batman had put sardine tins under each foot of the bed, filled with paraffin, to collect scorpions. The linen, which had been steamed in a tarpaulin 'bath' by the railhead, was crisp and white, the labels marked HOTEL BRISTOL, CAIRO. He'd enjoyed a glass of whisky and a cigarette – one of the elegant Black Russians his father had given him at the station in Cambridge when he'd waved him off. The entire effect, after a bath in hot water – admittedly under the stars – was of civilised luxury.

The night air in Gaza had been cold. He'd fallen asleep in the act of turning his head away from his half-finished drink. Of fourteen hours' sleep he recalled nothing. It was the last time he'd ever embrace slumber like that, as a fearless giving up of the day, as an innocent release. These days, when sleep came it was fitful and intermittent, sudden periods of total immersion lost between nightmares which left his heart pounding.

He woke in cell six with a start, both legs kicking out. Looking at the candle stub, he checked his watch: six forty-five. He'd slept for thirty-one minutes. The sun would be up.

He'd gone to sleep considering the lorries, and what might be stashed inside, and the missing drivers. He woke up thinking about the soldiers on the riverbank, wondering if PC Woods had found the pit on the riverbank meadows. The terrain, masked by willow and thorn, was a wilderness, but there had to be a pit, because they'd buried something.

Either way he'd make it his business to ask questions up at military headquarters at Madingley Hall, and given the army's bureaucratic obsessions, he'd take the time to put them in writing. He recalled the soldiers in the traces of the carts, and a fleeting coincidence: the soft guttural north country accent of the sergeant had its perfect echo in the mouth of Turl, the young man who had finally outpaced PC Cable.

CHAPTER NINE

Chris Childe, conscientious objector, lay awake in the dawn light of Romsey Town, haunted by the flickering images of a nightmare just passed: skeletons and corpses tethered by ropes in a stiff, mannered dance of death, watched over by hooded executioners. Up on one elbow, bathed in sweat, he drew comfort from the sleeping faces of his twin girls and his wife, all snug in the double bed. Outside, the only signs of life were the strange metallic percussion of a goods wagon on the railway, and the distant glass rattle of a milk float drawn by a plodding horse.

Downstairs in the front room he found his typewriter. He heaved it into the kitchen, closed the door and briskly typed a terse statement outlining what he had witnessed the night before. What had Henderson, the Party chairman, advised? 'If you won't tell us, Chris, then tell London. Tell the Party. Write it up, stick to the facts, and keep them in the right order. Then give it to Vera – she'll make sure it gets to headquarters at Cadogan Square. And keep a copy, but keep it safe.'

The envelope sealed in his pocket, he closed his front door behind him and set out through the serried rows of poor terraced houses, over the iron bridge towards the old city, which lay before him, shreds of mist flying like flags from college spires. The air still carried the fine ash of the incinerated barrage balloon, the acrid smell of the fire on the morning breeze. The Great Darkness had given way to a misty, autumnal morning, but even now Childe could detect the gleam of a blue sky beyond, promising that the Indian summer might last. On Regent Street, an early bus clanged past, while a line of soldiers unloaded sandbags at the corner of Parker's Piece.

Turning into Babylon Street, he paused. This short cul-de-sac formed the heart of the city's red-light district, a small quarter given over to prostitution. The houses stood five storeys tall, with deep basements and high attics. Even now, at eight in the morning, two men sat on the stone steps of one, smoking and watching him closely.

Childe walked purposefully to number 12 and knocked.

Waiting on the doorstep, he tried to recall the exact moment he'd realised Vera Staunton, branch secretary to the Party, was a member of the oldest profession. How had this knowledge become commonplace? In debates at weekly meetings she'd spoken up for women throughout the Empire, 'subjugated by man and money' to sell their bodies. Any direct acknowledgement she sidestepped, but no one doubted that she experienced the violent reality of the class struggle at first hand, a sharp contrast to the theoretical musings of the Party's academics.

Childe watched a figure approaching through the stained glass of the front door: shuffling, slightly bent, struggling with the latch.

An old woman's face appeared in the gap between door and jamb, bisected by a metal chain.

'A letter, for Vera Staunton. I need to hand it over in person.'

The woman shrugged and slid the chain, retreating to a door at the end of a tiled corridor. At the last moment, she turned to call back, 'Go on up. Fifth floor, front room. Her name's on the door.'

Climbing the stairs, Childe met a man descending, one of Vera's clients, perhaps, enveloped in a military greatcoat, chin down, a smart trilby wedged firmly in place. He stood to one side, and as Childe came level he tried to see his face, hoping to detect shame, perhaps, or a furtive hint of betrayal: but there was nothing, just the suppressed impatience of a middle-aged man having to wait, a transaction completed, money paid for services rendered.

Staunton opened her door in a thin Chinese print nightdress. When she recognised Childe, she drew it tight at her throat. 'Chris. What is it? What's happened?'

Childe gave her the envelope.

'That needs to go to the chairman, to Harry Pollitt, at Cadogan Square,' said Childe, stuck on the threshold. 'Today, Vera, either by hand or post. I saw something they should know about, something important. I don't know how you work it, Vera – with the Party. Is a letter alright? Should it go by registered post? Or do you take papers down? I could go down, in person, if you think that's my duty.'

'Calm down, Chris,' she said, smiling. 'Pollitt's gone, anyway, for backing the war. I've got the new man's name somewhere . . .'

'They need to know now, Vera, quickly. Henderson said we can't trust the phones . . .'

Staunton held up a hand, and then a finger across her lips.

She took his hand and drew him in, closing the door. Turning her back, she fussed at a record player until jazz filled the air.

Coming back to him, she stood a few inches away, and it

reached him then, the scent of the men who had gone before. What had Childe expected? Sweat, perhaps, and stale cigarette smoke. But this was less indelicate: scented soap, cologne, cigars.

The music made a songbird in a brass cage beat its wings, so that tiny feathers fell, caught in the light from the window.

'What does it say?' she asked, holding the letter up, finding it sealed, placing a hand lightly on his shoulder.

'I can't tell you, not yet. We're all agreed. London should know first. They must decide, the executive, at the highest level. It's not a decision for us.'

She weighed the envelope in her hand.

'Have you made a copy?'

Childe patted his jacket pocket and smiled.

'I can't go to London today,' he said. 'I'd take it myself, I would. But I'm digging this morning, the tribunal's this afternoon, then I'll have to go back to work . . .' He checked his watch. 'I can't duck it. I need a reference for the tribunal. But the Party must know as soon as possible, Vera. Today, if we catch the post?'

'You're right. Best send a letter.' She smiled, nodding. 'Wait here,' she added, retreating to a small side room, in which he'd glimpsed a single bed, a sink and a gas ring. He heard drawers being opened and closed. A light came on, and a chair grated.

'One moment,' she called.

The main room was dominated by a double bed, across which had been laid several throws, a pile of cushions and a patchwork quilt. Besides the record player on its table, there was a drinks trolley and a table which held three ashtrays, all of them empty. A bookcase revealed random titles, the walls anonymous prints.

Nothing gave a hint of Staunton's own story.

That first night, in the weekly meeting above the public bar of the Mitre, when they'd told her they needed her to join them in the Party, Henderson had asked the key questions: why had she worked for *Peace News*, why had she become a pacifist?

Corporal Harry Staunton, Vera's husband, had died at the Somme. Amid the carnage and the mud his body had never been identified amongst the corpses later buried in a mass grave. A letter from his commanding officer had failed to provide any details of his death, or any comfort. His unit had gone over the top at the sound of the whistle, and of forty-two men only seventeen had survived. The thirty yards won in the ensuing battle had been lost the next day.

'I don't believe in the glorious dead, do you?' she'd asked them. 'They left me a widow, with a son, and they left him so broken, ripped apart, that they couldn't put a name to his body. So he'll be in that pit with the rest, tangled up. They had the cheek to give him a medal, as if that helped me. No. I'm for peace. Peace at any cost.'

Staunton appeared with the envelope neatly addressed to the Party's London HQ.

'I'll post it, but I need stamps. We can't trust recorded delivery, especially to Cadogan Square. And they're watched, day and night, so I don't want to go in person, not unless we have to.' She checked a delicate wristwatch. 'I must fly.'

CHAPTER TEN

Brooke ate breakfast in the Masonic Hall, a hundred yards from the Spinning House, requisitioned by the Ministry of Food to provide cheap meals on a mass scale for workers and soldiers. The windows of what was known as the British Restaurant were clouded with condensation. Early workers, and a handful of soldiers, ate at trestle tables. Brooke chose an egg from a hotplate swimming in lard, a rasher of bacon and two slices of toast, and pocketed his change. The tea, stewed, was pungent and tepid. He drank it, freighted with sugar, under a ceiling decorated with moulded plasterwork, depicting the elaborate symbols of the Masonic order: compasses and trowels, and an unnerving single eye set in a ceremonial triangle. He smoked a single cigarette, drawing the nicotine deep into his lungs.

He'd have gone home to change and shave but Claire was still on shift at the hospital and the thought of the empty house was dispiriting. A change of clothes and a razor were always ready in his office at the Spinning House, alongside a spare towel and shorts for his clandestine swims. So by eight o'clock he was at his desk catching up on paperwork, including a note from PC Woods to the effect that there was no sight of a pit on the riverbank, or anything else untoward.

Brooke's office boasted two additions to the standard Borough issue: a set of wooden blinds, and a daybed he'd bought on the quayside at Suez before the desert campaign, which had once been decorated in blue and gold, depicting white cranes in the green bullrushes beside a blue Nile.

On the stroke of eight-fifteen, he picked up his phone and dialled zero.

'Mr Brooke. Good morning, sir.'

'Give me a line, please,' he said, sipping his water. 'Yes. Good morning,' he added.

He dialled a Cambridge number, which rang once before the phone was snatched up.

'Captain Kerridge.'

'At ease,' said Brooke, imagining his old friend standing rigid at his desk. Captain 'Rich' Kerridge had been Brooke's opposite number, his 'oppo', on headquarters staff in Cairo, the point of contact between his own battalion and General Allenby's staff. They'd built a friendship based on a willingness to break regulations, slip out of uniform and head out into the desert by car. Kerridge, who'd studied history at Oxford, was in search of ancient ruins to record his beloved hieroglyphs. Brooke, a natural scientist, was on the lookout for the famed Barbary lion and, along the Nile itself, basking crocodiles.

Kerridge, a career soldier, was now based up at Madingley, adjutant to the commanding officer. His voice was cultured, smooth. 'Skulking in your dingy office at this hour, Brooke. Last night must have been a blessing. All that darkness by government order.'

'Darkness in which you contrived to lose some barrage balloons,' said Brooke. 'That's careless. The one I saw was the size of a bus. I'm afraid there's more bad news, Rich. Very bad news.'

'Christ, really?' said Kerridge. 'The proverbial shite has been hitting the fan since dawn. These things are supposed to be the cornerstone of our defences, Brooke, against the Hun. Here we are letting them drift over a town packed to the rafters with military personnel, civil servants, not to mention evacuees. One of the sodding things is still aloft. It missed Ely cathedral by three hundred yards. It's still rising. The king's up at Sandringham. If he catches sight of it there'll be all hell to pay. So now what's happened?'

Brooke heard Kerridge's voice, muffled, before a door slammed.

'Sorry, Brooke. Commanding Officer wants a briefing. Tell me the worst, and tell me quickly.'

Did Brooke imagine a series of sounds: the metal twist of the cap of a hip flask, the faintest smack of dry lips? Kerridge started most days with a medicinal 'stiffner'.

The report on Brooke's desk, which he now summarised for Kerridge, lacked the forensic detail they'd have both wanted but the broad thrust of events was brutally clear.

An American called Lux, a research fellow at Michaelhouse, had enjoyed a drink with colleagues at the Eagle public house after a lecture at the Galen Anatomy Building. He'd left at a few minutes before nine, saying he was returning to his rooms. A constable on duty reported seeing a man fitting Lux's description – short, powerfully built, mid-twenties – passing the Senate House at just after the hour, no doubt heading for his college. But as Doric, the night porter, had reported, whilst he'd left with three fellow scientists, he had not returned before the gates had been locked.

There was evidence that Lux had encountered one of the drifting barrage balloons, or more precisely its webbing and trailing cables, on Senate House Passage. Broken tiles littered the passageway, a chimney pot had been demolished on the outer kitchen range of the nearest college, and a length of metal cable was entangled in the guttering. Several students reported hearing the tiles falling at shortly after the hour.

Lux's body had been discovered by a woman walking her dog at just after six-thirty that morning, half a mile from the Senate House, on the riverbank. It was partly clothed, and had suffered several severe traumas. The phrase used by the constable attending the scene was instructive: *He'd been torn apart*. The woman had been given a sedative and taken home in a police car.

'Save me the graphic detail,' said Kerridge.

In Cairo, Kerridge had specialised in logistics and communications. Before the big push towards Jerusalem he'd filled vacant hours with one other duty: vetting field commanders' requests from across the Middle East for acts of heroism to be marked by medals and commendations. Brooke had admired his ability to see the irony in this situation: that a man who effectively fought his war on paper had become the official arbiter of heroism. Kerridge had a gift for bureaucracy, a genius for intelligent administration and an aversion to the sight of blood.

Brooke had Lux's wallet, which included his college pass, on his desk, as well as the American's belt, the buckle of which depicted the Golden Gate Bridge at the entrance to San Francisco Bay, entangled with a length of material.

'I'm no expert,' said Brooke. 'But it looks like latex, lightweight, stretchy.'

'Colour?'

'Silver. There's some stitching too. I don't think there's much doubt, Rich. He's had a close encounter with a barrage balloon. A lethal encounter.'

'Right. Put out the sodding bunting. Not only do we let loose three barrage balloons, we manage to kill a scientist, a Yank Jew, I'm guessing. A good night's work. You know what this means. Whitehall, the powers that be . . .'

Brooke tried to visualise the moment of death: the drifting balloon snaring Lux, lifting him up, dashing him against stone and brick, dragging him, hopefully senseless, across the rooftops, before the return to earth. Damp earth, at least: the sweet-smelling riverbank.

'This can really happen?' he asked.

'Not the first time,' said Kerridge. 'It's not the cabling here, I suspect, it's the netting. Imagine a football goal without posts being trawled along the street. Once you're tangled up, you're not getting free until something gives.'

Brooke detected the intake of another snifter.

'Do you really need to get involved in this, Brooke?'

Brooke was tempted to let the military deal with the death. War had left the police force decimated. The halt and the lame, and long-retired, had been requisitioned to fill holes in the establishment. CID as such amounted to two detective inspectors, one of whom was about to volunteer for the RAF, and four detective sergeants. In a real sense Brooke *was* CID, in that above him was a single chief inspector with onerous administrative duties, and a chief constable who saw his role as principally ceremonial. A turf war with the military was the last thing Brooke needed.

But Lux's mangled body had been discovered on a public street, a world away from the theatre of war. Before he was reduced to a military statistic, Brooke felt Lux deserved a measure of civilian justice.

'The wheels will have begun to turn,' said Brooke. 'The coroner's been informed. You know the drill. I'll need to get a statement from the officer responsible for the barrage balloons,' said Brooke.

'Swift-Lane's the CO,' said Kerridge. 'But frankly he's a bit above your pay grade, Brooke. And mine. Second in command is your man – Major Joelyn Stone. He was in charge of planning for the blackout, so it's on his watch. RAF run the balloons, but there's nobody senior here, and this place is supposed to be all about interservice liaison. I'll fix it. I better sit in . . . Hold on . . .'

The line didn't go dead, but there was a sense in which the call had been shuffled into an electronic holding pen. The faint echoes of other voices could be heard against an institutional hum.

The line crackled. 'Brooke? Got to go. See you up here in an hour.'

CHAPTER ELEVEN

Ralph Edison was Brooke's new detective sergeant. Uniformed police officers switching to the detective branch always faced the challenge of becoming 'plain clothes', the protection of the insignia and the buttons, the stripes and the belt, swept aside. Most resorted to a strictly regulated version of 'civvy street', epitomised by a white shirt, black or navy-blue tie, dark two-piece suit and black leather shoes. (A tie could be purchased which simply clipped into the collar, removing the danger of being choked in the process of making an arrest.)

Sergeant Ralph Edison had found the transition more of a challenge than most. He had retired two years before the outbreak of the war after thirty years in uniform with the Borough. A whip-round on his last day at the Spinning House had produced enough cash to buy him a new set of tools for his allotment. Brooke recalled a short, gracious speech of thanks, which was remarkable for the fact that it gave the clear impression he was actually sorry to go. He had been called back to duty in the aftermath of conscription.

The suit still hung oddly from his rounded shoulders, the trouser legs too short, the shoes pinching. However, something about his calm, unhurried persona allowed him to project the *concept* of the uniform, even when it was long gone. A sense of confident authority radiated from his large, bony frame. Edison had a reputation for honest diligence, and a flair for dealing with ordinary people. He'd spent his last five years before retirement on the front desk at the Spinning House, on the day shift, a patient listener, the face of the Borough when the public called.

He paused now on the threshold of Brooke's office, waiting to be given leave to enter.

'Sit if you want to, Sergeant,' said Brooke. 'We don't stand on the niceties here.'

Uniformed branch had run on rigid rules, reflecting a pervasive hierarchy. Edison had been a plain-clothes detective for exactly three weeks, and old habits lingered.

'I'm just trying to sort out this incident last night, Sergeant,' said Brooke. 'The barrage balloons?'

'I heard. And I saw the fire,' said Edison, easing himself into a seat. 'Up at the railway station? We got a good view from our back yard. My granddaughter thought it was Bonfire Night. Bloody balloons are dangerous . . . There's hundreds over London, sir. Went down last week to see my son. All along the river, they were. Like clouds in uniform,' he offered, shaking his head, sipping a mug of tea he'd brought with him.

'Well, one of them killed someone last night, Sergeant. Right here in Cambridge. Proves your point.'

'Good God,' said Edison.

'Anything else from the duty book?' asked Brooke, keen to get on.

Edison gave him a concise summary of all other incidents logged overnight. Aside from a spate of traffic accidents, the hours of darkness had passed quietly.

'A suspected suicide, too,' he added, running a hand over his close-cut white hair. 'Body found at Byron's Pool. Male, fifties, decent country clothes, good shoes. He had a couple of bricks in his pockets to make sure. Uniformed constable attended after a local resident called it in. Poor bugger. Makes you wonder . . .'

'Get me a time on the autopsy, will you?' said Brooke, disturbed by the idea of death in such an idyllic spot. He'd once taken his son there for a swim, in the footsteps of the great poet, who'd haunted the spot as a student. The deep, green pool had a disturbing quality of apparently infinite depth.

Brooke stood and pulled up the blinds. Down in the yard stood the three lorries from Castle Hill, tailbacks down.

'This is your priority, Sergeant. Any news on the drivers?'

Edison shook his head.

The padlocks had finally yielded to the bolt-cutters to reveal insulated interiors. Once the tailbacks had been let down, blood had run out in a steady trickle. The first two lorries had been packed with freshly slaughtered meat – beef, pork, lamb, fowl – which had been removed and distributed to several city centre butchers with cold rooms. Broken necks for the fowl, but neat gunshot wounds to the skull for the rest.

The real mystery was Turl's truck. It was empty.

'What do you think, sir?' asked Edison, at his side.

'Black market,' said Brooke. 'We all know meat rationing's on the way. If you can bypass the slaughterhouses, the regulations, and stockpile enough, you can set the price, make a fortune. In business, Sergeant, it's what they like to call a killing.'

CHAPTER TWELVE

The barrier at Madingley Hall stayed resolutely down as Brooke flashed his warrant card from the police radio car. A redcap, bending down to make eye contact, peered into the detective's tinted lenses. The day was clear and bright, the mist long burnt away, so Brooke had upgraded to the blue glass pair, which gave the hall's manicured grounds a lush, exotic hue.

'Would you mind, sir?' asked the redcap.

Brooke slipped the glasses off, blinking in the light, revealing eyes the colour of falling water. The security was bizarrely tight, given he was driving a car with a light on top stencilled with the word POLICE.

The barrier flew up. To either side of the checkpoint stretched barbed wire: a double fence with a ten-foot gap between, topped with spikes. The sun glinted off a small watchtower in the distance, reflecting a gun, perhaps, or field glasses.

They swept through the grounds. Edison, left at the Spinning House to coordinate the hunt for the missing drivers, had expressed disappointment at missing the trip, as the gardens were by Capability Brown, the Georgian landscape genius. Brooke wondered how long the topiary, the parterre, the velvet lawns, the sickle-shaped lake, would survive in pristine condition under military control.

The medieval house lurked behind a Tudor facade of decorated brick. In the first minute Brooke spotted uniforms from all three of the services, plus Civil Defence, ARP, fire service, several motorcycle messengers and what looked like a gas decontamination team, loading up kit into an unmarked van.

Beyond a stone porch and open oak doors, a marble lobby led to a great panelled hall, apparently set aside as a make-do hangar. A deflated barrage balloon covered most of the floor of bare, polished boards, while at its edges women worked on their knees, sewing seams.

A sergeant took his name down on a clipboard and led him up an oak staircase to the first floor, into an office with double bay windows. Captain Kerridge sat on a wide window ledge, smoking.

Major Joelyn Stone, the deputy CO, introduced himself, but didn't abandon his desk to shake hands, leaning over the blotter awkwardly. He directed Brooke to a chair and told Captain Kerridge to join them. Stone was thick-set, bull-necked, with a round bony head, upon which his hair had been ruthlessly barbered. He emitted a constant sense of irritation and impatience. Giving orders, and having them obeyed, had clearly become second nature.

The contrast with Kerridge – handsome, loose-limbed, relaxed, with oiled black hair brushed back – was pointed.

'How can I help?' he said.

'Just routine, I hope,' said Brooke. 'There will be an autopsy, and I'll need to report on the basic facts. The coroner will need to be sure in his own mind that there will be no repetition of events.

Otherwise, he might issue a rider to his judgement, a warning if you like, of a more general nature. That might have repercussions, and would certainly make the newspapers.'

'Accidents happen,' said Stone briskly. 'I can assure you it will not reoccur. The military details are a bit technical, as well as classified . . .'

Kerridge shifted in his seat. 'Detective Inspector Brooke was in Palestine, sir. Awarded the DSO. He served with General Allenby. I think we can rely on him to be discreet. And he knows enough of the science: barrage balloons were used extensively on the Suez Canal to deter Italian air raids. Perhaps he could see your report to the War Office?'

Stone licked his lips. 'Palestine, eh? Technology was very different then, of course. They flew balloons in a line to support a net, high enough to stop the incoming enemy planes, which wasn't very high. What we call the operational ceiling. I was on the Western Front and we set 'em at 1,500 feet. This time round the bombers are a lot higher, twice that if not more. We need to be able to run the balloons up and down on winches above the clouds, and set them precisely at different levels, in formation. It's a highly sophisticated operation. And we're experimenting here with various innovations.'

'You were on the Western Front?' asked Brooke.

'The Somme – both times. And then Cambrai.' The major held up the hand he'd had hidden below the desk to reveal two missing fingers, a metal sheath over the middle digit. 'Sniper blew the gun out of my hand.'

Brooke was an aficionado of leaders. Edmund 'Bull' Allenby, his CO in the desert, had been a man of extraordinary temper and energy. T. E. Lawrence, despite the showy native costume, was a lesson in stillness and internal resolve. Both had won the affection of their men because they were genuine, in that their official personas were merely extensions of some core truth.

Stone, he judged, was a bit of a fraud. However, Brooke was more than prepared to accept that he might be a highly effective fraud, and that the successful military personality often incorporated several known psychological flaws.

The name Joelyn Stone had rung a bell. A scandal? He'd have to track down chapter and verse.

'We've got nearly two hundred balloons up in this zone,' said Stone. 'Another hundred down the line towards London. Various technical innovations are being trialled here for the War Office, as I said. It's early days. Bound to be some hiccoughs. The cables failed, as did one of the winches. The engineers are on the case now.'

'You mentioned a War Office report?' said Brooke. The nature of the American's death made him want to keep asking questions. Its violence, perhaps, or its sudden, God-like brutality.

Stone grabbed the white phone on his desk and instructed someone to bring up the relevant documents. He also ordered three cups of tea.

'I'd appreciate a measure of discretion, Brooke. The details are sensitive.' From a drawer he produced a map upon which he marked the spot where the three barrage balloons had been tethered. The missing third balloon had been located by a military messenger in a field ten miles short of the coast.

The tea arrived. Brooke balanced the saucer on his knee while Stone fussed with a cigar.

'We had reports, Major, last night, of a military working party out on the riverside. Army, certainly; Londoners, apparently. Your boys?' asked Brooke.

Stone nodded several times as if agreeing with the question. 'Middlesex Regiment, part of an anti-aircraft battalion,' he said finally. 'The guns are south and east of the city. When the real show starts they'll earn their keep. For now they're available for special duties with Civil Defence. We're keen to help when and where we can.'

'Why were they out by the river last night?' asked Brooke. 'Looked like a fatigue, digging trenches, maybe.'

'There's your answer,' said Stone.

An orderly arrived with the War Office report, which comprised a single sheet of A4. Brooke read the first two sentences quickly, finding them unintelligible, crammed as they were with military jargon, technical specifications and poor grammar.

'The man who died was called Lux. An American scientist,' he said, folding the report and slipping it inside his jacket.

'A foreigner?' said Stone. 'Unfortunate. But there we are. The War Office is likely to take a wider view of such casualties.'

For a moment Brooke imagined Lux entangled, bare hands pulling at the wires, tearing them away from his throat. The constable's report had mentioned the hands, lacerated; it was one of those words that made Brooke wince, a sympathetic pain reaching down to the fingertips. He thought of Claire's patient with his bandaged limbs.

'What does it entail, this *wider view*?' asked Brooke, acutely aware that to some extent Stone was trying to fob him off.

'We're wasting time on this, Inspector. This was one man,' said Stone, his good hand encircling his cup. 'This war, it'll kill thousands. You know that. Hundreds of thousands. They're the dead and the dying, Brooke, while we sit here. In Poland, out in the Atlantic. There's no rhyme or reason, is there? We didn't do that at Passchendaele, did we? Pick our way over the battlefield asking: and this one, how did *he* die? No one has a right to justice, that's what a war is, Brooke, a suspension of normal rights. What makes Dr Ernst Lux so special?'

Driving out through the checkpoint ten minutes later, Brooke played the conversation back in his head until he was finally sure: he'd never mentioned Lux's first name, or his doctorate. Perhaps Major Stone was more concerned about the American's death than he wished to appear.

CHAPTER THIRTEEN

The phoney war spluttered on. The Wehrmacht had made a lightning raid into French territory, teasing the massed allied armies. In Moscow, Stalin was telling the Finns the price they'd have to pay for peace. At sea, German U-boats had sunk a British merchant ship, although – according to the reports – the *Clement* had been carrying ballast en route to Rotterdam, and the crew had been rescued.

Brooke folded the *Daily Telegraph* away as Edison brought the Wolseley into a cul-de-sac on the southern edge of the city. The car was Edison's delight – a four-cylinder Wolseley Wasp. Brooke suspected that the mileage allowance, and the chance to drive despite petrol rationing, were among the benefits that had tempted the former sergeant off the allotment and back into the force.

Edison parked it with exaggerated care beside a grass verge dotted with cherry trees.

'A single shot? Just the one?' asked Brooke, surveying the street.

'That's it, sir. That's all he heard, man who rang it in. Number 29:

there . . . He reckons it's a Nazi parachutist, holed up in a garden shed.'

Brooke appreciated Edison's old-fashioned precision. There might have been more shots, but only *one* was heard.

The street was pure Metroland. Sub-Lutyens villas, semi-detached, with fake Tudor beams, sat back from neatly tended gardens, each one a miniature version of Madingley's sweeping artifice.

A crowd had formed at the far end. A uniformed constable ushered them back, while another, standing guard at the gate of number 29, approached the Wasp.

'Sir. Family's down the end of the street with the rest out of harm's way,' he said. 'We've cleared all the houses. Mr Reed, that's who spotted him, he's inside the house.'

Mr Reed was a cricket fan: there was a bat in the umbrella stand in the hall, and some boots by the mat. In the front room, a large print of a Test match at Lord's dominated the wall over the fireplace, while he sat on a dining room chair at the French windows, which were open. Across his lap was a rifle.

'I've got him covered,' he said, pushing a few wisps of hair back from his forehead. 'The constable said there were reports of parachutists with the raid last night. I reckon I've got one, maybe he's got the chute in there with him.'

He nodded down the garden, which was about fifty yards in length, dominated by an immaculate lawn, which had been cut in longitudinal stripes. At the far end was a shed, beside an air raid shelter, sunk into the ground so that only its curved roof, turfed over, was visible. In front of the shelter, obscuring the door, was a large iron grass roller, the handle sticking straight up in the air in the shape of a capital T.

'My youngest heard him cough when she took the dog for a walk. He's in the shelter, not the shed.'

'What time was that?' asked Brooke.

'Late. We all had a bit of a lie-in after the raid. 'Bout eight-thirty, I reckon. I slipped down there and had a listen,' continued Reed. 'Bastard was fast asleep. So I pushed the roller down the lawn. It's oiled up, coz I use it for the club, and we're near the mainline, so every time a train went past I rolled it twenty foot nearer. Last push I crashed it up against the door and wedged in a brick. He's going nowhere.'

Brooke considered the quiet suburban scene. Late roses bloomed on either side of the greensward while autumnal leaves fell from a line of plane trees. If it really was a German parachutist, he should secure the scene and ring Madingley Hall. Emergency orders, covering precisely this situation, had been issued by the military.

Brooke, however, relished the chance of meeting the enemy face-to-face.

'Tell me about the gunshot,' he said.

'Well, he shouted first. Said he wanted out, that I'd got nothing to fear. *I* said I'd rung the police. Then he offered money: five pounds, so he could get away. He said it was all a big mistake. He said that a lot. So I ignored him.'

'So he spoke English?'

Mr Reed nodded. 'If he's a spy he would do.'

Edison returned from a recce. 'All clear, sir. Back alley's got a constable on it, and then there's the railway line, with a six foot wire fence.'

'And he fired the gun then, did he, Mr Reed?' asked Brooke.

'That's it. There's a gap in the door panel, for ventilation, and I reckon he thought a potshot might help. Bounced off the back of the house. He said to let him out or he'd come out shooting. Tosh that, coz he's not going anywhere. Mind you, if he's got one bullet he's got more. So I'm staying here.'

Brooke took the rifle off Mr Reed and gave it to Edison, and then walked out through the French doors. The sun broke through the drifting clouds and lit the garden up in primary colours.

Brooke's footsteps were soft on the grass. When he reached the roller, he sat on the lawn with his back to it, the curved iron edge already warm with the heat of the sun. Whoever was in the shelter was less than six feet away, so he didn't need to raise his voice.

'Detective Inspector Brooke here,' he said, and heard a sudden shifting of weight. 'Borough police. I'm no expert but I'd say there was no way out of that shelter other than through the doors and there's a tonne of iron stopping you that way. There's twenty officers in the street, the back alley too, plus a platoon of armed soldiers. I can't roll the thing back until you chuck the gun out. Can you get it through the hole?'

There was a long silence. A cat came down the lawn and began to eat one of the bedding plants. A goods train clattered by on the railway line.

The silver bullet caught Brooke's eye as it fell on the grass, followed by four others.

'I can't get the gun out. That's all the ammo I've got.'

The voice sounded reedy, as if a dying man was begging for water. What if he was lying? One call to Madingley Hall would secure him a platoon of soldiers to surround the shelter.

He stood, kicked the brick away, and pulled the roller back a yard.

Running up the shutter, he was presented with the sudden impenetrable darkness within. He took off his glasses and for a moment doubted his decision as he saw the light catch a gun barrel, and then heard the distinct metallic whirl of the chamber being spun. Braced, he took a half-step back, and heard the trigger being pulled.

A face emerged into the light. It was Turl, the lorry driver from the night before. He showed Brooke the gun: a pistol with the chamber empty.

He opened his other hand to reveal a bullet.

'Old trick. Always keep a spare. You're lucky. I don't fancy swinging for killing a copper. But it crossed my mind . . .'

CHAPTER FOURTEEN

Blenheim House was an imposing nineteenth-century suburban villa, with a two-pillar porch and a great wisteria spreading out so that the windows had to be clipped free of tendrils. Major Joelyn Stone had liked it at first sight six weeks earlier. Officers' quarters had been set aside at Madingley Hall, but Stone's wife had announced her determination to set up household for the Duration. Stone certainly felt the house added an elegant air of confidence to their social position, a fitting residence for the deputy commanding officer. (Swift-Lane, his superior, was a Cambridge man, with a family house in a nearby village.) Stone had particularly liked the facade, until his own well-developed sense of self-knowledge had caused him to hastily move on to consider the other attributes of the house: a fine dining room, a renovated kitchen and laundry, and the electric lift, large enough to accommodate his wife's mother and her wheelchair.

The battalion driver swung the staff car in a circle on the gravel. Stone almost ran up the semicircular steps to the door, his knees rising smartly. The door stood open in the autumnal heat, the entrance hall thick with the sound of ticking clocks.

Taking the steps two at a time, he paused at the first landing.

His wife's bedroom door was open and he heard the chair legs grate as she pushed herself back from a writing table.

'Don't get up,' he said. 'The car's waiting. I'm due in court for the tribunal. I can't be late.'

Two changes of uniform hung in his dressing room.

It was twenty-one years since he'd lost the two fingers on his right hand. His middle finger had been badly damaged by the gunshot too, but the field surgeon had saved it, although the scarring was unsightly so he always wore a cover for the digit. Originally this had been a canvas sheath, but he'd hired a jeweller to make a brass replacement, the regimental badge engraved discreetly in the metal.

Buttoning up a tunic with one hand was one of the many skills he had honed over the years. If he'd had time he'd have run a bath and washed away the grit and dust of the day. But the court sat at one, and he was always punctual.

He considered himself in the full-length mirror.

Was Brooke, the Borough detective, a threat? At this point in Stone's plans the last thing he wanted was a complication of any sort. A civilian death was unfortunate, but the War Office seemed disposed to set that aside. For now, all he could do was make sure all the necessary paperwork was completed at top speed. The Ministry of War report, the coroner's statement, his log for the CO: everything was in hand.

The problem was that Brooke appeared oddly persistent. The affectation of the tinted glasses grated. Despite being a provincial policeman of no obvious intellect, he projected a haughty impatience. If he'd been in uniform, Stone would have suspected suppressed insubordination.

Stone, in a freshly laundered uniform, found Margaret at the bottom of the stairs, standing where she often stood, beneath the full-length portrait of her father. Stone had never met the general but the picture's lovingly recorded insignia and medals told the story of his father-in-law's life in exemplary clarity. Cut down by artillery fire in a now long-forgotten skirmish in India, he had come home a dead hero. The last honour, a starburst of silver and gold, had been awarded posthumously but was nonetheless included by the artist on the general's extravagant chest.

'Don't forget the Atkinsons, Joelyn. Tonight at seven. It's shoulder of lamb, your favourite.'

Ignoring her, he walked to a narrow mirror and straightened his tie. Somewhere in the building the lift was in operation, because they could hear the chains running in the shaft.

'Mother wants to go out,' said his wife, somehow implying that Stone had dodged a duty. Marriage to Margaret had brought him a fortune, and the priceless cache attendant on a being part of a famous military family. As yet, Stone had failed to make the most of these privileges.

'About six then, six-thirty,' she said.

A five-minute drive along leafy lanes took Stone into the city, past a roadblock holding back civilian traffic on Station Road. Beyond it he could see a line of fire tenders and a smudge of grey smoke lingering over Kew's Mill, where the balloon had come down in flames.

A few glittering military careers were built on bravery, initiative or intelligence. Most were built on an ability to lie low. The three errant barrage balloons represented a blow to Stone's reputation for diligent, *unremarkable* service. Damage limitation was, however, a military skill in itself.

The car slipped into the rear yard of the court of assizes. The high spiked walls radiated the autumnal heat which had been building up all day, so that as Stone got out he inveigled a finger of his left hand under his starched collar.

Lunch was a perk, served in the old Judge's Lodgings, with sherry and wine. Cold ham, a green salad and floury fen potatoes were laid out on silver plate set on a fine table in a bookcase-lined room. Stone's buttons were reflected in the polish. His two fellow tribunal 'judges' were a Labour alderman and a woman from the WRVS who'd been an ambulance driver in the Great War. The conversation was worthy, taking its cue from the morning radio news, which had set out a preliminary timetable for the further introduction of rationing.

The court clerk knocked three times and they took a moment to compose themselves. The woman said a prayer, which Stone felt was an imposition, but he sunk his chin to his chest nonetheless. Beyond the door was a damp wooden corridor which led them in a semicircle, until they reached a stone arch and a green-baize door. An usher appeared, the light flooding in behind him, and they filed past – the lady first – to the echo of 'All rise!'

The court list was laid out on each blotter: ten names, all applying to be registered as conscientious objectors. It was Stone's job – a temporary posting, due to illness – in concert with his two assessors, to place each applicant in one of four categories:

Armed Forces
Non-Combatant Armed Forces

Conditional Registered CO
Unconditional Registered CO

Stone studied the names, and then looked up as the first man was called: they came and went, each one judged, to be processed by clerks sitting out in the lobby of the court. On the whole, Stone thought them sincere in their belief that war was immoral. His own experiences on the Western Front had taught him that it took very little courage to hold a rifle and sit in a trench. Fear had a paralysing effect on the human psyche. What had terrified *him* was the appalling responsibility of leading his men. Running at the enemy, being the first to break cover, required a rare degree of bravery. To some extent the men before him now, who many classed as cowards, were leaders too, stepping out from the safety of the crowd.

An hour later the last name was called out.

'John Christopher Childe.'

The public gallery was packed, and Stone noted several women and two small children. Childe stood in the dock and glanced nervously up at the bench. Stone's heart missed a beat; he recognised the man instantly. He'd passed him that morning on the stairs leaving Vera's house.

CHAPTER FIFTEEN

Brooke sat alone in the Spinning House interview room, waiting for Turl, the lorry driver who'd fled the scene on Castle Hill, to be brought up from the cells. The furniture, brutally utilitarian, consisted of a desk and two chairs for the officers conducting the interrogation, and a chair opposite for the prisoner. A spare, for the duty solicitor, stood in one corner. A single unshaded light bulb hung above the table. One small lancet window let in the north light. On the south wall, a large map of the city had been taped up, revealing the way in which the river, rising in the southern hills, ensnared the city in a noose before swinging away north to the Fens and the sea.

Twenty years had passed since he'd been captured in the desert, but rooms such as this still made Brooke's palms sweat. The brittle sense of past tension permeated the air. The nightmare for Brooke lay in the rules set by his captors, that he must provide answers but was forbidden the freedom to ask questions. By day they'd tied him to an old cartwheel and set it out on the sand, so that he'd have to look up at the sky. At night they'd left him in a cell without light, then dragged him out, at random times, down a short corridor into a room just like this, save for the window. What came to him when he did sleep was the vivid sense that he was in that room, and the fetid, earthy smell of his own body, charged with the electricity of fear.

He'd been held in the ruins of an old telegraph station by an abandoned railway line. The interrogations were conducted in a cellar at the bottom of a short flight of stone steps. The lamp, within a silver reflective dish, blazed behind his interrogators; the men who'd asked the questions often changed, but the light was a constant, and so he never saw their faces. Towards the end of his captivity the electric lamp had merged with the sun, so that he was unable to distinguish them apart. The light from both cut into his eyes, past the glassy cornea, through the aching retina and deep into the brain beyond.

The distant sound of soldiers marching past on Regent Street jogged Brooke out of his reverie. He took a deep breath and opened the report which lay before him on the desk. Edison had summarised progress on the three impounded lorries from Castle Hill. The sergeant's prose style was pedestrian but accurate: the registration plates were false, the corporate branding – *Turl's of York* – bogus, as were all the drivers' documents recovered from the cabs. The relevant papers had been sent to the Ministry of Transport to see if other forgeries of similar standard had been found anywhere else in the country. All three vehicle engines were in first-class condition and had been regularly serviced to a high standard. One of the lorries had a fuel tank which had been patched with a piece of second-hand metal plate punched with a serial number and the stencilled words LOXLEY GARAGE.

Admin at the Spinning House comprised three young women

who shared secretarial duties. They had been directed to cable police stations in Manchester, Liverpool, Leeds, York and Nottingham with a résumé of the case file. Edison had added a priority request in each case to check local directories for Loxley Garage. He'd also got a photographer to capture a mugshot of the prisoner Turl for circulation by post.

Chief Inspector Carnegie-Brown, Brooke's superior, had helpfully sent one further document through the internal post for his private consideration. Jean Carnegie-Brown was a rarity, a senior police*woman*, who'd transferred to the Borough to take the post of chief inspector, having served in uniform in Glasgow for twenty years. In the Great War she'd used her degree from Edinburgh, in German, to work as a translator, interrogating POWs. This echo of Brooke's wartime torture brought a nervous edge to their rare encounters.

Carnegie-Brown was an efficient bureaucrat. The memo was her favoured weapon. The document she'd directed to Brooke's in-tray bore the Home Secretary's signature, and called on all forces to be alert to the emergence of a black market, manipulated by organised crime. Given Whitehall plans for rationing, a special note should be kept of any incidents involving petrol, sugar, eggs or fresh meat.

Carnegie-Brown had added, in a typically clipped copperplate, a line across the top of the page . . .

Home Office alerted to three lorry case from Castle Hill. Request daily update. Urge upmost priority in pursuit of national security. Copies to Sir Philip Game.

Brooke stretched out long legs and closed his eyes. Sir Philip was the commissioner of the Metropolitan Police. In Brooke's experience, catching the attention of Scotland Yard was not a helpful development in any inquiry.

A minute later, Turl, the lorry driver, sat opposite, slouched in his chair, as Edison asked perfunctory questions: name, home address, identity of the other drivers, the names of those organising the convoy. Because that's what it was, a *caravan* of black-market meat.

Turl didn't open his mouth. They could see now why he'd waived his right to a solicitor.

They pressed on. Destination? Payment? In terms of understanding the sinews of the crime, they were totally lost. Were there other convoys? Where was the meat going to be stored? That was the key, not to flood the market now, but wait for the real war to start, and for the imposition of meat rationing. Refrigeration plants on an industrial scale were rare. Deep freezer plants even rarer. It had been a chilly night, and the three lorries were insulated, but their eventual destination must have been within a night's drive.

Turl watched them with an intelligent eye. The role he'd played on Castle Hill, working an oily rag between his hands, had been replaced by something more multilayered: there was a lively intelligence in the restless eyes, and a deadly precision in the sinewy hands, which had been given leave to roll a cigarette.

Brooke and Edison asked him more than a hundred questions over the period of fifteen minutes without prompting a single answer.

Finally, he asked a question of his own.

'What are the glasses for?' he said, nodding at Brooke, who'd opted for the lightly tinted ochre lenses in the gentle light flooding in through the lancet window.

Brooke took them off. His eyes were so pale they looked like ice. Turl dropped his gaze, pretending to concentrate on rolling the cigarette.

'Seeing into the souls of parasites like you,' said Brooke. 'I'd make the most of that fag. If we don't get some answers soon, that's your last.'

Edison, sipping tea, grunted in approval.

'Have you found the others?' asked Turl, sitting back in his chair, rocking it on its back legs. 'If they'd sat tight we might have got away with it. But Ginger did a runner. Nev followed suit, did he? Couldn't keep their nerve under pressure. They'll pay for that.' This idea produced a smile. 'If – no, *when* you find them, I'll tell you this for nowt. They'll be burnt up, the bodies. *In-cin-erated*. But you'll be able to identify them alright, like. Otherwise there's no point, is there? It's our trademark. What'ya call it? Our brand. Death by fire.'

It was always a revelation, the extent to which prisoners thought that they could talk *without* revealing vital information. They failed to understand that this kind of catch-me-if-you-can game simply exposed the underlying geometry of the crime itself. It was clear that the drivers who had fled first had betrayed the gang by their loss of nerve. Turl saw himself as the noble victim of their treachery.

'Is that what waits for you?' asked Brooke. 'An execution?'

Turl shook his head. 'Not me, boss.'

He grinned at Edison.

'How old's granddad?' he asked.

'How stupid are you?' asked Brooke, and he saw a half-second flash of anger cross the eyes. 'I think you're very stupid. You're a minion. What's one of those?'

Turl's face had become entirely immobile. 'A follower of a powerful man,' he offered.

Brooke replaced his glasses. 'Especially a servile one. I think you've lost sight of your place in the world. You're a cog in the big machine. I'm not sure the fact that you kept your head when all those around lost theirs is going to weigh that heavily in the balance.'

Edison's pen scratched as he made a note.

'Does he write it all down?' said Turl.

'All except this bit.'

Edison laid down his pen.

'You've given me an idea,' said Brooke.

Turl tried a smile, pulling a thread of tobacco from his lip.

'We'll find out a bit more first, that mugshot we got of you is doing the rounds. Leeds, is it? Bradford? Manchester? Whatever. We'll strike lucky. Then we'll let it be known that you're helping us with some names, a few addresses. And when we do find some names we'll make sure you get the *credit*. Then they can start planning what they'll do to you when you get out. That'll be five years, maybe less. You can look forward to that when you're lying in your bunk at nights. That'll be a dilemma: do you spend five years doing your time, wanting it to end so you can get out, or five years hoping it doesn't end, because of what's waiting outside? When you finally walk through those prison gates there'll be a car waiting, a packet of fags, a bottle of whisky, leggy blonde on the back seat. But they won't take you home. Where do they do it? A garage maybe, then what? Is it a wrench to the back of the head and then the fire, or do they burn them alive? What's their modus operandi?'

Turl sucked at his roll-up, unblinking as the smoke drifted into his eyes.

CHAPTER SIXTEEN

Dusk was falling on Mill Road Cemetery as Chris Childe, conscientious objector, knelt before his parents' grave, marked by a flat stone, surrounded by a Gothic riot of ornately carved tombs, spreading ivy and statuary. A blackbird sang, perched on the head of an angel. The two sets of iron gates were locked, but the cemetery had been in a state of disrepair since the last war, and the wall was no real barrier to anyone who wanted to visit the dead out of hours.

He checked his watch: he was late for the Party's weekly branch meeting, so he stood, brushing his trousers clean of dead leaves. They could start without him, dispense with the drab formalities, then he'd arrive and take his place, briefly, in the limelight. Vera had the letter and she'd promised to send it to London, but for some reason he found himself unable to completely trust her. There had been something about her breezy efficiency which had left him feeling a fool, left him feeling insignificant, even *used*.

In contrast, the tribunal's verdict had been a liberation. He had been registered unconditionally as a conscientious objector. He was free to live his life as he wished. Which meant he could edit, and print, the news-sheet they planned to circulate with *Peace News*. Hundreds, potentially thousands, of copies could be distributed in the city.

The mere prospect of this had made him feel powerful, and it spawned an intoxicating idea. The letter could go to London; he'd done his duty to the Party. But tonight he would reveal its contents to his comrades in the Party, and he'd go further – he'd print the story in the news-sheet, and he'd make sure the local newspaper carried it too. Within days, even hours, he'd have made his mark: a footnote to history.

He forced himself to say one last prayer, standing at the foot of the flat etched stone. It had been decorated with the arms of the Machine Gun Corps: two of the menacing weapons crossed below the imperial crown. His father, George, had seen service in the Great War, the high point of an otherwise ill-tempered life. The only symbol of his mother was her name: Jennifer Maud McCulloch. She had insisted, in the Scottish fashion, on keeping her maiden name for the inscription – a final, insignificant victory over a violent man she must have hated.

As a child, he'd seen the bruises but never the blows, until one night when he was ten. He'd heard them coming down Gothic Street from the Spread Eagle. Summer, the window half up, so he'd looked out. No words were said. His father had gone ahead and stood below in the street, waiting for his mother, half-running to catch up. An argument in the pub, what he liked to call a 'flare-up', had no doubt led to his ejection into the night.

When his mother reached their door, she'd fumbled for the key and he'd delivered the blow from the side: a flat hand, with all his strength, knocking her into the gutter. On her knees, she'd searched frantically in her purse for the key, while he'd waited, leaning up against the lamp post, whistling 'The Happy Clown' – the Machine Gun Corps' official quick march.

Childe stood back, thinking about violence and how it couldn't be undone, and how it sent out ripples of hatred and regret. It had been violence which had made him take a stand for peace, and that too had profound repercussions, spreading out, reaching others.

A footstep very close, behind his back, made his skin prickle. Turning, he caught a glimpse of a figure in the tail of his eye. A single stride, the arm stiff, the oily click of a trigger: he never heard the shot that killed him, and despite a lingering sense of consciousness, his body fell like a puppet, its strings cut.

An image that had existed, in the sense of a series of interconnected electrical signals in his brain, flickered out of life: he'd seen himself at his printing press, holding up the still-damp news-sheet with its sensational story on the front page.

A hand slipped inside his jacket, searching the pockets.

Sight, certainly, had been snuffed out with the death of his brain. But the last image stayed reflected still in his blank eyes: his own blood, very close to his cheek, spreading out to fill the etched letters of his father's name.

CHAPTER SEVENTEEN

Brooke lay in the bath under a cone of light thrown down by an old standard lamp. The tub stood on four brass claw feet at the centre of a large uncarpeted attic room. Reflections from the water dappled the rough plaster of the ceiling, as if he were beneath one of the Cam's horse-leap bridges. Steam rose like a cloud from a thermal spring. Lifting his chin, Brooke turned his jaw to the right, pushing against the resistance of the neck joint until he heard, and felt, a satisfying rick as the bones fell back into place. Most of the peat had settled in the bottom of the bath, a minutely gritty residue of black particles. Examining his hands, he used a small file to tease out what remained of the soil beneath the nails.

The attic room had two dormer windows, which even in this mild autumn failed to retain the warmth of the day. It had been his mother's retreat, three clear floors above his father's laboratory in the basement, with its perpetually decanting flasks and tubes, its murky fume cupboard and hissing Bunsens.

Here, in her own realm, she had installed a chaise longue, a desk, the standard lamp still in situ and a large Turkish rug, upon which Brooke had played as a child. A memory of a lattice square of sunlight on the patterned carpet brought back an almost palpable sense of lost love. She'd died suddenly when Brooke was six, and the attic had been locked until his father's death.

A door opened along the landing and he heard feet on the threadbare carpet: a confident heel-first step, which heralded a fixed purpose, a sense of energy unleashed.

'Why are you lying in a muddy puddle?' asked his wife, bunching up a white linen shirt at her throat. 'I thought we'd agreed that swimming was over for another year.'

'I ended up in a ditch,' he said. 'I've been trying to wash it all away. Tenacious stuff, peat. Microscopic particles.' He worked his finger and thumb together as if searching for some minute trace of friction.

Slipping into the water from his mossy steps, he'd followed the river back to St John's Wilderness, and sought out the spot where the mysterious diggers had enjoyed their smoke the previous night. PC Woods had found no trace of a pit, but a pit there must be, so he'd edged through an old iron watergate into a deep ditch which led away from the river, into the meadows. Wading in this oily trench, he'd been aware of the viscous nature of the water, thick with weed, feathers and algae, the surface alive with night bugs.

Certain he was alone he clambered up the bank to look out across the marsh. A series of neat, low mounds ran in a military line, like the graves of giants, picked out by moonlight, between hawthorn and willow. Beyond them he could just see a sandy track, lighter in the gloom, twisting away towards open country. Across the wilderness nothing moved, so he slipped down the slope and knelt beside the nearest mound, thrusting his hand down into the loose soil, shocked that it had retained some of the heat of the day.

What lay beneath?

'What did you see on your swim?' asked Claire, rubbing her cheeks to wake herself.

Brooke tried hard not to bring his work home.

'Nothing much except the wonderful house of boxes, have you seen it?'

She shook her head, yawning.

'Just beyond Jesus Lock, on Midsummer Common. I could only glimpse the silhouette but it's quite the thing. Three stories, a ziggurat roof, all made of cardboard boxes. They're going to set light to it and invite us all to marvel at the skills of the Auxiliary Fire Service. Night after next, we should go.'

'I'm on shift. Tea?' said Claire, padding away down the stairs. 'Water that hot is bad for you,' she called back. 'It drags the blood to the skin. When you stand up you'll be dizzy. Post-posterior hypertension. You've been warned.'

A few minutes later she arrived back with a mug of tea and a heavy cut-glass tumbler of whisky, which she set beside Brooke's head on the enamel shelf of the bath. She set it down once, then returned to fine-tune its position an inch further from the edge. A compulsion to bring order to the world was one of Claire's defining virtues as a nurse. Outside the hospital she was unable to curb what could be a vice.

'By the way,' she said. 'I asked one of the surgeons about Doric's theory that the army is out burying civilian casualties from bomb sites. One's got a brother at the Victoria Infirmary in Glasgow. He said you were right; it's hogwash.'

Brooke nodded, putting his nose to the rim of the whisky glass.

The musty earthiness of the spirit was as intoxicating as the alcohol.

'I spoke to Joy,' said Claire, perched on the edge of a wicker sun chair. Their daughter, a nurse like her mother, had enlisted and been posted to Portsmouth to work in a dockside tented hospital examining troops before embarkation for France.

'Good God,' said Brooke. 'How did you manage that? It takes me half an hour to get a line to London.'

They'd been tracking their children by letter since the war began, but the post was unreliable, the missives rare and often terse.

Sitting up, he sent a wave down the bath which folded itself round the taps before sloshing back to his chest. He brought up his knee, massaging an area of white scar tissue just below the cap.

'I was told to ring the unit at Gosport,' said Claire. 'We've been ordered to do medical checks on the troops stationed on Parker's Piece. Have you seen it? It's like the Delhi Durbar. You watch, there'll be elephants soon, and the king on his dais.'

She sipped her tea. 'Anyway, I rang Gosport to request a copy of their protocol: the mandatory checks, what's critical, what we can leave. They went and got Joy!'

Again, she clutched the material of her shirt to her throat. She looked a decade younger than her thirty-nine years. It made him realise that but for this brief moment she too was a casualty of war, diminished by the absence of those she loved.

'How did she sound?'

It was a typical Brooke question, thought Claire. Not what did she *say*.

'Fine. Excited. She said she's applied to go over, to France. They're setting up field hospitals behind the lines for when it begins. It'll be trauma, wounds, burns, amputations. They'll be damn lucky to have her.' She put too much emphasis on this last thought, and had to hold a hand to her lips. 'I think she just wants to be near Luke.'

Their son's letters, when they got them, described an eerie rustic paradise of sleepy farms and distant church bells along the Franco-Belgium border where his unit was camped, part of the British Expeditionary Force, ready to hold the Germans back when the war in the west finally began.

Brooke took the whisky up. 'What did *you* say?'

'I said I might do the same, you know, try to go over, that is. Where I'd do some good.'

She tried to read his face.

'Will you speak again?' he asked. 'I mean . . .'

'Yes. Overnight, I think. She says it's been chaotic so they really need to settle on a protocol before they share it with us. She sounded very together. I'm proud of her.'

Brooke sunk his chin in the water.

'Tell her I love her. Tell her I miss her. But if she wants to go, I understand. There'll be POWs to treat as well. I think it helps if you see the enemy.'

The image of Turl, the lorry driver, letting cigarette smoke drift into his eyes without blinking, came to Brooke's mind.

'I hate all this . . .' he said, lifting his whisky glass and gesturing towards the window. 'The machinery of war. The civil servants up from Whitehall. The blackout. The lines of supply. The factories. Conscription. New weapons. It makes the fighting inevitable, but there's no courage needed, no sense in which you have to face the reality of it. It's just momentum, a collective inability to change direction. It's a dance of death, and you have to follow the right steps.'

'Quite a speech,' she said, kindly.

He shook his head, wondering what his father would think of

a world in which science was becoming one of the weapons of war.

She went to the window to look out at the moon.

'Cowardice is a great thing,' persisted Brooke, resurfacing. 'It's a brake on war, if it's hand-to-hand. It's an old cliché – *the whites of their eyes* – but it brings home the reality of combat. But this. Anyone can fight a war from a hundred miles away. Just press a button. There's worse to come. Rockets. Poisons. She's probably safer near the frontline than here. It's the civilians that'll cop it this time.'

He took another mouthful of whisky. 'If you want to go – go. I'll be alright. I'd be useless anywhere else. I'll fight my own little wars right here. The enemy within, and all that.'

She smiled, considering the pale form of his body in the murky water. The first time she'd touched him had been in the hospital at Scarborough: a bed bath, the face as brown as a nut, the rest white. Lying on his back, she'd had to force his hands away from his face, where they'd been shielding his eyes.

She took down a nurse's uniform from a hanger on the door.

'Are you home for the night?' she asked.

Brooke pulled the plug. 'No. I have two dead bodies to inspect. A lonely suicide found in Byron's Pool, and the mangled body of an American scientist, ripped apart by the drifting cables of a barrage balloon. Both victims, in their own way, of the Great Darkness.'

CHAPTER EIGHTEEN

'They're both as found, Brooke. I know you prefer that,' said Dr Henry Comfort as the Borough pathologist kicked open the double doors to the morgue. The room was bright and functional, lit by neon tubes, in keeping with the rest of the new Galen Anatomy Building. Two additional spotlights blazed down on a pair of dissection tables. Despite the intensity of the light, the twin sources of illumination could not banish all the shadows, so that the two corpses were substantial, although the process of the settling of bodily fluids and the relaxation of muscle and tissue did appear to flatten them slightly, as if they were melting, slowly, into the gutters which ran into the metal chambers set beneath.

'Where's your new detective sergeant?' asked Comfort.

'At this precise moment he is in a punt on the river, no doubt wishing he'd stayed in comfortable retirement.'

Brooke had obtained the punt from Michaelhouse, with Doric's assistance, and Edison's orders were to stay in the shadows on the bank opposite St John's Wilderness, and observe throughout the small hours. Brooke was convinced that the soldiers would return. What would be on their trundling carts?

'You know these men . . .' said Comfort, indicating his two 'servants'; Brooke could never recall the Latin term, but that was the gist of it. One would help haul the body over on to its side, the other perform the basic incisions and use the bone saw when directed. They hung back, cradling enamel mugs, a copy of the *Evening News* spread out on the bench.

Comfort struggled with his rubber gloves. Brooke, struck by the delicate, almost feminine hands, recalled the sudden iron grip the pathologist could exert on the tools of his trade: the rib-cutters, the euphemistic breadknife, the hooked skull chisel.

Comfort never bothered with small talk. He'd known Brooke a decade, and their relationship had gained a respectful distance. The Borough drew its pathologist from the university, the first such appointment listed in 1880 on a board in the Spinning House. Simple convenience lay at the root of this arrangement. And practicality. As a police district, the centre of the medieval city was hardly burdened by regular outbreaks of violent death, at least not in the current century. The county force, whose jurisdiction began just beyond the city's constricted boundaries, had its own resident pathologist, but the professional rivalry between the two forces precluded cooperation. In death, as in life.

'Lux, your scientist,' said Comfort finally, pulling the fingers on his left hand so that the joints cracked, then drawing back a plastic sheet from the face.

'He was here last night, in this building, alive and well,' said Brooke. 'A lecture, apparently, all hush-hush. Doubt he thought he'd be back so soon.' A thought struck. 'Did you attend?'

'I asked,' said Comfort. 'I was politely informed I was short of the necessary security clearance. Not for my ears. Some government project, apparently. Bloody cheek. They had food shipped in from the kitchens at Emmanuel, and a guard on the door.'

Comfort walked once round the corpse. 'We'll cut away what's left of the clothes, but the injuries are obvious, traumatic, lethal and inflicted pre-mortem.'

In Brooke's experience, this phase of the autopsy, the external observations, could last several silent minutes.

Around them, despite the hour, they could hear the building's own internal mechanisms, a pipe running with water, a lift whirring, the passing footsteps of a watchman. The Galen had been completed that summer. The university's old anatomy building stood opposite Queen's College, a museum now, draped in cobwebs. The Galen, by contrast, glowed with the white heat of modernity. The stone-cut white facia, rising up with the classically narrowing sightlines of the art deco, reminded Brooke of the Cenotaph, whose Greek etymology he knew to be 'empty tomb'. A chill irony, as Comfort's morgue was rarely empty. The corpses set aside for student dissection lay unseen in steel drawers along the windowless wall.

Comfort began to discourse on the body.

The dead man's left leg, below the knee, had been all but severed and lay an inch apart from the upper leg, connecting tissue linking the two, the bones disconnected, the trouser leg torn away completely from the upper thigh. The hands, set down in the gunnels to the side of the trunk, were bloody and lacerated. The left shoulder had been dislocated, flesh and bone, from the torso itself, leaving the body misshapen, crooked. The skull had been partly crushed and before Brooke could look away he caught sight of a dreadful wound, revealing a hint of the brain beneath.

Brooke closed his eyes, took a deep breath.

'Back's broken too,' offered Comfort, moving to the head. 'Blunt trauma. And here to the skull . . .' He used a scalpel to indicate the left eye socket, which was curiously oval. 'The alcohol would have helped, if that's any consolation. I've looked at a blood sample and it indicates a glass of wine, perhaps, a pint of beer. If he'd fallen down a flight of stairs the booze might have dulled the pain. But he's been *dashed* – that's the word. I think it's time I took a closer look . . .'

An imperceptible nod from the pathologist released one of the servants, who moved forward like an automaton, armed with a pair of large scissors, and began to cut away the clothes that clung to the corpse.

Brooke studied the ticking clock on the wall, then walked away to the door, where he lit a cigarette.

The ghostly life of Dr Ernst Lux played itself out in his mind, comprising a series of images assembled by Edison during interviews at Michaelhouse with the American's friends and colleagues. Lux was of German parents, now living in California, and had taken his first degree at the university in Berkeley. A bachelor, with a sweetheart who one friend recalled had been a volunteer nurse in Spain during the Civil War. The couple had met at a rally organised to raise funds for the anti-Fascist International Brigade.

Admired as an athlete, Lux had been a college rower and a keen climber, who took himself off to the Alps during the summer months with the university mountaineering club. The Fens, one of Europe's flattest landscapes, had been a profound disappointment, so he'd burnt off his surplus energies in term time each morning by running out along the towpath to Clayhythe, then back across the water meadows.

Lux lay naked now except for his shoes and socks.

The absence of the rest of the clothes focused Brooke's eye on the dead man's feet. Once, these shoes had been fashionable, he thought. They were in fact light boots, made of felt, which he judged had originally been green. The laces were dual threaded in red and white, reduced to grey by wear and tear. The boot shape was broad and workmanlike, but there was no mistaking the glaring error: they were on the wrong feet.

Brooke knelt down. 'Is it possible the shoes were removed in an earlier examination, and then replaced?' he asked.

Comfort had spotted the anomaly at almost precisely the same moment, and the pathologist's head came very close to Brooke's own, so that he could smell the faint aroma of pipe tobacco.

'No, as I said, he's as found.' The pathologist undid the laces and, with a swift rotation of his wrist, pulled the shoe clear of the foot on the left leg. From within the body came the slight grating of two halves of a ruptured joint.

Comfort knelt by the now revealed feet in their socks, which had been heavily darned at the heels.

'This is symptomatic,' he said. 'It requires great dexterity to slip on a sock, we underestimate our own precision and skill, but then we have years of practice, judging the action to the nicety required to get the sock straight, the heel engaged. You see here . . .' He tugged the material.

The coroner was right. Each sock sat uncomfortably at an angle, twisted onto the limb.

'This complicates matters,' said Brooke.

Comfort slipped off the socks. The tips of several of the toes on both feet were scratched and had bled badly. But the socks, turned inside out, showed hardly any bloodstains.

Comfort took notes and then, with the help of the servants, proceeded to the internal examination. Brooke retreated with a glass of whisky poured from a bottle stashed in what the pathologist described as the 'fume cupboard'. At the appropriate moments, Brooke held the glass close to his nose and breathed in the woody scent. He was in no order squeamish, but to see a fellow human being opened up, disaggregated and reduced to offal always delivered a shock to his system, an existential blow. The brain, removed from the skull and floating in a jar of chemicals, was held in place by a string noose: the pity, perhaps, that despite the preserving fluid all the memories were lost.

Brooke tried to divert his mind from the unfolding scene before him by asking himself the pressing questions: who had put shoes and socks on a corpse, *why* had they put shoes and socks on a corpse?

Finished, Comfort washed his hands and arms and poured black coffee from a flask. The assistants coaxed tea out of a metal pot.

They all moved down the room towards the second body. For the first time Brooke noted that while it too was clothed, it was bound in several strands of the vivid green river weed which characterised the river's upper stretches, where the bed was gravel and the water ran out of the chalk hills. He also noted a further anomaly of the feet, for one was shod in a reinforced boot, indicating a club foot.

'Our second customer tonight,' said Comfort. 'Pulled out of Byron's Pool. Two house bricks in his pockets. Edison said you'd taken an interest? I'll need to examine the lungs, of course, but it looks straightforward. No sign of foul play. Poor chap.'

Brooke examined the victim's profile, noting the prominent jaw, the false teeth, the large bags under the eyes, the fleshy neck.

There was no doubt: it was the sleeping driver of the lorry parked at the foot of Castle Hill. It was not difficult to imagine the prospect which had driven him to take his own life. Turl had painted a vivid enough picture: for losing his nerve he faced incineration, a ritual penalty exacted by the gang. At least he'd cheated them of that.

CHAPTER NINETEEN

Doric gave Brooke a glass of claret from the cellars, and a slice of Stilton. The porter, working by candle, was conducting an inventory of the keys, a simple act of housekeeping which he managed to imbue with the mystery of an ancient ceremony. Michaelhouse was Georgian, with some ugly Victorian additions, but Doric's sensibilities stretched back into the mythical past. He'd never let history stand in the way of his veneration for the college.

Every few minutes he'd break off from documenting the keys and make a move on a chessboard.

'Any news on my Londoners digging pits down by the river?' asked Brooke, making an effort to set aside for a moment the riddle of Ernst Lux's death and the identity of the man fished out of Byron's Pool.

'Duke of Cambridge's Own, they call 'em the Middlesex now.'

'Yes, I know, Doric. But what were they *doing*?'

'Long-term anti-aircraft duties. Bugger all going on for now, so they copped for general fatigues. Not the first time either. And they don't like it. Jenner, the porter at Trinity, goes in The Duke. The landlord's a cockney, so I guess the soldiers feel at home. Jenner says they're always moaning. Villains of the piece are the top brass up at Madingley. They keep volunteering for extra duties on their behalf. They were digging trenches on Parker's Piece for a fortnight, now they're digging out a bloody great hole for the footings of a Bofors gun out on the London Road. Up all night. Every few weeks they're back on that riverbank of yours. Fit to go AWOL, they are, but it'll all be talk.'

Brooke moved his bishop. 'I know they were digging holes, Doric. I want to know what they put in 'em.'

'Jenner said they clammed up when he asked questions. Listening's one thing. Asking's another. He'll keep his ears open. But no promises,' said Doric, whistling through his teeth.

They played in silence for twenty minutes. Brooke's mind was not on the game. The riddle of Dr Lux's shoes and socks overshadowed the intricacies of the chessboard.

'Any news on your situation?' he asked, forcing himself to make a move, sliding his rook into enemy territory.

The reorganisation of college duties loomed over Doric's life like the building itself.

'Fellows meet tomorrow. Three of the day staff have got the push, but they were all new, replacements for those that got called up. So maybe that's it for me too. Or, they're making room, and I'll end up on days . . .'

He shrugged, ever the fatalist. Brooke had never asked what particular aspect of the concept of *days* held such an aversion. Doric, in his army years, had been a regimental sergeant major. Cock of the walk. At night he was his own master again, so perhaps the prospect of being ordered around by the likes of the head porter was too much to bear.

Brooke surveyed the board, decided his position was hopeless, tipped over his king, collected his hat from the stand and wished Doric goodnight.

No air raid warning yet, so the streets were busy. Cars crept past with their slit eyes peering, seeking out the white-lined kerbs. Three bicycles, unlit but jangling, careered past as if he didn't exist. At the corner by the Round Church he saw Jo Ashmore up at her observation post, binoculars to her eyes, scanning the city's western edge.

Pressing on, he was eager to catch the tea hut in the square before someone, somewhere, imagined they'd spotted EA, setting off the whole farrago for another night. *By the time the bombs do fall*, he thought, emerging onto Market Hill, *we'll be inured to the prospect of death in the rubble, the siren will go off and nobody will care.*

Rose King was behind her counter, a gaggle of servicemen huddled in the light that fell out onto the square's flagstones. War was Rose's métier, allowing her to exhibit a genius for catering at short order on a mass scale. Facing thirty-five soldiers in need of tea, she lined up the mugs, added milk to each and then allowed the enamelled pot to swoop along the lines, pausing over each, but never righting itself to the point that the dark tannin was withheld. It was sloshing, but it was deft sloshing.

On a grill plate she had the full array of fried food encompassed by that bracing catch-all: full English. Sausages, bacon, fried bread, mushrooms, halved tomatoes. Eggs, already scarce, sat in their boxes waiting for an explicit order. But the soldiers, no doubt short of cash, wouldn't be enticed beyond tea, and headed off instead to sit on the benches in the graveyard of Great St Mary's.

'Here he is,' said Rose, seeing Brooke. 'The hero of the night. Grub?'

'A bacon sandwich, Rose. And tea.'

Mid-fifties, worn down by a life spent working on her feet, Rose nevertheless achieved a constant sense of performance, as if the rectangular open hatch of the tea hut was her own stage. A headscarf in gypsy colours held in place grey hair, a thread of which she tucked in as she poured Brooke's tea.

'Take a seat. I'll bring it out. I could do with a sit-down,' she said, an unlit cigarette bobbing in the corner of her mouth.

In front of the tea bar were arranged half a dozen round metal tables, salvaged from a pub, and matching wrought-iron chairs.

Rose brought his sandwich on a plate and took a seat herself, stretching out her legs, using the right shoe to lever off the left, to free wriggling toes in stockinged feet. She lit the cigarette and left it poised on her lower lip.

Then he saw what she had in her hands: a large china cup, which she began swilling with an almost religious precision, as a priest might clean the chalice before drinking the last of the communion wine. She swilled out most of the liquid into the wide gutter, then tilted the cup so that the light from the hatch illuminated the bowl.

It was the usual mumbo-jumbo and Brooke listened with as much good nature as he could muster. A snake, apparently, lay depicted in the tea leaves, or was it in the white spaces between? Either way: a snake pointed to falsehood. A house, its precise nature unspecified, indicated death.

Rose's shoes, kicked off with force, lay out on the cobbles. One had landed on its sole and heel, pointing back at them, while the other had toppled on its side, pointing away. Court shoes, worn to the point of obliteration, so that they gaped slightly.

Separated from their owner's feet, and set apart, they acquired a strange significance.

Brooke sipped his tea. By the time he'd finished he knew how Ernst Lux had died. The mystery was where.

CHAPTER TWENTY

In the year Brooke had spent as a student, before he'd set out for the recruiting station with a copy of the *Iliad* in his back pocket, he'd shared a set of rooms in college with a fellow natural scientist by the name of Peter Aldiss. Intelligence is a quality many people can emit, like a radio wave; Aldiss was an example of the opposite. Anyone of brief acquaintance would have guessed he was a not very bright builder's mate. His general slowness, of word and limb, seemed to indicate a mental process of glacial velocity. It took him a long time to say anything, and it was often mundane. But he specialised in a kind of relentless logic, and a brilliant capacity for devising painstaking experimental research.

It had therefore been a shock when Brooke had discovered, one summer's evening in 1913, that Aldiss harboured a daring secret. There had been clues: the night-time absences, the sudden reappearances in the small hours, the group of rather smug, cold-eyed friends who always swiftly finished a conversation when Brooke came upon them in the bar. It had been his *shoes* which had given the game away; a distinctive pair of pumps, which Brooke spotted one night at the foot of one of the college's stone buttresses, discarded behind a clipped hedge, the socks tucked inside.

He'd finally confronted his friend over a drunken lunch in a country pub the week before both left for service overseas: Brooke to Cairo, Aldiss to West Africa. The scientist, Brooke suggested, was part of a secret fraternity, members of which might be seen against the dark skyline of the colleges on moonlit nights, illicitly scaling pinnacles, chapels and towers. Secretive, because discovery risked being sent down, they combined two inhuman virtues: an ice-like calm in the face of death and vice-like strength in hands and feet.

The 'night climbers' dwelt in an almost legendary dimension: an elite club of gifted adventurers, careless of life. Brooke had always rather despised them, given that their passion exhibited a low appraisal of the value of their own humanity. There was something supremely arrogant in not caring about death.

Brooke had kept in touch after the war and recently Aldiss had begun a series of night experiments – or rather, a continuous experiment, on a rolling twenty-four-hour basis – which required him to camp out, as it were, in his own laboratory. The scientist was conducting research into the mysteries of circadian rhythm, the inbuilt clocks of the body, be it of a human or a fruit fly; work which had recently caught the attention of Whitehall, struggling to exact maximum efficiency from workers – and soldiers – forced to labour for days without rest. Brooke had simply added Aldiss to the list of nighthawks, and visited when he could, taking advantage of the fact that the scientist laid out the latest scientific journals for his students. Brooke may have abandoned his formal studies, but he was still in many ways an avid student.

Some nights, when Brooke called, Aldiss took him into the

lead-lined room which held the *Lampyridae*, the fireflies. They'd stand together in the dark, encircled by the gently humming green lights, until Aldiss switched on the solar lamps. Then, despite the hands over his eyes, Brooke would have to endure for a moment the incredible gilded sunlight.

Aldiss stood now cradling a mug of tea, his lumpen head, which had lost all its hair since their student days, nodding slowly.

But he hadn't answered Brooke's question, so he repeated it.

'I said: do you ever see Dollis, the chemist who was on H?' he asked, flicking through the October issue of *Science*.

Dollis had shared Aldiss's secret passion: they'd both been night climbers.

Aldiss blinked slowly. 'Glasgow, I think, to work on shell casings.'

'Ah. Plenty to climb there. The Highlands are up the road,' said Brooke. 'How about you, or have the years driven out the daredevil?'

'I'm long retired from such exploits, Brooke. Besides, the word went out after Poland. Men were dying – soon, *our* men would be dying. Young men should fight, or they should continue their studies if they were in the national interest. It was not right that they should put their lives at risk in what the authorities consider a student prank.'

He sipped his tea. 'The ban is complete: any student caught on the rooftops is out. For good. None of this being *sent down* for a term nonsense.'

Outside rain was falling, and the gurgling of lead pipes had reactivated one of Cambridge's most familiar soundtracks.

'My problem,' said Brooke, 'is that I have a young man in the morgue at the Galen and I think he died after a traumatic fall. He died barefoot, Peter. A young man you may know in fact: Ernst Lux.'

'The American? Good God – dead?'

'Yes.'

Aldiss pointed straight up in the air. 'Dr Frank's lab. Fifth floor, with the biochemists. He took an interest in my fireflies, came down for a look. Bit of government interest in his work too, otherwise he'd have been off home by now. There's not much patience for anything that doesn't *make a contribution* . . .'

Brooke nodded. 'If you can, could you find out more? The precise nature of that contribution would be helpful . . .'

'I'll try, but one of the many problems with war, as you'll know, is that asking questions is unpatriotic. We're supposed to follow orders. You're sure he was climbing? I'd heard gossip that there was a small group of enthusiasts . . . but I thought it was bar talk.'

'I'm pretty sure. You climbed barefoot; it's the preferred method?'

Aldiss nodded. 'Yes, a few used shoes but it is much safer without.'

'Lux's shoes were on the wrong feet and his socks had been pulled on by someone else. His body was found on the riverbank, which must be three hundred and fifty yards from the nearest building of any kind. So there's a narrative here, don't you think? A fall, a group out climbing and an attempt to cover it all up. I know about the draconian penalties but what if a few have risen to the challenge? After all, it's all about risk, isn't it? What greater danger is there, beyond losing your life, but to let slip your place in this gilded world, with its glittering prizes? One question left,' said Brooke. 'Where do I find these new enthusiasts?'

CHAPTER TWENTY-ONE

Brooke trudged along Regent Street under a starless sky washed clean by the rain, the night climbers dominating his thoughts. Had Ernst Lux fallen, climbing the rooftops of the city? The shred of latex material left on the body suggested deliberate subterfuge. Which implied guilt. Had his fellow climbers simply sought to divert attention from the college, or was there a darker motive? Brooke was not prepared to wait for answers.

As a uniformed constable in the years after the Great War, Brooke, and most of the Borough constabulary, had turned a blind eye to the night climbers. Curbing the adventurers had fallen to the college and university authorities, principally the proctors and their bulldogs. But the sport, such as it was, had thrived. There'd even been a book, published under some fanciful pseudonym, cataloguing the best climbs, the tricks of the trade, the delights and thrills which awaited those with the courage to climb.

Brooke's natural scepticism had led him to mistrust the narrative's self-effacing heroism. There were no pictures, and no real names, to verify the claims. Indeed, he'd harboured the suspicion that much of the legend was wildly overblown, an inflated Romantic illusion. He'd never doubted the ability of some to scale the walls when the porter's lodge was closed. But the pinnacles of King's College Chapel, the great tower of St John's?

Passing the blind facade of Emmanuel College, he noted that there was little to scale here, not even a challenging arch or giddy observatory perched on a brick tower. The Georgian buildings lay low and earth-bound. Classical pillars, ghostly white, marked the chapel just visible through the portico: an enemy to night climbers, surely, for they sought out drainpipes, and 'chimneys' – the narrow vertical chutes which allowed the nerveless to brace the body, feet to one side, back to the other.

Stone carvings also offered footholds, window ledges narrow pathways, empty niches a welcome place to rest. But Emmanuel's facades were fashionably featureless, its Georgian beauty the result of perfect dimensions arranged by golden rules, rather than fussy decoration. No routes to the summit here.

Parker's Piece, the city's great park, opened up to the east, presenting a vision of an armed camp on the night before battle. Lights showed, betrayed by lantern beams, the sources hidden, as if each was held in the cup of some unseen hand. Lines of pale bell tents had been pitched in rows. Duck boards, laid for trucks and armoured cars, criss-crossed the greensward. Along the northern edge a series of public shelters had been built; single storey, sunk to their roofs in trenches, offering protection to hundreds during the air raids to come.

A guard examined Brooke's warrant card by torchlight and waved him on down the line between the tents. At the far end he found Grandcourt, his one-time batman from Palestine, in his trench guarding the shelters.

He sprang to his feet, dropping down from a niche he'd carved in the clay, which boasted a neat shelf of wood, on which he'd stored candles, a tin cup, and the paraphernalia for his pipe. Like so many of short stature he always stood up straight, shoulders back.

'All's well?' asked Brooke, taking off his hat and running his hand back through his hair. During the long campaign in the desert Grandcourt had invariably given a cheerful reply to this question.

'So far, sir. There's plenty of room at the inn,' he said, indicating the open doors to the empty shelters.

'I'm thirsty, Grandcourt,' said Brooke. 'What about you? Can I persuade you to break the rules?'

The smile broadened on Grandcourt's face, and he pocketed the pipe and pouch. 'We'll hear the siren if I'm needed,' he said. The return of war had seen Grandcourt volunteer for civil defence work, overseeing the bomb shelters. The nights were long and, bar that of the Great Darkness, so far undisturbed, except by Brooke's welcome visits.

By his niche he'd engineered a set of steps in the clay which took them up to street level. Brooke led the way into a district of narrow streets and poor houses to the north of Parker's Piece, known as the Kite, bounded on four sides by main roads. In his head Brooke had a map of the route he needed to take as set out by Aldiss in the laboratory: down Elm Street, then left, left, right. The lanes reeked of boiled cabbage, the washed-out fumes choking every alleyway. Every corner had its pub or shop.

Their destination was the St Radegund, an inn which stood within the shadow of the college of the same name, at a point where the street divided, leaving the pub to stand on a flatiron site, widening from a wooden doorway. The blackout appeared to permeate the interior, leaving pools of half-light to fill booths in which students and dons huddled. A woman sat at a piano in the corner playing snatches of old show tunes from the West End hits. Brooke recognised 'Cheek to Cheek' from *Top Hat*, and as he waited for his pints, tapped his foot.

'How's the job?' Brooke asked, settling down. He had secured his former batman a position in the engineering department at the university after the Great War, running the stores.

'Good. Still steady, that's the thing. A place for everything . . .'

Brooke drank, and leant close. A feature of the St Radegund was its oddly narrow tables, long but just a foot wide, governed by the need to hold a few pint jars in a cramped space.

'After the Armistice, Grandcourt, when you came to the hospital at Scarborough to see me, there were patients there with certain injuries. Suspicious injuries. We talked about the trenches, about what it can drive a man to do.'

The buzz of conversation in the bar was enough to secure them a bubble of privacy.

'You're right, sir. The desert was one thing, but the trenches, that's another. I was only there for that last few months, but it was as bad as the rest of the war put together. Like living in a coffin, that's what they said. They shot a kid in our mob,' he added, taking a gulp of beer which left a white surf mark on his moustache. 'They had to tie him to a post. Coward? That's a funny word. He had more courage than the rest of us put together. It's about what you're afraid of, I reckon. He couldn't live with the wait for the whistle.'

It was the kind of straightforward wisdom Brooke had found so refreshing in the desert.

'There was talk in the hospital,' said Brooke. 'About an officer they'd treated after the battle at Cambrai, and you recognised the name. Joelyn Stone? A captain then, but I'm not sure I had the name right?'

'You had it right,' said Grandcourt, setting off a crackling inferno in his pipe bowl with a match.

Beyond the sudden cloud of smoke, Brooke could see a group of students with their heads together in the booth opposite. There was something in the urgent postures, the hungry eyes, which spoke of adventure. Above them a framed picture of the Alps was covered in scrawled signatures and the date: 1937.

It looked as if Aldiss's intelligence had been on the nail. Here was the new generation of night climbers, possibly planning their next night out on the rooftops.

'It was at Cambrai, alright,' said Grandcourt. 'The first battle. A runner comes through from up the line with orders for Captain Stone to go over next day at dawn, *before* the artillery. Element of surprise, they said. Element of pure bloody stupidity.'

Grandcourt took another inch off his beer.

The students drinking in the shadow of the Alps were becoming animated, one of them holding his hands out like claws.

'Anyway, that night the platoon sergeant goes to Stone's billet at some godawful hour and finds him on the field line to the top brass, trying to talk 'em out of it. But no joy. Three in the morning, this sergeant gets the men ready in the trench. Everyone's had a ciggy. A tot, too, and that's care of Stone, to give him credit. He was an organiser, apparently, one of the best.

'Everyone knows how this is going to end, Mr Brooke. They're going to die out in the mud. It's the full disaster and no mistake: men throwing up, crying, praying. It's all the sergeant can do to keep them from bolting the other way.

'Then there's a gunshot. The sergeant runs to Stone's billet and finds his bed's empty. Then he hears him, crying for help, and he's on the *far side* of the command post in the next section of trench. He's on the floor, half of his hand blown off, binoculars held in the uninjured hand. Said he was on a recce.

'Detail . . .' The batman stabbed his finger in the air. 'Sergeant says he held him up and he could smell cordite. If he'd been hit by an enemy bullet then the sniper would have been *two hundred yards away*. But the whiff of the gun was in the trench, Mr Brooke. Right there. He'd done for himself. There's no two ways about that.'

At the bar, buying refills, Brooke studied the corner where the students were huddled. There was a picture on the wall he'd missed because it lay half in shadow, a black-and-white shot taken from a rooftop across the city, catching the four pinnacles of King's College Chapel, each a red-hot poker in stone with a filigree-carved summit.

On his way back to Grandcourt, he skirted their table and stopped. Briefly, he had an insight into these young students' view of *him*: a tall middle-aged man, with a pale face, dark hair brushed back, eyes obscured by yellow-tinted glasses. They'd think of him as definitely the last war, an Edwardian, with the faded good looks of that lost generation. If, he conceded, they thought of him at all.

'I was looking for news of a friend,' he said to them, and watched their faces, the eyes turning down to examine a pack of cards which lay in haphazard hands on the bronze tabletop. 'He's a keen night climber.'

They were all men, but one was twenty years older than the rest. He wore a cardigan and a collarless white shirt. 'We're Am Dram, I'm afraid. College theatre club. *Hay Fever* is next up and we're casting. I think night climbing went out of fashion in the last century.'

They all laughed, nodding, and one of them pushed his way past Brooke to the bar.

'Really?' said Brooke. 'My friend was called Ernst. They found his body on the riverside. He'd been climbing and fallen and someone had dragged his body away from the scene. Injuries – well, you don't want to know. Left leg nearly severed, here . . .'

He ran a finger across his knee.

'Skull crushed, too. So we're all sure, are we, that we don't know Ernst Lux?'

Brooke leant over the table and set down one of his cards, embossed with the switchboard number: *Cambridge 0959.*

'If anyone can help, ring me. If I don't hear soon we'll be making enquiries, college by college, starting at Michaelhouse. Enjoy *Hay Fever.*'

CHAPTER TWENTY-TWO

Behind the front desk at the Spinning House, a board studded with hooks held the station keys. Taking a small bunch marked GARAGE, Brooke asked after the prisoner, Turl. The sergeant scanned the log. 'I checked on the hour, sir. Asleep. Ate his dinner at six. He's had tea, too, at eight. Doctor looked him over this morning. Apparently he's a "fine physical specimen".'

Brooke recalled the pace at which he'd fled the scene on Castle Hill.

He tapped a finger on the duty book. 'Anything happening, Sergeant?'

The highlights were quickly listed: a fire in a town alleyway, possibly started deliberately. A broken shop window on Girton Road, but nothing taken. And a gunshot, heard by several people on Mill Road earlier that evening at around seven-fifteen. Two constables conducted door-to-door enquiries, with no results.

'I'll be back to check on the prisoner in ten minutes, Sergeant,' said Brooke, heading out the back door into the station yard. An old corrugated iron garage made up one side of the square. Brooke slipped the padlock with the key and rolled up the slated door on metal rails. Strip lights revealed the three lorries from Castle Hill.

His encounter with the night climbers in St Radegund had left him frustrated and angry. If he didn't get a call in twenty-four hours, he'd take action: a visit to the college and a night in the cells might focus young minds on the consequences of failing to help the police with their enquiries.

In the meantime, the continued silence of Turl was proving intolerable. Brooke was determined to loosen his tongue.

He stood by an open tailgate, trying not to breathe in any trace of the dead meat. The professional consensus was that the animals had died within the last twenty-four hours, that the carcasses were of good to superior quality, and had been dispatched expertly by a trained slaughterman.

Profit from war was an ugly reality. *Black* market said it all: shadowy, evil, shameful. He thought of his son, in France. Luke's last letter had ended wistfully . . .

When it starts I can't write. We'll be on the move and speed is everything. Tell Mum not to worry, I'm a survivor. There's talk of leave by Christmas.

He collected a mechanic's spotlight from the sump pit underneath one of the lorries, and looped a twenty-foot electric cable over his arm.

At the top of the circular stone staircase which led to the cells, he kicked off his shoes, with their telltale Blakey's, and padded silently down the twenty-one steps. A little light from the stairwell illuminated a short corridor and six locked doors. Attaching the spotlight lead to a plug in the rotting wainscoting, he approached Turl's cell: number five.

In the twenty years he'd served at the Spinning House, he'd unlocked the various cells a thousand times; each one had a slightly different mechanism, but at a subconscious level he was able to adapt the twist of the wrist to each, so that the door of cell five flew open and crashed against the brickwork of the wall in less than a second.

At the same moment Brooke switched on the spotlight.

Turl stood frozen against the backdrop of his own shadow, a sheet still falling from his hand. Brooke waited to speak, knowing that in this moment, the prisoner had no idea who was behind the light.

The prisoner didn't move. Brooke wondered later if he was waiting for a bullet, or a flick knife to the guts. His face revealed a genuine expectation that he was about to die.

'Relax,' said Brooke.

'Don't you people sleep,' said Turl. 'What's this? The third degree?'

Brooke took the chair and set it in the cell doorway while Turl sat back on his bunk. They were six feet apart. Brooke attached the spotlight to a bracket on the wall which had once held a candle.

'We had some unanswered questions,' he said.

They'd confiscated Turl's tobacco and rolling tin when they'd charged him but Brooke had taken them from the possessions box.

He rolled one now, without offering Turl a smoke.

Turl had his hand up against the glare. 'This isn't very civilised, Inspector. There's a light . . .' He indicated the single bulb.

'Running black-market meat's a sordid crime,' he said. 'It's unprofessional to let personal considerations affect an inquiry, but my son is your age and he's currently camped out on the Belgium border, waiting for a war to start.'

He gave Turl the roll-up he'd made and a box of matches. 'I thought we'd talk for twenty minutes. Then you can sleep. Then I'll be back. Maybe tonight. Maybe tomorrow night. We'll cut this session to ten minutes now if you answer one question. You can roll ten fags too. You won't get a better offer.'

'Tell me the question if you want a deal.'

'Your first name. Your *real* first name.'

Turl dropped his hand, and narrowed his eyes. 'Jack.'

'Short for?'

'Short for nothing. It's Jack.'

'Alright, I'll believe you, Jack. While you roll your fags, I'll tell you a story. In the last war I was taken prisoner in Palestine,' began Brooke. 'It was my own fault. I'd come up with a plan to fool the Turks. All very *Boy's Own Paper*. We were going to attack Gaza from the west, and we wanted the enemy to use some of their men to defend their eastern flank. We contrived some coded documents and a map indicating a fake attack. We knew they'd cracked our codes, but they didn't know we knew.

'To cut a long story short, my plan was to let these orders fall into enemy hands, and then make a miraculous escape. I got the first part right. I waited by a desert oasis with the coded documents in my saddlebag until a Turkish patrol came into sight. I let them take a potshot or two and then rode away. I'd obtained a bottle of blood off the battalion surgeon, so it was easy to fake a wound, and drop the saddlebag. Clinging to the horse, I was supposed to outrun them back to our lines. I didn't make it.

'I spent six days in the desert being interrogated, by day and night.'

He paused, adjusting the tinted lenses, as Turl lit up.

'Did you tell them the truth?' asked Turl, his eyes reduced to slits in the glare.

'In the end, after six days, I told them a lie.'

'That was brave.'

'It was important. We attacked in the west the next day, the Turkish line collapsed, and the road to Jerusalem was open. The king gave me a medal.'

Turl tipped his head.

Brooke laughed. 'When I was in front of the light, at night in a cell like this, I wasn't alone. That's how I survived. How I got through it. There was a ghost with me. A man I loved, and admired. My father. He'd saved thousands of lives once, when I was just a child, and I saw that this was my chance to do the same. To match up.'

Turl's cigarette smoke hung over his head like a cloud.

'What did they do when the attack started and they realised you'd lied?' he asked.

'They shot me, in the knee, to make sure I couldn't get back to the battalion, then they left me for dead in the desert. They said I'd be food for carrion, for wild dogs and jackals. They said I'd be eaten alive. Or I'd die of thirst.'

Brooke retrieved his hip flask and drank some cool water.

'Make you feel good, does it? Bragging,' said Turl.

Brooke smiled. 'I'm telling you this because I didn't come to hate them, my interrogators. I hope you won't hate me. We were simply enemies, and it was war. There are many types of war. This is a war now, Jack. You and me. This is my war. It's not personal, but I take it very seriously.'

A tendon in Turl's jaw flexed as he drew nicotine into his lungs.

'There's been another change of plan, you see. If I don't get answers soon I've decided that once we've found your home city or town, we're going to charge you, put you up before the magistrates and then let you out on bail. Once you're free, walking your own streets, your friends will find you soon enough.'

'You can't do that,' said Turl, before he realised he'd said too much, that he'd exposed his fear.

Brooke smiled. 'I'll bend the rules for you, Jack. Before we let you go we'll make it clear you've been helpful. Then it's just a matter of time. Your mate, "Nev", he couldn't face the prospect. We found him in the river, Jack. A brick in each pocket. I wonder if you'll be tempted to take the same shortcut?

'Police bail of a fiver should buy your freedom. I'll pay, if it comes to it. We could even have a whip round. I thought it was only fair to let you know so you've got time to think it all through. This is going to happen, Jack. To you. Soon.'

Brooke stood and cut the light.

'I'm going to feed you to the dogs,' he said, closing the cell door.

CHAPTER TWENTY-THREE

A single window gave a narrow view of a topiary maze and a statue of Neptune standing in a mossy stone pool, all lit by the morning sun. The gardens of Madingley Hall lay beyond, running into a blue distance, a few spires rising from the haze that was the city. Brooke sat in a corridor leading to a polished door, along which had been arranged a dozen seats. Half an hour earlier he had been on the eleventh chair in the corridor, waiting his turn, having been picked up at home by a military driver in a black car, who had knocked on the door at seven, suggesting Brooke might have time to 'brief' the commanding officer up at Madingley Hall on an issue of relevance to the Borough constabulary. Now, an hour later, he was in the first chair.

It was one of the illuminating aspects of war that it laid bare these realities of power. He'd been summoned, and he'd obeyed.

'Brooke?' Captain Kerridge appeared at the door. 'Your turn,' he said, adding in a whisper, 'We don't know each other, Eden.'

The commanding officer's room was vast, a dining hall, perhaps, in its medieval heyday, with a single table set against a bay window, with its stunning view of the city. The contrast with Major Stone's stuffy office was stark. The army was an organisation which placed power precisely in the hands of those who held office. Deputies were for emergencies only, to communicate orders down the line, and to work diligently through paperwork. This was the office of an all-seeing commander.

A small, sinewy man in a flawless uniform shook Brooke's hand and sat down on a side chair, offering his guest another. The disarming informality put Brooke on his guard. Kerridge retreated to a discreet distance and began working through some papers on a side table.

'George Swift-Lane,' the CO said. Brooke noted the studied omission of his rank, designed to put the detective at ease. A well-scrubbed face, with ruddy cheeks, was offset by eyes which had the first rheumy opacity of old age. Swift-Lane had cut himself shaving and three small eruptions of cotton wool marked his attempts to staunch the flow of blood. There was a boyish energy to the man, which suited his slight frame, and a tendency to fidget. His hair colour was irrelevant owing to the application of oil, which lashed what there was to his narrow skull.

'Thanks for coming in,' he said, and Brooke felt instantly uneasy. Politeness as a prelude to authoritarian brutality was an English trope. The contrast between this bustling, impish officer and Major Stone, his stolid, bureaucratic deputy, was striking.

Brooke tilted his head to one side. 'Swift-Lane, I know the name?'

The effect of this enquiry on the colonel's face was startling. A look of settled hatred was immediately apparent in the eyes, and the colour drained from those schoolboy cheeks.

'Brother's in the Cabinet, other one's an admiral or some such.

Boys will play with boats. I did a bit of amateur exploring after the last war, the Arctic mainly. That made the papers. It's one of those names . . . But back to business . . .'

Swift-Lane glanced at one of the three phones on his desk. 'I rang the chief constable, and I don't want anyone thinking I'm in the business of going over people's heads as a rule, but this is a very sensitive matter.'

The colonel's eyes narrowed, noting perhaps Brooke's confident refusal to fill the silence which had fallen after this statement. In an anteroom, someone was typing at the steady rate of machine-gun fire.

'You'll have an idea what we're up to here. The vision is a simple one. Whitehall ministries, susceptible to attack in the capital, are being moved out to Cambridge. We're trying to bring the armed services together. The country's been broken up into regions and each will have a "capital" – so to speak – in the event of an attack. Cambridge will oversee the Eastern Region.

'We are given to understand that the Germans will attack next year. Then the real war will begin. It's far more difficult to predict its end. This will be a fast-moving, technological conflict. We may find ourselves isolated. It is a small risk, but we must be prepared for the worst. The unthinkable: an invasion.'

He let that idea hang in the air.

'In that unlikely event, regional government will become an absolute reality. As will military control. We need to be ready. I'm telling you this because we trust you. Your record speaks for itself.'

Patience and power are rarely combined in the military psyche. Swift-Lane's clasped hands came apart and seemed to propel him to his feet. Striding to the bay window, he looked out at the grounds.

'You've been asking questions about some work done on St

John's Wilderness,' he said, his back to Brooke. 'An official request for information has come across my desk.' He turned to face Brooke. 'Drop it. It's a distraction and it won't occur again. How can I put it? A line of action, a defensive line, has been abandoned. Some work was being done here, now it's being transferred to Oxford. There will be no further incidents. The chief constable was very considerate, but quite rightly asked me to make this request in person to you. Which I'm happy to do, and it is a request, Brooke. This is still a free country, after all, that's what we're all fighting for, in our own ways.'

Brooke took off his glasses and rested them on his knee. Decisive, direct, apparently competent, Swift-Lane was in many ways a model senior officer. In the desert, Brooke's life had been placed in real danger by a wide range of senior officers who combined stupidity with frantic manoeuvring designed to disguise their blatant shortcomings.

Swift-Lane went to speak, but Brooke held up a hand. 'We, the Borough police, are in the same position as everyone else, Colonel. Undermanned, and overworked. As a force, entrusted with imposing civil law and order, we are stretched to breaking point. No, beyond it. I'm being honest because I trust you.'

Swift-Lane kept his silence.

'I have no wish to enter a turf war, especially one I have no hope of winning,' said Brooke.

'Good man,' said Swift-Lane, shaking hands as Brooke stood. 'Captain Kerridge will show you out.'

'You asked me to remind you, sir,' said Kerridge.

'Of course.' Swift-Lane flicked open a file on his desk and extracted a single typed sheet, handing it to Brooke.

'Your chief constable mentioned a puzzling case, a convoy of lorries . . . Black market's one thing, a few lamb chops under the counter is what we expect. And fresh vegetables off the farms. If this war continues into its second year, its third, that will be an issue, of course: rural scavenging, urban starvation.'

Swift-Lane ran a finger along his lips and Brooke guessed he'd said too much. It was pretty clear the scenario of a successful invasion, in the sense of the Germans actually setting foot on British soil, had been rehearsed to some considerable degree.

'What we don't want – what we *can't* have, Brooke – is organised crime operating a black market. That would seriously undermine our ability to govern. Public morale would dip. We're all in this together, that's the prime minister's message. We won't tolerate the rich buying scarce food. This might help . . .'

Swift-Lane nodded, which appeared to be an accepted signal for his adjutant to take over the narrative.

'One of our men has gone AWOL. Corporal Stanley Currie. You've got all his details there . . .' Kerridge indicated the typed sheet. 'This man, Currie, has been interviewed by redcaps on three occasions for offences related to the procuring of petrol outside the ration system and selling it on to private users. That's in the last three weeks.

'He joined up in the Great War, saw service in the trenches, then became a full-time soldier in '37. Since then he's been in the glasshouse twice. Both times for pilfering, cigarettes the first time, gin the second, both from the mess.

'The chief constable said these lorries had full tanks and no paperwork relating to fuel, and the men had north country accents. On civvy street, Currie worked for the family garage business in Sheffield.

'The morning after your lorries turned up, he left Madingley on a pass-out to town. Never came back. Coincidence, maybe, but it seems he had a reputation for supplying scarce goods, and besides petrol he apparently offered a line in fresh meat. Perhaps he's the local man on the ground for this black-market outfit?'

Swift-Lane tapped the sheet of paper in Brooke's hand with his pen.

'If and when you find him you'll no doubt have your own questions,' said the colonel. 'But we'd appreciate the nod. Black-market offences are covered under Emergency Powers. Being in uniform won't save him from the law. Ten years' hard labour, I think. But we'd like to know when he's in the bag. Personally, and I say this only to make myself feel better, I'd shoot the bastard.'

CHAPTER TWENTY-FOUR

A woman visiting a grave with an armful of fresh flowers stumbled on the corpse of Chris Childe at just after ten o'clock, sprawled on the flat tombstone of his parents' grave. She'd let out a single, piercing scream, sending a flock of starlings up into the sky. She'd fled the spot, running out into Mill Road, flagging down a butcher's boy on his bicycle, who'd fetched a constable. Childe's body was cold, the limbs stiff. The head wound had bled across the gravestone. The victim's wallet contained three one-pound notes, an ID card and a membership card for the Peace Pledge Union. The address on the card was a poor street on the edge of Romsey Town, about half a mile to the east.

Brooke informed Chief Inspector Carnegie-Brown that the Borough had a potential murder inquiry on its hands, sent Edison to the cemetery with two uniformed officers, while he set out on foot for the dead man's house. As he crossed the iron bridge into Romsey Town, leaving the old city behind, he was followed by a long line of children: evacuees escaping London, each clutching a suitcase, all tagged with labels, the babel of excited voices rising as they were enveloped in the steam rising from a train as it thundered underneath.

Turning into Gothic Street, he saw a constable on the doorstep; relief, like a glass of wine, settled Brooke's pulse: at least he wouldn't have to break the news, wouldn't have to trade in euphemisms while a stricken wife began to realise that her life had changed for ever.

A woman police constable, one of two on the Borough force, joined her colleague on the threshold when Brooke arrived. 'Sir. Wife's in the kitchen, the children are with a neighbour. Twin girls. Her mother's with her, she lives in. Wife's able to talk, quite calm, really. She said she knew something was wrong when he didn't come home. The doctor's left a sedative but I don't think she'll need it. She's worried about the children . . .'

The front room held a wooden printing press, boxes of type, tools hung neatly across the wall like a flight of decorative ducks. The air was heavy with the acerbic aroma of ink. On one wall, a small desktop had been fixed with hinges and held a heavy Imperial typewriter. Brooke noted that some of the keys, the principal vowels, had been almost worn away, leaving behind a smudged, metallic fingerprint.

Through the open door, Brooke could see the kitchen, a back door ajar, revealing a flagged yard and a bicycle.

'Tea?' he asked: the ubiquitous English antidote to shock and grief.

'Pot's made, sir. I can stay if it's a help?'

Brooke shook his head, and went into the kitchen.

Mary Childe sat at the kitchen table, cradling an empty mug. An elderly woman with grey hair had an arm around her shoulders.

Brooke said he was sorry for their loss and added some other pleasantries he'd attached to the format over the years. His mind, on a separate track, considered the table, the way it embodied the family which had sat round it for meals: the dents and grooves, a circular burn, which told their own story of the lives led in a cramped terrace house.

Brooke gave the mother a shilling and asked her to fetch chips from the corner for the constable on duty at the front door, which they could all share. Straightening her stooped back she paused in front of Brooke. 'Did he do for himself?' she asked.

'It's too early to tell. I think food would help . . .'

The victim's wife was shaking very slightly, her hands held together to disguise the tremor.

'They said they didn't know anything. I don't know anything. I need to tell the children *something*. Can you help, please? Just tell me.'

There was a slight sibilance on every 's'. Her face was dominated by large liquid eyes which failed to hold Brooke's gaze for more than a fleeting second.

'Death would have been instantaneous,' said Brooke. 'A gunshot here, to the right temple.' He touched his finger to his skin and she looked up, the blood draining from her cheeks.

'The pathologist believes Chris died between five and eight o'clock. We have reports of a gunshot heard in the area at about seven-fifteen. Ballistic evidence suggests the weapon was held almost against the skin. We can't rule out the possibility the shot was self-inflicted; however, the gun's missing. We know that one bullet was fired, and it's been recovered from a tree bole by the grave. I'm sorry. Those are the facts.'

'Thank you,' she said.

Brooke swiftly established what she knew of her husband's movements. Two days earlier he'd left the house as usual at seven-thirty with a packed lunch. A conscientious objector, he'd been assigned to civic works. His duties that day had been scheduled as ditch clearing at Waterbeach, but he'd come home early to say that the shift had been reassigned to night work, digging trenches on Parker's Piece. He'd slept for two hours, had tea, and then left for the council works yard, returning in the early hours as the air raid siren had sounded.

'That was the night of the blackout,' she added.

'By the time he got back the siren had gone off, so we all got under the stairs, 'cept Mum. She's happy to take her chances, so she stayed up in the attic.' She pulled at a simple silver chain round her neck. 'Selfish, really. We'd have to dig her out if the bombs did fall.'

'Next morning?'

'Chris didn't sleep. We all went back to bed when the all-clear sounded, the girls in our bed, because they get scared, or excited. Chris got up at dawn and started work. I could hear the typewriter.'

'Is that unusual?'

'No, he's always working, Chris. When I took him a cup of tea he said he had to make a report, for the Party. Chris lives for his politics, for the Communists, and the PPU. He's a peacemonger, that's what he always tells the girls. That's why he'd been late that night, he'd met the other members of the committee because they wanted to help him prepare for court. He was up in front of the tribunal so he could print full-time. He had plans to edit a news-sheet for the Party.'

'What was this report about?' asked Brooke.

'He wouldn't say. He just had to get it down, and then get

the letter to London, to Party headquarters. Vera, she's the Party secretary, knew who to send it to. So he said he'd take it round on the way to the depot.'

'Do you have an address for Vera?' asked Brooke.

She fetched a small leather-bound book from the dresser, the entries in a neat copperplate. 'This is Chris's. Henderson's the chairman, Lauder the deputy, and Popper's the treasurer – they all helped with the tribunal rehearsal. Vera Staunton's the secretary.'

Brooke flicked the pages, finding addresses and a telephone number for Henderson, making notes as he went along. But under 'S' there was no Staunton.

'Any idea where Vera lives?'

She shook her head.

Finished, he looked round the room, noting the threadbare rug on bare boards, the tin bath on a hook by the grate. 'Who would want to kill Chris, Mrs Childe? Did he have any enemies, any fights or disagreements, with neighbours perhaps, or his comrades in the Party . . . ?'

A banal question, it produced a profound answer. It was clear that Christopher Childe was largely defined by a life constructed to anger no one. Printing, the Party, the PPU, his novels (unpublished), his studies in economics and politics for a degree which always seemed just out of reach, and his family: these were the sinews of a blameless existence.

Struggling to find any sense to his violent death, his wife finally settled on ideology. 'They argued in the Party. That got Chris mad. He'd come home het up. Chris liked the debates, the theory of it all, but he didn't like losing. And I think the others lost patience. But they were comrades, he always said that too, and comrades, in the end, would stick together.'

Brooke made a note. 'And he didn't return after he left with this letter?'

'No. He had the tribunal in the afternoon and he wouldn't have missed that. And he had to report to work, although they'd said he could have time off for court. Maisie, across the street, said he'd got what he wanted from the tribunal. Her son was up too. So if he'd come home we'd have celebrated . . .'

This thought made her stop in mid-sentence.

'The money they give him for the hard labour isn't enough,' she said, eventually. 'And it meant he didn't have time for printing, which used to bring in some cash. So getting registered would have changed his life, our lives . . .'

Her face lightened fleetingly. 'The last thing he'd do is take his own life. He wouldn't leave us.' She covered her face, but Brooke heard the addition: 'Not the girls.'

It crossed Brooke's sceptical mind that, for a pacifist, Childe had nevertheless inflicted considerable hardship on his own family, for while he pursued his obsessions, he had found little time to eke out a living to help make ends meet.

Mrs Childe got up to refill the tea pot, moving as if underwater, the weight of gravity almost too much to allow her to lift her feet.

She's thinking about telling the children, thought Brooke.

On the wall above the fireplace, Brooke noticed a framed photograph. A caption read: *The Anglo-Soviet Committee. Cambridge, 1938.*

The names were listed with appropriate positions, including *Christopher CHILDE, Editor, Anglo-Soviet Bulletin.*

Brooke slipped off his tinted glasses and studied the rest of the line-up: men, almost exclusively, mostly with glasses, mostly in late middle-age, if not older, in threadbare suits. But one woman stood out. Standing in the middle of the front row, she'd broken protocol with a smile, but there was nothing shy about the breach. She had a fine face, and very clear eyebrows, one of which was arched as if interrogating the camera. Mid-thirties, possibly older, but soft and sinuous where the men were stiff and upright. There was a certain challenge in the direct connection she'd made with the photographer's lens.

Brooke read the caption: *Mrs Vera STAUNTON, Secretary to the Committee.*

CHAPTER TWENTY-FIVE

Major Joelyn Stone took the train to London. As a senior officer at Madingley Hall, he'd been able to secure a first-class ticket. The carriage was empty, and he'd watched the harvest fields fly past, occasionally rereading a sheaf of notes extracted from a leather attaché case. The war had brought the countryside back to life, as the nation dug for victory. Pickers in lines stretched out along furrows, tractors raised clouds of red fen dust. Stone let the scenes slide past his eyes.

At King's Cross, the platforms were jammed with evacuees waiting for trains to the north. An air of a seaside outing pervaded, rather than panic, or even anxiety. Stone noted the smell, the stench of the crowd, something he'd forgotten since his pre-war days in India.

Outside, he watched the traffic on Euston Road. London, under low cloud, seemed to be wearing khaki. A wall of sandbags discouraged him from taking the Tube. Checking his watch, he calculated he had the time to walk to his appointment at the Army and Navy Club, so he set off down Gray's Inn Road. To the east he could see a few barrage balloons over the docks, and another, flying solo, to the west, possibly over Buckingham Palace.

Slipping across Trafalgar Square, he skirted the War Office: tomorrow he'd be there for the formal interview, but today was the real thing, a cosy 'chat' over lunch at the club.

Downing Street, when he reached the corner, looked as it always did, rather squalid and middle class, the paintwork grimy, a sandbagged machine-gun nest looking bedraggled under a camouflage sheet. A man in a morning suit and tails walked up the street, knocked and was admitted, the first gleams of a hazy sun catching the polish on the black door.

The Army and Navy Club – or The Rag as it was affectionately known – stood on Pall Mall. On his honeymoon with Margaret they'd stayed in a hotel on the Grand Canal in Venice and he'd bored her with a long walk to get a view of the Palazzo Cornaro, the architect's model for one of London's most imposing gentleman's clubs, the Good Old Rag.

Stone breezed in, trying to look at ease, avoiding the full-length military portraits in the lobby because one of them was of his father-in-law. Stone came from middle-class stock. His career had undoubtedly benefited to some degree from his wife's family connections, but he didn't like to be reminded too blatantly of the fact.

Brigadier Pearce was in an armchair, cradling a tumbler of whisky, and looked mildly out of sorts to be diverted from some inner reverie. Pearce was in his eighties, a veteran whose career stretched back into the previous century.

Pearce's hand shook slightly holding his glass, but his first question, after a few perfunctory remarks, was direct enough.

'This plan of yours has a certain brutal genius, Stone. I don't think anyone had ever realised you could use a barrage balloon as a weapon. Just drop the cables and let them drift away. It's cowardly, of course, don't you think? They can kill and maim, and spread chaos, but they're unmanned, aren't they? Delivering death by proxy. There's no sense of combat . . .'

The look on Stone's face must have shaken Pearce in turn. The word 'coward' seemed to have drained the blood from the major's face.

'And there's this American casualty, in Cambridge,' said Pearce, pressing on. 'Dr Lux. Unfortunate, to say the very least. One boffin, I know, neither here nor there. But it raised questions. It is rather careless.'

'The local police rang this morning,' said Stone, stretching out his legs to affect relaxation. 'The American's death is not down to us. I don't know what it is down to, the detective concerned is a difficult chap, and wouldn't clarify the issue. But he's pretty sure the balloon wasn't the culprit. An accident, perhaps; there were several during the blackout. And all three balloons are now accounted for. It won't happen again. The new winches are designed to allow us to release the balloons on order. There was a malfunction. They've been modified and the problem solved.'

'Don't misunderstand me, Stone. Everyone's impressed. Even the prime minister. In fact, *especially* the prime minister . . .'

'It's the perfect weapon,' said Stone. 'Properly organised, it could be devastating. And the Met Office will have to step up. Wind speed, wind *direction*, is critical. But there's no doubt the effects will be crippling for the enemy. A thousand, let loose at the right moment, could plunge the Ruhr into chaos. They're slow-motion bombs.'

The brigadier's eyes looked wary, as if this vision of the future was all too much.

'And the Germans can't retaliate,' said Stone, decisively. 'Wind direction's almost always against them. And the cost is minimal. Just compare it to a Spitfire, or a Wellington.'

'Quite,' said Pearce, summoning a waiter. 'A bottle of the Tsarine,' he said, pulling himself up straight in the armchair. 'You'll get the papers but, entre nous, the Cabinet has decided that funding can be set aside for your balloons, at least for six months. The chain of command will be short, so if it goes wrong it's your head that rolls. You're in charge. First, you'll have to work out of the War Office, then from somewhere on the south coast, that's up to you to map out.'

Stone thought he'd misheard. 'Command? But the other candidates?' Stone had been *hoping* for a senior role; second-in-command had figured only in his wildest dreams. It had never crossed his mind he'd be given command.

'Leave the other candidates to us. This is an organisational challenge, Stone. We don't need any flashy heroics. But for now, please keep the appointment to yourself. The other principal candidate has already been told of your appointment. You'll respect the niceties, this is all on the QT for now . . .'

'Of course.'

'Good man. You'll have to liaise with the War Office, of course. A production line is needed. Industrial warfare, that's the ticket. But yes, a thousand of these things drifting over Dortmund, or Mainz, has caught the spirit of the age, Stone. It's cheap, and it might work.'

Standing on the steps of The Rag two hours later, after an excellent lunch, Stone thought life couldn't get better. He'd booked a room for the night, but he saw Pearce to the door, as the old soldier shrugged himself into a greatcoat. 'Don't forget the formal interview tomorrow. Play it safe. They just want to feel they're in the loop.

'One other thing: given the scope of the command, we feel Lieutenant Colonel would be appropriate. It'll take time, wheels within wheels, but you'll get the notice in due course.'

He didn't shake Stone's hand – even the nod was limited to an upward dismissal with the chin – and then he was gone, bundling himself into a cab.

CHAPTER TWENTY-SIX

Detective Sergeant Edison swung the Wolseley Wasp out of the Spinning House yard into Regent Street, the pale sun catching the plum-red paintwork, which had been polished to a mirror-like patina. Slipping the engine into second, then third, they sped past Downing College and out beyond Parker's Piece, the old city passing in a blur. Brooke, in the passenger seat, held the map close to his eyes.

Their priority was to find Vera Staunton. The key, felt Brooke, to tracking down Chris Childe's killer lay in the letter he'd delivered to the Party branch secretary. But Staunton was proving elusive. They had uniformed branch checking out the Peace Pledge Union, and admin at the Spinning House trawling through the electoral rolls. So far, there was no sign of her. Brooke and Edison would try and locate her via her comrades in the Party: Henderson, Popper and Lauder, the three officials who'd put Childe through his successful rehearsal for his tribunal appearance.

They set out for Barnwell, a suburb clinging to the bank of the river, which had once clustered round a vast Augustinian abbey. In the crowded streets, medieval fragments survived: the monks' old treasury house in stone, and a chapel, now the local church. The place strived to be genteel, but down by the quayside there were slums. Lauder's address was a rooming house on Wharf Street. The skeleton of an old pram stood on the cobbles, and a small child chased a ball in the gutter. A neighbour said Lauder was a Scot, a brickie, and had not been seen that day.

His door, on the third floor of the block, was locked.

Edison knocked, then knocked again, as they stood listening to the house. Somewhere a radio played, while the ball bounced rhythmically in the street.

'It's a reasonable assumption that if Childe's dead then the lives of his comrades are in danger,' said Brooke. He took a step back, shifted his weight and kicked the door in, the jamb reduced to splinters.

There was no sign of Lauder, but the room had been ransacked. The bed was turned over, the drawers of a dresser pulled out, a rug folded back. The only surprise was a music stand, still upright, a violin set against the wall, and some music on the floor – a Mozart sonata.

Dr Jacob Popper, Lauder's comrade and branch treasurer, was missing too. His surgery operated from a semi-detached villa off Hills Road, a leafy prosperous suburb, overshadowed by the barrage balloons guarding the railway line. A bachelor, with a small flat in the attic of the house, Popper had last been seen at afternoon surgery the day before.

'He's a bloody good doctor, Jacob,' explained his partner. 'The problem is he can never remember to collect his fees. We're not a charity, are we? Jacob does twice the work, pulls in half the income. He's disappeared before, has Jacob,' he added, unlocking the door to the flat. 'Went off to some march in London when war broke out. Left a note on my desk. He'll turn up.'

Popper's flat had been searched too: books lay scattered, the clothes from a wardrobe thrown over the bed, a desk moved away from the wall.

Which left Henderson, the union convener and Party chairman. Brooke had tried the telephone number in Childe's address book three times from the Spinning House but there had been no answer. His address was listed as Abbey Island, a piece of land caught between the main line to Lynn and the branch line to Bury, not far from Cambridge Station. The V-shaped plot was cut off to the north by a goods line used to reverse trains. So: an urban island, surrounded by iron rails.

The Wasp rattled over three level crossings before they were on 'dry land', which comprised a single street of railway architecture: not housing at all, but dilapidated offices and workshops, many of the windows smashed, and doors off their hinges.

Edison stood stoutly in the street, such as it was, surveying the scene. The London train thundered past on the down-line, a goods train on the up-line following a few seconds later.

'If he does live here he must be a bloody heavy sleeper,' said Brooke.

At the far end of the street they found a set of steps which led up to a door marked:

Associated Society of Locomotive Engineers and Firemen
Office Hours: Monday–Friday
8.00–18.00

The door was locked. Inside they could see a desk, with a telephone. Filing cabinets obscured one wall, and a safe sat in one corner, on iron clasp feet.

Brooke rattled the handle. 'Steel frame,' he said. 'Maybe there's a fortune in the safe.'

Round the back of the same building they found a door at ground level marked: *J. R. Henderson: convenor.*

The blinds were down on a single sash window.

By the door stood a large flower pot, which looked so out of place that Brooke parted the leaves of a parched hydrangea to reveal a brass key.

The front room was spartan. An armchair, a fireplace, a coal bucket. Across the floor were scattered copies of magazines and newspapers. Brooke noted *Labour News*, *Picture Post* and *Peace News*.

Up a back-stair they found the now familiar scene. The small bedroom had been searched, the mattress set up on end against one wall. There was a sink, a gas ring and a desk, the drawer pulled out on the bare boards.

Edison patiently checked the scattered documents.

Brooke went outside and lit a cigarette, asking himself an increasingly urgent question: what were the chances he'd have another corpse on his hands before nightfall?

Edison threw up the sash window and called him back upstairs. The detective sergeant was examining the ceiling, which had been roughly plastered. 'Year I packed up the job I went to night school, up at the college: electrics for the householder. Edith said it would make the pension go further if I did more of the chores. No – *some* of the chores. Any road, that's not right, is it?' he said, pointing at a wire which came in through the top of the sash window, then, tacked to the wall, rose up to cross the ceiling, finally disappearing from sight for no reason right above their heads. Tellingly, it went nowhere near the central light fitting.

Brooke went outside to trace the wire's provenance. It ascended to the apex of the roof from the sash window, where it appeared to connect to a wind vane, which was badly rusted, and stuck pointing south to London.

Back inside, and balanced on a stool he'd dragged up the stairs from the front room, he discovered a small loft hatch had been expertly concealed by the plasterwork. Giving his glasses to Edison, he used the flat of his hand to lift it up. The hole revealed was no bigger than a roasting tin. He carefully raised his head into the dark space. Executing a cramped turn, he finally located a large radio, the dials indicating the principal European cities: London, Paris, Berlin, Rome, Madrid. Clipped to the side was a chrome microphone, which caught the light along its metallic bevelled handle.

Brooke turned the dial until he heard the bass note buzz of the power; the facia lit up, and the single word MOSCOW shone in the half-light.

CHAPTER TWENTY-SEVEN

The town's Civil Defence Depot, where Childe had been required to report for work, stood by the station: a collection of old warehouses and a redundant sugar beet store accommodating fire-watchers, ARP wardens, messengers – on bicycle and motorbike – and Childe's unit, the hard labour squad.

While the night of the Great Darkness had brought its challenges, and the blackened, smoking ruin of Kew's Mill still towered over the site, the phoney war had so far delivered no air raids, and despite the general panic over fifth columnists and spies arriving by parachute, Cambridge had been spared the sight of the enemy in any form.

As he entered the yard, unchallenged, Brooke encountered a general air of lassitude, if not idleness. A man sat outside a hut marked MECHANICS, checking a tyre for punctures in a bowl of water. Two fire-watchers were hosing down an auxiliary fire engine, although they were more interested in dousing a dog which ran in circles, unable to decide if getting wet was a good idea. The only sense of real purpose clung to a mobile tea van, where two women in WRVS uniforms were busy setting out rows of mugs and piles of sandwiches.

Brooke found a small hut in the old beet store, half-glassed and marked LABOUR OFFICE.

A man with straggly ash-grey hair had his feet up on the desk.

When he saw Brooke, he folded the newspaper he was reading but didn't take his feet down.

Brooke said he wanted to speak to whoever was in charge of the work squad of which Chris Childe was a member.

'Childe? The conchie? He's AWOL,' said the man, turning over what looked like a wad of tobacco in his mouth.

'He's not; he's dead,' said Brooke. 'And I'm in a hurry. What's your name?' he asked, flashing his warrant card.

'Hartnell, senior charge hand,' he said, lowering his feet.

Outside they heard marching and voices.

'This is Chris's lot now,' he said, standing. 'How'd he cop it, then?'

'A bullet to the brain. What was he like?' asked Brooke.

'A loner. Always had a book in his back pocket. But he could work alright . . . A bullet? Christ.'

The men were told to fetch tea and a sandwich and then Hartnell gathered them in the store, telling them to use sacking and old apple crates for chairs. Brooke counted fifteen, half of them teenagers, half of them too old for service, most of them smoking.

'I'm sorry to have to tell you that Chris Childe is dead,' said Brooke. 'His body was found in Mill Road Cemetery this morning. He'd been shot. We're now conducting a murder inquiry.

'I understand from his widow that you all went out the other evening digging on Parker's Piece. This would be the night of the blackout. I need to know what you did, and what Chris did. It's important.'

A teenage lad, lanky and confident, spoke up.

'Nah. Not Parker's Piece. It was down the riverside . . .'

Brooke took out his notebook, forcing himself to let the narrative flow from the witness, in his own time.

The riverside?

He nominated the lad to tell the whole story from the start.

The squad had left the depot at six-thirty. Despite the Great Darkness they'd been issued with lanterns, although they were the kind with metal shields, so that the light could be hidden. They were marched down to Magdalene Bridge by Mr Hartnell, then along to St John's College, where they were allowed to march through the courtyards to the college bridge, where they waited.

'The Bridge of Sighs?' asked Brooke, and the lad nodded. The detail struck a mournful note. The original, of which this was a rough copy, linked the Doge's Palace in Venice with the city jail. Prisoners, trudging over, would look out on the beauty of the city for the last time from its barred windows. On the night of the Great Darkness it must have been a forbidding sight.

'What happened next?' he prompted.

'A soldier met us and took over.'

Hartnell had a clipboard ready and handed Brooke a docket. The soldier who'd taken charge of the men was Corporal S. Currie: Swift-Lane's AWOL pilferer and would-be black marketeer.

Brooke made a further note. 'Go on, lad,' he said.

Currie had marched the men along the riverbank.

'That's when Chris asked this sergeant what they were going to be doing because he'd only volunteered on the promise that he wouldn't be involved in war work,' said the teenager. 'Defence was alright, but he couldn't support killing. That's what he said.'

'What did the soldier, this corporal, say?' asked Brooke.

'He told him to shut up and walk. They were a Civil Defence unit, so that's what it was. Defence work. So we all marched on until we got to St John's Wilderness.'

Then the work began. Pits had been dug and filled before them, because they could see in the dusk the neat mounds of soil. They were told to dig a fresh pit, six feet deep. The soldier set poles at four corners, creating a rectangle about twenty feet by twelve.

It took them two hours to dig the hole.

'The corporal, he was a bragger,' said one of the other teenagers. 'Couldn't stop himself. He said that his unit had dug the other five pits weeks back, and filled 'em in, but they'd complained about the work, and that's why we'd copped for the digging. So someone – you, Ron . . .'

A small elderly man cradling his tea looked startled at the sound of his own name.

'You said: "What did you bury?" and he said we'd to mind our own business. It was top secret, which sounded like bunk, and some of us laughed in his face.

'Then a messenger turned up on foot. They had a bit of a conflab and the corporal changed his tune after that. We'd done a great job, we deserved a rest and a decent meal. All gratis. Mind you, he didn't look pleased, he looked as sick as a dog.

'Then we heard the soldiers, coming along the riverbank from the other direction, from Silver Street. Cart wheels, you could hear 'em. He hears 'em too, the corporal, and marches us off pronto the other way.'

Several others joined in now to chart the squad's journey across Cambridge; back over the river by the Bridge of Sighs, up Trinity Street and through Market Hill, out past the Corn Exchange to the university science quarter, to a new building of white stone.

'The Galen Building, for anatomy?' asked Brooke.

'That's it,' said the lad. 'You got it.'

Brooke felt elated, even dizzy. It was like watching a jigsaw solve itself. Except this wasn't a solution, just a set of new questions.

How were the pits on the riverside linked to the three abandoned lorries? And how did Lux, the scientist, fit in? He'd been at the Galen that night, before his sudden, brutal death.

If anything, the end of the story was the strangest bit of all. They had been taken down into the basement of the Galen, where there was a boiler, and given a slap-up meal: roast beef, boiled potatoes, cauliflower and carrots, with herbs and a rich gravy. Each plate came with a tin cover to keep it warm, and they were told it was college food, and top quality.

Then Corporal Currie reappeared. He produced copies of the Official Secrets Act, and told them all they had to sign, and made it clear that under the Emergency Powers (Defence) Act they were to tell nobody what they'd done that night.

'We're guessing we can tell you,' said the lad to Brooke, and they all laughed.

Currie told them they'd be marched back to the depot in two hours, but in the meantime the basement was warm, so they were to make themselves comfortable.

Which they all did, except Childe.

'He tried the door when Currie buggered off,' said Ron, still sipping his tea. 'But it was locked. He said they couldn't do that. He said that was against natural justice, he talked like that a lot. He said you couldn't make a "pledge retrospectively", so there was no point getting us to sign anything. Flash bugger. He said when he'd signed the paper he'd used a made-up name anyway. "What's going into those pits?" He kept asking that, droning on.'

Upstairs, said the lad, they could hear a film running.

'A *film*?' asked Brooke. 'I was told there was a lecture.'

They all agreed: they could hear a newsreel-style voice, the bass note carrying. It was definitely a film.

Childe had been searching for another way out of the boiler room when he'd stumbled on a small lift in the corner, a dumb waiter, but slightly larger, used for hauling goods up and down to the laboratories above.

'Chris stuck his head in the shaft and said he could hear the film really clearly,' said the lad. 'He called us over, and he was right, although you couldn't make much sense of it. I don't know what got into Chris, but he said he was going to take a look, and if he could, he'd scarper.

'We said he was mad. The lift box was at the top of the shaft but he just grabbed the rope and started on up. There wasn't much to him, and he was no weakling. He went up it like a rat. It was dark, but we could see his shoes, crossed over around the rope. About fifty feet up he stopped for a minute, then there was this flood of light, and we could see him, leaning over, pushing the lift doors apart. Then he kind of swung himself across and out of sight. He might have been a conchie but he had guts.'

Fifteen minutes later he reappeared.

'He'd got himself one of those long rods they use to pull down blinds and he used it to snag the rope. He didn't bother shutting the lift doors so we could see him alright. As I said, fifty feet up, maybe more. Then he loses his hold with one hand and nearly falls. He'd have been dead as meat if he hadn't held on with the other. Then he shimmies down.'

'He looked shocked,' said Ron. 'He said he'd seen the film – or some of it, and that this wasn't stopping here, that people had the right to know what was going on. It was our country just as much as anybody else's. He was shook up, alright. I said to him, "You look like you've seen a ghost, chum."

'He said it was worse. He'd seen the future.'

CHAPTER TWENTY-EIGHT

Edison was waiting outside the depot at the gates, beside the Wasp, cleaning the side mirrors with his handkerchief. Brooke sat down on the running board, lit a cigarette and brought him up to speed on Chris Childe's adventurous evening in the basement of the Galen, or rather, his remarkable *ascent* of the Galen, via the goods lift.

'A film?' asked Edison.

'Indeed. Whatever he saw clearly made an impression. Presumably he described what he'd seen in the letter he gave to Staunton,' said Brooke. 'So, we return to the question: where is she?'

Edison shook his head. 'Brick wall so far, sir. The girls are still checking the electoral rolls. The woman who runs the PPU says Vera worked at the fallen women's shelter in Chesterton two mornings a week – I've asked a car to drop by. There's a rumour, at the PPU, that Vera works nights, if you understand me . . .'

Edison gave Brooke an old-fashioned look.

'Babylon Street, that area anyway.'

Brooke whistled. '*Babylon*. Good God.'

'Makes you think,' added Edison, tightening his tie.

The respectable Vera Staunton, secretary of the Party, might not be the woman Brooke had imagined. He thought back to the picture on the wall of Childe's bedroom; had he detected, and then put aside, a certain forthright sexual frankness in the eyes? An address in Babylon Street placed her at the heart of the city's red-light district.

'Get the local constable to knock on doors,' said Brooke. 'And let's ask County to check the records too; she might have strayed further afield in pursuit of punters. Come to think of it, we need to check our own files. We need that letter, Edison. In fact, I wonder if the killer's got it in their pocket.'

Brooke slid into the passenger seat and closed his eyes, deep in thought.

'One bit of progress,' offered Edison, turning the key on the Wasp's well-oiled four-cylinder engine. 'Our resident pathologist has a sharp eye,' he said, handing Brooke a typed sheet of names and addresses from his inside pocket. 'That's today's list of missing persons for the whole county. Dr Comfort gets a copy in case any of them turn up in his morgue. Note Neville Sneeth, Manor Farm, Horningsea. More to the point, note his distinguishing marks.'

Brooke tracked down the page to Sneeth's name: beside it had been written *CTEV.*

'Congenital talipes equinovarus,' said Edison, proudly. 'Club foot, sir.'

'Just like our runaway lorry driver, later found floating in Byron's Pool,' said Brooke.

'That's it. And a farmer to boot. Looks like he'd found a good way of making a markup on his meat. Uniform have sent a car out to bring in the wife, Elspeth, to identify the body. But there's not much doubt,' said Edison. 'I thought we could take a look at the farm, sir. We'd have the place to ourselves . . .'

Foot down, Edison got the Wasp up to fifty, leaving the city behind, arrowing out into the country along a lane between parallel lines of poplars, the weak sunlight flashing between the trees.

A village, a pub, a sliver of green by a war memorial, and then they were out again, the road snaking up a slow hill on the edge of the Fens.

Edison had clearly memorised the map, as he slowed suddenly and turned down a rutted track to a pair of farm gates. The overnight storm had left the lane awash with ribbons of black water, the surface psychedelic with engine oil and petrol.

Clambering out of the car, Brooke filled his lungs with country air and set out for a barn. 'Let's leave the house until last,' he said, leaving Edison to struggle with a pair of wellington boots.

Manor Farm comprised thirty acres of grassland on a clay hillside. There wasn't an animal in sight, except two horses bent down with the weight of damp blankets, tethered to the gate of the first field. The barn was full of beet on the ground floor, the loft with sacks, carrots spilling out.

Brooke paused at the open doors, surveying the farm. 'Field's full of cow dung,' he said. 'There's a pigsty somewhere, unless my nose deceives me. But where are the animals, Edison? Well. I think we know, don't we. And those' – he pointed down a drove which ran to the woods – 'are the tracks of a lorry . . .'

They led across the field into a narrow defile cut by a half-hearted stream. A small deer, no larger than a dog, stood on the path for a moment and then appeared to dissolve into the shadows with a single visual ripple. Crows cawed above the canopy but were reluctant to land, simply circling in a holding pattern over their heads.

The light levels plunged as they trudged down the valley.

An S-bend brought into sight the ruins of an old water mill. Tarpaulins, draped from a crossbeam, formed a tented area open to the air at both ends, upstream and downstream. The truck tracks stopped at the mill, while downstream they could see the path had been wrecked by the hooves of cattle coming uphill from the fields.

Edison stayed on the edge of the light, peering into the ruins, surveying a blood-stained wooden bench. A raised floor had been constructed of duckboards and extended out over the stream, so that they could just see the water below.

'Abattoir?' asked Edison.

Brooke adjusted his hat. 'Maybe. Or a slaughterhouse. I think they killed the animals here. All the carcasses on the lorries were whole. The butchery's for later.'

Brooke didn't believe in ghosts, but there were places that seemed scarred by time. The trees were rustling and there was a slender soundtrack of water flowing, but on the edge of hearing he thought he could detect the sound of the animals that had queued here by the water: wall-eyed, spooked. Fear ran through the old mill as palpably as the stream.

'We'll need a constable on the spot to preserve the site until we have a full record. Get them to haul the bench back to the station, and the duckboard where it's stained.'

Walking back towards the car, it was Edison who saw something move at the upstairs window of the farmhouse.

'Sir,' he called, pointing. 'A face, just ducked away, looked like a kid.'

The front door was open, the house within a surprise: whitewashed walls, colourful rugs, a vast hearth in the kitchen glowing red with coals. In a pot on the range a stew bubbled.

Edison led the way stiffly up the stairs, calling out, his warrant card held up like a lantern.

They heard a hesitant footstep and then a boy appeared in pyjama bottoms from a bathroom: *boy* was wrong now that they could see him, because he had a sturdy build, and must have been a teenager, although his face was pale and child-like.

His name, he said, was Jed, and he was Neville Sneeth's son.

'The horses are mine,' he said, taking them to the window which looked out across the field. 'Dad said I could keep them.'

He padded back to bed, explaining he'd got a cough and a cold and the doctors were worried about influenza, so he had to stay warm.

The bed looked like a nest, and a fire burnt in a small grate. A blanket lay on the floor where he'd been polishing horse tackle: bits and bridles, and a line of brasses.

'They took the rest of the animals in the lorry, did they?' asked Brooke, but the question remained unanswered.

Jed lay back and closed his eyes. 'Did they find Dad? Mum said I'd best be ready for the worst. He's been worried about money, about the farm. It got him down. I wanted to go with her but she said I should rest. I've been weak, but I'm better already. Maybe I should have gone.'

Jed closed his eyes.

Brooke thought the teenager was being devious. 'The body of a man was found in the river, Jed. Your mother is going to see if it is your father. Until we hear, we don't know for sure.'

The boy nodded, eyes still closed.

'I asked a question, Jed. Where did the pigs and cattle go?'

'I've been out of it,' he said, meeting Brooke's eyes. 'I need to rest now,' he added, shutting his eyes again, although Brooke could see movement beneath the lids.

'We'll make you a cup of tea,' said Brooke. 'My sergeant is just going to look round . . .'

Edison set off along the landing to check all the rooms while Brooke slipped into the bathroom to wash the dirt of the slaughterhouse off his hands. An old bath stood on wooden blocks, beside a porcelain washbasin. Turning on the tap, he watched the clear water wash away a neat line of three bright red drops of fresh blood.

CHAPTER TWENTY-NINE

That night, Claire took Brooke to the pictures to see *Goodbye, Mr Chips* at the Regal, just a hundred yards from the Spinning House. She had a shift off, and they always tried to use the opportunity to establish the ghostly outline of a real life. Brooke took his third pair of glasses, the ones tinted a deep shadowy blue. They gave the black and white film a surreal marine hue.

Sitting in the flickering light, he tried to weave together the threads of the various cases under inquiry into some kind of coherent pattern. Earlier, in his office, he'd resorted to his blackboard and chalk, drawing what was now being called a Venn diagram, in honour of the gifted young scientist who'd invented the concept not half a mile away, at Gonville and Caius College. Three circles: one for the meat wagons on Castle Hill, one for the riverside pits and one for the American scientist Lux. Besides the fact that they had in common a moment in time – the Great Darkness – what else linked them all? In the space where the three circles overlapped he'd written a single word: *film*, and a single name: *Currie*.

Goodbye, Mr Chips passed him by, except for a scene towards the end in which the eponymous schoolteacher stood in a chapel reading out the daily list of former pupils killed in the trenches, pausing to add the name of a German friend, met on a teenage Alpine adventure, who had fallen with the rest. The audience in the cinema, packed beneath drifting cigarette smoke, respected a tense silence.

Later, at home, they ate liver, a rice pudding, and drank another of his father's bottles of wine. In bed, the window open as always, they listened to the distant whisper of the river: not one stream here, but several, diverted into mill streams and ponds, backwaters and pools, finally falling over the weir downstream. The view from the bedroom was more water than land.

Sleepless, they played out a small ritual which had become a drug, imagining precisely the scene at that moment if they'd been with Joy and Luke.

Brooke went first: his son would be outside, under the stars, with the small telescope he'd given him as a farewell gift at the station.

Claire took Joy's last letter as a starting point, in which she'd mentioned a young doctor called Ben. 'I hope they're in bed too,' she said, and Brooke affected a gasp.

'The real war's coming,' said Claire, by way of explanation. 'They should seize the day.'

Brooke slept fitfully, transported back in time to a hospital bed; precisely, a sanatorium a few miles outside Scarborough. The scene recalled was vivid because he knew what was going to happen next. The door at the end of the ward would open and an officer – a captain – would walk down the aisle between the beds and, calling for attention, announce that the war was over, or that it would be over, in under ten minutes.

So: 11th November 1918, around 10.50 a.m.

At that moment Claire was sitting on the edge of his bed. He'd called her Little Nurse Tidy persistently, until she'd given up her resistance and revealed her real name. Romantic rubbish, of course, but as soon as he heard the word itself, it seemed astonishingly familiar.

'Tell me a fact and a secret and I'll do the same,' she'd said, surreptitiously taking his pulse.

They'd made him glasses with an odd purple tint and it gave the sunshine a sickly quality, which made him ache for air, but all the windows were shut. Earlier, he'd asked her what the surgeons thought about his knee, if he'd walk again, and she'd evaded any answer.

'I've been awarded a medal,' he said. 'That's a fact. The secret is I don't deserve it.'

'What medal?' said Claire.

'Well, the DSO. The Distinguished Service Order. I'm not sure there is actually a medal.' He looked out of the full-length window, searching for the broken shard of blue light which revealed the sea through the screen of trees. He imagined a beach, with white sand, and a view to the horizon. 'It's an award. An order. It's for bravery.'

'Why don't you deserve it?'

'I was captured. I didn't talk. But I was scared, terrified really. I don't think I knew what the truth was. I hardly deserve a medal for that.'

'One of your visitors said you'd saved the lives of hundreds of men, maybe thousands.'

He closed his eyes, knowing that for a few seconds it would relieve the pain, which felt as if it ran along an electric wire around his skull.

'Now you,' he said.

When he opened his eyes, she was walking back from the window where she'd lowered the blind. A minute may have passed, or just a few seconds. The man in the next bed whimpered in his sleep and his left foot appeared from under the sheet.

Claire checked her watch. 'I have five brothers, that's a fact.'

Brooke immediately understood, because he could imagine the chaos and the swirl of family life, and the need to impose order and neatness and calm.

'And a secret?'

She came round the bed to tuck in the sheet and her lips were close to his ear.

'The surgeon says they'll fix your leg, that you'll walk again, and that the road to recovery begins tomorrow in the pool in the basement. They're going to make you swim.'

CHAPTER THIRTY

At his desk by six, Brooke felt revitalised. The blackboard still held the circular patterns of the Venn diagram he'd scrawled the night before. After a breakfast at the Masonic Hall, he made a series of calls, until Edison appeared, rubbing puffy eyes, a bacon sandwich in one hand. 'Nothing to report from the riverbank,' he said, stepping over the threshold. 'I stayed till well past midnight. Quiet as the grave. And bloody cold.'

'Fancy a drive?' asked Brooke. 'Petrol on expenses.'

'The Wasp's in the yard, sir. She's got a full tank.'

'A treat, then, Edison,' he said. He gave him a set of the photographs they'd had taken of Turl, with orders to deliver them to Sheffield, the hometown of their runaway black marketeer, Stanley Currie. The corporal was now at the heart of their enquiries into black-market meat. Had he run home? Was he in cahoots with Turl and the rest?

'Put your foot down and you'll be there and back by nightfall,' said Brooke. 'I've rung the station at West Bar and they're expecting you. Check out the Currie family garage in the city centre. Do what you can. We've got Turl, Sneeth's in the morgue. Maybe they know where we can find the third driver, the one Turl called Ginger?'

A note from the commissioner's office, Scotland Yard, reiterating the Home Secretary's personal interest in the case, had come to Brooke via Carnegie-Brown, so he gave Edison that as well. 'If they're not cooperating, show them that. If they don't help us crack this case, Sergeant, Scotland Yard will be heading north.'

Edison vanished, taking his bacon sandwich for the journey.

For the rest of the morning Brooke tried to track down Vera Staunton, but she was proving an insubstantial presence. Door-to-door enquiries in Babylon Street had raised nothing. There was no record of her at the magistrates' court, or in their own books, although the county police force was still checking its files. Finally, he'd made a call to the identity card centre at the Home Office: but that could take months to produce a result.

Sipping his third cup of stewed tea, he reluctantly decided that they might be dealing with an alias. Finding Staunton's missing comrades in the Party presented a similar challenge. Where were Henderson, Lauder and Popper? More to the point, what was their fate? Had they fled before their rooms were searched, or had they been hauled away? Were they, like Childe, victims of a calculating killer? Brooke had circulated their ID numbers to the ports, and informed Henderson's employers. He could do little else but wait, and hope.

Which left him with the film shown at the Galen on the night of the Great Darkness. What was its subject? What had been buried in the riverside pits? What was the link between the two? A briefing was necessary, and the commanding officer at Madingley Hall was the perfect man to deliver the facts. Colonel Swift-Lane's assurances to leave well alone now looked threadbare. It was time to come clean.

Brooke rang Captain Kerridge.

'I'd ask his deputy if I could,' said Kerridge. 'Major Stone's more likely to tip the wink if it saves time and effort, but he's off at the War Office for a two-day briefing, all hush-hush. Which leaves us with Colonel Swift-Lane. He's hardly the type to offer up classified information. I'll try. If I get anywhere I'll ring, but he's already laid down the law on this to you in person. For now, just leave it with me.'

By nightfall, Brooke had reread the relevant files and made a brief summary report for Carnegie-Brown. Then he set a lamp over Elspeth Sneeth's statement and speed-read from the top for the third time, his eyes travelling vertically down the middle of the typewritten page. It was an unremarkable story, but for the fact that it led – ultimately – and with a remorseless logic, to the body on Dr Comfort's autopsy table, the white limbs tangled in the green river weed from Byron's Pool.

Neville Sneeth was the third son of a Lincolnshire farmer. He'd married Elspeth, a dairy maid, in 1925. After saving a down payment of £100, they'd secured the lease of Manor Farm, Horningsea, in 1937. The land had been recommended to them by cousins who ran a smallholding near Newmarket. It had not been a sound piece of advice. They'd struggled to meet the rent, and had only managed to stay afloat in their third year thanks to a loan from one of Neville's older brothers, the owner of an agricultural haulage business in Gainsborough.

Brooke had a map of England up on the wall and found Gainsborough exactly on a level with his eyes, just thirty miles from Sheffield.

The causal connections between Sneeth and the black market were compelling: debt, a loan, Sheffield, livestock, meat, cash – or, more pertinently, the lack of it. Mrs Sneeth's summary hinted at what she'd guessed: *I didn't ask too many questions. Nev said he'd got a good deal and that 'needs must'. There'd be cash, he said, and a surplus for new stock in the spring. I knew about the slaughterhouse by the mill, I'm not blind. He said to keep away. He said it meant they didn't have to pay for the red tape, that he could go straight to market. All Nev had to do was provide the meat, and drive the lorry.*

Brooke was rereading the statement when his phone rang: one of Dr Comfort's assistants informed him that the autopsy on Christopher Childe was about to begin in the Galen's mortuary. Five minutes later Brooke was looking at the young man's body, laid out on its metal table. The exit wound had destroyed the back of the skull, but his face was strangely untouched, except for the entry wound at his temple. Brooke struggled to concentrate on his facial expression of mild surprise, and the fact that his lips were parted as if about to speak. It was difficult to escape the conclusion that this was the face of an innocent victim. Brooke endured the external examination, but left when one of the servants stepped forward with the breadknife, the saw designed to lop off the top of the cranium.

Back in his office, he returned to the paperwork under a desk lamp. Outside a siren wailed, and the lights of the city began to flicker out into total darkness.

As Great St Mary's struck ten he heard a car dashing gravel in the yard below. Looking down, he watched Edison get out of the car, straighten his back, then pat the roof, as if the Wasp were a family pet, with which he had just completed a long walk.

'How was the city of steel?' asked Brooke when Edison appeared, carrying a tray on which lay the night shift canteen dinner: meat pie, mashed potatoes and carrots. Brooke cleared his desk so that his detective sergeant could eat in comfort.

'I took the Great North road; I flew,' said Edison, stabbing a piece of nameless meat. 'Currie, our vanishing sergeant, is permanently AWOL, I'm afraid; body turned up yesterday on some waste ground in the Don Valley, a mile or two from the city centre. Always famous for it, Sheffield, gang wars, but I thought they'd got it under control. Place is infernal.'

Edison shook his head, only stopping to ladle some potato into his mouth. 'There wasn't much left of him either. Body burnt beyond recognition. They chucked his wallet on top of the cold corpse so everyone would know it was him. Just as Turl predicted.

'Police surgeon gave me ten minutes. Body appeared to have been "primed", his word – grease maybe, a heavy engine oil. Signature killing, that's the ticket, used by one of the gangs. They've never found the scene of crime, but they're reckoning a garage sump, vehicle pit, that kind of thing. Roll the body in, there's evidence of ligatures, add some accelerant, and then a match. Effective, sir, not a scrap of evidence. So, they did the obvious and checked out the Currie family garage,' he said, brushing pastry flakes from his shirt.

Edison consulted his notebook, set down beside his plate. 'Bit of a tip. Moorfoot Motors, but the sign was new, and you could see the old name underneath: Loxley Garage, same as the name on the patched-up fuel tank underneath the lorry on Castle Hill. West Bar will get forensics to give the place a check but the place was dusty, so I don't think we'll get much. Currie didn't die there.'

He took a breath, forcing himself to sip his tea. 'And they came up with an ID on our friend in the cells,' he said. 'By sight. Took them less than a minute. He's a gang member. Real name's Jack Gretorix. They think they know this Ginger, too – so they'll keep an eye out. There's a whole rat king of 'em.'

Brooke smiled: it was such a good phrase – *rat king* – a tangle of vermin, teeth sunk into each other.

'At least he told us his true first name,' said Brooke. 'That's arrogance, of course. It'll be his downfall.'

Edison put his tea down and ran a finger through the gravy left on the plate.

'They'll help us if they can but they've got the Home Office on *their* backs,' he said. 'Government's terrified of sabotage, that a Jerry spy might bomb one of the munitions factories. They've got this piece of kit, sir, in one of the steelworks, which can punch out a cam shaft for a Spitfire. One blow. Only one in the country. Whole war could hinge on it. A stick of high explosives and there'd be no new Spitfires in the air.

'No police leave, everyone out on the streets, CID and uniforms, on the lookout for strangers. Which explains why the gangs are back in business.'

For a moment they sat in silence.

'If the meat was going north, and there's more than one convoy, then they'd need a refrigeration plant,' said Brooke. 'A big one.'

'They took a note on that. But as I say, sir, they're stretched . . .'

'I've just come from the autopsy on Chris Childe,' said Brooke, checking his watch. 'But there's not much to know. A bullet to the brain is a bullet to the brain. And no gun found.'

'I better turn in, sir,' said Edison, standing. 'I picked this up downstairs just now,' he added, producing a note. 'From County: they've found our Vera at last. Babylon Street, so much for door-to-door enquiries. Two previous convictions for soliciting out at Strawberry Fair. It's a way back, mind you – 1920, 1921. Since then there's nothing.'

Edison checked his watch. 'She'll be working now,' he said.

'First thing, then,' said Brooke. 'And Edison . . .'

'Sir?' The sergeant leant on the door frame.

'Well done.'

CHAPTER THIRTY-ONE

Brooke, on the bunk in cell six, closed his eyes and let sleep fall like a blow, obliterating his world: the narrow stone room, the medieval building above, the city beyond, his house by the river. This release came so rarely that he smiled as he fell away into the darkness.

A confused dream threaded its way through his subconscious. A dark, grey sky lowered over a city that didn't look like Cambridge. From a rooftop, he glanced up and realised they weren't clouds at all, but balloons, massed in their thousands, jostling, and just beyond them, in the stratosphere, the sound of cart wheels turning: mighty, celestial cart wheels.

Looking down, he saw a lake and, just beneath the surface, the pale outline of a woman swimming naked. Although her hair was dark he knew it was Claire. Gliding towards him, she reached the water's edge and, hauling herself up on the bank, looked him in the face. In her eyes he saw fire, a single flame burning in each.

He woke up and heard the echo of his own cry. For a moment he lay still, listening for movement through the stone wall from Turl's cell.

By his watch the time was four. Switching on the light in the outer corridor, he selected the key for cell five from the bunch he'd used to open six.

This time Turl was ready for him.

'I heard the scream,' he said, nodding to the connecting wall with cell six. 'Bad dreams?'

'I promised I'd be back,' said Brooke. 'We try not to disappoint.'

'No spotlight; you're losing your touch.'

'The wheels are in motion, Jack,' said Brooke. 'A new plan for a new man: Jack Gretorix. You're a crook, Jack Gretorix. The police at West Bar know your face.'

Brooke gave him back his tobacco and rolling tin.

'Your confederate, Stanley Currie? I hope he wasn't a friend, because he's dead, Jack.'

Turl couldn't hide his reaction to the news, his skin stiffening over the bones of his face.

'Body soaked in oil, then lit, as you predicted. So presumably he cocked up too. Not very forgiving, are they?'

Gretorix just shrugged, but he didn't deny knowing Currie.

'So here it is, Jack. The time has come. I'm going to ring West Bar in the morning and say that I'm releasing you to their custody. You'll go north. They'll make it known you're back on the manor. Then they'll let you go. They'll also make it known that you've given us names, places, times. That's either going to loosen your tongue, or it's going to lead with some certainty to a garage somewhere; you'll have a mental picture, I'm sure. A garage with a sump or a vehicle pit. This is your last night here, Jack. After that, it's out of my hands.'

Turl ran a pale tongue along the edge of his cigarette paper. 'Do what you want, copper. When I'm gone you'll still be having the nightmares.'

'True. But you'll be in a grave somewhere on a hillside, Jack. Bunch of wilting flowers in a jam jar by the headstone. Think on that, Jack. And this: the world will be a better place when you're gone. You know that, so do I.'

He left him with the tobacco tin, as if a cigarette was his last wish before execution, and climbed the stairs.

The sergeant on the duty desk said the night was a quiet one, but he'd been asked to point out a note from switchboard in Brooke's pigeonhole which was untouched.

Brooke retrieved the slip of paper. The call was timed for that day at five in the evening and was curt:

Caller refused to leave full name or contact details but said the message was from the NIGHT CLIMBERS. Message related to Ernst Lux. ASK FOR MARCUS ASHMORE AT MICHAELHOUSE.

Brooke wondered which one of *Hay Fever*'s thespians had broken rank. The message itself was startling enough: Marcus Ashmore, Jo's older brother, was a research student, like Ernst Lux, at Michaelhouse College. Was he a night climber? Had he been aloft when the scientist fell to his death? What had his sister seen from her rooftop observation post?

CHAPTER THIRTY-TWO

Jo Ashmore had one shoe up on the parapet, binoculars to her eyes. She was scanning the western horizon, ignoring Brooke's brisk arrival up the vertical ladder to her rooftop observation post.

'The kettle's in the hut,' she said, without turning round. 'Help yourself.'

Even now, even here, she cut a stylish figure. Her gas mask sat nicely on the hip, perfectly judged, a cardboard box transformed into an item of fashion.

He mashed tea in two mugs, using evaporated milk from a little can and adding sugar to both.

'It had been bothering me,' said Brooke, carefully. 'The night climbers are back on the rooftops of the city but you haven't seen them. And you're such a diligent lookout.'

She kept the binoculars to her eyes.

'Does it matter?' she said.

'A man's died.'

She took up her mug of tea.

'The man we thought had been killed by the drifting barrage balloon had been climbing. He fell. Then someone dragged his body clear of Michaelhouse College, and dressed the corpse with a scrap of half-burnt latex. The town was covered in the stuff from the blimp that exploded by the station.'

Brooke turned, sitting on the parapet. 'I've just checked the victim's file. It contains a plan of his set of rooms at Michaelhouse with the names of the other students pencilled in; my sergeant's the painstaking type, slow but sure. Room opposite Lux's is your brother Marcus's. There's a list of Lux's friends and everyone thinks Marcus and he were close. There's a girlfriend too, but she's a bit shadowy. Marcus was a bit cooler about Lux, said they were colleagues, and that the American "kept to himself", which is a bit of a tired cliché on the best of days.'

Jo bent her head back to study the sky, where occasional stars fidgeted between clouds.

'Which leaves me with the same question, and still no answer,' said Brooke. 'If the night climbers are back, why were they not spotted by a bright-eyed observer with her own rooftop eyrie?'

To the south, the sound of a plane's engine pulsed a few times, fading fast, but Ashmore didn't react.

'I must talk to Marcus, Jo. I don't want to turn up at the college and set any bells ringing unnecessarily. I understand the risk: that if he's caught, they could chuck him out, which would end his career. I don't want to do that; I don't need to do it. But I do have to talk to him. So I need a go-between. On this occasion, Jo, that's you. I think that's a pretty a decent offer from your brother's point of view.'

Jo went over to the conical post hut and came back with a half-bottle of brandy, pouring a shot in both their cups.

'You've never asked, either you or Claire, why I'm up here, why I've left the life I had. Glamorous, wasn't it? The parties, the late nights in London. I was having rather a good time.'

She took a gulp from the mug, masking a wince as the spirit kicked home.

'Oddly, all this' – she indicated the OP – 'is about keeping a low profile. Daddy's words. You won't have heard, it's only important in the world he lives in, but the chair's up soon and it's his by rights. *Professor Ashmore*. Someone once asked me why academics are so nasty to each other. It's because there's so little at stake. I rather like that.

'There was a scandal, Brooke, but not a public one. I caused this scandal. There, that's me taking *responsibility for my actions*. That lifestyle of mine. I met a man at the Criterion one night. There's a jazz club on Kingly Street, behind Liberty's. I was seen with him, often seen with him. Mistakes were made. I took a risk. I needed help, medical help. It's been . . .'

'You don't have to tell me, Jo.'

'I'm enjoying telling you. No. Enjoyment's not the word. But it is doing me good. You're that kind of man, Brooke. People want you to think well of them. So this helps . . . I think I'm looking for forgiveness.'

'You're forgiven,' he said.

She knocked out a cigarette from a packet and, shading it from the night breeze, lit it in the dark shadow created by her lapel.

'A *public* scandal, a hint of one, might have got back to the college, to the department.'

'What of the man from the Criterion?'

'If you could call him a man.' She gave a bitter laugh, and Brooke thought he saw her future, after the war, regretting a night out in London.

'I didn't see the night climbers during the Great Darkness, but they often avoid the roofline, so that's no surprise,' she said. 'But I've seen them this autumn. My shift is three nights on, three nights off. Marcus knows the schedule. Marcus is bored; he wanted to fight, but Daddy pulled strings. The government needs gifted mathematicians. So that's him for the Duration.

'So he's kicking his heels, and prepared to risk it all, including Daddy's reputation, with his silly, deadly night games. Perhaps we're more alike than I ever thought. He wanted to climb, for the thrill of it. In his case, a slightly chilly thrill. I think it's one of the few things that actually lights up his life. He's tried gambling, but apparently it doesn't even come close. He asked me to turn a blind eye, for Daddy's sake, which was a nice touch.'

She turned to face Brooke. 'Sorry,' she said.

'Apology accepted.'

'Where do you want to see him?'

'My house. Tomorrow, at six? He can use the old gate from the meadow, the back door's open. Tell him I just need to know the truth.'

CHAPTER THIRTY-THREE

Peter Aldiss was in what he referred to as the 'roach room', monitoring changes in habit related to light amongst several hundred specimens of the *Blattodea*. The study of circadian rhythms was a ceaseless labour. Brooke had long ago declined the opportunity of seeing them in the flesh, as it were. Even here, in the coldly lit laboratory, he thought he could hear the insects through the door, the strange, almost metallic rustle of their carapaces touching the concrete floor as they fled into the corners, like shadows. The fireflies, behind their door, were silent.

Aldiss appeared with a single cockroach in a glass beaker which he set on the bench-top, cleaning his hands with a cloth.

'Did you find our night climbers?' he asked.

'I'm close, thanks to you.' Brooke sat at one of the sturdy laboratory benches. 'You said you'd try and find out more about Lux's work . . . ?' he asked.

The manner of the American's death, or rather its mysterious concealment, disturbed Brooke. He wanted to know more before confronting Marcus Ashmore. Had he simply dragged the scientist's body away from the college buildings to protect his own academic career? It was the coincident death of Childe which rankled. Lux had been at the Galen that night, and he too had seen the film. Brooke was on the trail of a motive for something darker than an accident; could it lie in the American's work?

'I asked,' said Aldiss. 'They're a bit jumpy, as you can imagine, the powers that be. The professorial class is not exactly given to idle chat. In the end I was honest, often a disastrous tactic, but it worked this time. I said you wanted to know about Lux's field of study. The name helps. Your father's still . . . what's the word, Brooke? Revered.

'So I was allowed an answer of sorts. Let me show you,' said Aldiss, walking over to the light switches and plunging them back into darkness.

'See?' Aldiss's voice came from the corner.

What was clear was the illuminated face of his watch, swinging from side to side like a pendulum.

The lights, restored, revealed the watch, free of the scientist's wrist, now laid out on the bench like an exhibit.

'They get women to paint the numbers on these watch faces, there's a big factory in the States. United Radium. They're the market leaders. So, imagine I am such a woman in such a factory . . .'

He put his empty mug to one side and from the bench drawer produced the finest of paintbrushes.

'I put glowing dots on the backs of the roaches with this. I can see certain individuals in the dark. Imagine my mug holds the paint.'

He picked up the brush, put it in his mouth and drew it back through his lips, then pretended to dip it in the paint, acting out the precise craft of configuring the tiny numerals on a watch face. Then he licked the brush again, repeating the procedure.

'Do that every time and you can imagine the result. They called them the radium girls, the victims. They were told the paint was harmless, so for fun they painted their nails, and lips. Piecework, of course, paid 1.5 cents per watch dial. Hundreds contracted radium poisoning. The symptoms are off the scale in terms of unpleasant, necrosis of the jaw being perhaps the worst. The company said those who claimed the radium was to blame had in fact contracted syphilis. Five took the company to court. They won, thank God. Now we know the truth.'

'And Lux?'

'An expert in bioluminescence. Nature's *natural* electricity. Imagine, if we could work out how that works. Even I'd be grateful; I'd know how the firefly glows, Brooke. And no more horrific deaths at United Radium . . .' He thought the idea through. 'Better, no United Radium at all.

'So that comprised his research area, and I'm sure there was ample funding, especially from the US. But the best chemists are here. So that was the link-up. When the war broke out he was persuaded to offer his services in some form to that great collective: the War Effort. In what form, I do not know. I am simply gratified he shared some of the findings of his own research with the rest of us. He put a circular out to all the labs last year on the hazards.

'I never lick the brush.'

CHAPTER THIRTY-FOUR

Claire was back on nights, and their house at Newnham Croft was intolerably empty without her, but Brooke sensed a further episode of momentary sleep was circling. He needed to find a place to rest. A return to cell six, beside the prisoner Turl, was out of the question. Leaving Aldiss to his roaches, he set off across Parker's Piece, past Fenner's, the university cricket ground, and down a cul-de-sac at the end of which stood a tall house. For a year now there had always been a night light at the bedroom window on the third floor of the narrow facade.

The front door, unlocked, led into a hallway in which a mirror reflected Brooke's silhouette: a tall figure, narrowing to the shoes, the hat slightly tipped forward. Climbing the steps softly to the third floor, he slipped into a bedroom across the landing where a body stirred in the dark shadow below the open window, the feeble night light on the ledge.

'Frank,' said Brooke, by way of introduction. 'The bedside lamp?' he asked.

'Why not?' said a voice, unfurred by sleep. 'Light, dark, day, night. I've lost my place in the world.'

Former Detective Chief Superintendent Frank Edwardes lay revealed by the electric lamp, propped up on a bolster, his usual pallor, a kind of damp marble, perhaps a little more pronounced than usual.

Edwardes, a stalwart of the Spinning House for thirty years, was Brooke's mentor. After the war, when Brooke had come home from the hospital to take up his studies again, he'd discovered the allure of the natural sciences had faded, and his wounded eyes left study a struggle. Besides, he felt he'd left his student self somewhere out on the sands beyond the oasis east of Gaza. A return to his former life would have been surreal.

Detection, the logical art of securing the victory of good over evil, caught his imagination. But for his extreme sensitivity to light, diagnosed as photophobia, his body had made a sound recovery from his capture in the desert, and he'd passed the Borough's medical with flying colours. Given he was never asked how he slept, his insomnia went unrecorded. His actual vision, in terms of focus, was rated 20:20, but the tinted lenses were needed to reduce the intensity of light. Edwardes, newly promoted on *his* return from Flanders, contrived to make sure the two years Brooke faced in uniform, before moving on to the detective branch, were largely restricted to the night beat. The necessary medical documentation mentioned only a prescription for sunglasses, a category of disablement not covered by the constabulary code.

Edwardes, diagnosed with stomach cancer, had taken sick leave a year earlier. Brooke called at the house to keep him up to date on current cases, and use the armchair for rest.

'I presume you've been swimming?' said Edwardes, a note of genuine irritation in his voice. 'I'm told there are deluded individuals who use the river for sport.'

Brooke's night-time swims were a subject of suppressed scandal at the Spinning House. As a constable in his first year on the force, Brooke had been put on a charge, discovered by his sergeant bathing in the river with his uniform neatly folded on the bank. Edwardes had set the penalty aside, but a sense of moral indignation lingered.

'Not tonight,' said Brooke. 'Soon it'll be too cold.'

To one side of the bed, a bank of electronic equipment filled a wall. Gadgets hummed, not with a single note, but an array, so that the overall effect was of a group of singers trying to produce a chord a cappella style. Several of the upper boxes had the half-lit facades of radios.

Edwardes was one of several thousand 'hams' – amateur radio enthusiasts – recruited across Britain to monitor the ether. These official duties allowed them to keep their radios, which would otherwise have been confiscated. Any traffic considered of interest had to be recorded and logged. Given his illness, these new-found duties were a blessing, in that they gave his hobby a frisson of genuine excitement.

Tonight, while the radios hummed, the airwaves were silent.

The old man was in pain. He held himself with a certain tension, calculating each move of hand or head. Reaching out, he located a glass of milk by the bed and sipped it, leaving a white tidemark to match the others encircling the tumbler.

They heard the rattle of a kettle on a stove below.

'How's Kat?' asked Brooke. Edwardes' wife had worked at the hospital with Claire, as a geriatric nurse.

'Thirty years on the ward and she gets to retire in time to find her home's not her home at all, but a one-bed hospital. She's taking it well.'

Brooke made himself comfortable in the deep chair.

'Sleep if you want,' said Edwardes. 'If not, what's the case?'

Brooke tried to focus. 'You'll know all about the conchie, shot dead in Mill Road, at the cemetery?'

Edwardes nodded. 'A conchie? I didn't hear that bit.'

'Member of the local communist party too. Three of his comrades have gone missing to boot. Puff of smoke, and they're gone. Where, why? Either they've done a collective runner, or they're dead too. In which case we've got a killer loose on the streets. I need to find them, Frank. Find them quickly. We've tracked down a woman the victim saw on the day he died; we'll speak to her tomorrow. But I'd like to find her missing comrades, too . . . Especially as one of them had a radio in his loft.'

'Really?'

'Tuned to Moscow. It had a microphone attached too.'

'That's a transmitter, so he could get messages out. Blimey. Let's hope he didn't know anything he shouldn't have . . .' Edwardes struggled to sit up straighter against his pillows. 'Not that easy to disappear these days. Tried the ports?'

Brooke nodded.

'Did they have coupons for petrol? Did they have a car?' asked Edwardes. 'Trains are the best bet. If they had a head start maybe they travelled together.'

Brooke nodded. 'One of them, with the radio, is a union man on the railways.'

'There you are, then. They get free travel. Kind of thing a ticket collector would remember. A nod, a chat, a moan about wages. If they've gone south to London you can kiss goodbye to 'em. But west, east or north, you've got a chance.'

A distinct regular beep suddenly came into sharp aural focus in the room. Edwardes calmly picked up a log book and began to jot down five letter groups. But the beeps faded quickly, and then were gone.

Brooke rubbed his eyes and wished Kat would bring up some tea.

'Slept tonight?' asked Edwardes.

'An hour, a bit less.'

Brooke's eyelids closed, his brain slipping into neutral for a fleeting second: he let the unfamiliar sense of falling overwhelm him, like the tumbling giddiness of the drunk. His body spun but never seemed to complete the three hundred and sixty degrees required to return to its starting place.

Waking up was what he remembered next, as if he'd fallen into the room from another dimension. The beeps of a fresh transmission filled the air. Edwardes' hand flew, adept at transliterating the dots and dashes, setting down letters on paper.

Kat appeared with two cups of tea and set one beside Brooke, taking away one which was cold, and must have been left for him earlier.

Catching his eye, she looked at her husband feverishly taking down the code, then rolled her eyes. 'That'll be Goering, trying to reserve a punt for Goebbels. Love to Claire, if you ever see her,' she said, retreating.

From under the bed, Edwardes retrieved a silver cigarette box. Brooke stuck to his Black Russians.

The old man blew a smoke ring. 'Here's a thought, young Brooke. Officially, there's a few hundred of us radio hams across the country, but there's *six of us* in Cambridge. We meet up. It doesn't say you can't. Apparently, a place like Hull – a port city, and in the frontline – has got just one operator. Six here. Why?'

'You tell me,' said Brooke.

'Half the university's on government work. Classified this, classified that. One of the other hams has got a son who works at the labs on Free School Lane. He told his dad that he'd had to sign all sorts and he couldn't tell him a thing. But he gave him this . . .'

Edwardes showed Brooke the book he'd been leaning on: *A Trip to Catch the Sun* by H. G. Wells.

'Science fiction, Frank, no more,' said Brooke.

'But you haven't read it, have you?'

Brooke felt like the new boy again in the Spinning House. Edwardes had a gift for spotting bullshit.

'It's about what Wells calls a *perpetual bomb*,' said Edwardes. 'It never stops burning, Brooke. The force of the sun held in a particle so small it's invisible. An atom. The world's at war again in this story, and it makes the last lot look like a picnic, this lot too – so far. Then, at the last moment, Wells has all the governments get together and see sense. Wells is an optimist, Brooke. That's the only bit I don't believe.'

He tossed the book to the floor.

CHAPTER THIRTY-FIVE

Sergeant Edison waited on the corner of Babylon Street in the early morning rain, his eyes – under cover of a wide black umbrella – searching the windows and doorsteps of the red-light district with a keen interest. The street itself, a hundred yards long before it came to an abrupt full stop demanded by a railway embankment, was deserted. The gutters must have been blocked because the rain had formed an unbroken mirror of the road, reflecting low grey clouds. Brooke, approaching from the Kite, noted again Edison's ability to look like a policeman even in plain clothes.

'Sir,' said Edison by way of welcome, lifting the umbrella to accommodate his superior.

'Number twelve's our girl . . .'

They knocked loudly for a full minute before the door opened.

A young woman in a nightdress finally appeared, rubbing her eyes.

'We're looking for Vera Staunton,' said Brooke, and held up his warrant.

'Try Ida,' she said, opening the door and nodding down a tiled corridor to another door, half-glazed. 'She keeps an eye out for all of us. Sees who comes, who goes. She'll know if Vera's free.

'Mind you, it might be Ida's day for the clinic,' she added. 'She's ancient, and her heart's dodgy, even if it is in the right place.'

She slipped back inside the ground floor front flat.

They knocked on Ida's door, but all this produced was a chorus of cat meows from inside the flat. A beaded curtain blocked the view through the glass pane set in the door. On the mat, Brooke noted a letter with a Glasgow postmark and a neat copperplate name and address.

'Let's find Vera on our own,' said Brooke, leading the way up the stairs.

Each floor had three rooms, all marked with names hand-printed on cards: Marge, Gilly, Esther, Bethy . . .

Vera Staunton was at her door when they arrived, her face bisected by the security chain. Brooke offered his warrant card and said they were making routine enquiries, and they'd like to take ten minutes of her time.

The main room held a double bed, a drinks trolley, a changing screen and a large mirror. She offered them seats, while she slipped into a stylish art deco chair. Edison stayed on his feet and asked some perfunctory questions – name, date of birth, ID number – while Brooke cradled his hat, considering the woman.

She wore a nightdress, which had fallen open to reveal a slip; unworried by the intimacy, she stretched out her bare legs, slender feet and wriggling toes. Her hair was artfully dyed, but her skin – despite some face powder and blusher – revealed the lines of time.

Edison dragged one of the stools back a yard and sat down abruptly, making the pair of songbirds in their silver cage beat their wings against the bars.

Brooke took up the interview. 'You'll have heard the news? About Chris Childe?'

'Yes. The Party looks after its own. There's only four or five active members, but we've twenty or more on the books. The news is out. But it's difficult to know what to think.' She examined her nails, in what Brooke thought was a show of studied indifference. 'Poor Chris. How's Mary?'

'We think Chris was murdered,' he said, ignoring her question. 'We need to know why someone would do such a thing. Mrs Childe said he came to you with a letter, an urgent report she called it. Two questions: what was the content of his report, and did you post it as he asked?'

She wrapped the loose nightdress closer around her shoulders.

'He said he'd been a witness. That he'd seen something important and that the branch committee had decided he should make an official statement. I simply addressed the envelope to our Cadogan Square offices in London, for the attention of the general secretary, and went out to get stamps to post it. Chris suggested recorded delivery but I said – if anything – that might be more likely to get intercepted en route. Better lose it in the millions of letters posted every day.'

She looked around her room. 'Chris didn't stay long . . . he may have found my circumstances offensive.'

Setting a hand on the bed, laden with a variety of throws and blankets and silks in exotic patterns, she brought her legs up under her in a single fluid movement. 'Chris was excitable, a bit of an innocent. Some of us have to live in the real world. Clever, alright, that was Chris, but a bit disappointed at his life, this life . . .'

She kissed the back of her hand and examined the trace of lipstick on her skin. 'I must be a sight,' she said.

'He didn't know you were a prostitute?' asked Brooke, running out of patience with the euphemisms.

She rocked back a little on her seat, then shrugged. 'I think they all knew, or they guessed. Chris? Maybe not – as I say, an innocent. There have been times I've spoken up for the girls, women like me, at meetings.'

'This letter, the addressee . . . ?' prompted Brooke.

She threw her head back. 'Chris wanted me to send it to Pollitt, but he's been given the elbow. The new man's Palme Dutt.'

She spelt out the name letter by letter, as Edison took a note.

'Hardly matters, because he won't see it anytime soon. I've been to Cadogan Square, Inspector. It's a tip. Books, papers, everywhere. Meetings in every room, generating more paper. And Palme Dutt's abroad. A secretary will have filed it under "urgent", and that will be that.'

Suddenly energised, she leant forward. 'I told Chris he could go himself, get on a train that morning if it was all so important, but I'm not sure he had the guts, frankly. Guts isn't right – gumption, perhaps. He had his tribunal hearing, of course. But if it was *that* important . . .'

'And he left when . . . ?'

'Before nine, for the depot. He had to go to work.'

'How did he seem?'

'Nervous, even excited. Chris studied, always had his head in a book – history, economics, politics. God, he loved the politics. He'd always give you a long word where a short one would do.'

'You didn't like him?' asked Brooke.

The brown eyes hardened. 'I didn't like him coming here. I live in two worlds, Inspector. More. I like to keep them all apart.'

'He said nothing of the possible effects of making the report?' asked Edison.

'He expected to be summoned to the Party's offices to give a verbal account. But as I say, that was his secret hope. He may have overestimated his place in history.'

'The letter?'

Again, the visible hardening of the stare. 'As I said, posted that morning.'

She slid her feet to the frayed carpet.

'He didn't mention seeing a film?'

'A film? No. Bit early for the pictures . . .'

Brooke shook his head. 'Did you tell anyone else about the report?'

'No. Henderson knew, and Popper and Lauder. Chris wouldn't tell them the details. He'd started, then clammed up. Some rubbish about seeing the future and that soldiers were a thing of the past. That sounds like Chris.'

Brooke stood. 'Forgive me. Politics seems a strange choice for . . .'

'For a woman? Or for a woman like me?'

Brooke waited for an answer.

'They *asked* me to join, Inspector. They'd seen me working for the PPU – the Peace Pledge Union. I've been a member for twenty years. My husband died in the last lot. I think he would have registered as a conscientious objector if he'd been alive today, but back then, Your Country Needs You and all that . . . He didn't come back. Even his body didn't come back.'

She shook her head. 'It's no great sacrifice, is it, taking a few notes, pushing round agendas, keeping ahead of the paperwork. Before the war I worked in an office. So I know how to deal with paper. Believe me, that's what the Party does best. Paper soldiers, all of 'em.'

'Your husband: rank, unit?' asked Edison.

She blinked twice and Brooke thought, *She's calculating, wondering where the facts will lead.*

'My husband was Corporal Harold Staunton. The Cambridgeshires.'

'And what was his trade when he met you?' asked Edison.

'Harold worked on the river, a bargee, but he had ideas, ambitions. Most nights he'd be down on Mill Road at The Settlement, that's the workers' school. Bettering himself: I liked that. He said we'd all be able to thrive if the rich gave some of what they had to the poor. He said we had a future, after the war, together. Then he put on a uniform.'

Now, for the first time, she appeared desperate for them to leave. She stood, walking to the dormer window, looking down on the street in the rain.

'A widow's pension is not sufficient?' asked Brooke, pleased with the inference buried within the question.

She turned and smiled. 'I said we had ambitions. The war destroyed them. Frederick, our son, is everything now, all that's left. It's what we talked about before Harold left. We promised each other then, the child would have a chance in life, an education. So, boarding school. It's not been cheap.'

She ushered them to the door.

'Childe didn't have a carbon copy of the letter?' asked Edison on the threshold.

It was such a good question that her eyes showed a flash of alarm.

'Yes. I asked him about that and he just patted his chest pocket. It'll be on his body?'

CHAPTER THIRTY-SIX

Chief Inspector Carnegie-Brown called the full complement of the Spinning House's day shift – CID and uniform – to the old hall on the third floor. Her first name was Jean, but nobody on the Borough had ever heard her called anything but 'ma'am'. Neat, confident, at ease, she stood before her troops like a general before the battle is joined. As she took up her position on a small raised dais, she squared her shoulders, briefly examining the complex carpentry of the fine wooden ceiling.

It had been in this room that poor young homeless women had been put to work at their spinning wheels. Something about Carnegie-Brown found an echo there; she radiated puritan values of fresh air, exercise and abstinence. A keen angler, Brooke had often spotted her on his summer swims, on the bank at Fen Ditton, fly-fishing where the river swung north and the dead water lay in a black pool by the towpath. Perhaps she found there a memory of her native home in the Scottish Borders.

She surveyed her audience until there was silence.

'Delightful news from Scotland Yard,' she said, and the room fell silent. 'The Auxiliary Fire Service is conducting an exercise this evening on Midsummer Common, an event already on our calendar of wonders. A house, as you will have all noted, has been constructed of cardboard boxes, and is due to be set alight at eight o'clock. The AFS's two fire tenders are to tackle the blaze, exhibiting a high level of efficiency and skill.'

The AFS was not known for its efficiency or skill. It had also failed to work smoothly alongside the town's existing brigade. Its inability to put out a fire was almost certainly going to be matched by an equal inability to start one.

'The development of the AFS is a government priority. Fleet Street's finest have been invited to step out into the provinces to witness its skills. The Cabinet wishes to show its support. The minister of labour, the Right Hon. Alfred Brown, will therefore be a guest of the civic party.'

There was a universal groan.

'All leave is cancelled,' she said, raising her voice. 'Day shift will run until midnight. County will provide a motorcycle escort and twenty uniformed officers to shadow the minister. We will be responsible for crowd order at the event. This should not be a problem as there has been no advance public notice of the event, or the VIP visit. However, given it is the minister, we will perform our limited task with aplomb. Thank you. Let's get to work, shall we?

'Inspector Brooke: a moment, please, in my office.'

Brooke watched her heels, and the seam on her stockings, as they climbed a metal spiral stairwell into her office, the bay window of which looked out directly into busy Regent Street, with a view of Emmanuel College's chapel beyond. Wren's exquisite six-sided lantern tower caught a shaft of sunlight, which had broken through the clouds, only to be washed away by a fresh squall of rain.

'The Childe inquiry?' she asked, sitting at her desk, touching a plain folder on the blotter.

Brooke offered a brisk, logical summary: Childe believed he was a witness to something of great importance, almost certainly the classified film shown in the Galen's theatre on the night of the Great Darkness. He'd made a report, outlining what he'd seen, which had been sent by the secretary of the local communist party to their London headquarters. A day later Childe was dead. The Met was endeavouring to find the letter. Questions crowded in: had Childe told anyone of the contents? Was he killed to ensure his silence? Who had the copy of the letter, given it was *not* on his body?

'The case has disturbing subtleties,' said Brooke, and left it at that.

Carnegie-Brown closed her eyes. She expected her senior detective officer to make sense of life, to bring her solutions, not intricate problems.

'The chief constable has received a series of calls from Madingley Hall,' she said, flipping open the folder.

'Yes. I made enquiries about the soldiers digging on the riverbank – at St John's Wilderness, on the night of the Great Darkness. The CO, Swift-Lane, warned me off,' said Brooke. 'I was happy to comply. I'm not happy now. Childe was in the work squad which dug the pits. I've asked for further information: I'd like to know what was in the pits. We are dealing with a murder inquiry, ma'am. This young man leaves a wife and two children. He has a right to a proper investigation.'

'I'm perfectly aware of the gravity of the case, Brooke. Tread carefully. The chief constable advises cooperation, not confrontation.'

'A meeting place has been agreed on neutral ground,' said Brooke. 'Swift-Lane is keen to "clear the air", apparently. We'll see.'

She stood up and produced a silver cigarette case from inside her tunic. This had been a rumour in the Spinning House for some time: that she had a weakness, a human frailty, even if it was a common one, but no one had ever seen her indulge. She lit the cigarette with a lighter and stood by the window.

'Those pits on the riverbank, Brooke. What do we really think?'

'Take your pick of the town gossip,' said Brooke. 'Are they shooting mutineers? I doubt it. Are they burying the mangled dead from air raids, all hushed up by Whitehall? I doubt it. Are they testing weapons out on Thetford Chase, or in some forsaken corner of the Fens? Are there casualties they wish to conceal? It's all talk.'

'Talk?' said Carnegie-Brown. 'Now *there's* a weapon we should fear.'

CHAPTER THIRTY-SEVEN

Rain on the Backs, with the river brimful with the flood, lapping at the banks. Brooke always felt that on days like this the water might start welling up, through drains and ditches, creeks and basements, until the city was reduced to a series of reflections in a mirror-like maze. A Fen *acqua alta*. Even the cattle on the water meadows looked soaked, with straggly beards where they'd chewed the grass.

Colonel Swift-Lane, wrapped in a full-length oiled coat, sat upright on a bench, looking across the meadows to a distant school playing field. As Brooke approached, the referee's whistle signalled the start of a rugby match.

'Look, I'm indebted we could meet, Brooke,' offered Swift-Lane, shaking hands vigorously. The man was a ball of suppressed energy. 'I think the time has come to pool our resources. The death of this conchie changes everything. The chief constable briefed me, and felt it might help if we joined forces. Has there been any progress in the inquiry?'

Brooke lit a cigarette, calculating how much was in his interests to tell the colonel. 'So far there is no trace of the letter at Cadogan Place, the Party's London headquarters.'

Brooke watched the boys form a line-out in the rain.

'Christ, what a mess,' said Swift-Lane. He jumped up, walked away to the river's edge, then came back to his seat. 'It goes without saying that we wish to limit the degree to which this information is circulated. It is highly classified.'

Brooke noted again the slight wiry frame, the barrel chest, out of proportion to the short, powerful legs. The colonel had mentioned an Arctic expedition and Brooke pictured him man-hauling a sledge. It occurred to him that this might be the successful physiognomy of the explorer: wiry, compact and low-slung.

'Military intelligence are involved, Brooke. They were there on the night, at the Galen, and they've been on the case from the off. They keep a watching brief on all classified projects. After the last war I did a stint with them, before returning to the general staff. I know how they work. If they think any sensitive information has leaked, we won't know what's hit us . . .'

He turned in his seat as if about to deliver a confidence. 'I appreciate the update. You know you can ring Kerridge at any time. For my part, I have some news. The intelligence services picked up three of Childe's fellow travellers. They're in custody up at the Castle Gaol. Names of Henderson, Lauder and Popper. I got notification this morning.'

Brooke, angry, lit a cigarette with exaggerated calm. 'Any chance they might have informed me, the officer in charge of the murder inquiry?'

Swift-Lane concentrated on the distant sports field. 'These men may have been under surveillance for some time. I'm not privy to the full file. The central point remains, Brooke: these three men saw Childe *before* he sent his report. They met up that very night. They claim Childe told them nothing. Are they lying? If so, who might they have told . . .'

'You know what was on this film?' asked Brooke.

'I don't know the precise details.' Swift-Lane ran a hand over his oiled hair. 'Look. The film and the pit are part and parcel of the same . . .' He searched for the right word. '*Project*. Whatever it is that's buried on the riverside is just that, buried. It's the past. That really is all you need to know, Brooke.'

The colonel buried his head in his hands.

'Can I interview Childe's three comrades?' asked Brooke.

'I'll clear it,' said Swift-Lane. 'We need to know why Childe died. Is it the letter? Or are there other, hidden motives? The hard truth is that if we can't clear this up, military intelligence will take on the case, lock, stock and barrel. Either that or they'll pass it to Special Branch at the Yard, then we'll never know the truth.'

Brooke adjusted his tinted glasses, watching the rugby play out in a vivid green light.

Swift-Lane was up again on his feet.

'One detail you should know,' added Brooke. 'Henderson, the local party chairman? We searched his house and found a two-way radio transmitter, and receiver.'

Swift-Lane looked stunned. 'His house was checked. They all were. How could they have missed a radio?'

'It was in the loft space, under the roof.'

A ragged cheer greeted a try scored in the distant rugby match.

'Then we really must keep in touch, Brooke,' said Swift-Lane, as if it was a threat.

CHAPTER THIRTY-EIGHT

Detective Inspector John Solly, of Sheffield CID, stood on Fitzalan Square, watching the first snow flurry of the year accumulate on the bronze shoulders of Edward VII, who looked north from his central plinth towards the distant high line of the white moors.

Solly, a big man in a heavy overcoat with the collar up, studied the principal building across the square; since he'd been a child he'd never heard it called anything but the White Building. While the rest of the city centre was layered in a fur of soot, it defied the grime. The facade's glazed tiles recorded the city's fame: men aglow at an open furnace, men at lathes, men at drill jigs, men at steam hammers.

Solly's brothers had gone into 'the steel'. He was smarter, no one's fool, so he used his brain, not his muscles. And his eyes: for twenty minutes he'd kept watch on the public bar door of the Elephant Inn, right next to the White Building. Spotting his quarry at last, he skipped between a pair of black cabs on the rank and plunged into the pub, to be engulfed in a warm fug of humanity, rank with damp clothes and coal smoke.

Three crowded bars led to a snug which was so full he had to thread his path to the bar as if trying to get a decent view on the terraces at nearby Bramall Lane, to watch his beloved United. He'd rolled a pound note up tight and slipped it into the top pocket of a man who stood at the end of the bar.

'I'll get that,' he told a barman who'd just delivered a pint. 'And another.'

They were in a corner, and at head height they faced a line of open modesty screens, small glazed panels of fogged glass. Solly deftly closed two so that they couldn't be seen from the other bars.

'I can't talk,' said Solly's informant, revealing tobacco-stained teeth. 'It's too dangerous.' Clossick owned a cab, and boasted bat-like hearing and a mind sharp enough to recall minor details. The city's infamous gangs used taxis to keep one step ahead of CID, which regularly circulated lists of suspect licence plates.

Clossick heard a lot, but said little, unless paid.

'Too late now, pal,' said Solly. 'Might as well make it short and sweet and enjoy the pint when I'm gone.'

The cabbie had wide, flickering eyes, with which he kept a constant vigil over the detective's shoulders.

'The lorries?' prompted Solly.

'That's it. I did hear . . .'

It was Clossick's signature: *I did hear . . .*

'They set up a convoy, Mr Solly,' said Clossick. 'They went down south to pick up meat at farms. All under the counter, no paperwork. None that's legit.'

Clossick tapped the bar top. 'Left here at dawn, back by dusk, that's the way of it. They've done half a dozen trips in the last few months, and no problems. Plan is to stockpile the meat then play the market when rationing starts.'

Clossick drank, then set his empty glass on the bar top.

Solly flipped open one of the screens, ordered a refill, sipping his own pint.

'This last time it's a right lash-up,' said Clossick, lifting his drink. 'Local uniform in Cambridge catches 'em parked in the street, two of the wagons full. One of the drivers panics, makes a run for it, when the coppers arrive. Another follows suit. Wouldn't give a lot for their chances if either shows their face back in the city. If they'd sat tight they might have got away with it.'

Solly put an elbow on the bar, pivoting, so that his lips were close to the cabbie's ears. 'We need to find the meat, Clossick. How many times have they done this run? Half a dozen? So there's lorry-loads of the meat somewhere. And that's if it's one convoy. What if there are more? Find me an address, pal. It's worth a fiver.

'And if you get the chance, let it slip that the driver's being transferred back home. He's turned informer. Arrests are imminent. He'll be at West Bar in a cell by tomorrow night. I'm going down to pick him up, make sure he gets here safely. Then he'll be out on bail. Spread the news, Clossick.'

Solly left, ricocheting off the other customers, until he fell out into the street. The snow was an inch deep. He looked up into the low sky, which seemed suspended just a foot above his head, and watched the shadows of the falling flakes, already smudged with soot.

CHAPTER THIRTY-NINE

Brooke climbed Castle Hill, past the spot where the lorries had been parked on the night of the Great Darkness. At the top stood the County Gaol, amongst the ruins of the castle. It was a mathematical gem: eight-sided, an elegant octagon, each wing afforded its own central spine, within which lay a three-storey high corridor and a soaring, iron-framed skylight roof. The views out were mean, the small cell windows criss-crossed with bars, imposing a latticework frame on the college spirelets spread below. Rain fell across a slate-grey city.

Henderson, Lauder and Popper, the principal activists of the city's communist party, had been allocated cells in B Wing, but on different levels. They were forbidden to join the 'wheel', the circulating walk in the prison yard which afforded prisoners an hour each day to fraternise. The deputy chief warder was the only member of staff authorised to enter their rooms; their food was eaten alone, delivered through the door by the governor's personal kitchen orderly.

Brooke felt here the brutal imprint of authoritarian discipline. The risk these men posed to the state was surely limited: they claimed, separately, that they had no insight into the scenes Childe had witnessed. Vera Staunton had been clear: he was determined to tell London first, in writing, and no one else.

Henderson, the trade union convener, was on his feet in shirt, tie and jacket, standing by his bed when the warder opened the cell door. A linen towel covered a bucket by the sink, but the stench was a shock, despite the open window.

'On whose authority am I being held and under what law?' he asked, before Brooke was fully through the door. 'I demand to see a solicitor, and I wish to exercise my right to appear in front of a magistrate.'

To an extent, the art of confrontation was Henderson's business as a union official, but the forthright delivery, the summoning up of a sense of moral right, was nonetheless impressive.

Brooke gave him a copy of the Emergency Powers (Defence) Act, having anticipated the request, and circled the relevant clauses. Carnegie-Brown had a pile of copies set out in the hall at the Spinning House, an eloquent reminder of the locus of power in a time of war.

Henderson retrieved a pair of glasses from his suit pocket and read: '"Threat to national security"? In what sense? Christ, I fought for this country, Brooke, more than the bastards who write this rubbish ever did . . .' He flung the paper in the air.

'We searched your house, and the attic,' said Brooke.

Henderson took the news like a blow, subsiding to his bunk, head held between his hands, which he slowly ran back through thinning hair.

'It's not a crime.'

'It is, actually. Your grip on the legal code isn't exactly vice-like, is it? Unless you are registered as part of the government's own radio monitoring scheme it is indeed illegal to own a transmitter.'

Henderson shook his head. 'The Party has its own network. It's a contingency, in case of invasion. We'll need to organise, keep abreast of the situation. I listen to Moscow; we've never transmitted. Is that a crime, man? In a free country? We're ready to fight if the Nazis come, Brooke, a darn sight harder than the fascists will. Sod *Peace News*: we'll fight the Germans on home soil, don't you worry.'

Brooke had come armed with a packet of Woodbines, a habit he'd learnt over the years when visiting prisoners.

A single exhalation of smoke filled the box-like cell, catching a beam of light which came in through the high, narrow window.

'Thanks,' said Henderson. 'I needed that. Sorry, it's nothing personal. A tirade does me good . . . They took all my fags. They've banned visits, too, although the governor claims he's trying to get that lifted. We'll see.'

Brooke tried to focus the anger in the room. 'The problem, the reason you're here, is Childe's letter. It hasn't arrived in London. Further, Vera says he made a carbon copy, a black. That should have been on his body. It wasn't.'

Henderson shook his head. 'I tried to get Chris to tell us there and then. Not telling us was illogical. The London office is a bloody sieve. Tell 'em anything and it'll be chit-chat on the docks in half an hour. Much better to speak to us – then, if needs be, go to London and *tell* someone. Why put anything on paper? In the end we agreed to the letter, only because that way at least someone would get to hear the bloody truth, whatever it was.' Henderson lowered his voice. 'Thing is, Brooke. The idiot changed his bloody mind.'

'Childe?'

'Yes. Rang me at the office from a phone box and said he'd tell us the lot at the weekly meeting that evening. Seven o'clock in the Mitre's private room as always. What with the coins clattering there wasn't much time. But he did say he'd thought it through and decided the best thing was to go public. Christ knows what he had in mind. Speakers' bloody Corner?'

Brooke felt this nugget of information would have given Swift-Lane a heart attack. Childe's letter was dangerous enough, but if he'd decided to talk, and tell others, then he'd certainly put his life in danger.

'Do you think Vera actually sent the letter?' Brooke asked, changing tack.

Henderson studied his face. 'What, you think she's a wrong'un, Vera? A spy within? No way, Brooke. Don't forget we recruited *her*. No. Vera's sound.'

'So where's the letter?' persisted Brooke.

'Ask me, it's at the Party office, or a safer place. Think about it. If someone at Cadogan Square opened the letter and read it, and it's that big a deal, why the hell own up? Why tell the police anything?'

Brooke thought the logic of this was powerful.

Henderson sensed his moment. 'Do me a favour,' he said. 'Make sure we don't disappear. I can face a court, I can face a charge, but I can't face that. Left to rot in some godawful forgotten cell. You know who to ask, Brooke. You know how to keep tabs. I've no idea what they've told you, about letting us go, but I think someone wants us out of sight. There'll be a truck in the night. Then? Christ knows. So look out for us, please.'

'Alright,' said Brooke, unable to decline. 'But they know about the radio, so expect visitors.'

He promised cigarettes, too, and then rapped on the door to be let out. He dogged the warder's steps, along the landing and down a flight, to see the other prisoners. Lauder and Popper confirmed Henderson's version of events: Childe had kept his secret, at least from them.

Finally the warder steered Brooke back towards the main gate.

The corridor led to an outside door, and a small shadowy garden.

A man dug the clay soil with a fork, in full-length black overalls, and it was only when Brooke came level that he realised it was the governor. His hairless domed head was shiny with sweat. Brooke felt sure the meeting had been contrived.

'Inspector. Give my best to Carnegie-Brown. Haven't seen her since last year's Rotary dinner,' he said. 'My haven,' he added, indicating the neat garden plot and a series of trellises threaded with winter jasmine and a woody wisteria.

Looking up, the governor surveyed the sky. 'Always makes me think of Wilde's little tent of blue.' He set his spade aside. 'About these three prisoners,' he said. 'I'm not happy. Lockdown is inhumane. They keep telling me there's a war on. It's the devil's excuse. I wanted you to know I don't approve.'

The complaint lasted several minutes more.

'One favour,' said Brooke. 'If the order comes in to move them can you let me know? And insist on seeing the warrant, and a note of their destination. If they won't comply, can you secure a record of the licence plates, anything you can.'

The governor looked shocked. 'It's come to that?' he asked.

CHAPTER FORTY

Brooke stood at the French windows, watching mist creep out of the river, finding a foothold where the cattle had worn down the bank. A lone horse was slowly disappearing: hooves first, then fetlocks, until only the noble head remained, a suspended chess-piece knight hanging in mid-air. Out of this whiteness, a hunched figure approached from the towpath towards the house: Marcus Ashmore, night climber, mathematician and the studious brother of the party-loving Jo.

A strange boy, thought Brooke: such an English epithet, a catch-all for so many unspoken peculiarities of manner and action. It had been the Brooke family's universal verdict from the day Marcus had first come to the house with his parents. The children had formed a close-knit club: two girls, two boys, left alone while the adults ate at the long table in the dining room. The old house had become their playground, the shadowy attic and the dripping cellar the backdrop to shrieking games of sardines or hide-and-seek. When the Ashmores had moved to a grander college house, the children had kept in touch, if not the adults.

Marcus approached the back gate, lifted the snicket with practised ease and made his way to the kitchen door.

'Tea?' called Brooke, trying to ignite some warmth in his voice as a reminder of past times.

'Please,' said Marcus, taking a seat at the plain deal table. 'It's good to be back,' he added, and smiled. A small, neat figure, he succeeded in conjuring up the ghost of the child he once was.

Marcus would be twenty-two, Brooke calculated – in academic terms, the intellectual prime of his life. His physical stillness always suggested a whirring brain, betrayed by the rapid movement of his eyes, which danced round the familiar room, perhaps trying to detect the unfamiliar: a new watercolour print, an addition to Brooke's collection of framed maps of the city, or a gleaming coffee pot.

'How's Joy?' Marcus asked.

For a minute they swapped family updates until Brooke could pour the tea. The biscuit tin, a family treasure, he placed between them in an effort to summon up the informality of childhood treats.

'Jo said you wanted a word,' said Marcus finally.

'Yes. About Ernst Lux – a friend, a colleague?'

'A friend. We played Russian roulette . . .' Marcus smiled, and Brooke was reminded of the many times he'd seen the innocence of that face reveal a cruel streak.

'No guns,' said Marcus, holding up both hands. 'Ernst used a book, instead. Clever, really. We'd set various parameters against certain outcomes. So: you would open the book on the basis that picking an even page number would result in a payment of £100, an odd page number an immediate call-up for military training. Or, a page number divisible by five, which would give you £1,000, but any other page would result in being sent down. We played for hours. It reveals character.'

His eyes met Brooke's for a second, then took up their tour, continuing to compile an inventory of crockery and cups, glasses and pans.

'On the night Ernst died, you both went night climbing. A regular event?'

Marcus examined his teacup, waiting for further clarification, perhaps, of the risks he faced if he gave the detective the truth.

'I can't prove anything,' said Brooke. 'This is a private conversation. I'm the last person to play custodian of the university's rules. I need to know how he died, Marcus. His work was classified, at least in part. There's interest from my superiors, your superiors, in how he died. They need, I need, to be sure. An accident's an accident. But if I don't get the truth I can take other measures. We could talk formally, in college, but I'd need to seek the agreement of the master.'

Marcus nodded, as if he'd expected as much. He held his fingertips together as if using the ten digits to make the fine calculation of probability required to make a decision.

'Ernst was drunk that night,' he said, finally. 'Oiled, certainly. So we didn't go out for some time. A little alcohol can work wonders, actually. It disinhibits, lends a fluidity to the limbs. But he was giddy, so we talked. He was in a very strange mood.

'On the way back from the pub, he'd gone for a long walk – to think. By the time he got back to college the gate was locked, so he climbed over the wall by the cedar tree, an easy task for Ernst. He turned up at my room in a state. So we sat out on the roof edge. He was very quiet: introspective, certainly.

'I asked if he was alright. He said it was his work, that he'd been to a lecture at the Galen, and it had taken an unexpected direction. That was his phrase: *an unexpected direction*. I suppose he was depressed. That's the aspect of alcohol everyone forgets, that it enhances the mood, it doesn't create the mood.'

'He said nothing more about why he was upset, nothing specific?'

'No. And I didn't labour the point. We'd never swapped any ideas on an academic level. He's a natural scientist. Or a chemist, or both. My work is very different. And classified. So I guess we'd agreed a subconscious truce on the subject of our work.'

Outside, in the milky dusk, they heard the *plosh!* of an oar breaking the surface of the river.

'We hit upon the idea of climbing,' said Marcus, as if exposing yourself to the possibility of instant death was the equivalent of a game of bridge. He seemed to understand how ludicrous this might sound. 'I know. It's the thrill of it, I guess. It lifts the spirit. I think he really needed it, like a drug. I'm no different. You can't live a life entirely inside your own head.'

There was an intimate note to this revelation, as if he was making a confession. Brooke felt strangely moved by the insight.

'You knew the consequences?' asked Brooke.

'Well, it's always been *verboten*,' said Marcus. 'But Michaelhouse has notched up the penalties and the moral opprobrium, in line with the rest. So the risks were very high. But I think we both felt that rather helped. I'm not sure Ernst cared at all, and he certainly didn't care that night.

'There's a relatively easy route from the chapel over into the North Court. We got ready in my room and set out along the gutter's edge, which is cheating, really, but it meant we were clear of Doric's baleful vigilance . . .'

He smiled, confused perhaps by Brooke's refusal to match the mood of jovial adventure.

'He left his shoes and socks in your room?' asked Brooke.

'Yes. I climb in shoes, but Ernst always went barefoot. The experts differ . . .'

Brooke nodded.

'Anyway, we stopped below the roofline and looked out over the city. In retrospect, we'd underestimated the effect of the blackout. Even with cloud cover you get some light bouncing down, but that night it was particularly dense, the sense of the dark pressing in.'

He held his hands in front of his face as if for illustration.

'I thought Ernst's mood had lifted. But I may have been wrong. We decided to plough on and traverse the facade of the West Range, then come down using a chimney . . . That's not a real chimney, you understand? It's a vertical gap, between buttresses. You put your back one side, feet the other. Routine for us. Halfway down you can cross over to a drainpipe, but you have to use a narrow decorative ledge. You need good fingers.'

Marcus flexed his left hand. For the first time, Brooke thought he might have underestimated him. Did the almost childlike facade hide a more calculating mind?

'We were keen to get down because the air raid siren had sounded. The college has fire-watchers, although frankly they're as phoney as the war itself . . .

'I wasn't looking when it happened, I was still in the chimney, but he'd reached the ledge, to edge across. I heard his feet scrabbling, and his hands. That's important, I think, if you're looking for evidence. If he'd decided, at that instant, to end his life, he'd have just dropped. But his hands, and his toes, were frantic for a moment, and then he was in the air.'

Brooke was shocked by this new suggestion, that the studious American might have taken his own life.

'I saw him then,' said Marcus. 'His face, quite calm, actually, falling away from me. There was light in the sky, from the fire at the station, so I could see his eyes.

'It's fifty feet to the stonework over the porch. There's a line of small pinnacles and he fell onto those. He had no chance of surviving. It was very quick. That's what they always say, isn't it? I'm not so sure about painless.'

'No rope?'

That ghost of a smile again. 'No. That's pretty much de rigueur.

'It was a disaster, of course. They'd have sent me down, chucked me out. So when I reached his body I checked his pulse, but there was no doubt he was dead, his body was broken, shattered, really. Then I went to a friend's room, and we got together a group of six. The porter does his rounds at dawn so we had time.'

'And the noise, of the fall?'

'As I said, after the siren they sent up a couple of fighters. Hell of a racket. So it was mayhem, which was perfect, because everybody stayed indoors to maintain the blackout.

'We carried him rolled up in a rug. Someone stole the key to the watergate years ago and had copies made, so we slipped out onto the riverbank, and got him a few hundred yards away. Shreds of the balloon were everywhere. We thought it might provide . . .' He searched for the right words. 'An explanation.'

'Dr Lux's wounds were extensive. There must have been blood – worse.'

'Yes, we cleaned up the stonework on top of the porch and

at ground level. If you look higher, on the pinnacles, there'll be *evidence*, but you'd have to know where to look, and there's been rain and sun.'

Blood, bone, muscle, brains, so lightly dismissed as mere evidence. Brooke felt the chill of the river mist seeping into the old house.

'Why do you think Ernst fell?' he asked.

'I think he lost concentration. That would be fatal. It *was* fatal. You need a cool head. But we knew the risks. At least, in that sense, it was his decision. It's better, I think, than getting cut down in a foreign field because a superior officer has told you that you have to fight. That's a situation in which someone else has calculated the risks. And his family will have his ashes, so that's a comfort, I suppose. And he'd done his bit, which is more than most will ever do. I think of him as a casualty of war.'

'And what did you feel?'

'That I'd lost a friend, and that I'd miss him. I don't have many friends at all. It makes the work very lonely.'

CHAPTER FORTY-ONE

The house of boxes on Midsummer Common stood nearly thirty feet high, a strangely solid form in the misty night, with a doorway and windows, and a roof constructed in the fashion of a ziggurat, with each layer of boxes a few feet narrower than the last, until an apex was achieved with exemplary skill. The Auxiliary Fire Service's two engines stood ready to tackle the self-induced blaze. The crowd, herded along the bank of the river, had congregated around the Fort St George, a riverside pub.

Brooke's presence was merely symbolic. The inspector in charge of the uniform section was in control, busy directing the city's constables, grouping them ostentatiously in a cordon below the VIP vantage point, a balcony on the Fort St George, which had been draped with a Union flag and the arms of the AFS, and was currently empty.

Two military guards stood in the far meadow beside the house of boxes, presumably alert to the danger that some miscreant would attempt to start proceedings early. Brooke suspected that news of the minister's flying visit had spread beyond the top brass, as the crowd numbered at least a hundred, and was growing at a visible rate.

Edison ducked the barrier, down on one arthritic knee. 'Sir. Sheffield have sent down an inspector to pick up Gretorix, a car and a police driver too. They've put the officer up in the Bull Hotel. Message said he'll be at the bar, by the name of Solly. Said he'd pick up the prisoner at eight tomorrow, but he asked to see him tonight. Didn't think I could stop him, really?'

Brooke nodded, pulling down the rim of his hat. 'Tomorrow, Edison, first thing, we need to review the Childe inquiry.' Control of Gretorix's fate was slipping from their hands, and Lux's death looked like a reckless accident, but Childe's cold-blooded murderer was still on the streets of the city. 'There's pressure to hand over to the Yard, or military intelligence, if we don't make progress. We've got a day, maybe two, before we lose the case. It's not one I intend to lose.'

Edison nodded, producing his pipe, excavating the bowl with a small knife. 'The Met rang. They've finished turning over the sorting office at Mount Pleasant and there's no sign of Childe's letter. They've hauled in everyone from the communist party's back office, and the assistant general secretary. Bit of a stink, apparently, and Whitehall's jumping. So far they've kept it off the commissioner's desk. But that won't last . . .'

'Let's talk to Childe's neighbours, get a wider picture,' said Brooke. 'Staunton's a mystery in her own right. Why don't we insist on a list of her clients, Edison? I don't care if it's bad for business. She just doesn't add up.'

'There he is!' shouted a voice in the crowd. A cheer, several cheers, pulsed up and down the line. On the balcony of the Fort St George, the minister for labour waved cheerfully.

'Bring the grandchildren?' asked Brooke.

'Wouldn't miss it,' said Edison. 'They love a bonfire.'

Brooke was unable to suppress a brief return of a nightmare image: Claire's eyes, with flames flickering.

Up on the balcony, the minister had been joined by a contingent of the great and the good: Brooke spotted Colonel Swift-Lane and Carnegie-Brown, who at that precise moment leant over to offer the visitor a pair of field glasses.

A platoon of soldiers mounted a smart march past, before the shadowy form of what might have been the lord mayor, a new arrival on the balcony, delivered an inaudible speech. The minister said a few words in response, of which Brooke caught 'great city', 'noble honour' and 'flying visit'.

The first flame finally flared. The pyrotechnics were spectacular and almost certainly totally unplanned. The air within the boxes was in effect fuel, so the result was not so much a blaze as an explosion. The fire service's hoses played ineffectually into what became a single huge flame, the threads of water incinerated to steam in mid-air. The fire, a vibrant yellow at the heart, appeared to reach up into the low misty cloud. The noise was terrific, a whirlwind, battering at eardrums.

Each box blazed only for the length of time it took the heat to destroy its fragile cardboard strength. The layers collapsed, one by one from the bottom up, until the ziggurat roof finally folded itself down into a bed of ashes.

An uncertain ripple of applause greeted a scene of total devastation.

Brooke hadn't watched. As soon as the first flame flickered he'd turned his back and watched the dignitaries on the balcony, lit in an increasingly lurid light. The minister's spectacles became two small circles of fire. It was Carnegie-Brown who reacted first, suddenly stepping back to disappear from view; then the Lord Mayor's hands came up to cover his mouth. Swift-Lane actually staggered to one side as if his legs had buckled, so that someone had to grab his arm to keep him on his feet.

The crowd, which had been in a state of awestruck silence, gasped. A single scream cut the air.

Brooke turned back to the fire. A figure stood within the ashes. As he watched, it seemed to grow taller, rising – phoenix-like – from its knees. Brooke would never shake off the immediate sense that this man had been resurrected, drawn up from the earth perhaps by the sheer power of the heat of the blaze. For a moment the figure was still, flames licking its outstretched limbs, fluttering about its head. Then it took a step towards them, the hands beginning to act out a kind of deathly semaphore, its strides mechanical, as if the limbs had been fused at the joints.

At last, exhausted of energy, the figure knelt at the edge of a trench which had been dug to contain the fire. A single flame sprang from the chest, before – finally – he fell backwards, into the damp, steaming grass.

The shocked silence was profound.

Brooke ran forward and, picking up a fire bucket from the edge of the safety trench, managed to step across. With three paces he'd reached the blackened, scorched body. In death, the limbs visibly stiffened. Smoke drifted from a charred foot. Brooke avoided looking at what was left of the face, and set the bucket down.

CHAPTER FORTY-TWO

Claire had set a candlestick on the card table by the fire, with two wine glasses, the bottle on the hearth, warming. Brooke had phoned, so she knew he'd be late, and he'd described the scene on Midsummer Common. Was the candle, with its guttering flame, a mistake? She thought not, adding the silver cutlery neatly, and two place mats showing pictures of York Minster, a wedding present from her sister. The pewter salt and pepper pots were Brooke's mother's, as was the linen cloth.

Food, the little rituals, provided a handhold on the world they'd lost. Claire always laid the table, her methodical obsessions rewarded by the final symmetry of silver and crystal. Even the crease on the tablecloth was at just the right angle.

War, and the imminent imposition of widespread rationing, had transformed their diet. Claire, condemned to mass catering at the hospital, was prepared to meet the impending challenge head on: they'd tried stuffed hearts, tripe and various reinventions of offal. Tonight, the food came in a casserole dish and, with a stir, revealed that it was pretending to be chicken.

Brooke arrived, throwing the door open with the key still in the lock, and calling out, 'Home!' In all the years the children had been with them they'd never kissed in the hallway; now it was a ritual.

'That poor man . . .' said Claire, taking his hat.

'That's the one surprise,' said Brooke, shrugging off his coat. 'It's a woman.'

They'd taken the charred body to the Galen and Dr Comfort had undertaken a brief external examination. A woman, certainly, aged between seventy and eighty-five; dressed in good quality, if worn, clothing, of which there were several layers: a wool housecoat over a shirt, over a vest.

In the ashes of the 'house', Brooke judged that he'd found the spot where she'd been hidden away, marked by a blackened blanket, and two empty glass bottles of cider, which had partly melted in the extreme heat.

'Do you think we'll ever know her story?' asked Claire, standing by the fire. Life, for her, was largely illuminated by teasing out these narratives, tracing back the threads of character and fortune into the past. Having been brought up in a small village, in a large family, she was used to knowing everyone's story.

'A roadster, perhaps,' said Brooke.

Vagrants, tramping between the towns and villages of the Fens, had become a regular feature of the city since the outbreak of war. Free soup kitchens for the workers had proved a honeypot. A few slept out, begging at college gates or on Market Hill, under the stalls.

'A box is home for some,' said Brooke. 'The insulation is remarkable. A cold night, a wet day, perhaps she'd just slipped in and fallen asleep. The thing had been up for a day or two, how was she to know its purpose? There were no guards until the last day. Perhaps she thought she'd take her chance, then move on before nightfall. If the cider bottles are hers she might have been beyond caring.

'Anyway, case isn't mine. It's an accident, hardly a job for us. Uniform branch will take over tomorrow.'

Claire shivered and threw a half-log into the grate. Brooke followed her gaze into the soft flames, troubled by that image of the woman's arms, the fiery semaphore, as if it might contain a message.

'What a way to die,' said Claire.

'There's a letter from Luke; I've not opened it,' she said.

'Let's wait. Food first. Rabbit?' he asked, sniffing the air and walking to the fire. He picked up the bottle from the hearth and poured two glasses.

'Hare,' said Claire, placing the casserole on the table and using her fork to test the tenderness of the flesh.

They ate in silence for a moment.

Brooke poured more wine. 'With luck I can get back to the Childe murder, a case which seems to slip through the hands like sand, and not just ordinary sand, more like the stuff they put in egg timers. At the moment I can't shift the idea that I'm being made a fool of by the military. Which makes me angry, given we're at war, and I'm not the enemy.'

He prodded a piece of meat. 'It's not bad, is it? Gamey. As if it's been hung with the pheasants and the partridge.'

Claire sipped her wine and then dabbed at her lips with a serviette.

'In a year, you see, we'll be reminiscing about this casserole,' she said.

'Necessity and all that . . . The French ate horsemeat during the siege of Paris,' said Brooke, which was a misstep, because it reminded them of Luke, camped out in some field in north-east France.

He cleared away the plates while Claire fetched down their son's letter from its position of honour on the mantle.

'Go on,' she said. 'It's best in your voice.'

In detail, Luke described the arrival of British materiel at the border, a convoy emerging through the gloom of perpetual autumnal rain. He'd slept under a tank despite the absolute instruction not to, preferring a dry night to the outside chance the vehicle would sink in its tracks, crushing him to death.

I woke up refreshed was the line they enjoyed.

Brooke said it was remarkable how mild discomfort, the damp soft grisaille of France, could eventually accumulate into a form of slow torture.

Outside, the mist pressed up against the cold glass of the windows. The old house was draughty, so the candle guttered. Brooke sheltered it for a moment with his hand.

Claire sighed. 'I hope she was drunk, your roadster – oblivious, at least, until the last moments.'

'In the last lot,' said Brooke quickly, 'the Germans bombed London and started these fires. I was told that when the heat gets to a certain level the fire starts to suck air into itself, like an engine drawing fuel. *A fire storm* – that's what I heard. Civilians died, in the East End. It's always the East End, isn't it? The poor in the frontline. The Kaiser, and this is hearsay . . .' He sipped his wine. 'Hearsay, but nonetheless. Apparently he intervened, stopped the raids because he said it was *uncivilised*. So perhaps we'll be spared this time.'

Brooke checked his wristwatch. 'I have to go. Sheffield have sent down a car for our cocky lorry driver. I should hand over . . .'

'How was Marcus?' asked Claire, keen to preserve the veneer of domestic conversation for a minute longer.

'Not much different from the boy we used to know.'

Claire helped Brooke on with his coat, running a finger along the collar to turn it down, where he often had it turned up, in a fashion she found irritatingly military.

'I always felt sorry for him,' she said. 'That awful father. There was very little love in that family, no wonder he's so fond of numbers.'

She offered Brooke the last of the wine. 'Last night, when I got home, it was nearly dawn. I couldn't sleep so I got a pot of the whitewash from the shed and started on the far attic room, the old nursery, where the kids used to play.

'The walls are covered in all their secret plans, the boys' adventures. They were going to run away to the Wild West, do you remember? They even had a schedule for the boat from Liverpool. Marcus was out there in the lane, satchel packed, ready to go at midnight . . .' She shook her head. 'He was eight. Luke was fast asleep in bed with the map for the journey crushed in his hand.'

'Look at them now,' said Brooke.

CHAPTER FORTY-THREE

Detective Inspector Solly was in the Bull Hotel. Brooke's estimate was that he'd been at the bar for several hours. As he crossed the room he could hear his accent, that peculiar nasal burr he now knew to be unique to Sheffield, relaying a lurid story of his home city's infamous gang wars to a group of men in suits – travelling salesmen, Brooke judged, all past the age to fight.

'That's what you've got to do, see,' said Solly, pointing at several empty glasses for refills. 'Meet violence with violence. These thugs cut up rough. So we cut up rough back. If you know you've got a villain, treat 'em like a villain. You don't want to end up in a cell at West Bar for the night, believe me.'

Brooke introduced himself, accepted a whisky and drew Solly away from his audience to a quiet corner.

The Bull had seen better times. A plaque by the door in brass said an inn had stood on the site since the reign of Edward V. The interwar years had dented its regal pretensions: the Axminster lay threadbare, the gilded mirrors milky and mottled.

'Heard about your fire. Has your minister buggered off back to London?' said Solly, spreading his wide shoulders along the back of the worn velvet banquette.

'Flying visit,' said Brooke. 'You've seen the prisoner, I understand?'

'Gretorix? Oh, aye. I know Jack Gretorix. Heard of the Skye Edge gang? He's in what's left of it. Scum, Brooke. People like him tore the city apart in the twenties, we're not gonna let 'em do it again. We had murders in broad daylight. Bodies dumped on street corners. Not this time, Brooke. Not on my watch. I know Jack Gretorix, alright. More to the point, he knows me.'

Solly got closer. 'We'll get the truth out of him, don't you worry. I reckon he's gonna blab once he knows he's really heading north. We'll go with your plan. Tell him he's set for bail.'

Brooke felt Solly had underestimated his foe. 'He won't talk,' he said.

'He has,' said Solly, pulling a face at his beer. 'I reckon he's been playing a long game. Sweating it out. Waiting for his moment to spill some beans.'

'What did he say?' asked Brooke.

Solly took another pull on his pint. 'He said he knew where they were stockpiling the meat.'

'Just that?'

'Aye. Credible, too. He reckons they're using the old city abattoir in the valley. Derelict for years, mind, since well before the last war. But who knows? We'll check it out. If it's legit, perhaps we won't let him go after all. The next question's the big one. Can he name names? The top men, not the middle men. If he does, we might have to reinvent Jack Gretorix, give him a new life. If not, we'll turf him out. Pick up his body with the rubbish.'

He turned his pint upside down and put it on the table. 'Your round.'

CHAPTER FORTY-FOUR

The concept of the sacrifice had always eluded Doric. Perhaps it was his pragmatic military training, or the precarious lifestyle of the soldier, but the college porter found the idea of deliberately offering up materiel on the field of battle, as it were, was a gambit beyond his rank.

The porter's hand hovered over the rook Brooke had placed in jeopardy. Whistling tunelessly, he grabbed it, tossing the piece into a balsa-wood box with a satisfying *toc!*

'Some bad news, Mr Brooke,' said Doric. 'Jenner's heard the latest on your soldiers digging on St John's Wilderness. Whole unit's been posted north, end of the road, Scapa Flow. That's all of 'em. No explanation, no nothing. Like they'd never been here.'

Brooke swung his queen along the diagonal cleared by his sacrifice to confront Doric's king, and considered the implications of this latest news. The determination of the military to neutralise any potential security threat was remarkable: Henderson, Lauder and Popper were in the County Gaol, the soldiers who'd dug on the riverbank banished towards the Arctic Circle. What on earth was in those pits?

The porter adjusted his trousers, pulling on the creases, and shuffled his shoes under the table. Then he got up and fetched a plate of leftovers from the small kitchen: a tray of cheese and bread and what he called 'monnits', anything applied to bread or toast: jams and marmalades, honey or, a college favourite, Gentlemen's Relish. Brooke had checked his two-volume *OED* and been unable to find the word monnits, or anything like it.

Doric considered the food spread out on the platter.

'This fire. A woman, you say? A roadster?'

'That's the theory. Well, definitely a woman, probably a roadster.'

Doric shook his head. 'After the war we had a victory dinner here. A frosty night, January 1919 that would be. Eight courses. The soup was turtle, that I do remember. We all had a taste in the kitchens. Ever had it?'

Brooke shook his head, breaking some bread and pairing it with a piece of cheddar.

'Overrated,' said Doric, with some satisfaction. 'You can live for a long time on a good dinner, Mr Brooke. When I took the bins out that night after the feast there he was, a roadster. I've seen men dead, men dying. But that . . . Froze to death, they reckoned, on my doorstep, rolled up in a curtain, in the alcove by the post box, like a church mouse . . .'

He wiped his hands on a creased napkin. 'That reminds me.' He strode out to the post room, returning with a bundle of letters tied up with a blue ribbon. 'The day staff cleared Dr Lux's room. They've packed up his stuff in a tea crate. Head porter told me it was all done and dusted.'

The head porter, never afforded the dignity of his name, was a byword for incompetence and shoddy standards.

'So I checked his pigeonhole. Sure enough . . .'

Doric tapped the bundle.

Two students arrived, wanting to book the college boat for an early morning row on the river. While Doric completed the paperwork with a flourish, Brooke pulled the ribbon to release the post.

Item number one: a form and covering letter from the Bureau of Internal Revenue, postmarked Washington DC.

Item number two: a scribbled note from a Dr Stern, with a series of academic articles under Lux's name published in scientific journals. Brooke noted one entitled 'The role of aequorin in the chemical reaction between luciferins and luciferase: a case study in bioluminescence'. The note was on a slip which bore the arms of the University of California, Berkeley.

Item number three: the August–October copy of *The Cordillera Climber*, an unillustrated magazine of close-printed notes on routes through what Brooke would have called the Rocky Mountains.

Item number four: a postcard showing a stretch of grey choppy water with an island in the mid-distance, dominated by a large institutional building, a tower and a lighthouse. A boat occupied the foreground, its V-shaped wake stretching back towards a quayside.

Doric had dealt with the rowers, so Brooke read the postcard out loud:

Ernst – all our love. A trip up the coast. It's your father's arrow. That was his cell! He's so proud, even if it is ancient history. He claims Al Capone got his room! We think of you always. Travis

says he'll join up if it comes to it. You can imagine the ructions.
Try to write, you've no idea how much it means. Your mother. xxx

Brooke flicked the card over and there it was, an inked-in arrow pointing at the building on the island. The scale was far too small to identify one window, but the serried rows were certainly jail-like.

He turned the postcard back over. At the foot in italics was a pre-printed legend which read: *US Federal Prison, Alcatraz. CA.*

CHAPTER FORTY-FIVE

After midnight, a light wind blew away the mist so that by the time he got to Frank Edwardes' house a group of students had started playing cricket by moonlight on Fenner's. From the window of the old man's sickroom, Brooke watched a slice of the game, six students clustered round the bat as a tall young man bowled spin from the Gresham Road End. A moon-shadow clung to a fielder as he ran to the boundary to fetch the ball, reminding Brooke of a childhood production of *Peter Pan*, with the hero flimsily attached to his alter ego.

'Silly sods,' said Edwardes, propped up on his pillows, his eyes closed. Sheets of paper were scattered across the bed, each crowded with the dense five-letter phrases of Morse code.

'I need help,' said Brooke, standing at the window, and Edwardes nodded, setting aside his pad.

A brief outline of the Childe case took five minutes: from the events of the Great Darkness, the pits on the river, the film in the Galen, the letter posted to London, to the murder itself in Mill

Road Cemetery. 'It seems to me that the motive is unavoidable: Childe knew too much, so he was killed, and the copy of his letter taken. But that makes no sense if the top copy was on its way to London by post.'

'This woman, Staunton. How sure are you she posted it?'

Brooke shrugged. 'She might be lying. But then what could be *her* motive? You're right, though, she's a mystery in herself. We're trying to find out more about her. Then there's her missing comrades in the Party. They're up at the castle, held under Emergency Powers. Someone thinks they may know too much. Maybe they do. But killers? No, Frank. I'm missing a vital part of the picture. I can't help thinking the military's holding back, there's a major – name of Stone – he's a pen-pusher, but he's not been entirely honest about the night of the blackout, and those drifting barrage balloons. His boss – the CO – is a career soldier too, name of Swift-Lane. He's all charm and energy, but I wouldn't trust him as far as I can spit. Brother's in the Cabinet, another one in the navy, so maybe it's just all sibling rivalry.

'I could let the file go like that,' said Brooke, clicking his fingers. 'For all I know I'll be off the case in the morning anyway. But there's something about it that lingers in the mind . . .'

'Here's my advice, if you want it . . .' said Edwardes. 'I'd go back to the scene of the crime. Someone heard gunshots on the night? Send out uniform door-to-door. Perhaps someone saw your killer. Why not put a man in the cemetery after dark? You're not the only night walker, you know. Most places like that end up being used as lovers' lane. Maybe someone clocked the murderer, alright, but they don't want to come forward. Shoe leather, Brooke. That's what this case needs.'

Downstairs they could hear Kat at a sewing machine, the

rhythmic pedalling like a racing heartbeat. The sensation of the regular speeding palpitation made Brooke feel feverish, so he took the armchair, knowing it might invite a moment's sleep.

He leant over from the chair to pluck a sheet of paper from the bed, noting the neat circles drawn around groups of letters. 'What's all this?'

'Nothing clever,' said Edwardes. 'We've had our orders from the Home Office to watch out for groups of letters which repeat themselves in a set pattern. A tip-off from Madingley Hall, no less, via London. It's called a crib. A key. If you had radio traffic and you knew it was about Cambridge you'd look out for nine-letter groups. See? CAMBRIDGE – nine letters. Once you've got that, you're into the code.'

'But you're after seven?' said Brooke, suddenly awake, letting his eye run over the encircled letters.

'That's it. They've given us the actual word in case someone panics and sends an uncoded message. That's not as daft as it sounds, because the point about Morse is that it's fast, and the operator can hear it as if it's the spoken word. So if you're in a hurry, and you think no one's listening, then you might take the risk. It's called "chat".'

'What's the word?'

'Pegasus.' Edwardes was laughing. 'I know you're trustworthy, Brooke. But if you let that slip they might shoot me, which come to think of it might be a blessing. So, yes, Pegasus. You're the one with the classical education.'

Brooke shook his head. 'Pegasus was a god, a mythic horse with wings. I think he carried another god as a passenger in pursuit of the chimera, a dazzling beast made up of several parts of other beasts: the head of a lion, the body of a goat, the tail of a snake.'

Edwardes nodded, shuffling some sheets of paper. 'Other than that it's the usual chatter. The minister's visit caused some traffic, but nothing sinister. Nasty shock, that old girl in the fire. What's Dr Comfort say?'

'Hardly a mystery. The poor woman burnt to death, pretty much in front of our eyes. We're working on the hypothesis she was a vagrant, a roadster, probably a drinker.'

'But a woman?' said Edwardes. 'Roadsters are usually men, Brooke. Women are very rare; I pity them all. Ever put 'em in the cells?'

Brooke shook his head.

'Next time it's frosty, think about it. Charity doesn't have to start at home.'

CHAPTER FORTY-SIX

Rose King's hut on Market Hill was doing brisk business; a gaggle of shop girls had formed a scrum in front of the counter, vying for the chance to add sugar to tea.

'Your luck's changed, Rose,' said one, and they all dissolved in laughter, watching Brooke approach.

'Tall, dark and handsome,' said another voice. 'Just the ticket!'

Brooke's narrow steps brought him into the pool of light spilling from the hatch. He tipped his hat, and the girls fled, giggling.

'Your man's over there,' said Rose, half a cigarette bobbing at her bright red lips. 'Gives me the creeps. Oily's the word, and I know he's a friend . . . I don't think it's my tea that brings him to town, do you? It's the glassy eyes that gives the game away.'

Brooke surveyed the market. The stalls were mostly bare, a patchwork of shadows, the awnings just now beginning to glimmer with the first signs of a frost.

'By the fountain,' said Rose, signalling with her eyes.

Captain Richard Kerridge sat on the edge of a stone bowl, a

cigarette leaking smoke at his fingertips. Out of uniform, he looked rakish, even dissolute. He loosened a red silk tie at his throat and brushed some ash from his lapels.

'Rich, thanks. You got the message,' said Brooke.

Kerridge nodded. 'Summoned by the hero of the desert. How could I refuse?'

'A favour if you can, Rich,' said Brooke. 'I need to check out the story of a soldier, in the last lot, who won a medal, could you trace the citation? Name of Corporal Harry Staunton.' Brooke spelt out the surname. 'That was your beat in the Middle East, wasn't it, medals, awards. Still got the contacts?'

Kerridge executed a lazy salute and nearly tumbled into the fountain.

'Bit of a party somewhere?' asked Brooke.

'Gathering intelligence,' said Kerridge, pouring a mug of Rose's tea into the fountain. 'And I must get back. My duties are ceaseless.'

The gaggle of girls was out of sight but they heard a wave of delighted screams bounding and rebounding down distant streets.

'Tell me about Swift-Lane,' said Brooke.

Kerridge sighed. 'What's to tell? A soldier trying to match the exploits of his elder brothers. Did I say trying to match? Perhaps *desperately* trying would be more accurate.'

He met Brooke's eyes. 'I didn't tell you this, Brooke. You heard it on the grapevine. Swift-Lane has a reputation for flakiness. Before the Great War he led an expedition to map Baffin Island, up in the Arctic. It was so badly organised he and his men had to be rescued by the Canadian Navy. Copybook blotted.

'In the war he was at Gallipoli – ditto – then various theatres of war, all far-flung. Russia after the Armistice, one of Churchill's anti-communist volunteers. Then a spell in military intelligence, then back to the War Office. Marriage ended in divorce, another black mark.

'This is his last chance, Brooke. But that's the great thing about war if you're a soldier. Right place, right time, you can remake a career. Wrong place, wrong time, you get shot. Madingley's a little cauldron of schemers, believe me.'

'So Swift-Lane's distrusted?'

'A loose cannon, Brooke. Lethal in action, but only to his own men. There's nothing a soldier despises more than the reckless hero. You can see why he hates Major Stone. He might be second-in-command but at least he *can* organise a piss-up in a brewery. Talk about chalk and cheese.'

'Hate's a strong word.'

'They communicate by paper. Total loathing, Brooke, believe me.'

'Why's Swift-Lane so interested in the fate of Chris Childe?'

Kerridge brushed his greatcoat down, buttoning the collar under his chin, so that what little light there was caught his profile, and Brooke saw a glimpse of what the drink would do to his face in ten years' time.

'Swift-Lane's interested in Childe because if sensitive information gets out it will cost the colonel his career. The operation on the riverside, the lecture at the Galen, it's all part of military weapons research and it's under Swift-Lane's direct oversight.

'The night of the Great Darkness was a five-star cock-up. The civilian unit should never have been allowed to dig the pits, but Corporal Currie wanted to give his lads a break. Currie's got previous with Swift-Lane, by the way – he was his driver at Gallipoli. Anyway, he goes to Swift-Lane and pleads his case and the colonel obliged by signing the order.

'Crucial mistake. Worse, Major Stone spotted it, and took action. Currie had to sprint down to the Galen and read the Riot Act. Not that they'd seen anything. But they couldn't take a chance. Which might have all worked, but Childe, as you have discovered, was a persistent man. He got sight of the classified film.'

Kerridge ditched his cigarette in the fountain. 'If there is a major security failure, if the contents of the conchie's letter do reach Moscow, then Swift-Lane will carry the can. Stone will make bloody sure of that.'

CHAPTER FORTY-SEVEN

Vera Staunton sat opposite Brooke in the slated morning sunlight which fell through his office blinds. She'd called at the Spinning House duty desk at eight o'clock, asking for the inspector, explaining that she wished to make a statement in relation to the death of Chris Childe. They waited patiently in silence for tea, and Edison, who'd been summoned to take down a record.

At Staunton's feet sat a wicker basket of shopping: a loaf of bread, a butcher's parcel of folded brown paper, a tin of soup. On her lap was her purse and a copy of *Britannia and Eve* magazine, showing a young woman at the wheel of an open-topped sports car, cherry-red lipstick matching the paintwork, a beret set at just the right angle.

Staunton wore a full-length coat, slightly frayed at the cuffs, and a pair of leather flat-soled shoes. She looked tired: a tradesman's wife perhaps, with children still at home, and a day of chores ahead. The easy confidence she'd displayed in her rooms on Babylon Street was gone. Her face, free of make-up, looked puffy, as if she'd been crying.

In the war, Brooke had seen many women forced into prostitution. In Cairo, he'd often met Captain Kerridge in a bar in the Birka, the city's red-light district, to swap gossip and so-called 'intelligence'. Shops, bars and brothels fronted a lake. The atmosphere had been febrile, with good reason, for in the first years of the war a riot had broken out, sparked by the discovery of an English girl dancing naked in a club. A mob of soldiers had tried to 'rescue' her, and were promptly ejected from a fourth-storey window.

The women of the Birka were cowed, not only by their clientele and by a palpable sense of shame, but by the men who hovered by every stairwell, their eyes constantly scanning the crowd for approaching customers. Vera Staunton radiated a very different aura: there was more of the scent of the cool courtesan, a working woman visited at appointed times. There had been no pimp at her front door on Babylon Street, just the intermittent vigilance of the aged Ida in her bedsit at the end of the corridor.

Edison arrived with tea and biscuits, and set them down before subsiding into a chair himself. He'd been out since dawn organising the door-to-door on Mill Road, trying to track down, without success, a sighting of Childe's killer. Several residents had heard the shot, at a time between seven and quarter past, but seen no one.

'You wanted to make a statement,' prompted Brooke. Edison had his notebook unfolded on the desk before him.

'I have a friend,' said Staunton. 'A Major Stone. He visits regularly.'

'I see,' said Brooke, nodding his head as if this statement were not as startling as it was. Amid his confusion, the euphemism 'friend' almost worked: how clever to choose it, ahead of visitor, acquaintance or client.

'And he pays, to visit, and to be your friend,' he said.

'Yes,' she said, her voice cracking. 'He pays.'

The only sound was the scratching nib of the sergeant's fountain pen.

'This is Major Joelyn Stone, of Madingley Hall?'

She nodded. 'The morning Chris called with the letter he bumped into Major Stone on the stairs. Major Stone – Joelyn – had been with me, for several hours. Later, around five, Joelyn returned. He'd seen Chris at the tribunal at the court. Joelyn sits on the bench.

'He was convinced Chris had recognised him. He wanted to know if he'd been back since the tribunal to ask questions. I said he hadn't; I said that he'd simply seen a soldier on the stairs in the half-light. He was hardly likely to recognise him on the bench in court. But Joelyn wouldn't have it . . . He's an ambitious man whose career depends on the opinion of others,' she said.

Brooke thought it was a devastating verdict, and wondered if she'd prepared it, along with the rest of her story.

'He insisted that he couldn't just let the issue lie. The timing, he said, was particularly bad. I think he planned to offer Chris money for his silence. I said he should just wait. But he said that wasn't an option.'

'Major Stone is married?' asked Edison.

'Yes. To a general's daughter. I think the relationship's a cool one.'

'What do you mean – *I think he planned to offer him money*? Why do you suspect that?' pressed Brooke.

'He asked several questions about Chris: his house, job, family. I said he was often pressed for cash and had two young girls. The house in Romsey Town is a poor one, a slum, at least to some eyes, if not to mine.'

'Did Childe come back at all that day?' asked Brooke.

The events of the last day of Childe's life were still unclear. He'd taken the letter to Staunton, reported for work at the depot, appeared in front of the tribunal, then returned to work on Midsummer Common. His body had been found the next morning. Had there been time to go back to Babylon Street?

'I didn't see Chris again, not after I went out to post his letter,' insisted Staunton.

'A letter which never arrived, Mrs Staunton,' said Brooke.

'I can't answer for the Royal Mail, Inspector. Or our central office,' she said, shaking a bangle which encircled her right wrist.

'Why tell us about Major Stone now?' said Brooke. 'Do you think the major is a murderer, that'd he'd take a man's life to protect his own position?'

'I don't think he'd plan such a thing,' she said carefully, and Brooke thought how damning *that* line would have sounded to a jury. 'But I think that if he did offer Chris money he would have turned it down. Thrown it in his face. And he might have said more: about my life, about the men who visit, about the evils of money and power. Once he started, Chris just spewed it out. They might have fought. It has to be possible.'

She appeared genuinely moved. 'I had to tell you. I visited Mary last night. There is *no* money. She's a widow with two children, as I was a widow with a child when Harry didn't come back. Her life is ruined, Inspector. Every day will be a struggle. I should have told you sooner. I'm sorry.'

The brown eyes flooded. 'Mary deserves some justice. I thought I should tell the truth, whatever it costs me. The children should know what happened to their father. It's all I can give her.'

'I see,' said Brooke, keeping his voice neutral, reminding

himself that this complex woman had mixed political activism with working as a prostitute. Perhaps she did feel deeply for Mary in her plight. Perhaps she had other motives. 'How many *friends* do you have, Mrs Staunton? I ask only in the interests of the inquiry. Was Childe ever such a *friend*?'

'Good God, no. Chris loves Mary. Mary loves Chris. Frankly, he seemed to emit no sexual . . .' She searched for the word. 'No sexual signals at all. As to my friends, Inspector. Six, sometimes eight. It depends . . .'

'I see,' said Brooke. 'We'll need to confront Major Stone with this allegation. We may need a statement.'

Edison had one last question. 'Are any of your other clients military personnel?'

Staunton stood, an easy fluid motion, and Brooke thought she'd simply ducked the question, but she stopped at the door and turned back. 'They're *all* military personnel.'

CHAPTER FORTY-EIGHT

The key to the case, at least to its successful prosecution, was the murder weapon. If Major Stone was their man, and he had not disposed of the gun in the river, then it was either at Madingley Hall or hidden at his private home, a leafy villa on the city's southern borders. Brooke dispatched Edison to the magistrates' court to obtain a warrant to search the house, while he waited to set out for military headquarters at Madingley.

The phone rang on Brooke's desk.

'Inspector?' Brooke recognised Dr Comfort's blunt vowels. 'I've completed the external examination of the woman burnt to death last night. A surprise, I'm afraid. Can you?'

'It's urgent?' he asked the pathologist.

'Oh, yes, Brooke. I'd say so.'

It would take Edison an hour to get the warrant, so Brooke grabbed his coat and rushed out into the autumn sunshine. The Galen's white facade was stark in the morning light, students crowding into the lobby, heading for a lecture. He took the steps to the fifth floor two at a time, bursting through the doors into the light-drenched morgue.

'I'll keep it brief, Brooke, as you're clearly in a rush,' said Comfort, by way of welcome. 'Several points, but you do need to see this . . .'

A surgeon's face mask covered Comfort's mouth and nose, fogging his speech. Brooke declined the offer, instead holding his linen handkerchief to his nostrils.

The badly burnt naked body was laid out on the metal table.

Comfort moved towards the head, to which a few threads of hair were still attached.

'Overall she's suffered eighty per cent burns. The skull is particularly badly affected, the bones charred, but it does reveal this . . .'

Brooke had no choice but to look. Carefully he removed his spectacles, leaning in to examine an area of exposed cranium.

'Do you see? A depression, a wound, I'm afraid. What? A centimetre in depth at the centre, indicating a forceful blow. Our old friend the blunt instrument, very blunt actually; you can see that the wound is in no way concave, it's a flat depression in a curved surface. And I found this, just a few particles in the wound, most definitely associated with the trauma.'

He had a Petri dish, within which was a small amount of a sticky material noteworthy for its colour, a metallic, blanched blue.

'Ceramic paint, mixed with a little blood,' said Comfort. 'My guess, from the colour, is that it's the paint used to cover a lot of heavy-duty tools. A wrench? A hand vice? Unconsciousness would have followed within seconds of this blow, certainly within a minute, and would have lasted several hours. It would have killed her eventually: unfortunately, we know it didn't.'

Brooke saw again the flailing semaphore of the jerking arms, the oddly inhuman erratic stumble, then the collapse into the grass.

'A few other details,' said Comfort.

A box stood by a microscope on the pathologist's desk. Inside were a pair of glasses, misshapen by the heat.

'Badly melted, of course, but they're reading glasses. And she had her own teeth, showing signs of dental work, a filling, certainly, within the last five years. Her general physical condition, given her age, is actually excellent.'

Comfort rocked his head from side to side. 'If she was a vagrant I'd say she was a pretty unusual one. The internal examination shows no signs of alcohol abuse. The bones show no signs of rheumatism or deformation, and certainly not in the feet, which would be symptomatic of a roadster. You might have to think again, Brooke. Sorry. The good news is that there's a shop mark on the frame of the spectacles. Here, see? Goodall's. Silver Street, I think, so that might help. Here . . .'

The detached lenses of the glasses, slightly distorted, lay in Comfort's hand as he slipped them inside an envelope with the frame. 'With any luck the prescription will do the trick.'

The pathologist threw open a window. The morgue filled with the sound of the city's church bells marking the hour.

'I know you like the wider picture, as well as the detail,' said Comfort. 'There were several other items found in the ashes of the box house. A tobacco tin and cigarette roller, a couple of chicken bones. A two-bob bit. None of it seemed pertinent. I assumed it was either litter, or it'd been left by the crew who put up the boxes. That was the Auxiliary Fire Service. When I asked, they pointed out they weren't the only crew on the site. The safety trenches on Midsummer Common, around the box house, were dug by a labour squad from Civil Defence. Which, if I'm not mistaken, brings us back to your man Childe, on the day he died.'

CHAPTER FORTY-NINE

Edison, with a newly issued warrant, took the Wasp to Major Stone's house. Brooke commandeered a radio car with a uniformed driver and sped out to Madingley Hall along dappled lanes. At the barrier he passed Colonel Swift-Lane, leaving, at the wheel of a black polished Bentley.

'Inspector. Anything I can do?' called the colonel.

Brooke asked the constable to wind his window down. The situation was hardly conducive to a candid update on the inquiry. 'No, sir. Still on the case; a few loose ends. Major Stone will do. If I need you later?'

'Absolutely. Ring the adjutant's office, they'll track me down. I'm off for a Whitehall briefing, but I'll be back by dusk.'

Swift-Lane appeared almost childishly excited. Brooke recalled Kerridge's expert summary of his career, the almost boyish enthusiasm for adventure. He actually bobbed in his seat. 'How can *Stone* help?' he asked. 'He's just ahead of you, back from London.'

'I won't keep you,' said Brooke, nodding to his driver.

They swept on, leaving Swift-Lane at the gate.

The forecourt of the hall was busy, with trestle tables laid out on the gravel covered with order papers. Motorcycle couriers came and went with document bags.

'Bit of a flap,' said Stone, still standing by his staff car as an orderly took his small case out of the boot. 'Invasion exercise at the weekend. No doubt you'll get the bumf in town. Bloody chaos here . . . CO's off to get further orders from the Regional Comptroller, no less.'

'I need a moment,' said Brooke, and Stone nodded amiably, heading back up to his office. The wary lack of confidence, palpable in their first meeting, had evaporated. Perhaps, Brooke thought, he revelled in the idea of being a man of action, even if it was entirely administrative action.

'This about your Yank scientist again?' asked Stone, installed behind his desk, relighting the stub of a small cigar in a tin ashtray.

'Lux: Ernst Lux. No, this is an entirely different matter.'

Stone walked to the open window and filled his lungs with the country air.

Brooke contemplated his broad back. 'Do you know a woman called Vera Staunton?'

Stone turned, tried a smile, but it slid away to leave a sudden look of anger. He slammed the mullioned window shut.

'What is your interest in Vera?' he asked, coming back to his seat.

'I know it's a bore, Major, but I'm afraid I'm the one who asks the questions. Colonel Swift-Lane is as keen as I am to find the killer of Chris Childe. I can—'

Stone's hand rose quickly to dismiss the idea of involving the CO.

'I think we can take the basis of your relationship with Vera Staunton as a given, Major,' said Brooke. 'I'm not here to secure a minor conviction for soliciting. You—'

'Vera is not a common prostitute,' said Stone, almost in a whisper.

'In what sense is she uncommon?'

'She observes certain proprieties,' said Stone, although he sounded uncertain that he'd done her justice. 'She is a decent woman. A war widow. A—'

'And a member of the communist party, and the Peace Pledge Union . . .'

Stone inflated his chest. 'I think you'll find her role in the coming revolution will be restricted to filling envelopes. The Party meetings provide her with an intellectual escape. They recruited her, you know. She's a pacifist at heart, not a Bolshevik. And it is a free country. Isn't that the point of all this . . .'

Brooke sensed Stone was trying to deflect the course of the interview. 'You'll be aware a man was found shot dead in one of the city cemeteries. The newspapers have noted the bare details. He was a conscientious objector by the name of Chris Childe. Killed by a bullet to the left temple.'

Stone had been nodding, a very slight movement of his square jaw, and this continued, although Brooke felt it was a cover for a certain level of shock. Had Swift-Lane failed to keep his deputy fully briefed on the case?

'I see,' said Stone. 'Am I in some way a suspect?'

'Mrs Staunton has made a statement to the effect that on the night of the Great Darkness you visited her rooms and on leaving the next morning bumped into a man on the stairs. She further alleges that this man was Childe.

'You returned to her room unexpectedly later and told her you'd seen him again, in the dock at the assizes, pleading for unconditional registration. You feared recognition, and – presumably – blackmail. Mrs Staunton says she got the impression you were going to try and offer Childe money for a measure of discretion. Did you?'

'No.' He rearranged his hand on his desk, lifting the metal finger with his undamaged hand.

For a few tumbling seconds Brooke thought that would be it: a series of flat denials, but the major's shoulders slumped, and he met his eyes.

'I felt an approach was counterproductive, Brooke. Why signal my anxieties? If he had the guts, and tried to use what he knew, then, and only then, I'd have offered money, yes. Or devised a counter-threat. The decisions of the tribunal are open to review, after all. He didn't hold all the cards.'

'Did you take any direct action?'

'Yes. I felt Childe had been less than honest with the tribunal about his political affiliations. Vera was able to fill in the details. I left a note with the clerk of the court, to be copied to my fellow assessors on the tribunal, making it clear I might wish to revisit one of our recent decisions. I gave the clerk Childe's case number. He'll have a note.

'I trusted Vera's judgement. Childe wasn't a troublemaker. But if he tried to use what he knew against me, I would have had a riposte at least. I had no need to kill the man, Brooke. None at all. I had the situation under control.'

Brooke considered the image of Childe's shattered skull on its steel pillow in the morgue.

'Did you fire the shot that killed Chris Childe?'

Stone managed the smile this time, and a short laugh.

'I'm not sure panic, or overreaction, is a sound military virtue,' he said smoothly.

'I'm sorry, this is a serious enquiry. I can continue it at the Spinning House. Did you fire the shot?'

'No.'

'You have a pistol?'

Stone unbuttoned his leather holster and placed it on the desk. Brooke noted the affectation of his initials on the grip, and the regimental crest. He wondered if it had been with this gun that he'd mutilated his own hand in the trenches.

Brooke's jacket had a ticket pocket from which he extracted a bullet, which he placed on the desk.

'That is the bullet which killed Chris Childe; it was embedded in a tree, having passed through his brain. It is, remarkably, intact. A simple matter to match it with the murder weapon.'

'No doubt,' said Stone, sliding the pistol in its holster over the desk. 'Help yourself.'

'I have obtained a warrant to search your home. That is in progress. Do you possess other weapons?'

'You're searching my house, now?' Stone, normally florid, seemed to drain of blood. 'Will my wife have been offered an explanation?'

'No. We simply need to find any firearms and eliminate them from our inquiry, and take a statement from her on your movements on the night Childe died. My question, again: do you possess any other pistols capable of firing a bullet of this calibre?'

'Not that I'm aware. My wife's father collected pistols. They're all boxed, and spiked. There's a gun-room caisson on the upper landing. They're all mostly Indian Army antiques, frankly.

There's a shotgun in the kitchen, but there's no ammunition.'

Brooke made a note.

'If the bullet doesn't match, is that an end to it?' asked Stone.

'No. But if no other weapon comes to hand, and you can adequately explain your whereabouts on the night of the murder, I think we're done. Can you?'

'I was in court until five. I walked home via Vera's flat. I'd let the driver go and it's only a mile. We had dinner at eight-thirty with friends. My wife can confirm that. Our guests left at eleven. I got a cab to the station the next morning, and we dropped by at the court to leave a note for the clerk . . .' He shrugged. 'I caught the 9.17. I spent two nights at my club. I returned just now, you saw me.'

Brooke nodded. 'We'll make the necessary checks. In the meantime, I can take it you will be on duty here at the hall? No urgent, top-level military exercises planned outside the county?'

Brooke had let a slightly mocking tone enter his voice, and he could see Stone swell slightly with bruised self-importance.

'In the short-term, no. No plans, Brooke. But I've been given a new command, by the War Office, by the prime minister, actually. It's classified, I'm afraid, otherwise I'd share details. I'll be gone by the end of the month.'

'Let's hope so,' said Brooke.

CHAPTER FIFTY

Major Stone, having given Brooke permission to search his office and a small dormitory room in the attic where he was able to sleep when working late, promptly commandeered a staff car to take him home. He wished to 'oversee' Edison in the search. A suspicion lingered in his wake that the major's eagerness to return to the house, in the midst of a top-level military exercise, was the result of anxiety over his wife: what would she think? What would she be told? What did she know? Brooke recalled wise words from his father: never judge a marriage from the outside. Perhaps she knew it all: the indiscretions, the kept woman. To what extent was she also dedicated to the upward trajectory of her husband's career?

First, for Brooke, came Stone's office. He noted its neat, bureaucratic simplicity, with the desk and chair set to impress beneath a regimental flag. The two phones, red and green, placed precisely at one o'clock, and two o'clock to the blotter. A black fountain pen lay at right angles to the pile of documents. A framed picture, to the far left, was turned so that any visitor could glimpse the scene: the steps of the Old College, Sandhurst, a group of cadets at attention, as perpendicular as the white pillars which held the pediment above.

The overall effect was of a sanctum, and the extent to which the room resisted the sounds of the outside world was extraordinary. The atmosphere was stifling, claustrophobic, almost quilted with silence. Brooke thought of Stone seated in this peace, considering perhaps what lay ahead: a new command, rank, even a title, while his hands lay on the blotter, the disfigured fingers a reminder of the hint of disgrace which might now, finally, be consigned to the past.

Had Childe threatened this glorious future?

Brooke searched thoroughly but there was no second gun. The attic room proved to be one-time servants' quarters. The book beside the bed was *A History of the Punic Wars*, the blanket neatly folded, the pillow smooth and unruffled. Brooke wondered if the creation of this billet had provided Stone with the camouflage required to visit Babylon Street. He imagined a late-night call from the black phone to home, complaining of the workload, the necessity to use the cold attic bed.

Here, under the roof, Madingley's bucolic silence was even more profound. It was into this cotton wool world that a single sound *did* impinge: a gunshot, dull and muffled by a silencer. Brooke went to the window and opened it, breathing in the country air laced with pine scent, listening: five shots more rang out in a stilted, imperfect series.

Taking directions from the staff sergeant on duty in the Great Hall, he set out around the perimeter of the building, a bewildering zigzag path past walled gardens, ice houses and a dilapidated orangery, into the grounds beyond.

The officer class at Madingley had kept its pleasures close to hand. A groom led a pair of handsome horses into the old stables, while two men played tennis on a court bordered by hedges of copper beech, although the net was partly perished and roughly patched. Under the rusted iron canopy of a small bandstand, a pair of young men in braces played violins in front of a music stand.

A path led past a dovecote into the formal gardens, and Brooke followed it to a fork, took the left way, and left again at a statue of a god blowing a wind with puffed cheeks. The woods finally cleared to reveal a large rectangular piece of open grass which the staff sergeant who'd given him directions had referred to as the old polo pitch.

Here a shooting range had been set out. The targets to the right, the butts to the left, a wooden pavilion beyond in the colonial style. Reaching the verandah, Brooke watched an elderly man in a shirt and breeches firing pistol shots, then testing his accuracy by examining the distant target with a small brass telescope. The targets were made of straw, and roughly assembled in human form.

Inside, the pavilion revealed its original purpose: a series of heraldic devices decorated a long bar, while half a dozen battered leather couches were arranged in a convivial nest around a large open fireplace. At the bar, a private in fatigues worked with dubbin, softening an ammunition belt, while a spread cloth held several pistols, each one glistening with newly applied polish.

Brooke held his warrant card in the soldier's face. 'Major Stone asked me to pop down and pick up his pistol. Just routine elimination. He said I was to ask for Private . . . ?'

'Goodman.'

'Right. Goodman. That was it. He said you had everything running smartly.'

Goodman smiled. 'Good shot, the major – old school of course. You can tell the ones who did their bit last time. Competitions, with a crowd watching, or a wager on the outcome, they get better. Rest of 'em fold under pressure. And the gun's not important. The major has an old Webley .45, but he can outshoot the cadets with all their new kit.'

Reaching back, he slipped a padlock key off a board painted with numbers.

'Gun's booked in, is it? You keep track?' asked Brooke.

'No need. The estate's secure, you came through the gates, you'd have seen. Tight as a duck's arse . . . The perimeter wire's seven foot high. We trust the officers. These keys are spares.'

Brooke was directed to the changing room, which was lined with lockers and reeked of damp clothes, polish and sweat. Stone's locker was number 34 and, besides a padded jacket and a box of ammunition, contained a revolver folded in a green cloth.

Brooke requisitioned everything in a felt bag provided by the amiable Goodman.

Outside, on the verandah, he watched the elderly soldier fire a final round at the distant straw man. The first five shots missed but the sixth caught the target's head, so that it flipped back only to sag forward on its chest. A skein of blue cordite drifted across the green landscape, all the more vivid when viewed through Brooke's lenses.

Now he was out in the clear light, he slid the pistol out of the bag using a pencil through the trigger guard. While he'd been a decent shot himself, he'd never coveted guns, never found that their metallic heft held the special fascination it did for others. So he was no expert. But he was absolutely sure he wasn't holding an antique Webley .45.

CHAPTER FIFTY-ONE

While Brooke searched Madingley Hall for the murder weapon, Edison was back at the Spinning House, typing up an inventory of items removed from Stone's home: a total of thirty-two guns, all ceremonial, and none in a condition to fire.

He was about to add a summary of Mrs Stone's testimony when the desk sergeant shouted up the stairs that he should pick up the phone as CID at West Bar, Sheffield, were on the line, insisting on speaking to Brooke, on an urgent matter.

Edison scribbled down a brief outline of the message.

The car which had taken Gretorix – aka Turl – north, with Detective Inspector Solly and his police driver, had stopped for petrol on the A1 at Newark. It had then pulled into a roadhouse on the edge of Sherwood Forest. Solly had left Gretorix and the driver in the car, while he used the toilet and ordered a round of sandwiches.

Returning ten minutes later, he found the driver unconscious at the wheel. A head wound, delivered with a heavy blunt object, had cracked his skull. The prisoner, despite being handcuffed to a restraining bar in the rear of the vehicle, was gone. The cuffs' chain had been severed with bolt-cutters.

The driver, on regaining consciousness at the Royal Northern Hospital, said he'd noted trailing headlights when they'd turned off at Newark, and later at the roadhouse. He had determined to mention his suspicions if the car had followed them out onto the A52. The car? A black Ford, with two men in the front. A general alert had been issued across Yorkshire to find Gretorix.

The caller was a desk sergeant relaying information on behalf of Solly. Finished, Edison adopted a weary tone in reply. 'A sorry tale indeed,' he said.

The line went dead.

Edison sat quietly for a moment, watching the second hand of the clock tick by, wondering whether Gretorix was still alive, and how the driver of the following car had known they were moving the prisoner and what route they would take. Perhaps the city's infamous gangs had survived so long by making sure they had ears inside West Bar police station.

He was up on his feet, hat on his head, looking forward to a late lunch, when the phone rang again.

'Detective Inspector Brooke's office,' he said.

He heard the desk sergeant mumble something, then the line cleared. 'Eden?'

'Detective Sergeant Edison.'

'Ah. It's Corby, at the *News*.'

Drew Corby was the editor of the local evening paper.

'Tell him for me, will you? One of the city reporters has just been in to my office. He got a call from this fella who's been found shot, name of Childe? He wanted to meet a reporter. Had a story, he said. Promised it was a corker. So my man Dodds fixed up a meeting at the Maypole, on Portugal Place, at nine, the night he died. No show. He waited an hour, then gave up. Tell Brooke.'

CHAPTER FIFTY-TWO

Jesus Green Pool stretched for a hundred yards into the distance, a narrow pencil of reflected light, just a dozen lanes wide but a hundred yards long. Built by the Victorians on the meadows of Jesus Green, its meagre width was designed to echo the joys of swimming in the nearby river. The facilities were functional at best, a match for the men who swam here each day throughout the year. In the winter, the breaking of ice was seen as an added attraction.

Brooke liked it best in autumn, when he'd swim through a floating carpet of leaves. From water level the view was limited to a surrounding screen of pine trees, the walls of Jesus College just visible across the grass. The college had been founded on the ruins of a nunnery, the chapel tower of which still broke the skyline, and he often wondered what the nuns would have thought of the sight of half-naked men lying on the grass.

Today, the water held its own light, cold and blue, dappled by the breeze which made the pines whisper and flex.

A phone call to Doric had produced four of the college

swimmers. These volunteers had collected deckchairs from the pool attendant and were lounging in the pale sunlight, affecting to read dusty books but in fact watching Dr Comfort as he set about what looked like an arcane exercise in trigonometry. The pathologist had begun construction of what he insisted on calling the 'marksman's station', a heavy-duty tripod with clamps, its three legs anchored in small nests of sandbags.

The particular dimensions of Jesus Green Pool had presented considerable problems. Most swimming pools have a deep end and a shallow end: not Jesus, which was deep in the middle. It was at this point that one of the swimmers, a pale bony student with red hair, had been invited to dive in and run two floating lines across the narrow pool, creating a test range two yards wide, from side to side. The marksman's station was set to one side, the angle of the shot regulated by a wooden protractor hastily constructed in the lab by Comfort's servants, effectively creating a makeshift theodolite, to which he now clamped not a telescopic sight, but a gun.

Not a gun, *the* gun, discovered in Major Stone's locker at Madingley Hall: the weapon identified easily enough as a revolver designed originally for the Russian Imperial Army.

Now, judging the angle of the weapon, Brooke doubted Comfort's calculations. 'You're telling me a bullet fired into the water at that angle won't reach the bottom? What is it – eight feet, less. It's water, Doctor. Not concrete.'

'You of all people should never doubt the soldier's lore,' said Comfort, screwing the gun into the tripod and checking the angle for the third time. The pool attendant, who had been dragooned into allowing the test firing, stood anxiously in the lee of the changing rooms, looking on and chain-smoking.

Comfort was finally content with the preparations. 'There was an incident in the war, Brooke, on the Meuse, I think: a platoon on recce got caught on the far bank. They tried to swim back but a Jerry machine gun opened up. They held their breaths, kept six feet down, and lived to tell the tale. Not a scratch until they tried to get *out* of the water on the far side. The forces on a bullet hitting water are not appreciably different from hitting concrete. But for our purposes it has one outstanding advantage: it won't destroy the bullet.'

The four Michaelhouse swimmers waited for the sun to reappear from behind a bank of cloud before sliding into the water at the far end and, no doubt following a prearranged plan, racing to the mid-point, employing expert butterfly strokes.

Comfort braced himself at the tripod.

'Right. Brooke, your job is to keep your keen assistants clear of the firing range. I'll fire six bullets. Ready?'

Brooke directed the swimmers back another yard.

'Ready.'

The first gunshot cracked, the track of the bullet marked by a sudden silver thread in the blue water, which – almost miraculously – fell geometrically away from a straight path, weakening, dying, fading away into the depths.

Comfort, unhappy with the angle, readjusted the tripod by a few degrees and braced himself anew. The next five shots came rhythmically, each silver thread unique, but all falling within the narrow range and all petering out of violent energy long before reaching the shimmering pale tiles on the bottom of the pool.

Brooke unleashed the mermen of Michaelhouse.

Suddenly the pool was full of them, taking air like goldfish before sinking down to the pool floor. It was quickly clear that some kind of rudimentary competition had been agreed, for the water was white with thrashing limbs, hands scouring the tiles.

Within a minute they had all six bullets.

Brooke, at a trestle table, set out glasses and a bottle of sherry, the best Doric could find.

Comfort held a bullet in one hand, an eyepiece magnifying glass in his right eye. His head, neck and hand froze as he deftly turned over one of the bullets retrieved from the pool. Then he repeated the exercise with a bullet in a small plastic see-through envelope, the one which had passed through Christopher Childe's brain.

'Result?' asked Brooke, accepting a sherry from the red-haired swimmer.

'As I say, I don't want to be quoted as yet, but visually, and therefore *provisionally*, there are matches both in terms of the striations on the bullet and the imprint of the firing pin in the soft metal primer.'

'It's the gun that killed Childe?'

The light swept away as a dark cloud slipped over the pool.

'Looks like it, Brooke. And this is interesting too . . .' He led Brooke to the marksman's station. 'Now we can see the gun in the sunlight at this angle, it appears to have quite a history – considering it was made for the Imperial Army of Russia. Do you see?'

Because it was set at an angle on the tripod, the base of the grip was revealed. It was crudely stamped with the Delphic inscription *ACEF*. And across this had been scratched the iconic outline of a hammer and sickle, the enduring symbol of the Russian Revolution, and of the Bolsheviks who had brought down the Tsar.

CHAPTER FIFTY-THREE

Brooke slipped from his mossy step into the river. His body welcomed the shock, his heartbeat picking up, the warm blood rushing to toes and fingers. Once the winter frosts really bit, the water would be too cold, but for now the autumnal sun provided just enough heat to keep the Cam bearable in the hours after sunset.

On his back, drifting, he let the tension flood out of his body. The afternoon had been spent in a frantic effort to assemble the evidence required to support a charge of murder against Joelyn Stone. Dr Comfort had finally rung Brooke's office at dusk to report that the ballistics results were not in doubt: Stone's gun had fired the fatal shot. Formal statements had been taken from Stone's wife, and a request had been made to the War Office for details of the major's forthcoming appointment to head a new unit charged with developing balloon warfare.

The key evidence, however, would be Vera Staunton's. Brooke and Edison had returned to her rooms on Babylon Street. Was she prepared to give evidence in court? She was. Her contribution, Brooke was confident, would put a rope around Stone's neck. It had been a nasty, brutal, selfish, tawdry killing. And a disappointment: Brooke had been convinced the young pacifist had died because he knew too much, the sad end of a thrilling tale of political intrigue. But in reality it had turned out to be no more than another seedy domestic tragedy.

Leaving Babylon Street with Staunton's signed statement, he should at least have felt some satisfaction, but something of the house's downbeat despair troubled him: the threadbare carpets, the stifled voices, the joyless name cards on the peeling doors. Standing on the doorstep, he sniffed the air in the corridor, noting the smell of decay, stale food, cigarette ash and a sour note: milk, gone off. The memory troubled him now as he slipped under Trinity Bridge, but he let the thought pass, distracted by the silky embrace of the river.

Clear of the bridge, he rolled over and broke into a crawl. Soon, alongside St John's College, he caught the unmistakable sound of Formal Hall: scholars, dons and visitors dining by candlelight at long, polished tables. In full cry, it was a cacophony of cutlery and glass, china and chairs, and voices raised in that strange murmuring chorus, so distinctive of argument, conversation and alcohol. But not a single light betrayed the outline of the dining hall on the bank.

He struck out along that stretch of the river which ran in front of the college boathouses. Each was adorned with a flagpole of imperial dimensions. Opposite, Midsummer Common stretched away in the moonlight. Here, the previous evening, he had watched the house of boxes burn, and the cruel, violent death of an elderly woman.

Opposite the Fort St George, he noted the pile of ash, all that was left after the blaze, and ahead of it the narrow trench Chris Childe and his fellow labourers had dug only hours before his own death. The coincidence had irked, so he'd sent Edison back to the depot to double-check the details. Hartnell, the senior charge hand, had given a brisk outline of Childe's duties that final day: he'd been on site from ten with the rest of the squad, with a few hours' leave of absence after lunch to make his appearance in court. They'd been dismissed at six, the safety trench completed.

Had Childe walked directly to Mill Road Cemetery, en route to his weekly Party meeting and his appointment with Dodds from the *Evening News*? Had Joelyn Stone followed, armed with his pistol? Brooke pictured the major slipping through the iron gates, using the trees and monuments to shield his presence, until the moment the gun was drawn. Had he shown the courage to look his victim in the eyes?

Brooke doubled back, swimming hard, making his heart creak with the effort. Opposite St John's Wilderness, he spotted the glint of a rifle butt where a sentry stood on the bank. With silent strokes, he crept upstream and found two more guards, at one-hundred-yard intervals.

While the manner of Chris Childe's death was now clear, at least in outline, the mystery of the riverside pits remained impenetrable.

At the narrow riverside ditch, Brooke squeezed through the iron grating, as he had before, and slipped fifty yards inland, climbing the bank, to look down on the meadow. The moon, which had been playing cat and mouse with the clouds, broke free, and he saw the reed beds, the rough grass, the dotted thorn trees and the mounds which marked the pits.

But he could go no further: along the top of the bank had been laid a spool of barbed wire and a series of posts. On each had been attached a sign depicting a skull with the blunt warning:

LIVE FIRING
KEEP OUT

An hour later he was back at the Spinning House, the cold of the night beginning to make his bones ache. A terracotta pot stood on the duty desk, brimming with what Brooke recognised as winter jasmine.

A note in an envelope confirmed the sender as the green-fingered governor of the County Gaol:

Brooke. I promised. The birds have flown. A Black Maria turned up with a warrant and two plain-clothed sergeants from Special Branch. Destination: Barlinnie, Glasgow. Abandon hope . . .

CHAPTER FIFTY-FOUR

Brooke was on the doorstep of Goodall's, the optician's, at eight-thirty, the town centre's various clocks marking the half hour in a variety of ways, orchestrated by the musical chimes of Great St Mary's. The window dressing was discreet, a few pairs of ladies' spectacles laid out on a velvet shelf, the gold lettering on the glass door crowded with Jacob Goodall's professional qualifications: *FBOA, BOA (Disp)* and a motto – *Aequis oculis videre*.

He rapped smartly on the glass door.

Walking through the waking city, he'd considered the fate of the three communists: Henderson, Lauder and Popper. Barlinnie was a grim jail, a pile of bleak stone on moorland to the edge of the city. How many men, he thought, were in England at that precise moment, locked up for no more reason other than posing a threat, a threat undefined, or only dimly understood? He'd made a promise that he'd not forget them, and he intended to keep it.

Brooke thought he saw a shadow move at the back of the shop. He adjusted his glasses, trying to peer inside, while the polished window insisted on reflecting the street scene behind him.

Sidney Street was jammed with two-way traffic, students spilling out from the college lodge into Rose Street, and towards the University Library. In the half-distance, towards the Round Church, an army lorry was being divested of several hundred sandbags.

Suddenly the optician, Jacob Goodall, was there – narrow face, eyes cast down – attacking the lock with a practised twist of the wrist.

'Problems?' he asked, readjusting his own pair of upstairs-downstairs spectacles. Brooke's precarious eyesight was of professional interest to Goodall, who'd studied the detective's medical files from the sanatorium in Scarborough, and had since provided several pairs of specially designed lenses. Jacob was a craftsman, an artist in optics.

'No, no, Jacob. A brainwave – at least I hope so. All thanks to a fen cat.'

After his visit to the Spinning House the night before, he'd eventually gone home, pouring himself a glass of water in the kitchen before turning off the lights, so that he could see the towpath, and a feral cat picking its way along the top of the bank. Burly, with rounded heads, these animals stalked the open country north of the city, the distant progeny of ratters. Something about the way it held one paw above the ground before bringing it down to earth reminded him of a chorus of cats behind a bedsit door on Babylon Street, a worn carpet and the smell of sour milk.

Goodall was nodding his head but walking away, around the counter and down a short corridor, so that Brooke had to follow. A light came on to reveal a thirty-foot-long gallery, at the end of which was mounted a Snellen chart, with its signature pyramid of letters, the largest a capital E at the top. Brooke had been here before, as much in his nightmares as in real life. Haunted by the letters, he often saw them circling in front of his eyes in the dark as he lay trying to find sleep.

'You stay there,' said Jacob.

'It's not me, Jacob. I'm fine.'

'Yes. But it's months since your last test. You're here. I'm here. You can ask your questions – your man Edison dropped round the glasses – the old woman in the fire . . .'

Producing a pointer, Goodall selected letters in the third and fourth ranks and Brooke read them confidently enough: T, Z, P, D.

'But you couldn't help with identifying the owner?' said Brooke.

'That's right. The heat had melted the lens, so the prescription code was not decipherable. We have hundreds of customers, Brooke. And many come once, and never again. It's a needle in a haystack. Now. This?' He pointed at the sixth line.

Brooke narrowed his eyes. 'F?' They tried several other optotypes on the same line, and then the one below that.

Goodall switched the light out without comment and they wandered back into the shop. Brooke felt like a naughty schoolchild following the headmaster to his office.

'But if I had a name you could check a list of customers?' he asked, trying to wrest back the initiative.

'Of course, Brooke,' said Goodall, lifting up a tome from under the counter.

'Mrs Trew,' said Brooke. That first time they'd called at Babylon Street he'd seen her name on the letter he'd picked up from the mat. 'Ida Trew,' he added.

Goodall leafed deftly through a ledger. 'Ah. Here. Babylon Street?' he asked, looking over the top of his glasses.

Brooke saw her then, stepping stiff-legged from the flames, staggering out of the ashes, until she folded herself down into the damp grass. Sour milk, the scent of it in the downstairs corridor at Babylon Street: that was what he'd put to one side of his mind when he should have simply stopped and asked after Mrs Trew, the vigilant gatekeeper with her cats.

Brooke took down the details from Jacob's ledger. Ida Trew had been a customer for fifteen years.

'Good heavens, Brooke. A smile!' said Goodall.

'Yes. Thank you, Jacob. I must get on.'

At the door, Jacob rested a hand on Brooke's sleeve. 'A proper test, I think, soon. Your eyes are no better, maybe worse. We should explore other treatments, even alternative diagnoses. We need to focus on the problem.' He smiled at his own word play.

'Insight's the thing, Jacob. The inner eye. Have you a Snellen chart for that?'

'What does your inner eye tell you now, Brooke?'

'It tells me that a man who can kill once, can kill twice,' he said.

CHAPTER FIFTY-FIVE

The door of Ida Trew's flat was locked, a beaded curtain still obscuring the view through the pane of glass which served as her window on the world. Brooke considered breaking the flimsy door frame, but then remembered the young woman they'd met on the doorstep, who'd slipped into the ground floor flat. She answered his knock with a stealthy silence, opening the door by an inch. A series of smells wafted out into the damp corridor, oranges and cinnamon, stale sweat and pipe smoke.

'It's still early,' she said, and behind her a voice, muffled perhaps by a bedspread, said something indistinct.

'Mrs Trew?' he asked, looking towards the locked door. 'There's no answer.'

'She goes away the odd night; she usually lets us know.'

As she spoke her hand rose up to the top of the door, disappeared, then reappeared with a key.

'We've all got one, in case there's trouble. It's a safe place.'

She gave him the key. 'I want it back.'

As Brooke walked away, she called after him, 'You got a warrant?' But the muffled voice must have beckoned her back inside, and she closed her door.

Ida's room was deserted, but he could hear the cats, on the far side of a door which led into a scullery. Once released, they swarmed to drink from a series of bowls, each one filled with milk, which had curdled and dried at the edges.

What little light there was limped into the room through a mean window, revealing a sink, gas cooker, box bed, sideboard and dresser. He flicked the light switch but nothing happened. A minute's search revealed the meter on the wall by the door. It took florins, so he pumped three into the slot, waiting for the mechanism to register the cash. A dull clang brought light, and then the radio sprang into life, the volume low, but loud enough to identify the clipped tones of the BBC's Home Service. The cats milled around his feet, their insistent pawing unsettling and vaguely threatening.

Sitting by the pillow on the bed, in a nest of old cushions, he found that he had a comfortable view down the corridor to the front door. Ida was certainly the gatekeeper. A semi-official role, clearly, to monitor the punters, coming and going. Was she paid for the service? And what had the woman in the downstairs flat said? *It's a safe place*. Really? The tawdry rooms of an eighty-year-old widow?

From the bed he could see that under the table lay some broken crockery, around which the cats circled. On his knees, Brooke tried to reassemble the lost cups but the task was beyond him, although he did identify two handles, and the residue of sugar in a shard of china. At floor level, he saw the cooker door was ajar, and, tracing its edge, he found a smudge of blood on the metallic rim and a flake of ceramic blue paint.

A gloomy yard led by a gate into a back alley. Coal brimmed over a wooden bunker. A privy door stood open, revealing the china bowl. Out in the alley he noted tyre marks in the cinder path.

On the back step he found a pint of milk, which he emptied into the three bowls once he'd cleaned them in the sink. The cats purred in unison.

Switching off the radio, he sat at the table. The only items in the room of any real note were a Chinese tea caddy in splendid gold and ebony, and a telephone, which was a new model in Bakelite. Above it, taped to the wall, was a sheet of paper with a series of three numbers opposite names:

Pete: 4409
James: 3007
Jim B: 4888

Brooke took a note, presuming them all to be local.

The cats, sated, were back around his ankles.

'Sorry,' he said. 'I don't think she's coming home this time.'

Standing there, on the worn patterned carpet, he could almost feel her fading away. There was a sense in which a personality held a room together, linking its disparate characteristics: the phone, the cats' dishes, the teacups, the picture framed over the gas fire of a horse-drawn tram passing Parker's Piece in a snowy dusk, splashes of sunset mingling with the newly lit gas lights. The smell of a human life was fading too: the tannic edge of the perpetual teapot, the warm mustiness of the box bed.

He picked up the phone and dialled 4888.

'Crown,' said a female voice against a background of voices.

Brooke introduced himself: 'I'd like to speak to Jim B?'

The phone clattered, and there was the distinct sound of someone pushing a carpet cleaner.

'What is it?' said a man's voice.

Brooke explained that he was a policeman and standing in Ida Trew's flat, and that she was missing, and he was concerned for her well-being.

'I'm sorry, you are?' he added.

'Her son. Eldest son. You asked the girls? Any trouble, they go to Ida and she rings us.' The background noise suddenly faded as a door slammed. 'Christ, hang on.' The phone buzzed, then fell silent. 'Sorry. Pub's full of cleaners. You say Mum's gone, but for how long?'

'A day, maybe two. You're at The Crown, on Mill Road?'

'That's us. I'll ring round the brothers. She's good on her feet. Maybe she just stayed over for a night if she's feeling under the weather. She'll be alright. Grew up in a pub in the Gorbals; a night out in Cambridge ain't gonna knock her over.'

Brooke would need a doctor's records to identify the corpse in Dr Comfort's morgue. After that he'd send a constable round with the bad news. For now, he'd leave Jim B to ring his siblings.

'Let me know when you find her,' said Brooke, giving him the Spinning House number. 'Any of the girls particularly close? There's one in the front room, just down the corridor.'

'Nah. She's new. Polly, they call her. Mum wasn't keen. That's why she got the ground floor flat, see, easier to watch. No, Vera's the girl. Mum looked after her kiddie on and off for years. They're close. Top flat. Vera's sound.'

CHAPTER FIFTY-SIX

Brooke climbed the dreary flights of steps to the fifth floor. Vera must have heard him earlier, talking to the girl on the ground floor, because she had her door open an inch in the half-light of the landing. Stepping out, she looked wary, clutching a flimsy nightdress to her neck against the chill in the house, which seemed to condense here, beneath the attic, where the reek of damp was tangible.

She clutched her shoulders. 'What now? I've answered all your questions,' she asked, resting a hand on the door chain.

'Ida's missing. I've talked to one of her sons. She knew Major Stone, presumably – he was a regular visitor?'

'Yes. For three years. Ida always kept an eye out and we give her names so she can keep track. She does go away to stay with her son, and see her grandchildren. I wouldn't panic, although she usually tells us.' She bit her lip. 'What about the hospital? Her heart's not strong. Maybe she's unwell?'

'I'll check,' said Brooke. 'Do the clients know that she keeps tabs on you all?'

'No. They may suspect. If Ida's in, she makes sure they know she's seen them, coming and going. Some ask who she is; I always lie and say she's the landlady.'

'How well did Stone know Ida?'

'He brought her tea. He's kind to people he doesn't see as a threat. But, yes, packets of tea. There's an estate in India. He never said but I bet it's hers, the wife's. He used to bring the stuff for me, but I can't stand tea. Hot dishwater. But he kept Ida sweet.'

Brooke replaced his hat.

'The Yard has news on your letter, by the way,' he said, watching her face. 'The addressee was Palme Dutt, you said?'

'Yes. The new general secretary. The last one – Harry Pollitt – he's long gone now. Ructions over Russia, in-fighting I bet. I didn't think he'd read it anyway; I thought there'd be . . . *minions*.'

'Scotland Yard's trying to track down Palme Dutt,' said Brooke. 'The principal secretary says if the letter arrived it would have gone to one of the deputies, a man called Hamilton. At the moment *his* whereabouts are fluid. No doubt he'll surface, but he was last seen boarding a boat for Ireland.

'You may have a visit, from London, from the Yard, or military intelligence. There's concern, naturally, that the letter may have reached the Comintern, the international party. Which means Moscow, of course.'

Brooke tried to hold her gaze. 'They won't talk to you on the landing, Vera. There'll be a car. You should be prepared.'

He touched his hat.

CHAPTER FIFTY-SEVEN

Dusk spread over Cambridge, a smog of river mist and coal smoke brewed up by the setting sun, blurring the mid-distance so that the view from Brooke's office, over the university laboratories, was reduced to a roofscape of grey, with splashes of electric light. At one window he could see a white-coated technician, lit by a Bunsen burner, over which he patiently held a test tube with a pair of tongs. The Galen stood out, the white tiled exterior of the anatomy building oddly luminous.

Brooke thought of the pale bodies within, allotted their sightless metal coffins. Death in the Galen held a certain nightmare twist: the bodies of Lux, Childe and Sneeth faced intermittent exposure to the light as they were slid out for re-examination. Suspended in this strange purgatory, they would be denied peace until their cases were finally closed.

Brooke ordered Edison to bring Major Joelyn Stone up from the cells. Unlocking his handcuffs, they sat him down and left a bottle of Bell's by a tumbler. Stone's undamaged hand was steady as he sipped the spirit. His uniform had been removed to test for gunshot residue, along with clothes from his house. Shorn of his military carapace, he looked oddly vulnerable.

'We found this gun in your locker at the firing range at Madingley,' said Brooke. He let the weapon tumble out from its green felt bag.

Stone reached out a hand, then stopped, looking up at Brooke.

'Help yourself. There are no fingerprints; even our modest resources stretch to charcoal powder and a brush. It's clean, in fact so clean, I'd say it's been wiped.'

Stone held it easily in his hand. 'But not mine, Inspector. I've seen them, back at the end of the war. German prisoners had them, souvenirs from the Eastern Front. They'd pick them off the Reds.'

'I'm more concerned that you denied having any other pistols, but failed to mention the one you kept on the range.'

'The one in my locker is a Webley .45 – ancient, bloody museum model. Slipped my mind. Sorry.' He tipped back the whisky and refilled the tumbler.

'*This* gun was in your locker, Major. How do you explain that?'

'No. Mine's a .45 Webley,' he said flatly.

'This gun killed Chris Childe,' said Brooke. 'There's no doubt. I asked you twice if you'd fired the shot that killed him, Major.'

'I didn't fire the shot,' said Stone, examining the pistol closely, until he found the inscriptions. 'I've never seen this gun before. What do these letters mean?'

'Ah. Oddly, your wife solved that mystery.'

For the first time Brooke could see fear in Stone's eyes: an intimation, perhaps, that the rest of his life might be spent in a prison cell. Or was it the shame, the public downfall, that suddenly loomed large?

'My *wife*. What the hell does she know about guns?'

'She's a general's daughter. I don't think I need to remind you of that. The general collected pistols. He had three sons. They all served in the armed forces, and they all brought back interesting weapons for their father. One of them was a captain in the Armoured Car Expeditionary Force in Russia. The ACEF. All very swashbuckling, a band of brothers, let loose on the Red Army after the Great War. The White Terror, and all that. Glory and medals.

'To be fair, your wife couldn't identify the gun per se, but there's no doubt a jury would find the coincidence persuasive, don't you think?'

Stone took a gulp of whisky. There was an air of desperation now, a sense, perhaps, that the life he'd had was indeed slipping through his wounded fingers.

He made an effort to regain his dignity, brushing imaginary dust from the white shirt front.

'If you're going to charge me, do it.'

Edison leant back heavily in his chair until it creaked, one hand caressing his pipe in his jacket pocket.

'I'll tell you what happened,' said Brooke. 'You bumped into Childe that morning at the house on Babylon Street. A few hours later he's in the dock, in plain sight, and you were on the bench. No wigs, no gowns. You recognised him, so did he recognise you? There was a lot at stake: not just your marriage to the general's daughter, but a career. You said yourself you anticipated a new posting. A chance to shine at last, perhaps.'

Stone's good hand closed in a tight fist on the tabletop.

'You went to see Vera Staunton after the tribunal. You thought you'd buy Childe off. You thought money would solve the problem. How did you track him down to the cemetery?

'Vera Staunton knew that Childe was working on Midsummer Common that day. I think you made a visit to the site. It would have been easy enough to follow him to Mill Road . . . Did you try to offer him money there, or was the opportunity too good to miss? A deserted graveyard in the failing light?'

Stone started to speak but Brooke held up a hand.

'Then I think you went home for dinner. Later, you drove back to Babylon Street in your car. My sergeant tells me it's a black Ford, and it's in the garage behind Blenheim House. We're just checking if the tyres match the tracks left behind Ida Trew's flat. Because it was Ida you went to see.'

'What has any of this got to do with Ida Trew?'

'She's dead, Major, as you well know, because you killed her.'

Stone stood up, but Edison was ready for him, using his own weight to settle him back into the chair.

'If you stand up again we'll put the cuffs back on,' said Brooke. 'Yes. Ida the gatekeeper. She'd seen the comings and goings. A chat, perhaps, a cup of the fine tea? She'd seen Childe, a stranger, so she'd have remembered him. What else had Ida seen? What would she have said if asked about Vera's clients? Did you mean to kill her? I got the sense she was a determined soul.'

'Ida? Brooke, she's an eighty-year-old woman. You think I killed her to protect my career? This is ridiculous.'

'The body was the problem,' continued Brooke. 'I think you got her out into the car and drove to the riverside. There's blood stains in the boot of the Ford. We're testing those too . . .'

'A holiday in Scotland, Brooke. We went shooting. I had a boot full of pheasant.'

Brooke ignored him. 'It was your job to set a guard on the site, but I checked, he wasn't due on duty until midnight. So there was a window of opportunity. The great fire would leave no trace.

'One mistake. She wasn't dead. A note of panic there, I think. Did you even bother to try her pulse? But your career is not entirely unblemished by fear and panic, is it?'

Stone was beginning to shake, a high frequency vibration notable in his fingers: 'How dare you.'

'You might like to think about Ida tonight in your cell, Major. She was unconscious, almost certainly, so there's some comfort there. Left alone she'd have died in time. Her heart was weak, it would have faltered and failed. But then the fire was lit, and that's what brought her to life, Stone: the pain of the fire, the flames and the heat.'

CHAPTER FIFTY-EIGHT

Brooke let the great oak door of Michaelhouse bang shut behind him. The *boom!*, embellished by the metallic clatter of the lock and latch, faded away in a series of diminishing echoes. The street was empty, its high kerbs teetering over damp cobbles, the only noise the dripping of water from the iron gutters. Doric had provided a leftover ham hock which they'd picked apart in convivial silence, aided by half a bottle of the Coulange. Brooke felt replete, his steps buoyant.

As he walked, Brooke manipulated in his mind the pieces of the jigsaw which made up the murder of Chris Childe: the motive, the opportunity, the evidence from the scene and the car. With luck they'd have a formidable case, including a corrosive motive: ambition. Although it occurred to him that the real wellspring of the crime had been Stone's cowardice, the constant pressure to excel at being a soldier drove him on, in a desperate attempt to offset his inability to *be* a soldier when it had really mattered to his men.

The zigzag route took him between high walls. In his imagination he hovered overhead, watching his hat navigate the maze, like one of Aldiss's pouch-cheeked hamsters trapped in a laboratory experiment. The concept was unwelcome: the idea that he might be condemned to wander in some vast unperceived puzzle created by others made him feel like a helpless victim.

Distracted, he at first failed to note the footsteps behind him; a fleeting coda to the sharp double-crack of his own shoes.

At a corner he paused in the gloom, adjusting his collar, and glanced back to see a figure following him. He stepped out of sight into a doorway slick with mud which must have led into some college gardens. He waited, his heartbeat steady, the footsteps finally passing. He watched her go: a uniform, tweaked at the waist, gave her identity away, as did the immaculate pair of tailored fatigues and the pale-stockinged calves.

'Jo?' he called.

Ashmore stopped and turned, a look of pleasant surprise on her face, and not a trace of discomfort.

'You're following me,' said Brooke, offering her his arm.

'I tried the station; they said you used the phone at Michaelhouse, at the lodge. I missed you by a minute. The porter said you were heading to the river and home. He gave me a very knowing look; he fears for your moral soul, Brooke. Am I the only young woman on your trail . . . ?'

'You are unique,' said Brooke.

She clasped a lapel at her throat. 'It's winter already. I hope to God you're not planning a nightly swim.'

They walked onto the bridge over the weir, white water racing beneath them. Upstream, in the half-light, they could see the complex wooden geometry of the Mathematical Bridge, a construction of wooden beams which, according to legend, effortlessly spanned the Cam without the need of a single nail. It appeared to hang over the water by some trick of the light.

Together they breathed in the intoxicating air. Brooke explained that the latest theory, being tested right here in Cambridge, was that falling water molecules released charged particles – new-fangled electric ions – which might explain the exhilarating effects of waterfalls.

'That's the problem with you scientists,' said Jo. 'Where's the romance in an ion?'

She stood close to him in this state of inward reflection.

'It's Marcus; he's disappeared,' she said finally, lighting a long cigarette with a gold band on the filter using a slim mother-of-pearl lighter.

'In what sense?' asked Brooke. 'I saw him last night at the house.'

'In the sense that he's not in his rooms, Brooke,' she said, in short temper. 'In the sense that the college claims he has given notice of leaving to take up unspecified government work in London. In the sense that he left by cab last night at midnight from home, according to Father. The last train to London is before eleven. So his destination was, in fact, unknown.

'It's a cruel verdict but I'd have to say my father doesn't care where Marcus has gone. The responsibilities of the new chair are, apparently, overwhelming. He's become a potentate and we have been relegated, finally, to mere subjects.'

She ditched the cigarette, half-smoked.

'It makes no sense. If he'd left Cambridge he'd have taken the car. That MG is his teddy bear, he'd never go anywhere without it, but it's sat in the garage at home. And there's his room, next to mine: his books, his notebooks, everything's untouched. His college room is empty, but then there was never much there besides paper and pencils.'

The water churned beneath them, sweeping under the bridge.

'I talked to Marcus,' said Brooke. 'About Ernst Lux's death. He said they went climbing together, and the American fell. Do you think he was capable of lying about that?'

'Marcus doesn't live in the real world, you know that,' she said. 'Mathematics isn't a discipline, it's an escape route from everyday life. Within himself – of himself – he's an innocent, Brooke. The only person he'd ever put at risk is Marcus Ashmore. But he's always been susceptible to manipulation by others; *easily led*, that's the verdict.'

It was a curiously even-handed answer to the question.

Ashmore drew savagely on a fresh cigarette so that it actually flared in the dark, emitting a tiny blue flame. 'I don't do melodrama, Brooke, but I can't shake the sense, the conviction, actually, that I may not see my brother again.'

CHAPTER FIFTY-NINE

At Madingley Hall, despite the blackout, slivers of light betrayed the great Tudor windows. Curtains, blackboards, tapestries, all had fallen, literally, short. So now the lamps were being doused, floor by floor, room by room. The house was fading into the night. Even the guards patrolled with downturned torches, securing the half-mile of perimeter wire.

In his attic bedroom, Captain Rich Kerridge read a file, delivered by a motorcycle messenger from the War Office, Awards Department, Whitehall. Medals, gongs, ribbons: he'd rather enjoyed the work in Cairo, desk work admittedly, sifting citations from senior officers, witness reports and recommendations from commanders. One of his wartime subordinates was enjoying the current conflict from the comfort of London SW1. He'd located Corporal Harry Staunton's file in the dusty tomb of the third basement level, where the stories of past heroism were laid to rest.

A faded brown ink hieroglyph on the front of the file yielded some meaning under a magnifying glass:

Reading the three-page report, he didn't touch his glass of whisky, but he drained the spirit in a gulp before reading it a second time. A third reading consolidated a vivid picture of the events of those few days in December 1920, nearly two years after the Armistice had been signed, bringing hostilities to an end in France.

Harry Staunton's unit had taken refuge on the edge of a village, no more than a Jewish shtetl, close to the Pripet Marshes, three hundred miles south-west of Moscow. They were all volunteers in the buccaneering ACEF, the Armoured Car Expeditionary Force. Their three vehicles were hidden in the barn, iced in, the fuel frozen in the engines, the ruts in the muddy farmyard like iron. For some days they'd witnessed birds falling, frozen, from the sky. At night, trees cracked in the forest, their woody veins turned to ice.

The officer on the spot called the men into the barn. The unit's position, he told them, was precarious. They were being left behind by the White Army, which was retreating south, to reform around Lutsk. Radio contact had been lost, and besides the Red Army would be listening for any airwave traffic to the rear of the fleeing ACEF. They could not abandon the cars, as they were valuable military materiel in a motorised war fought against the Bolsheviks, who were generally poorly armed. It was imperative to get someone out through the woods on foot to a nearby railhead, which the White Army had hoped to hold in order to protect the rear of their positions. There was a telegraph post at the station. A call for help could be made. It was a twenty-mile hike.

A volunteer was needed, and Harry Staunton promptly stood. He left at dusk.

After ten days, they reasoned that Staunton's sortie had failed. The rest of the ACEF would now be more than a hundred miles distant. Defending the farm, and the frozen vehicles, was not feasible. They decided to spike the engines and make a dash south.

At dawn the next morning they set out, the officer leading the line, his pistol drawn.

Two miles south the woods thickened, transformed by ice into a maze of chandeliers, the twigs and branches tinkling in random, atonal accompaniment. Every few minutes a tree would crack with a sharp report. Starvation had left them all in a dreamlike state of exhaustion.

They found Harry Staunton half a mile along the track. The pines had given way to birch, and he was up in the canopy, about thirty feet above the forest floor, wedged between the bole of a tree and a branch. Staunton was an athlete, they all knew that, because he'd won the battalion medal for the mile. The climb, up the branchless bole, was of itself a feat of strength.

The officer used his field glasses to examine the body: Staunton had run his belt around the tree to hold himself in place, probably after sustaining a series of gunshot wounds, four of which were evident from the ground, including one in the neck. His right hand clutched his chest, but his left still held his gun, frozen in his frozen hand, held with frozen fingers.

In the snow, they collected more than a hundred and fifty cartridge shells around the base of the tree. Clearly, once his own ammunition had been spent, Harry Staunton had provided a sitting target. Had he saved one for himself, to avoid capture and the inevitable interrogation? They would never know.

It took six of them to rock the tree. Ice fell, and the branches played their strange tune, but the dead man clung on. Then, long after the silence had returned, the pistol fell from Harry Staunton's hands.

There was no chance of digging him a grave, even if they had been able to dislodge him from his crow's nest. So they left him aloft. The gun had been Staunton's special prize of war: taken from the body of a soldier they'd found hiding on the docks at Archangel after they'd disembarked the armoured cars. Staunton had told his comrades that the man, in his fifties with broken pince-nez, had been the first Bolshie he'd ever killed. The first, he hoped, of many.

Kerridge, reading, drained his glass again. The window stood open and he heard, quite clearly, a perfunctory 'Who goes there?' from one of the guards below.

The last lines of the report were particularly poignant: *The unit reached White Army positions in eight days. Staunton's commanding officer undertook, with the enthusiastic support of the men and the cooperation of battalion headquarters, to return Cpl Staunton's pistol to his widow and to enquire into her means. Mrs Staunton indicated that there were no dependents and she was in receipt of a military pension. The sum of one hundred pounds was paid over from monies collected from his comrades in the unit and beyond. Mrs Staunton wished her thanks to be placed on record.*

Kerridge turned off his light and stood at the window, looking out over the pinewoods, and raised his glass for a toast.

'To the frozen hero.'

CHAPTER SIXTY

A banner, hung across the stage of the city's newly built Guildhall on Market Hill, shouted in letters a foot high:

WELCOME BREAKFAST
THE SPANISH RELIEF COMMITTEE

When Brooke arrived, the children were all at trestle tables, finishing boiled eggs, toast, jam and margarine, clutching tumblers of milk or watery squash. Patriotic music blared from loudspeakers set either side of the vast array of organ pipes which dominated the stage.

A man began formal proceedings by climbing onto a dais and reading out a list of names, prompting a line of children to come forward amid applause, before each was allotted to a local family which would provide a foster home.

A light touch on Brooke's shoulder, and he turned to face a woman, standing close. 'Mr Brooke? Detective Inspector Brooke?

I got a message at the hospital? I'm Ginny Waites, Ernst's friend.'

She'd brought with her two glasses of the anaemic squash. For a woman of perhaps twenty years of age she exuded a remarkably fluent sense of confidence, in her voice and in her body.

'You were Ernst Lux's girlfriend?' asked Brooke.

She nodded. 'Yes. We'd been going out for a couple of years – well, two years one month, but I suspect I was the only one counting . . . Once, on a long walk by the river, I thought he was going to propose. Now I'll never know.'

'I'm sorry,' said Brooke, giving the platitude a few seconds to gain some meaning, as they watched another child climb the steps.

'It's just that one of his friends, Marcus Ashmore, has disappeared,' Brooke went on. 'Did you ever meet him? He had a room opposite Ernst's?'

'Yes, once or twice. That world, the college, was not my world. We spent most of our time together at my flat, or walking, the pictures, a country pub. I left him to his work, left him to get on. I'm a nurse, so I understood. Work's important, isn't it?'

She let her eyes stray to the unfolding ceremonies on stage.

'There's gossip at Michaelhouse,' she said. 'I met one of the graduates in the street. It might be bunk, but he said there were rumours that Ernst had been climbing on the night he died. That he was with someone else: was that Marcus?'

'Yes, I'm sorry.'

She nodded. 'I see. So he betrayed me in the end,' she said, and Brooke was astounded at the anger in her voice.

'How?'

'The night climbing. It's juvenile, and it risks life. I'm a nurse. Ernst was a scientist dedicated to saving the lives of exploited workers. It's what brought us together. We sound appalling, don't we? Do-gooders.' She laughed, shaking her head. 'These children, their parents died – or they're missing, or worse – in pursuit of an ideal. Ernst died for a thrill. I'm going to struggle forgiving him for *that*.'

She looked up at the stage as the children posed for a photograph.

Brooke produced the postcard which Doric had retrieved from Lux's pigeonhole.

'This intrigued me,' he said, letting her read the brief message. 'Do you know why Ernst's father was once in a cell at Alcatraz?'

She laughed. 'I met Frank last Christmas, with Milly. They both came over, Ernst's parents, on the *Normandie*. Very glamorous. The family made its money exporting oranges, apparently. It sounds idyllic, doesn't it? Pacific beaches, orange groves, snow on the Sierra Nevada.

'Frank's very proud of his spell behind bars. So was Ernst. Frank refused to fight, you see, in the Great War: a conscientious objector. A rare breed, I think. The island was a military prison back then. A few months behind bars, and then they got him out cutting lumber in the hills.'

'Ernst had sympathy with his father's views, political sympathy?'

'Yes. A pacifist, certainly. I went to Spain in '37, just a month, at a hospital in Tarragona. Ernst thought that was quite wrong, supporting the war effort, despite the fact the people needed us. Of course, *he* worked for the government here. But he justified that, at least to himself. On one hand it meant he was able to continue with his research, and on the other he secured some kind of assurance that the project was humanitarian. But he didn't ask too many questions.'

The crowd stood to sing an anthem Brooke didn't recognise.

'I wish now he'd come with me to Spain. There was a beach in front of the hospital in Tarragona and at night the waves were luminous. There's some small marine algae which glow. Ernst knew the science, but he missed the sight of it; it was beautiful, watching the waves break and fall, lit up within. I'd like to have shared it with him.'

CHAPTER SIXTY-ONE

Brooke found Captain Kerridge asleep on a bench in the lobby of the Spinning House. The desk sergeant explained that he'd turned up to see the inspector just after dawn and said he was happy to wait. The faint scent of malt whisky hung in the air, battling against the bleach the cleaner used in the cells beneath.

Gulping coffee in Brooke's office, Kerridge produced a file from his greatcoat.

'This changes everything,' he said.

And it did.

At his desk, an hour later, Brooke tried to assess the precise impact of Corporal Staunton's story on the wider case. Vera Staunton wasn't the widow of an unknown soldier from the trenches of the Great War; her husband, a volunteer, had died fighting Bolsheviks in the Russian Civil War. He had been part of the ACEF – the Armoured Car Expeditionary Force, a swashbuckling unit, an enthusiastic component of what had become known as the White Terror. Rather than a human victim of the slaughter of the Western Front, a symbol of the pointless brutality of war, he'd been a reactionary warrior, a man who had sought out a battle, half a continent from his native land.

And then there was the pistol. It had been returned to the widow. Could there be any doubt it was the gun Brooke had found in Stone's locker? Had the major taken it from Staunton's flat? Had she *given* him the weapon? If so, why then go to the police to reveal his corrosive motive for wanting Childe dead? The questions swirled, the jigsaw back in motion.

The file also suggested that other lies had been told. Mrs Staunton had informed her late husband's comrades she had no dependents. Where was young Frederick?

Staunton had said her son had enjoyed a private education. So, a fee-paying *public* school, with boarders. Ida Trew, the lookout at Babylon Street, had looked after the boy as a child, when needed. Had Staunton decided to keep her son close by, in the city, as he grew up? Edison retreated to the sergeants' room on the ground floor to use the phone, ringing round the city's many fee-paying schools, where the children of the rich could enjoy a fine education, in the shadow of the great university many of them would eventually attend. If the search failed, they'd haul Staunton in for questioning. For now, Brooke wanted to keep her innocent of the knowledge that her lies had been revealed.

Brooke turned back briefly to Ernst Lux and the hunt for Marcus Ashmore. Ringing Michaelhouse, he asked for Professor Ashmore's rooms. The conversation was brief and adversarial. Once, they'd been neighbours, even friends. Now, it seemed, Brooke's place in the world was defined entirely by his rank. The *professor* was busy. He had no idea where Marcus was, but had understood he'd left Cambridge on government work.

'When I find him I'll let you know,' offered Brooke, but the phone was already dead.

Detective Inspector Solly, at his desk at West Bar, Sheffield, was loquacious by comparison.

'Brooke? No, no sign, I'm afraid. Gretorix has vanished. Best forget him. Currie, your AWOL squaddie, was buried yesterday at Sharrow Vale. We had a man there, but it was just family. Lot of flowers, most of them probably from the men who killed him. They'll look after his family; they always do. Makes you sick. There's no sign of Ginger Thorpe, by the way: he was your third driver. He made it back to Sheffield, apparently, but now he's disappeared as well.'

Brooke listened as Solly drew on a cigarette.

'Better news on the meat, so listen up.'

Sheffield CID had found the manpower to run a twenty-four-hour surveillance of the old corporation abattoir, a now derelict industrial ruin in the valley of the River Don. The abattoir itself was a wreck, without power. Lorries came and went from the old vehicle depot, while a pack of German shepherd dogs patrolled the perimeter. The current theory was that the meat was being brought to the site, butchered there, and quickly redistributed for storage across the north.

'We're trying to get a man on the inside,' said Solly. 'For now, it's wait and see. Top brass want to know who's organising it, the big picture. I'll keep you posted.'

Brooke broke for lunch and walked to the Masonic Hall, taking his usual table at the far end so that he could eat a sandwich in peace, making notes on the Staunton file. Edison appeared, helping himself to a wedge of cottage pie before joining his superior.

Edison surveyed his food and smiled. 'Got him, sir,' he said. 'Young Frederick Staunton. Headmaster sends his regards. I told him you'd like a chat and he said that would be a pleasure because it's your father's old school, sir. St Botolph's?'

CHAPTER SIXTY-TWO

Brooke had not sat in the chapel since the day of his father's memorial service more than thirty years earlier. Snow then; bright sunshine now, streaming through the stained glass, splashing the reds and purples and blues over the polished wood. Stupidly, he found himself shocked by the unheroic dimensions of the building, for the chapel of his memory was vast, a cathedral in white stone, crammed with pews, the giddy roof a spider's web of vaulting. Front row, next to his mother, the lectern set before them, it had felt as if each speaker, every reading from the Bible, or Tennyson, or Kipling, had been chosen for him alone.

Today, he sat alone in near silence, the only noise the swish of a broom somewhere beyond the open door of the sacristy. The chapel felt mean and – to use a favourite phrase of Claire's – jumped-up, its neo-Gothic kings and saints misplaced, its draped regimental standards out of scale.

The school porter who'd shown him in had located the plaque at Brooke's request, in brass, set in the tiles of the floor:

Prof. Sir John Brooke
1833–1908
Pupil, governor, patron
President of the British Paediatric Association
Nobel laureate in medicine 1903
For his work on serums and infant diphtheria

The porter leant on his broom. 'Saved lives, he did,' he said. 'That's what they say. Thousands – millions even, in the Empire, India and such. You a doctor, are you?'

'He was my father,' said Brooke.

The porter rearranged his broom. 'Blimey. That's a thing.'

Embarrassed, the man fled.

Near the plaque, a glass box had been set on a wooden board, a gun inside, and a brass plate recording the exploits of its owner, a young subaltern in the Sudan who'd single-handedly quelled a revolt. It made Brooke think of pistols in boxes, locked away, and the extent to which an alibi can rely on the precise whereabouts of an *object* – particularly the murder weapon – as much as a person.

He let the idea flourish in the cool silence.

Footsteps echoed down the nave and, glancing to the west doors, he saw a man approaching at a clipped, military pace. He introduced himself as Dr Paget, headmaster.

'Inspector? They said you'd be here.' Paget sat awkwardly in the choir stall facing Brooke, straightening a narrow tie at his throat. 'Your father brought great honour to the school,' he added.

Brooke executed a fractional nod. 'Frederick Staunton,' he said. 'More to the point, his mother. You know her well?'

'Yes. A widow. She visits the boy often, but he never goes home. In the holidays he attends cadet schools, outward bound. Several of the boys have families here in Cambridge; it means they can take part fully in the life of the school. A few day boys, certainly, but they're, how can I put it, on the fringe?'

'You taught him?'

'Teach – Freddie's in the lower sixth, he's just sixteen, young for his year; in fact the youngest, I think. Small lad, but tough. He'll finish next year but there's already talk of a commission if he doesn't go straight up to university. Bright, too, so a scholarship's within his grasp, which would dispense with the fees, of course.'

Born in 1923, Brooke calculated: three years after his father's heroic death.

The chapel clock struck the hour and Dr Paget raised his eyebrows as if that might mark the end of their conversation.

'Fees always paid on time?' said Brooke.

'Like clockwork,' said Paget, and Brooke could feel the icy cold sense of disapproval in the words. He wondered how much the staff of St Botolph's knew of Mrs Staunton's trade.

'I'd like to talk to him if I may,' said Brooke.

'That is not so easy,' said Paget. 'As I said, he's a keen cadet, and they're out beyond the nets on the range. A good shot, Freddie. And popular, all things considered. And I'd have to get Mrs Staunton's permission for you to see him. School rules, you see, given his age . . . I'm sure you understand. Or you could get his guardian's permission.'

Brooke could not resist the bait. 'Freddie has a guardian?'

'Yes. One of our governors here since the last war. I've always understood that he was the late Mr Staunton's commanding officer. He takes an interest in Freddie; not a keen interest, but there it is.'

'I'll need the name,' said Brooke.

CHAPTER SIXTY-THREE

Brooke slept for a precious hour in cell six, his subconscious mind working all the while to fit together the intricate puzzle that was the fate of Chris Childe, so that when he woke, at just after two in the morning, it seemed, if not straightforward, then at least darkly visible in its barest bones. The heart of it all was Vera Staunton's false story of her husband's tragic death in the Great War. Once he'd understood that, and why she'd lied, everything else stood in a clearer light.

The test of fire, as it were, would come in precisely eight hours' time, at ten o'clock the next morning, at an appointed place: a place, in fact, of execution. He'd yet to summon the guilty, but he had no doubt they would come, eager to incriminate others, and return to the scene of their crime.

First, he had to set an innocent man free.

Despite the hour, he found Major Stone reading in his cell. Brooke noted the cover: Clausewitz, *The Art of War*.

Brooke produced the gun, with its etching: *ACEF*.

'The irony is that it's this weapon which proves you couldn't have killed Chris Childe,' he said, commandeering the only chair in the cell. He'd brought down a bottle of whisky from his desk and poured two shots into tin mugs. 'You're free to go, Major, but please hear me out, by way of apology.

'The gun belongs to Vera Staunton, you see. At first, I admit, it seemed probable that you'd taken it from her rooms. Then I realised it was the weapon itself that was your alibi . . .

'It was at Madingley Hall when I found it in your locker two days after the killing. You left the hall *before* the killing, and spent three days in London, returning through the gates just ahead of my own car.

'Do you see? The hall is secure, and all visitors have to log in and out. You could not have *returned* the gun – certainly not in person, and I don't think anyone has suggested you have a horde of accomplices.

'Whoever placed the gun in the locker, and disposed of the Webley .45, was trying to frame you. From that certainty we can begin again . . . The fact of the matter is the killer proved your innocence in the process of trying to put a noose round your neck.'

Brooke gulped the malt, wincing.

'It's late, so if you wish to sleep, do. I'll leave the door open, and the duty sergeant has his orders. You have my apologies again. I've no doubt that if the case had gone to court, a jury would have found you guilty. So it's a narrow escape for us both.'

They shook hands. Brooke left, and didn't look back. Stone had uttered not a word.

The streets were dark, a few pedestrians hurrying home, the shopfronts already boarded. The last bus edged along Regent Street, standing room only, faces pressed glumly against the glass.

A squad of soldiers building a sandbag wall outside the post office had stopped for cigarettes, lounging, one of them wolf-whistling as a young woman sped by on a bicycle.

At Frank Edwardes', he drank tea, and while the radios beeped with their Morse code messages, he consulted the house copy of *Who's Who*, and then discussed the approach of winter, a hint of frost in the city air, leaves scattered across the outfield of Fenner's, already gathering in drifts amongst the trees beyond the boundary.

The siren remained mute, and so later, when he reached Market Hill, it was crowded, and Rose's tea hut in full swing. Hot fat laced the air as she studiously riddled a battalion of frying sausages.

Taking his own mug, he walked away to the fountain.

At the corner of the square, where Peas Hill ran past the assizes, he noted five black cabs parked on the rank. Jo Ashmore's voice was in his ear, trying to impress on Brooke her fears for the safety of her brother, Marcus: '*He left by cab last night at midnight, according to Father.*'

He spoke to the cabbies. The first hadn't done a job out at Newnham Croft for a week. The second said that at that particular time it would be the night shift. So Brooke waited, and the five cabs were taken, and there was a halcyon lull in which a group of students sang an ethereal madrigal on the steps of Great St Mary's.

Then three cabs climbed Peas Hill. Climbed? It was such a subtle incline that it was impossible to tell which way was up, which way was down. Except for Castle Hill, the city was a fitting gateway to the flat Fens.

All three cabbies were adamant they had not picked up a fare from one of the big houses at Newnham Croft.

The cabs were taken; the rank left empty.

After waiting twenty minutes, Brooke was about to walk on

when a cab crept into the square, its swaddled headlights hardly distinguishable at all. It was only the polished black paintwork which gave it a physical reality, the reflections on its surface shimmering as it took pole position on the rank.

Yes, the cabbie had picked up at the house the night before. A young man, a suitcase, a suit on the back seat.

'He'd had a drink,' offered the driver, tilting his wrist.

'Destination?'

'Madingley Hall. The big house . . .'

CHAPTER SIXTY-FOUR

Sleep was now impossible, even in the fitful fleeting form that Brooke endured, so he threaded his way through the maze of the old ghetto to Doric's lodge, and with a pair of powerful torches they set out through the college's linked courtyards. Crossing Great Court, Brooke told the porter what he knew of the night Ernst Lux had fallen to his death.

'Never liked young Mr Ashmore,' said Doric, leading the way under the arch and into North Court. 'His father's no better. Knighthood next, you see. One of the great and good, and about as deserving as the rest.'

The court lay in moonlight, all the student rooms blacked out. Brooke positioned Doric by the small fishpond at the centre and told him to play the torch on the facade of the West Range, across which Ashmore and Lux had climbed on the night of the Great Darkness.

The route, as related by Ashmore, was still fresh in his mind: down the chimney – a narrow niche between two buttresses – then across, using a thin decorated ledge for a series of handholds, before descending the drainpipe. That, at least, had been their plan.

Lux had fallen from the decorated ledge, his body destroyed by the pinnacles of the porch below. Brooke levered himself up onto the small roof over the door, using a short stretch of the same drainpipe. Pinnacles of stone rose around him like stalagmites. The thought of human flesh falling onto these vicious spikes sent sympathetic pains bolting through his limbs. In the moonlight he could detect dried patches of blood, and worse. Recalling Lux's corpse, laid out on Dr Comfort's metal table, he could see again the ugly trauma to the skull: the bone splintered like eggshell, revealing a hint of the brain within, the glazed and bloody tissue with its maze-like pattern.

'According to Ashmore, they got the body down and carried it out through the watergate,' said Brooke, returning to ground level.

An arch was set in the east wall, obscured by weeds and a rose covered in thorns. Brooke pinned it back with his arm so that Doric could get to the lock. They both had to set their shoulders against the oak but when it finally gave way it shot open, so that they were both pitched out onto a path which ran beside the river. In five minutes they'd reached the spot on the Backs where the early morning dog-walker had found Lux's tangled body.

Marcus Ashmore's story fitted the ground plan perfectly.

Doric stood very still, and it was only when the moon came out and Brooke could see the porter's lips that he realised he was praying. It wasn't that Brooke had no faith of his own, just that in his daily life he found the existence of a god of little practical help. And he certainly didn't believe in the efficacy of prayers. In the desert, in his cell, he'd said many, with little result. They walked back in silence, a funeral procession without a body, locking the watergate behind them.

Back in the North Court, the porter led the way towards the lodge but, in a gesture of farewell and resignation, Brooke looked back one last time at the spot where Lux had fallen. This time he saw the truth. It had always been in plain sight.

The porch, which had taken the force of Lux's falling, flailing body, was *not* beneath the narrow decorative ledge, with its delicate handholds. It stood directly under the chimney down which, Ashmore had explained, they braced their bodies, feet to one side, backs to the other. Such a descent was meat and gravy to them: simplicity itself, a manoeuvre without danger or, indeed, a requirement for a strong nerve or concentration.

But it was here, at this precise point, that Ernst Lux had fallen to his death.

CHAPTER SIXTY-FIVE

Brooke arrived first at the Mill Road Cemetery. A dawn mist had thickened, reducing visibility to a few yards, so that crosses and statues, tombs and sarcophagi, looming grey to black, came into intricate focus and then faded into white. The path, which led from the broken iron gates, slid past a chapel with a single spirelet and then split three ways. Brooke turned right to the tumbledown cemetery wall and circled the graveyard until he reached a bench opposite a stone, set flat in the ground, marked by a police lantern and a single bunch of flowers. In the stone was etched the military crest of the Machine Gun Corps.

By the bench stood an old gas lamp, a monster of Victorian ironmongery in black and gold, with the arms of the city crudely cast. Brooke noted the three boats under a gilt bridge, supported by hippocampi: Neptune's steeds, half horse, half fish. The heraldry seemed to chime with the liquid morning, the thickening fog depositing a million miniature globes of water on Brooke's overcoat and skin. He imagined tiny seahorses suspended in each drop.

The cemetery, comfortably able to swallow a dozen football pitches, had been reduced to the intimacy of a Turkish bath. Close by, he could hear buses idling on Mill Road, the wet swish of cars crawling through the gloom, and the chiming of clocks to mark the hour. Chris Childe had died at this spot, his body slumped across the gravestone of his parents.

Brooke shivered, turned up his collar and lit a cigarette.

Out of the mist, with a martinet's military step, came Colonel George Swift-Lane. He took his place on the same seat, but at the far end, leaning on the iron armrest so that he could turn his small, wiry frame to face Brooke, slipping off a pair of leather driving gauntlets.

'The Bentley?' asked Brooke.

Swift-Lane ignored the question, producing a silver cigarette case. It was probably the mist but in profile the colonel's face seemed covered in bead-like sweat.

'Why are we here, Brooke? I'm a busy man. Do we have news?'

'I'm intrigued by your passion for vehicles,' persisted Brooke, setting his hat down on the seat, refusing to be hurried. 'Did it start in Russia, with the ACEF? I looked up your *Who's Who* entry; you've had an adventurous career. A whole army of armoured cars to direct – it must have been heaven. Or was it the élan, so to speak, of the expedition that took you to Russia, or the politics? Then off to military intelligence when you returned home, very rakish. Calls for something stylish, certainly, but isn't the Bentley a bit over the top?'

'The Bentley's new. But don't let me stop you. You're obviously enjoying yourself. Is this why I've been summoned here, to discuss my choice of vehicle?' The simple set of four sentences had left him breathless.

'No. I wanted to talk about why you killed Chris Childe, right here, on this spot.'

For half a minute the colonel was silent, staring straight ahead into the mist.

Finally, he laughed, checking his watch. 'I'll give you five minutes, Brooke. Then I think it's time I visited the chief constable in person. I think your career is about to come to a premature end.'

'It all goes back to Corporal Harry Staunton,' said Brooke. 'His story leads us here, to this spot. The facts speak for themselves. You were his senior commanding officer in Russia, although you were several hundred miles away on the day he died. A heroic death, and a promise made by his pals to return his gun to his widow. It fell to you to do the honours, because you're a Cambridge man, and you were going home. Stop me if I go wrong . . . And so you met Vera Staunton.'

Swift-Lane seemed to make a decision then, visibly relaxing his shoulders, leaning back in the seat.

'Alright, let's play it your way,' he said. 'I'll tell you what happened, Brooke. Then it's over.'

He kept it short, and brutally to the point.

Yes, he'd tracked down Staunton's widow, and brought with him her late husband's pistol. And there was a small sum of money, raised by the battalion, to supplement the pension.

'It was clear to me that Mrs Staunton had found her feet . . .' He let that hang in the air.

'She was on Babylon Street?' interjected Brooke.

'Yes. She was not in any pressing need. I gave over the hundred-pound annuity. There were other officers in pursuit of . . . what shall we call it, Brooke? *Female company*. I effected introductions. That is the extent of our relationship.'

'I see,' said Brooke.

'I doubt that very much. It was a matter of honouring the dead. Her husband was a brave man.'

'Very much so. But not the father of Frederick. The dates don't match. I've been to the school. You are on the board, I see. You're the boy's guardian. In fact, I think it's possible you're his father. Were you in pursuit of female company? You were certainly in a position to pay.'

Swift-Lane tilted his head upwards to let the mist fall on his face.

Brooke stopped there because he heard approaching footsteps. At a turn in the path Vera Staunton appeared, walking under an umbrella. The colonel half stood, reached out a hand and then sat back down, adopting a curious slow-motion descent.

'Is this really necessary, Brooke?' The thin military lips were set murderously straight.

Staunton sat on a bench opposite. 'You said you'd be alone,' she said, addressing Brooke directly. 'Why have we been summoned here?'

She fussed with a loose thread at her hem, and Brooke was struck once more by how odd she looked out of the soft, ordered world of her rooms. The mist, which hemmed them in, seemed to make her nervous.

'I had two things to show you both,' said Brooke, taking out the gun that had killed Chris Childe and placing it on the seat beside Swift-Lane, set on its green felt bag. The lustre of the polished metal, enhanced by the droplets of water in the air, was almost luminous.

'Joelyn Stone has been released from custody,' Brooke said. 'He didn't kill Chris Childe. I suspect all his vices are dull. He's certainly not a cold-blooded murderer. Trying to frame him by planting the murder weapon up at Madingley Hall was a crucial mistake.'

Vera Staunton's mouth hung open, and she went to speak, but checked herself, intimidated by a glare from Swift-Lane.

From his greatcoat Brooke produced a manila file, tattered and tied with a discoloured tape.

'Second item. A comprehensive, and official, account of the heroic death of Harry Staunton. You'll both be familiar with the contents.

'Let's consider the glaring contradiction at the core of this: a woman widowed by the Red Army, whose husband volunteered to fight communism, finds herself at the heart of the local communist party. How can we reconcile these facts? Let's try.'

'This is a farce,' said the colonel. 'You'll pay for this, Inspector.'

Brooke smiled at Staunton.

'I think that when the colonel brought back your husband's pistol you began, what? A relationship, certainly. Frederick was born, and the school fees were paid. But your new mentor wanted more, didn't he? By then he was working for military intelligence. You, I suspect, revealed a violent hatred for the regime that had left you a widow.

'It's a classic – if patient – strategy. The key is never to *apply*, to always be approached, that way there is never any suspicion. So you joined the Peace Pledge Union first; a perfectly respectable protest against the horrors of war, bolstered by the story you invented to underpin your convictions, that your husband was a victim of the horrors of the Western Front.

'You made yourself useful; no doubt you expressed further sympathy for the wider political cause: international socialism, and an end to war on a global scale. Most of all you were efficient, clerical. Eventually, inevitably, they approached you. That put you in an exalted position, an invaluable operative for any intelligence officer. No doubt you were also expected to report back on your clients as well, all those military officers seeking female company. All that indiscreet pillow talk.

'Which is why, when Chris Childe's letter fell into your hands, you thought it might be politic to keep it safe. It was never posted. I think you used Ida's phone that morning to ring the colonel and fill him in on Childe: that he was a witness, that he was determined to get information to London. Did Ida hear that conversation, by the way?'

'What's Ida got to do with this?' asked Staunton.

Brooke left them a few moments' silence. 'At first there was no need to panic over the letter. Chris had his copy, but had no plans to divulge its contents until London gave its orders. But then it all changed. Buoyed up by his success at the tribunal, and perhaps wary that his letter would simply disappear into the Party machine, he decided to bypass London entirely.'

The mist, thickening, began to drip from the trees around them.

'I think Childe returned to Babylon Street after his tribunal and told you he was going to tell his comrades at the meeting what he'd seen, that he'd go to the newspapers too.

'Either way, the cat was almost out of the bag. He had to be stopped. So you rang the colonel again. Or did he call round? Yes, to pick up the letter? While he was there you took the time to bring him up to date on Joelyn Stone as well: his ambitious junior, determined to silence Childe himself, but for very different reasons.

'I think the colonel saw his chance. I think he helped himself to the gun and its ammunition. Then he went to Midsummer Common and followed Childe after work to the cemetery, where he put a bullet in his brain. If Childe had a copy, he took it off the body.'

'It was *you*?' she said.

'Vera, enough. Remember the boy,' said Swift-Lane.

Brooke nodded. 'You thought it was Stone all along, Mrs Staunton, although I suspect you were eventually encouraged to make your helpful statement of incrimination. The colonel here stole the gun, not Major Stone.'

'If I'd wanted to stop Childe I'd have made a citizen's arrest,' said Swift-Lane. 'Why kill him? He was a clear and imminent danger to national security. I could have had him in the Castle like that . . .' He clicked his fingers. 'That's where I dumped his comrades. Murder is murder, Brooke. I've no protection in any court. Why would I kill the wretch?'

Staunton had subsided back into her seat.

'Indeed. *The* question,' said Brooke. 'Certainly not to protect national security, although I'm sure we will hear that defence. No, you took the chance because you saw a way of securing that glittering prize: a heroic, even historic, command.

'I rang the War Office, you see, to check on Stone's new posting. A surprising, innovative appointment, in that they'd passed over the favourite for the job, an officer of higher rank. A certain George Swift-Lane. Your reputation for erratic command could not be lightly discarded. They'd rung you with the bad news *on the day Childe died* . . .

'How did you react on the phone? *Fine, officer, perfectly understandable, younger man, total support, et cetera, et cetera* . . . But how did you feel when you put the phone down? This wasn't any old posting, was it? The Cabinet was behind the scheme, the prime minister himself. What lay ahead? A title, honours. Equality at last with those dazzling elder brothers. You'd worked, with your diligent junior, to perfect the scheme, and now all of this had been snatched from your grasp.

'And then this opportunity fell to you, to kill Childe, shore up the security breach your lax command had allowed and put Stone behind bars. Irresistible to a man of action.'

Swift-Lane swung round in his seat. 'Evidence, Inspector? Or do we take all this on the basis of your moral authority? The hero of the desert has divined the truth, so that is enough, is it?'

'Then you killed Ida Trew,' said Brooke.

Staunton half stood, her face oddly tilted down so that she could level those brown eyes at the father of her child.

'Vera. The boy's future is in *my* hands,' warned Swift-Lane.

She sat, finally, turning to Brooke. 'Ida was a good friend. We just wanted to make sure she didn't blurt out George's name. I . . .'

'But she'd seen too much, heard too much, hadn't she, Colonel? Childe's second visit, Stone's visit, not least your own. The telephone calls. Perhaps, at first, you tried to plead discretion. I can't see you initiating the violence. She was rather fond of Stone, of course. The presents, the kind attentions.'

'She had a weak heart,' said Staunton. 'You said she collapsed, George.'

'Shut up,' said Swift-Lane, this time brushing spittle from his bottom lip. For a moment he seemed to struggle for breath, pressing a handkerchief to his mouth.

'Maybe she did fall,' said Brooke. 'There's a trace of blood on the oven door. Either way, you had to get rid of the body. The Bentley, I think, down the back alley, after dark. I can only assume she *appeared* lifeless. Or didn't you care?

'Once they were both dead all you had to do was cover

your tracks. The awkward witnesses were taken care of; Childe's comrades were already in the Castle Gaol, the soldiers who'd dug the pits posted to Scotland. Even the runaway Corporal Currie had to be tracked down and silenced. When you couldn't find him, you enlisted my help. Very cool and calculated.'

'Any evidence to support this fantasy?' asked the colonel. 'It will never get to court, Brooke. Think it through, man. The implications . . .'

'It will go to court if I tell the truth,' said Staunton, on her feet. 'You made me tell them about Joelyn. You lied about Ida. You've used me, George. You *used* me.'

At a low angle, the sun had appeared through the mist at last, a pale but waxing gold.

'I think Frederick's old enough to stand on his own feet now, George,' she said. 'He's a rather remarkable young man. One day you'll be proud of him. He's never going to be proud of you.'

CHAPTER SIXTY-SIX

Twenty-four hours later, Brooke found himself summoned to Carnegie-Brown's office. He'd submitted his eight-page summary report on Swift-Lane to the chief constable the day before. Edison had typed it, while Brooke dictated. Five carbon copies had been made, and he could see one of them on Carnegie-Brown's blotter. Swift-Lane, on a holding charge, was in cell five.

'Good work, Brooke,' she said. 'A comprehensive job; well done.'

She gave him a glass of sherry, decanted from a bottle made of what looked like milky glass, until Brooke realised it was simply encased in dust.

'I had your report couriered to the Yard. Special Branch have just rung the chief constable. I want to brief you on developments. Everyone is aware that this is very much your case.

'A car's on its way for the prisoner, although there may be a slight delay, as he is complaining of a sore throat and giddy spells – the doctor suspects a chill, so we'd better take care: he's no spring chicken.

'When he does go south he'll be signed off our books. A meeting's been called in Whitehall for tomorrow, with the Yard in the chair. Military intelligence, and Downing Street, wish to be briefed. The precise location is to be advised. I'm to represent the chief constable, and the Borough.'

'I could charge him now,' said Brooke, downing the sweet sherry in a single gulp. 'I have the evidence,' he added. 'Putting aside the tyre prints on Swift-Lane's Bentley, which match tracks behind the house in Babylon Street, and the gunshot residue on the right sleeve of a jacket we found in his rooms, we have the letter – Childe's eyewitness account, *and the copy*. Both were found in Swift-Lane's private papers, hidden away in his attic room at Madingley. And then we have Staunton's testimony. She's ready to take the stand.'

'Indeed, Brooke. But a trial? What kind of justice is that? The case would be held in camera, with no jury. And what would the defendant say from the dock? That he was motivated to protect national security. Item: the letter, and its copy. The tone of his defence is not difficult to predict.

'I know he's guilty of murder, Brooke, and so do you. He could have frogmarched Childe to the nearest police station, not shot him at point-blank range. It was a desperate attempt to cover up his own shortcomings in leadership, and to frame his rival. But he'll want the content of the film divulged; that's his right. Even in a closed court that may be asking too much.

'We may never know his fate, Brooke, but I can tell you that we've been assured, at the highest level, that he will never regain his freedom, let alone his career.'

She drummed her fingers on the desk. 'You need to let go of this, Brooke. You've done your job. The in-tray's full. Why don't we get on with *our* jobs?'

'At this meeting,' said Brooke. 'At a location to be announced. I'd like you, if you would, to indicate that I'm content for them to proceed as they wish. I have little choice, although they will need access to our files, our notes. But I'd ask you to make three requests on my behalf.'

He tilted his head to make sure she knew he was asking a question. She nodded.

'The first is easy. I'd like PC Cable to receive a commendation. If he hadn't spotted the dodgy paperwork on Castle Hill, none of this would have come to light. It was diligent police work. It always comes back to that.

'Second: Swift-Lane may, technically, be a *former* member of the military intelligence, but he seems to have been active nonetheless. I think he was a recruiter here in Cambridge after he left the service, focusing on the university. He may have gathered up a research student called Marcus Ashmore. I'd like to know where Marcus is, as he's gone missing, and I'd like to speak to him. His family's worried. It's an entirely personal matter.'

'And the third?'

'I want to see the film.'

CHAPTER SIXTY-SEVEN

Three days later, Brooke sat alone in the Galen's lecture theatre, watching the flickering black-and-white square of film, a soundtrack crackling, until the picture cleared and a handwritten blackboard appeared, with chalked letters reading:

MINISTRY OF WAR
EXPERIMENTS ON HOAY
JULY 21st–25th 1939

A blurred frame, then the blackboard rewritten:

CLASSIFIED
RELEASED ON AUTHORITY OF PORTON DOWN

A voiceover cut in, the tone pure Whitehall mandarin.

Hoay, the audience was told, was a 'remote island of the St Kilda archipelago, more than sixty miles further west than the

Outer Hebrides. An Atlantic island, a day's boat journey from the Isle of Lewis.'

The voice pronounced the word 'Hee-brides' in the classic manner.

The spot had been chosen because even Hirta, the main island, was uninhabited, and had been since the evacuation of the entire population in 1930. The distance of site from Lewis meant that offshore westerly winds posed no lethal threat to human beings.

Why, Brooke asked himself, could a wind pose a threat to life?

Research was under way into 'BWs' at both Oxford and Cambridge, the commentary continued. A serum had been developed, Vollum 14578, and it was hoped that the experiments on Hoay would determine whether its spores could survive delivery by mortar, or a 4 lb bomb, and proceed to infect a population.

Brooke's brain didn't process this information; it simply registered it, suspending analysis, or questions of any kind. What were BWs?

The film sprang to life, at the slightly manic speed characteristic of a silent movie. Hoay and Hirta could be seen from a pitching boat. Thousand-foot cliffs lowered over a choppy grey sea, while the sky was alive with wheeling masses of birds. Despite the grainy film, the scene projected an extraordinary inner light: the white horses of the ocean and the circling gulls emitting a neon-white intensity against a grey, shifting world.

'The chosen infectious agent is anthrax,' said the announcer. 'This film begins at Base X on Hirta.'

Anthrax. The first question forced itself upon Brooke's conscious mind: what did he know of anthrax? A bacterium, certainly, which leads to infection and lethal disease, by the agent of its spores – its *seed*.

BWs – *biological weapons*.

Hoay – Gaelic, according to the voiceover, for 'windy island' – proved to be a rocky outlier of the main island, dominated by a sloping high moor. A boat moored in a bay was loaded with sheep at a wooden jetty, then towed by landing craft towards the islet, where the animals were herded ashore by dogs.

The film jumped to a new scene. Here the sheep were up on the moor, being wedged into crates, from which only their heads protruded, and these were hooded. This final indignity made Brooke shift in his hard wooden seat. Hoods led to execution: the obliteration of sight, the loss – perhaps – of emotional empathy. There was a suggestion of the shameful about the use of such a device.

The voiceover, by contrast, coolly explained that the crates and hoods were designed to ensure that any resulting fatalities were the result of inhalation of the spores only, and not by any other agency, such as physical contact, or infection of one animal by another.

The men were hooded too. An adapted gas mask had been produced, with a wide tarpaulin bib, which sat over a full-body suit. The crates were lugged out onto the hillside and set in three parallel lines so that the beasts would face the cloud when it came. The voice tried to impart a certain nobility to this, as if the victims had a choice.

The various delivery systems were discussed with a note of schoolboy excitement. A bombing raid had been tested, although the 4 lb bombs had plugged into the deep peaty soil without detonation. A night-time exercise was considered, with a luminescent agent added to the anthrax so that the drifting cloud could be visibly tracked. This had proved feasible, and further work was being undertaken at Porton Down to find a suitable isotope of uranium.

Luminescent agent: had this, thought Brooke, been Ernst Lux's inadvertent contribution to the project?

'But today's live firing will be delivered by inverted mortar. A shell will be fired into the ground from a wooden gallows.'

A long shot of the open moor showed the gibbet stark against a white sky, supporting an upturned gun barrel rather than a felon's corpse. A sudden spasm marked the firing itself, and then a wisp of dirty smoke drifted away from the spot, towards the crated sheep. Within a second or two it was not visible, the blustery Atlantic air dissipating it into the atmosphere.

'Now it is imperative to monitor the effects of the agent.'

The film shifted, and the blackboard announced: THE NEXT DAY.

Hooded men worked at freeing the sheep and then tethering them to rope lines. One or two broke free and the announcer's tone shifted. 'Anyone who thinks that a sheep is a docile, placid animal should try herding one which has ideas of freedom!' Men chased animals in a jittery comic opera.

DAY THREE

'Fatalities have begun.'

Several of the animals lay unmoving on their tethers. These were cut free and tossed onto wheelbarrows. Brooke noted that the men never seemed to look at the animals which were left.

DAY SEVEN

'Only a few remain alive. It is now essential to undertake autopsies in order to make sure death is the result of inhalation of the anthrax spores.'

A few sheep had their ears cut off to produce blood smears on microscope slides, but most were simply cut open on a rock beneath a convenient waterfall.

Three hooded figures gathered round as each was eviscerated, the gas masks turning to each other as some kind of animated conversation took place.

The carcasses and entrails were burnt on site in an incinerator on the beach, the men's suits and masks stuffed into hot chemical disinfectors set up along the stony shore.

One final twist made Brooke look away.

'It is of interest to further examine the physiology of those sheep which survive the test.'

A hooded man caressed a sheep before producing a small pistol, pressing it to the side of the head. The inaudible shot produced a spasm, and then a second later, the animal flopped.

'The results indicate that the Hoay expedition was a success,' said the announcer, his voice rising to signal a sense of peroration. 'The agent can be delivered and is effective. Further research is now needed to see if the death rate can be maintained when the target population comprises large, complex mammals. Initial research at institute level will proceed on horses. Operation Pegasus is already in its initial stages.'

Six men, exhilarated at being freed from their protective suits and masks, were shown standing round a fire, drinking tea. One of them had put on a woollen hat, and he lifted it now, as if in celebration of a victory.

The film closed with Porton Down's insignia, and – briefly – a fluttering Union flag. Then it spooled off the projector. The light became a beacon on the square of white paper, and Brooke recalled the shots he'd heard from St John's Wilderness on the night of the

Great Darkness and had dismissed as the sound of poachers. Then he saw again the men, straining to pull the empty carts.

'Horses,' he said out loud.

They'd infected horses as part of the anthrax experiments. Some had died, others had shown no symptoms, but they couldn't take chances. They'd buried the slaughtered horses in the pits, and then shot the others who'd hauled the carts.

The film had left him with a sense of powerless despair. But what got him to his feet was an idea, a terrible idea, as deadly as the anthrax seed. And this idea sprang forth fully formed from the back of an empty lorry parked on Castle Hill.

CHAPTER SIXTY-EIGHT

The city, when they saw it laid beneath them from the edge of the high moor, seemed to shimmer with fire, sparks rising from flights of chimneys, the sudden glare of furnaces glimpsed along a snaking valley. The hellish lights played on a low ceiling of sooty cloud. Brooke thought what an inadequate word *city* was, in that it had to embrace the liquid reflections of the Cam on medieval stone, and this – the city of Sheffield – a flickering crucible of brick and steel.

Edison, at the wheel of the Wasp, peered at the scene as the road slid downhill, telling Brooke that he had relatives in Leeds and *they* said that the only time anyone in Sheffield had seen a clear sky in living memory had been during the General Strike. The place was a byword for miasmas of sulphur and pitch, for canyons of windowless brick and sudden glimpses of distant high moors.

By a series of plummeting turns, they descended into the city. Brooke noted what must be the city hall, a tall Florentine tower wreathed in dirty smog. A fine neo-Classical concert hall faced a brightly lit department store; a fountain in white stone depicting a dolphin shot a plume of water skywards. Trams slid by, clanking on iron rails.

West Bar, home to the city's police headquarters, lay in a trough leading down to a canal which glowed with a luminous orange light. Behind the station building, a yard ran up to a stone cliff, down which water ran in intermittent waterfalls. Cambridge, thought Brooke, floated on the fen-edge, whereas this place felt as if it had been hewn from the rocks.

Detective Inspector Solly appeared, armed with a map and a torch, directing Edison to take the Wasp to the tail end of a convoy of eight unmarked vehicles, which included two large black vans and a lorry.

'Mob handed,' said Solly, smiling, getting in the back. 'They'll have flown, mind. We were gonna get a man on the inside like I said, Brooke, to find out who's at the top. Too late now. Can't keep anything secret now, can we? Still, you've called foul, Brooke. This is down to you. Let's hope you're right. If you are, there'll be fireworks . . . You say this meat's infected?'

Brooke half-turned in the passenger seat.

'Just the horses,' said Brooke. 'There were carcasses to bury, and the soldiers had to do the work. Currie had a better idea. Get the carts down to the pits, then beyond to a sandy track on the far side, load the horsemeat into a lorry, then fill in the empty pits.'

The convoy pulled away from West Bar through half-lit streets.

'On the night of the Great Darkness it all went wrong,' said Brooke. 'Our sharp-eyed constable stopped the convoy. Currie had to call it off. Which left one empty lorry on Castle Hill. But they'd made five earlier trips, maybe more. The meat is not for human consumption. It's lethal.'

A wide street swept past, then a railway station, as they drove under a great set of stone arches. Here the city's industrial district began, miles of straight road running like an arrow between towering factory walls. When the air war began, Brooke imagined the bombers following the thin silver thread of the river to this vast metalworks. For every bomber they sent to Cambridge, they'd send a hundred here.

They passed rows of terraced houses before the ground opened out before them into an area of derelict one-storey factory buildings, the cars bumping over iron rails, before sweeping between a pair of grand, dilapidated concrete gate posts.

The old abattoir lay ahead. Solly told them that in the city it was always called the Meat House. Two administrative blocks in identical classical style, with mock pillars, stood on either side of the drive, which led towards a complex of low buildings, skylights catching the moonlight.

'We'd smell it as kids,' said Solly. 'Even from the top of a bus you'd get the stink. Iron, like rust, on the wind. And the sound, of course, the lowing and the odd bellow. They know, course they know, that death's coming, because there's a stench of burnt bone from the saws.'

The cars, trundling forward, cut their lights. Past the gates, they killed the engines too, rolling to a halt. To one side of the main building stood an old vehicle depot, comprising a high shed with a pitched roof and a glass canopy over the entrance, the great doors wide open.

Brooke heard a pistol chamber being spun on the back seat.

'How many guns?' he asked.

'All the inspectors, that's six. Paperwork's all done, Brooke. It's no big deal in this city. They carry, we carry. Just make sure you stay behind me.'

He leant forward and Brooke caught a whiff of beer on the detective's breath. 'We find anyone in that place tonight we're takin' them back to West Bar. If they want to travel in a bag that's all well and good.'

The two black vans came to a halt, open at the back, to reveal squads of uniformed constables, who were set back in reserve by a wall, night-sticks drawn.

A chief inspector by the name of Garside was directing his forces like a traffic policeman on point duty. A rapid search of the vehicle bay revealed it to be deserted. A silent order must have been given because several of the constables began to smoke, and the whispers of the plain-clothes men grew louder.

Solly wandered back to find Brooke and Edison standing by the Wasp. 'Told you. They've pissed off. They got wind, alright. We should 'ave waited.'

A pair of arc lamps, run from a generator in one of the police vans, lit the garage up, the oily concrete floor glistening like frost. Garside and Solly were called over to examine one of the sumps in the vehicle bay. Here, mechanics had been able to work under the lorries in a low trench, greasy and dark. The mood changed again. A doctor with a black bag was fetched from one of the waiting cars.

Solly was back. 'They've done for someone in the pit,' he said. 'Farewell gift for the pathologist. By what's left of the hair I'd say it's your missing driver, Brooke – Ginger Thorpe. Christ . . .' He fumbled for his cigarettes. 'Stink's foul. Up close. They've burnt him, alright, rolled him in the oil and chucked in a match.'

Garside marched over, his outline distinguished by the lack of a neck, scrum-wide shoulders and the whiff of peppermint.

'Brooke? The Yard rang. I'm to assist, apparently. Well here I am, assisting. Looks like the lot of them have scarpered. But we'll search the place. What are we looking for?'

'Fridges. A meat store big enough to establish a market in illegal supply.'

Garside crunched a mint between his back teeth. 'This place closed in '36. We've had a car on surveillance for a week since your first call. Nowt. Fuck all nowt. And listen to that . . .'

He held a hand up to a cauliflower ear. 'Silent as the grave. No power. The meat'll be on counters by now. Here, Leeds, up the valley, Manchester.'

Garside looked at his shoes. 'Still. Thorough, that's us. To a fault.' He filled his lungs. 'Where's our man the key holder?' he shouted at a group of detectives clustered by a radio car.

The site, Garside explained, had been rented by a haulage company. A man in brown overalls, representing the owners, led them to a set of metal doors and, after struggling with padlocks, swung them open.

'Lead on, McDuff,' said Garside. 'Let's get this pantomime over with.'

Torches played over a large room, perhaps thirty yards long, with three parallel lines of metal tables. Overhead, a pulley system had once run a railway of hooks. At the end stood three industrial lifts, the buttons listing three floors:

GROUND

BASEMENT

COLD ROOMS

They took a staircase to the basement. It ran under the whole of the ground floor factory area. Brick corridors led to a series of rooms still cluttered with tool shops, vats and finally a power room. A set of three large electric generators stood caked in dust.

Garside left a trailing line with his finger through the grime on the metalwork. Brushing dust from a seat he perched, retrieving a hip flask which he offered to Solly after he'd taken a gulp.

'Told you,' said Solly. 'Your meat's gone, Brooke.'

Brooke thought about telling them there and then what that meant: that hundreds, thousands, could die.

But it could wait, because as he'd come down the stairs from the ground floor he'd felt it: the trace of iciness, a degree, perhaps two, but perceptible nonetheless.

'I'd like to try the cold rooms,' he said, leading the way back to the staircase.

The lowest floor was much deeper below the basement than the basement had been below the ground. Six switchback flights emptied into a room less than ten feet square with a single locked door. The key man caught them all up and struggled with the padlock.

Garside silently showed Brooke the dust on his hand from the banister. Underfoot, the tiled floor was gritty.

The door opened to reveal three mobile generators, the new metal fittings gleaming in the torchlight, and beyond them a set of lift doors. Beside one, a tall metal stool had been set by the controls, a copy of the *Sheffield Star* on the ground beside a ceramic mug. The front-page picture showed Neville Chamberlain waving from an open car. Cigarette butts littered the ground, the crushed paper dry and white. Rats' eyes flashed in the shadows.

Garside filled his lungs. 'Petrol-fired generators, to power the fridges and the lifts. Right, the fuel tank must be upstairs. So we missed that. Amongst other things.' He turned to Solly. 'Get the sparks down here. I want one of these working. I want lights. Now. And get the uniforms too, fast.'

Brooke realised that the left-hand wall of the narrow room was in fact a series of metal doors, each one padlocked.

'These are new,' said the keyholder, examining the locks. 'I'll need the cutters.'

Brooke put a hand on the nearest door and felt the icy cold.

It took two electricians less than twenty minutes to start the first of the three generators. The bolt-cutters took longer, so that by the time the first padlock lay in pieces the lights were buzzing.

Edison gave out face masks they'd brought in a satchel from Cambridge, care of Aldiss's storeroom at the laboratory.

Brooke put his weight down on a lever and prised the first door open, releasing trapped air with an audible hiss.

He'd never forget the sight: this fridge, which would turn out to be the first of six, contained the unbutchered meat. To one side, whole carcasses of beef hung from hooks. But on the other, an open space had been set aside for the horses. An image flashed into his head from the Western Front, the blasted winter fields of Flanders, the stiff limbs of bloated horses crooked in the air. Frost glittered from frozen eyes.

Edison followed him into the room, buttoning his coat to his throat.

Kneeling, Brooke reached out a hand to the neck of a horse whose teeth caught the light as if they'd been studded with diamonds.

'Right. You better tell me what I should know,' said Garside, his voice slurred by the mask.

Brooke took out a notebook, although he'd memorised the key facts. 'The horses died of a lethal bacterium. One of the reasons it's so dangerous is that it spreads by using spores – seeds, really.

They are tough. They can survive low-temperature freezing.'

He let that sink in. 'They can't survive fire. An incinerator would work. But beware. Human beings can catch this bug, it's called anthrax. There's one of three ways – skin touch, breathing in spores or eating infected meat. The one class of people most at danger are abattoir workers. You need to find the men who did this. You need to make sure they've just been storing the meat, that it's not already on the market. And you need to destroy all this . . .'

In the white light he could see Garside's eyes for the first time. They narrowed now, as he tried to find a way out, an easy fix.

Surveying the dead meat, his shoulders sagged. 'Alright. Let's see inside the others . . .'

Fridges two and three held pork and lamb carcasses. Four held poultry. Five held split carcasses of beef. The generators must have been down only a matter of hours because nowhere did they see any signs of melting flesh. Skin shone with a crisp frost.

It was in five that Edison called out. Walking between two lines of hooked pig carcasses, Brooke came to a halt beside his sergeant.

Side by side with the slaughtered meat hung Jack Gretorix. His face had frozen in an ugly mask, one eye closed, the other dimly reflecting the electric light. They'd put a hook through his belt to haul him up on the pulley and then tied his hands to the line. There was no sign of any wounds, or violence. The frost had turned him, and his clothes, the same colour as the beasts on either side.

'Jack,' said Garside, as if greeting an old friend. 'Well, that's one less to worry about. Cut him down . . .'

Brooke considered the irony of young Gretorix's death: that he'd lived his last days in fear of the flames and the heat, the baiting of his killers, only to meet it here in the icy silence, surrounded by the glassy stares of innocent animals.

It was Edison, again, whose keen eyes took them back to the first fridge. Leading them into the mass of stiff bodies, he pointed out two horses which they'd all overlooked; they'd been part-butchered, a leg missing on one, a flank on another, the red flesh pale and bloodless.

'I saw pigs too, in the third fridge, part-butchered,' he said. 'Someone's taken meat off en route. Eaten it by now,' he said.

Garside looked stunned, perhaps by this revelation, but possibly by the sight of the horse's frozen guts, bowels curled neatly around pale organs.

He put a cigarette between his lips but left it unlit. 'If someone catches this . . . What are we looking for, Brooke?'

Aldiss had given him a brief summary. It depended on the route of infection: by touch, by air, by food.

'That's complicated. But we need to look out for ulcers on the skin, stiff limbs, vomiting blood, nose and throat pains – swelling up, difficulty breathing. Shock: toxic shock, then death.'

An hour later, in the car, after they'd dropped Solly off in the city centre, Brooke made the final connection. Did Edison recall Jed Sneeth, stretched out on his bed at Manor Farm, sickening, complaining that his limbs were always stiff? And Brooke's private memory: a white china sink, splashed with drops of blood.

CHAPTER SIXTY-NINE

Six hours later, they picked Aldiss up outside his laboratory in the heart of Cambridge. The scientist climbed aboard with a set of lab coats over his arm, a box of rubber gloves and a four-gallon carboy of a clear liquid. Edison had already collected a single A-frame sign: *POLICE – KEEP OUT*. A radio car, sent to Manor Farm before Brooke left Sheffield, was already at the scene, with instructions to let no one in and no one out. 'Say it's quarantine,' Brooke told Carnegie-Brown by phone. 'Don't say anything else.'

Leaving Cambridge at just after dawn, they followed the river north, a single skein of white mist marking its winding course through flooded water meadows. The first police checkpoint was on the edge of Horningsea, where a uniformed constable with white cuffs directed a tractor onto a back road. The village itself was still asleep, save for a farmworker trudging north by the roadside.

At the entrance to Manor Farm they found the radio car blocking the road, and PC Cable at the farm gate.

'Sir.'

'Cable. Anything here?'

'Nearest neighbour's there . . .' He pointed across two fields to a single set of two terrace houses. 'Farm labourers. They heard about Sneeth's death; it's local gossip. The wife – Elspeth – has not been seen since she identified the body. I've been here an hour and nothing's moved.'

Cable looked back down the lane to the farmhouse.

Not a cat, not a dog. Even the sky was empty.

'Stay here; we'll take a look,' said Brooke.

They left Aldiss at the gate too, and set off for the farmhouse, the face masks around their necks, but hanging loose.

'Dr Comfort's view is that it is pretty difficult to catch anthrax from another human being,' Brooke explained. 'All we need to do is avoid direct skin-to-skin contact, keep our distance if anyone coughs and resist the urge to accept any home-made meat pie. Got it?'

Edison nodded.

The front door of the farmhouse was unlocked, and as they crossed the threshold the air felt colder, the white light of dawn in chilly splashes on the wallpaper. Checking the ground floor, they found nothing. The door to the boy's room upstairs was open, as it had been on their first visit. The bed was empty. Brooke was wondering if they'd find a fresh grave out in the fields when they heard the distinct sound of a horse cantering, a joyful rhythm to the hooves.

Brooke threw the sash window up as Jed Sneeth emerged from the woods on a bay horse, riding up the valley, urging it on, coaxing the last ounce of energy from its muscles before reining it in at the door of the barn.

The boy was actually whistling by the time they reached the stall. With a brush in each hand, he worked strong, curved strokes over the sweating flanks.

'We thought you were ill,' said Brooke, holding the face mask to his chest.

'No, I said I'm on the mend.' He ran his hand through the mane, puzzled by the face masks. 'What's going on?'

They didn't answer.

'This is Broomstick,' said Sneeth. 'My horse, for today anyway. Mum says we have to sell her, and everything else that's not nailed down. We're off back to Gainsborough – my uncle's farm. There'll be other horses, but I'll miss her.'

'The horsemeat your father butchered was contaminated,' said Brooke. 'It's lethal, Jed. We thought it was killing you . . .'

The boy shook his head, dropping the brush. 'Dad called it *cheval*, but that doesn't change what it is. I couldn't . . .'

'We can't find your mother,' said Edison.

'She's been staying with her sister in Newmarket; she'll be back by noon. She didn't eat it either.'

'Is there any left?' asked Brooke.

He took them into the kitchen and opened the pantry door. Brooke found the meat under a muslin cloth, a broad cut of exceptionally lean flesh, the grain of it like best beef.

'Dad loved it,' he said. 'That's our perk, he said. None of the others got a cut, just us and Currie, the soldier. He was the organiser. Dad said that was a risk: dead meat, not slaughtered meat. Shouldn't really touch it. But he had a taste for it. Currie said the horses died trying out a drug, a medicine, and that the meat was fine. Fit for consumption. I didn't like him, but he always bought a few bottles of beer for Dad.

'We ate the rest, alright. A cut of pork, mutton, a pheasant. Dad said it was like the Ark, only backwards. Half for us, half for Currie, and that included the horsemeat.

'He didn't eat it either. He said he had a special customer up at Madingley Hall, and they paid well – top rate.'

CHAPTER SEVENTY

Brooke passed the doctor on the stairs down to the cells. A former GP, called out of retirement for the Duration, he took the stone steps carefully, a metal pail in one hand, a cloth draped over the top to conceal the contents, but Brooke could smell blood, and something sour which made his stomach lurch.

'He's given up,' said the doctor: 'Otherwise we'd have a better chance. Comfort's recommended a serum, but he won't have it. If he was healthy, and he wanted to recover . . . As it is. He can't stop here. Addenbrooke's can't take him. There's an isolation hospital at Ely, that's favourite, but the paperwork's to be done. I'll get to it . . . For now, don't touch him. Don't go near. Got that, Inspector?'

Brooke nodded, standing back to let the doctor pass.

The cell door was open. Swift-Lane lay propped up on a bolster on the bunk, his shirt open. Any visible skin was bathed in sweat, and his eyes seemed to have burrowed back into his skull.

His neck was badly swollen, and at one corner of his mouth his lips were disfigured by a small ulcer.

'Inspector. I think this is what the classicists would call nemesis . . .'

He dabbed at his mouth with a cloth stained with blood and mucus.

'You should let them try the serum,' said Brooke, taking a chair and placing his hat on his knee.

'Why? So that I can be fit enough to stand trial? Or worse, fit enough for some godforsaken cell in some forgotten jail. Christ, I'd rather be dead. And that's wishful thinking, Brooke . . .'

'I presume Currie played supplier when it came to the meat?'

The colonel nodded, then fought a series of wracking coughs.

Recovered, he took a few moments to fill his lungs with air. 'Useful man to have around, Currie. Spares for the car, cigarettes and, yes, the odd lean cut of meat. The steak was exceptional. He said he'd got a supplier in Suffolk. I believed him.'

He shook his head and winced with pain.

'I used to eat up in my attic room, bottle of claret, just like the old days. Kitchens didn't mind, how long does it take? A minute either side. Rare, always bloody. Fatal, Brooke. The doc said they'd check the kitchen staff but there's been no reports of illness. I'd never forgive myself . . .'

Brooke almost laughed at that: the idea that in this whole affair, the inadvertent infection of the cook might be his only real crime.

Swift-Lane folded up then, as if he'd taken a blow to the stomach. Brooke actually heard the gut in spasm.

As he swept the sweat off his brow, his fingers shook violently.

He gestured to a pile of documents on the floor.

'A letter: to whom it may concern. There's a file at Madingley, in my room. A will; everything goes to Frederick. I've no one else.'

'Vera?'

'She sent a note. Frederick will decide on his own future. She's taken up the rent on Ida's flat. A retirement of sorts . . . Admin up at Madingley are looking for secretaries, and I've put in a word. If not, the widow's pension will have to be enough, because she won't take my money, but it will fall to Frederick come what may . . .'

In the silence they heard a bus rumble by overhead on Regent Street.

'My life's been a failure, Brooke. It's maudlin, I know, because the past is just that: *past*. There'll be a fine funeral, of course; my brothers will see to all the details . . .'

He stopped for a full minute, regulating the rise and fall of his chest.

'At least there won't be a scandal,' he said at last. 'I know how these things work, Brooke. The sooner I'm nicely buried the better for everyone. By the time the church is empty, I'll be forgotten. Anonymity is mine. The irony is brutal. I spent my whole life trying to make a mark.'

Brooke heard footsteps on the stairs, and voices, negotiating the strategy for getting a stretcher down the spiral stone descent.

Fear brought a light back to the colonel's eyes. 'I'd like it noted that I did prevent a disastrous failure in intelligence. That must never be forgotten. Henderson could have used the radio. It could have got to Moscow. I want that on the record.'

Brooke felt he couldn't let him have the last, self-serving word. 'Marcus Ashmore, was he a final recruit?' he asked, standing.

'Marcus? He'll serve his country well, Brooke. There'll be no medals, but we can't choose our war, that's the lesson I've learnt.'

'But Ernst Lux?'

'The American? It was the Great Darkness, Brooke. Some things it will hide for ever.'

CHAPTER SEVENTY-ONE

A white world stretched beyond Cambridge's northern limits, where snow-covered fen stretched towards a crisp, frosty horizon. Station DA, a series of three huts in a damp fen field, lay surrounded by a double line of barbed wire, from which icicles dripped in the cold sunlight. An army guard, stamping boots on frozen peat, gave Brooke's pass a desultory check and directed him to park on a stretch of old concrete runway where a line of motorcycles were accruing snow on leather saddles.

The ruins of an abbey stood on a slight rise of ground. Brooke's historical grip on the 'fen islands' was shaky, but he seemed to recall a link with the Knights Templar, and that the estate had been granted to the order in lieu of a debt. It still radiated the sad depleted energy of a lost time. Beyond the old wall, several swans sat in a field of peat, their necks held high like question marks. Overhead, a V-shaped flock of geese flew north towards the sea.

Marcus Ashmore was waiting for him in the car park

allocated for visitors, each bay outlined by whitewashed bricks set on the concrete.

'Brooke,' he said. 'My office?'

He pointed to one of the huts. The boy had changed, thought Brooke as they walked in silence. A month ago, when they'd met at the house, he'd been a shy, introverted version of his childhood self. Now, striding towards the huts, he radiated a proprietorial confidence, as if he'd finally found a place to be himself.

The hut contained trestle tables covered in papers, at which worked about twenty men and a solitary woman, although she had assumed what appeared to be an informal uniform of tweed jacket and white shirt, with tie. Pipe smoke clogged the air, while a mean gas fire emitted a glow of amber warmth.

Brooke noted what had become the leitmotif of the phoney war: the aroma of stewed tea.

All heads turned to examine the new arrival.

'This is Detective Inspector Brooke,' said Marcus. 'His security clearance is A-plus.'

Brooke raised his hat.

One of the men, in a suit – but daringly tieless – coughed, and this seemed to be a signal for them all to return to their work.

As they walked towards Marcus's office, a half-glazed box, Brooke glanced at some of the paper scraps on the tables; numbers, in box-like paragraphs, dominated the scripts. And there were newspapers, several of which had German titles, although he caught sight of one in the Cyrillic Russian script.

'I can't tell you what all this is about, Brooke. It's actually pretty tedious, and not at all dramatic. But it's the start of something; a seed, if you like.'

'A spore?' asked Brooke.

Marcus shut the door.

'I've been instructed to be as helpful as I can,' said Marcus, ignoring the question. 'There is no question of prosecution. I take it that's your understanding too?'

Brooke nodded. 'I didn't know military intelligence had an interest in undergraduate high-fliers while they were actually still at university,' he said.

Ashmore laughed, his eyes focusing on some secret mid-distance, where the landscape was only revealed to men of his calibre and intellect.

'I admit that there has been enthusiastic interest in recruitment at the university,' he said. 'I think, as a cadre – if I can call us that – we will make a difference to the service, to the country. I was approached; I was honoured to accept. That's all I can say.'

'Swift-Lane,' said Brooke.

'Indeed. He has contacts at the college. Are there any more details of his fate?'

Brooke shrugged. 'He died in Ely. Anthrax, the gastrointestinal strain. He was alone. Not a man to court friendship. The boy visited, Frederick, so that must have been some consolation.'

'What a mess,' said Ashmore, neatly consigning the events to the category of history's forgotten disasters.

On the wall behind his desk was a planner for the months of 1939, 1940, 1941, 1942. The idea that there were years of this weary, bureaucratic dullness made Brooke feel suddenly old.

'Was it strictly necessary to kill Ernst Lux?' he asked. The act of accusation was important. Just posing the question made him feel better than he had for a month.

Ashmore steepled his fingers. But his eyes betrayed him, flitting to the escape route offered by the office door.

'His girlfriend said you and he were close. Did you *get* close? An American on research work, he must have alerted your intelligence antennae. Did he mention his father, a hero of pacifism, locked up for his principles? If we take all that and set it against what he saw in the Galen that night, the film that I too have now seen, we can see his dilemma.

'Obscene, isn't it, the idea that biology, the science of life, can be harnessed for death? A single forty-pounder dropped on the Ruhr would result in, what, a thousand dead? Twenty thousand? A fifty-bomber raid, a hundred thousand dead?'

Ashmore glanced at the clock.

'Ernst was an intelligent man,' said Ashmore. 'He wanted to continue his research. There was a price. The war demands . . .'

'But what did he say, Marcus? What did he plan to do? Denounce the work publicly? Another Swift-Lane slip there, letting an American citizen see the film. Not much point in getting *him* to sign the Official Secrets Act, was there? He could have said what he liked once he stepped off the boat in New York. Or, maybe not a public denunciation. What if he'd gone to Washington? In fact, it's a bloody good question, Marcus. Do our allies *know*?'

'The Germans don't know, that's the point, Brooke,' he said, clearly tiring of the polite tone of the conversation. 'Meanwhile, the Nazis are developing their own weapons. I've seen the aerial photographs, and we have people on the ground.'

Brooke noted the *we*.

'There's a village on the Luneberg Heath where they've made a nerve gas called tabun. It's the same facility which produced mustard gas in the last lot. You think they won't use it? Where's Luke? Jo said France, so he'll be close to the front line.'

'I'm a simple policeman,' said Brooke. 'I'm concerned with the

343

death of Ernst Lux. I've examined the scene and he most certainly didn't lose his grip on the narrow, decorated stone ledge. When did you decide that it might be opportune if he fell? When the siren sounded? When he told you what he planned to do? Or when you realised you'd played your own part in the security breach? He'd promised his fiancée that he'd never climb again. Did you persuade him to go out that night on the rooftops? A last climb, perhaps, before booking the boat home.'

Ashmore stood up, both his hands manipulating a pencil.

'You'll never know,' he said.

It was the closest he was ever likely to come to a confession. Brooke wondered if he might be haunted by the falling image of Ernst Lux's upturned face, and the last expression in his eyes. Betrayal, or simply surprise?

'Your rise has been meteoric,' said Brooke, surveying the workers at their tables as he was offered the door.

'There are great problems to solve. Puzzles, Brooke, beyond the power of men. We're going to need machines that think.'

Brooke adjusted his hat. 'We need men that think, Marcus. Remember that.'

CHAPTER SEVENTY-TWO

Brooke unlocked the Michaelhouse punt from its manacles on the wooden dock by Mill Pond. A slim pole, attached to a fitting in the prow, suspended a lantern over the slatted seat. Snow lingered on the banks, and Claire lay wrapped in a picnic blanket, as Brooke, standing in the stern, edged them expertly under the Bridge of Sighs, with one hand on the stonework overhead.

'I nearly forgot them,' said Brooke. 'The three commies: Henderson, Lauder and Popper.'

'And you'd promised to look out for them,' said Claire.

They couldn't run to champagne, but Brooke had found a Chablis in the cellar. The icy night air had kept it crisp.

'Yes. And we keep our promises, the Brookes. They'd moved them again – to Lincoln. I drove up with Edison and caused a fuss. The union man, Henderson, had suffered most. He was thin, and nervy; I doubt he'd have lasted too long. They had to fish him out of solitary. We got them in the back of the Wasp and took them home. If they report regularly to the station they can see the war out as free men.'

'So that explains the celebration?'

'Yes. No one had bothered to unravel Swift-Lane's orders. They could have stayed there for the duration. Now they're free to agitate for worldwide communism. Although Henderson's radio has been removed. No point in going too far . . .'

Claire threw her head back to look at the sky.

'That's one thing you can say about the blackout. It's given us back the stars,' she said.

'And that's not all,' said Brooke. 'The colleges have been persuaded to set up their own fire-watch scheme, a warden for each, for all the hours of darkness. Doric has been placed in a position of giddy authority. The prospect of working days has been miraculously lifted.'

A minute later they were opposite St John's Wilderness, a skull-and-crossbones sign just visible in silhouette against the sky. A platoon of soldiers had uncovered the pits and found all of them empty, except the last. The decaying bodies of the horses, encased in lime, were burnt in the pit. All the meat in Sheffield had been destroyed. The West Bar team had made a series of arrests across Yorkshire. There was no evidence any of the meat had made it across a butcher's counter. But, as Solly had predicted, the shadowy gang leaders had melted away.

'One day,' said Claire, 'our grandchildren might play on that riverbank.'

She raised her glass.

'Read it again,' said Brooke.

The letter from Joy had come in the post that morning. A wedding was planned for February. A child was due in June.

Claire read, catching expertly the note of suppressed excitement, emphasising the promise to come home for the birth.

'Boy or girl, do you think?' asked Brooke, edging down the punt to take a seat and a glass.

'Don't mind,' said Claire, rearranging the picnic blanket.

'Aldiss wants to run an experiment on me,' said Brooke. 'He thinks he might be able to make me sleep; apparently, I have much in common with his cockroaches and fireflies. I have circadian rhythms. They need establishing anew.'

'Sleep would be good,' said Claire. 'I worry you're living life too fast, that you'll get to the end before me. Your hair's going grey, but that looks distinguished. And it makes you look like your father, the picture in the hall?'

He nodded, trying to hide how absurdly pleased he was by this observation. 'Rose, on the market? She read the tea leaves and said she'd spotted Hypnos, the god of sleep. I'll let Aldiss know; he'll be thrilled.'

Claire unfolded Luke's latest letter.

'Now for the son and heir,' she said, snapping it open and passing it to Brooke.

The letter was a model of Luke's style, full of detail and colour, but no real sense of how he felt. They'd been moved back fifty miles, then forward again, to a point on the border a mile from their original camp. There were rumours the Germans had rockets. They'd seen a shooting star and they'd all grabbed their gas masks. The corporal made them wear them till dawn, but they were stifling, and blurred speech, and the sweat trickled down the plastic visor.

It was hell, he wrote.

They slipped under the Mathematical Bridge.

'Ginny Waites, Lux's fiancée, did you find her?' asked Brooke, his voice echoing.

'Yes, Rene knows the ward sister; she's down in geriatrics. What do you want me to do?'

'A message, if you would. Just tell her Ernst died for what he believed in, that he didn't fall. Tell her I don't think she was betrayed. It might help.'

For a moment they were quiet and Brooke knew she was memorising the words, the phrases, so that she'd get it just right.

The punt slipped downstream, accompanied by the strange mechanical *brrr! brrr!* of a nighthawk.

ACKNOWLEDGEMENTS

I'd like to thank Mike Petty, doyen of Cambridge local historians, for his help in researching the wartime background to this book. Anyone wishing to dig deeper should visit www.mikepetty.org.uk. The College of Optometrists provided expert analysis of my hero's eye problems, and the history of eye care: individual thanks should go to Neil Handley and Daniel Hardiman-McCartney. Lawrence Holmes, of the Royal Observer Corps Association, offered a rare insight into the realities of this key service. I also relied on Bradley and Pevsner's *The Buildings of England – Cambridgeshire*. Everyone at the Cambridgeshire Police Museum at Monk's Wood went out of their way to bring to life the story of one of the country's smallest forces – the old 'Borough'.

Four books must be noted, *Cambridge at War. The Diary of Jack Overhill 1939–45* edited by Peter Searby; *The Last Crusade: The Palestine Campaign in the First World War* by Anthony Bruce; *The Night Climbers of Cambridge* by Whipplesnaith; and *Conscientious Objectors of the Second World War: Refusing to Fight*, by Ann Kramer.

Several friends offered helpful insights into the manuscript. I must thank – in the order in which they read the work – Rowan Haysom, Richard Reynolds, Chris Simms, and Robert Jones. The first reader was my agent, Faith Evans, who again steered the literary ship clear of the rocks. Midge Gillies, my wife, also read the text and was a guiding light. Susie Dunlop, publisher at Allison & Busby, and her expert team, have shown faith from the start in Eden Brooke.

I should also mention that the film featured in *The Great Darkness* was in part based on that produced by the government to mark a series of experiments carried out on an island off the Scottish coast, between 1942–3. It is freely available to watch online. My film, and the tests it chronicles on Hoay in 1939, are entirely fictional.

Jim Kelly was born in 1957 and is the son of a Scotland Yard detective. He went to university in Sheffield, later training as a journalist and worked on the *Bedfordshire Times*, *Yorkshire Evening Press* and the *Financial Times*. His first book, *The Water Clock*, was shortlisted for the John Creasey Award and he has since won a CWA Dagger in the Library and the New Angle Prize for Literature. He lives in Ely, Cambridgeshire.

jim-kelly.co.uk
@thewaterclock